# THE WEDDING WALLAH

## Farahad Zama

ABACUS

First published as a paperback original in 2011 by Abacus

A CIP catalogue record for this book
is available from the British Library.

ISBN 978-0-349-12268-7

Typeset in Bembo by M Rules
Printed and bound in Great Britain by
Clays Ltd, St Ives plc

Abacus
An imprint of
Little, Brown Book Group
100 Victoria Embankment
London EC4Y 0DY

An Hachette UK Company
www.hachette.co.uk

www.littlebrown.co.uk

To my sister Nilu,
my brother-in-law Babur
and my nephew Ashiq

# Newlyweds kidnapped

**Usha Malladi, reporting from Vizag district**

A wedding ceremony ended in terror and chaos yesterday as Naxalites struck at Chittivalasa village, thirty miles from the city. Guests of the two wealthy landlord families were about to sit down for lunch when approximately thirty suspected activists of the Communist Party of India (Maoist) swooped down and abducted the newlyweds, Srinu Kankatala and Gita Marredu, and several of their guests at gunpoint. The guests were later freed, but Mr and Mrs Kankatala were taken away to an unknown destination. Family members said they could not think of any personal vendetta as the reason behind the kidnapping.

'We found empty cartridges of self-loading rifles from the spot. Only Maoists have SLRs in this area, which is a definite indication of the rebels being behind the incident,' Police Inspector (Rural) Mohan Verma said. He added that raids were being undertaken in several nearby areas to apprehend the kidnappers.

Naxalite is a loose term used to define groups waging a violent struggle on behalf of landless labourers and tribal people against landlords and other members of the country's wealthier classes. They claim to represent the most oppressed people in India, those who are often left untouched by India's development and are bypassed by the electoral process. While the militants have a great

*Farahad Zama*

deal of power in parts of rural India, they have little day-to-day control outside of isolated forests and villages.

'They are nothing but terrorists who use violence to try to achieve their objectives,' Inspector Verma said.

# CHAPTER ONE

Mrs Ali could have sworn that the thief had a sneaky look in his eye as he crept closer to his target. She watched the crow drop on to the ground from the lower branches of the guava tree. She was in a cane chair, on the verandah, looking out on to the front yard where she had laid tamarind on an old sheet to dry in the spring sun. Mrs Ali was aware that modern women like her niece Nafisa bought their tamarind in little plastic packets, as and when they needed it, from a supermarket. They even stored it in the fridge. But Mrs Ali wasn't like that. She still stuck to the old, proper ways and bought her entire year's supply fresh, when it was in season, and cheap, like now. After shredding the long pods into small pieces, she removed the seeds, mixed in some sea salt and dried them out properly in the sun for a few days until the moisture was gone. The tamarind could then be kept for a whole year in an earthen pot without going mouldy or smelling stale. Mrs Ali still used the same glazed earthen jar that she had inherited from her mother-in-law. What was the point of putting everything in the fridge and fretting about power cuts?

Mrs Ali was a fair-minded woman. She had to admit that one didn't have to worry about crows if food went straight from the shopping bag into the fridge. She looked across the verandah to her husband. He was sitting behind the table, deeply immersed in the newspaper. The years had been kinder to him than to her. His hair was grey and he had a slight stoop to his shoulders now, but he had maintained his weight and was still sprightly. Her hair was grey too, and she had put on a bit of weight over the years. Not enough to be called fat, she was certain. Her arthritic knees were what gave her the most trouble. When she was younger, she would get up at five and squat in front of a heavy grindstone making the batter for breakfast dosas, but those days were long gone. She used a motorised wet grinder like everyone else these days. Age suited men better than it suited women, she thought. There was no point in getting upset about it, however – that was just the way of the world.

Her eyes flicked back to the front yard. The crow was now walking on its curiously ungainly legs towards the tamarind. Its claws clicked on the cemented ground, crazy-paved with broken granite stones left over from the flooring when the house was built. It made its approach cautiously. When it was still a foot away from its target, Mrs Ali waved her hand and said, 'Shoo!'

The crow flew back into the tree. Mrs Ali relaxed. She wondered where her son, Rehman, was. He had gone out in the morning, telling her that he was meeting some friends and wouldn't be back until dinnertime. Since he had left his job as an engineer with a local building company, he had been out of work.

The crow, back on the ground, was making its way purposefully towards the sheet again.

'Go away, you silly bird,' said Mrs Ali, waving her arms like a windmill in a gale. 'Tamarind is sour and you won't like it.'

It seemed to understand what Mrs Ali was saying because

it flew away over the house and out of sight. Mrs Ali smiled. Not only was she a good cook and housewife, she was an excellent scarecrow too.

It was March and winter was over. The fan above them was whirring away, its brief two-month annual holiday already history.

She heard a caw and looked out quickly. 'This is ridiculous!' she muttered.

The crow had come back with a friend. She wondered why Allah had created crows. What was the point of their existence? Ugly raucous creatures that poked their beaks into anything that was not theirs. Parrots were beautiful and could be trained to talk; pigeons could find their way home and carry messages; sparrows were small, chirpy and not a nuisance; but crows . . . She shook her head.

Her husband turned the pages of the newspaper noisily, attracting her attention. She still kept half an eye on the birds – she was too experienced to forget them entirely. Mrs Ali read the headlines and some news stories daily, but she could not understand the devotion that some people, like her husband, brought to the task of newspaper reading. It seemed to her that they were so interested in what was happening in the wider world that they sometimes did not see what was occurring right under their noses.

'These rascals are getting bolder every day,' said Mr Ali, finally looking up.

Mrs Ali nodded, deciding that she had been unfair to her husband.

'It's hard to get rid of them,' she agreed.

'They have started moving around in broad daylight,' her husband said.

Mrs Ali frowned. 'Well, of course! They are not big-eyed owls to see in the dark.'

'What have owls got to do with anything?'

Mrs Ali had a suspicion that, not for the first time, she and her husband were talking at cross-purposes.

'Aren't you talking about crows?' she asked.

'Why would I talk about birds and beasts?' her husband said, putting on the expression, as she knew from past experience, of a patient man in trying circumstances.

'Don't give me that look,' she said.

'What—' he began, but went no further.

Mrs Ali had whipped her head round and saw to her horror that the crows had reached the tamarind. 'Shoo! Shoo!' she shouted, from her chair, making a throwing motion with her hands.

Indian crows are intelligent birds that have learned over hundreds, if not thousands, of years just how much liberty they can take in the face of human activity. The pests in Mrs Ali's front yard had obviously decided that the old woman did not pose a serious threat and carried on pecking at the juicy, brown, fibrous fruit.

Mrs Ali had no choice but to rise from her chair, wincing at the twinge in her knees. As she came out of the verandah and on to the yard, the crows retreated but only up to the front wall, each carrying a piece of tamarind in its beak. There they gave a grating caw and dropped the sour fruit. Mrs Ali took out a long bamboo stick from under the stairs and waved it threateningly. The crows took wing. Mrs Ali laid the stick across the tamarind. For all their bravery, she knew that crows never came near a stick. She should have put the stick there in the first place. As her grandmother used to say, a long time ago, 'Lazy people end up doing more work.'

Mrs Ali came back into the house and said to her husband, 'Look at what you did. Your silly talk made me lose my concentration on the crows and they managed to get to the tamarind.'

Mr Ali shrugged. 'And how is that my fault?' he said, not unreasonably. 'I was talking about the Naxalites. They have kidnapped a young couple from their marriage altar in broad daylight.'

Mrs Ali's anger fizzled away. She shook her head. 'Poor things . . .'

Before her husband could get back to the paper, the phone rang. 'Mr Ali's Marriage Bureau,' he announced, picking it up.

He listened for a little while and then said, 'Yes, sir. We have lots of matches in your caste. In fact, we have Hindu, Muslim and Christian brides and grooms on our books. Widest variety, sir. I am sure there'll be somebody who is perfect for your son.'

The conversation continued. Mrs Ali had heard her husband's patter many times before. She picked up the newspaper and sat back in the chair. Mr Ali finally put the phone down and there were a few minutes of silence, broken only by the honking of cars and scooters on the road outside.

'Isn't Chittivalasa close to Kottavalasa?' she asked.

'Yes, the two villages are just a couple of miles from each other,' Mr Ali replied, even though Kottavalasa had long outgrown its humble village origins and was now a market town that sat at the junction of two major roads.

'Rehman is going there soon,' she said.

Mr Ali raised his white eyebrows quizzically.

'What's the point of reading the news and missing the important bits? I am sure that it was a man like you who read the whole Bible and then asked, what was Mary to Jesus?'

'What is it?' said Mr Ali, looking irritated.

'The couple were kidnapped by the insurgents in Chittivalasa.

I hope Rehman doesn't get into any trouble when he goes to Mr Naidu's village near by.'

'He should be all right. He's already been there several times before and he gets along well with the villagers.'

'I hope so,' said Mrs Ali. 'But I am still worried.'

'You should be more concerned about why your laadla, your dear son, has thrown away a perfectly fine job and gone back to his crazy campaigning ways. How long can he act like a student? He needs to grow up.'

Mrs Ali sighed. Rehman had indeed grown up, though her husband didn't know it. He had fallen in love with that TV journalist, Usha. Something made her look at the byline on the news article about the kidnapped couple. Usha Malladi – yes, it must be the same woman. So, she had now started writing for newspapers . . .

Their son, Rehman, had an engineering degree from a prestigious university, but no interest in following a career. It was on Usha's family's insistence, after they had found out about Rehman and Usha's engagement, that Rehman had not only taken up a job but also started thinking about money to buy a flat and a car and all the other 'normal' things that Mr Ali liked. In the end, it had not been enough and Usha had broken off the engagement. Rehman had gone into a deep depression for weeks and recovered very slowly, once again taking an interest in the affairs of a poor villager who had committed suicide. The villager, a farmer, had been the grandfather and guardian of a little boy called Vasu, whom Rehman had been trying to protect for some time. Unlike her husband, Mrs Ali was not unhappy that Rehman had thrown away his job. She was just glad that their son had found something to interest him again.

Mrs Ali looked into the front yard again. The stick had definitely scared the crows off and they hadn't returned. If only all problems could be solved so easily! She glanced at her husband. Neither of them had been privy to Rehman's engagement and it was only by luck and some clever questioning that she had managed to find out that it had been broken off. How was she going to tell her husband about the reason for their son's depression? How would she reply if her husband asked her why she had not told him earlier? She had only wanted to keep the peace between her husband and son.

Should she tell her husband? It was like meeting somebody vaguely familiar at a wedding, she thought. If you don't ask their name within the first few minutes of starting the conversation, it becomes too late and you just have to smile brightly and keep up your side of the chat even though you know that each word you speak is sucking you deeper and deeper into a lie. No, she couldn't tell her husband now.

Across town, the same spring sun that was drying Mrs Ali's tamarind shone down on an old bungalow on the Daspalla Hills. Once upon a time, the house had stood in solitary splendour, with the steel-blue of the distant Bay of Bengal visible from its front door. The house was now hemmed in by tall buildings, put up in haphazard fashion with complete disregard to aesthetics or even urban planning rules. The house and its surrounding garden seemed today like a relic from a different age.

The mistress of the house, Mrs Bilqis, waited until the maid had poured the milk from the silver pot into china cups and left the elegant drawing room. She then turned to her dearest friend and said, 'Nadira, you won't believe the news I have to tell you.'

'I heard,' said Nadira, infuriatingly. 'What a clever thing you've turned out to be, darling, but I hope you haven't found a dragon. It is better that Dilawar doesn't marry rather than get hitched to some unsuitable creature.'

Mrs Bilqis frowned. 'How did you know? Anyway, there's no need to dismiss my son's prospects so easily, Nadira,' she said.

Nadira looked at her with a smile. 'Darling, don't get so serious. We've known each other since we were teenagers. If I don't tell you the truth, who will?'

Mrs Bilqis fell silent for a moment. It was true that they had known each other for years and years. Nadira had always been blunt to the point of rudeness.

'I have found an absolutely delightful girl for my son,' Mrs Bilqis said finally. She opened the top drawer of an antique teak side table, took out a photograph and passed it to the other lady. 'This is Pari.'

Her friend gazed at the young woman in the picture, dressed in a dark-maroon sari and smiling unselfconsciously. A long, oxidised-silver earring could be seen dangling from the one ear in view. 'Lovely,' Nadira said. 'She is beautiful. Such an elegant neck and what a nose!'

Mrs Bilqis smiled. She decided not to tell her friend that the fair-skinned, dark-haired Pari was actually the child of a poor couple who had given her up for adoption because they had too many mouths to feed already. After all, she was sure that there was noble blood in Pari's lineage, somewhere.

'If you've got such a suitable match, why did you cancel the wedding?' asked Nadira.

A few months ago, in a rush of blood, Mrs Bilqis had fixed a date for her son's wedding, organised the venue and told a few friends about it before she had even found a bride for her son. As the time ticked away closer to the deadline, she had joined Mr Ali's marriage bureau in desperation. No member had been suitable, but she had seen Mr Ali's niece, Pari, at their house and known that she was the perfect bride for her son. Everything she had found out since then had only confirmed her initial view.

'It's not a done deal yet,' she said. 'Pari has only agreed to think about the match. She hasn't fully consented to the wedding.'

'How dare the slip of a girl refuse? Doesn't she know how lucky she is to get a proposal from a family like yours?' Nadira said loyally.

Mrs Bilqis sighed and looked across the room to where a framed gold medal and a certificate hung on the wall. They had been personally presented by King George V himself to her husband's grandfather at the Delhi Durbar in 1911.

'What does family status mean nowadays?' she said. 'My son sells soap to common people.'

'Nonsense,' said Nadira. 'Aristocratic blood is aristocratic blood. Give me her address. I'll talk to her parents.'

Mrs Bilqis shook her head. 'Her parents are dead. She lives with her aunt and uncle.'

She was reluctant to explain that Pari actually lived by herself opposite Mr and Mrs Ali's house and was bringing up a boy that she had adopted.

Nadira said, 'Tell the girl's uncle and aunt to convince her. They are her guardians, aren't they?'

'She is a widow,' said Mrs Bilqis. It was well established in Muslim law that while parents and guardians decided a maiden's match, a second wedding was within a woman's own control.

'Oh,' said Nadira. Both women were silent for a while. Then Nadira continued, 'Even so, I am sure they can persuade her. Did you tell them how much your son earns?'

'I think that's part of the problem,' said Mrs Bilqis. 'Pari doesn't care about money. She works in the call centre and earns a good salary herself.'

'Which one? The call centre near the university?'

'Yes,' said Mrs Bilqis.

'You are in luck,' said Nadira. 'Anees works there.'

'Who? Your older sister's son-in-law?'

'Yes, darling. He's quite a senior officer there. Let me give him a call and the girl's job will be history. He won't say no to me.'

Mrs Bilqis was shocked. 'That's wrong.'

'Darling,' said Nadira, patting her friend's hand, 'you are too gentle. It's in a good cause.'

Mrs Bilqis nodded slowly as she considered the idea more fully. 'Thank you,' she said, after a moment.

'Anything for you, darling. Just make sure that this Pari doesn't meet your son before she agrees.'

'Oh, Dilawar isn't that bad.'

'Your son is so handsome and smooth that any girl will fall for him. If he wants her to, of course. Nobody will notice any problems.'

Mrs Bilqis drew in a sharp intake of breath, and Nadira slid over the ottoman to hug her. 'We all make plans, darling. But Allah also has plans that He doesn't reveal to us.'

Mrs Bilqis dissolved into tears on her friend's shoulder.


'Have you finished eating?' shouted Pari from the bathroom.

Mornings were hectic when she was on the early shift. Collecting water, preparing breakfast, packing lunches for Vasu and herself, doing the dishes, taking a bath and twenty-five other things gobbled up the time. She finished brushing her hair and quickly applied moisturising cream to her face. Pari had given up all other cosmetics when she became a widow. Now her angular face looked thin and her nose more prominent than ever. Her dark eyes did not really need any mascara.

She walked briskly into the one room where she and Vasu – the two orphans, as she sometimes said to herself – lived. She sat on the folding chair by the small table and served herself four idlis from the batch that she had steamed earlier. Vasu had taken the other steamed rice-and-lentil cakes, even though he hadn't finished them all.

'Come on, finish what's on your plate. What happened to the brown shorts, by the way?' she asked.

'They tore when I was playing football,' he said, coming back to the table.

Pari nodded, deciding not to pursue the point further. Vasu went through clothes the way a chameleon goes through colours. She would have to ask chaachi, Mrs Ali, if all boys were the same. She wondered what Rehman had been like as a boy. Had he been naughty? She herself didn't have any experience of boys. She had been adopted as a baby and had grown up as an only child. Was that why she had been unable to resist adopting Vasu when Rehman had brought him from the village after Vasu's grandfather died and nobody else was willing to look after what they considered an 'inauspicious' boy?

After a moment, she pushed these thoughts aside and started thinking about work. Her probationary period was coming to an end shortly. Her manager had told her that she had done well and could be assigned to the follow-up team. She looked forward to that. The work there was more interesting and varied than in the cold-calling unit.

'When can I go to a proper school?' Vasu said, interrupting her silent munching. He went for a few hours to a retired teacher's house, but not to school.

'Soon,' she said.

'The boys were teasing me because I didn't go to school. They said I must be dumb . . . or a servant.'

Pari looked up in surprise at the child, eight but soon to be nine. 'Oh, Vasu,' she said. 'People always talk; you have to learn to ignore them. There is just one more formality left to complete. I've already spoken to the principal of that school we visited.'

'That's what you've been saying for a long time.'

Pari sighed. 'Government work always takes longer than we think,' she said. 'Don't worry.'

Vasu turned away from her, his face set. Pari didn't know what to say. She had been trying to get Vasu admitted to a local school but without much success. Vasu had started living with her quite recently and she did not have all the paperwork that the schools were insisting upon. Having heard of one school that was willing to bend the rules and accept Vasu without the necessary papers, she had gone to visit it.

She had entered a courtyard crammed with children on long benches. The walls rang with the sound of a hundred boys and girls reciting their lessons. The open area was divided into two classes. There was a blackboard and a teacher behind a table at either end; half the children faced one teacher and half the other. There was a narrow aisle but no other partition between the classes. The teachers had long bamboo canes in front of them that Pari eyed uneasily. As she followed an attendant towards the headmaster's office, the teacher nearest to Pari picked up her cane, pointed towards a girl and then tapped one of the questions on the board – 'How many rivers are there in the Punjab?'

'Five, madam,' said the girl.

Pari relaxed. I've got the wrong end of the stick, she thought, pleased with her pun. A cane was obviously not just for beating kids.

'Welcome, welcome,' said the principal when she walked into his office. After the introductions, Pari asked whether the lack of a birth certificate or transfer certificate from Vasu's previous school in the village was a problem.

'Not at all, madam,' said the principal. 'As long as you pay the fees, we won't ask for any certificates.'

Pari smiled uncertainly, not sure whether the man was joking.

Several minutes and questions later, they stood up.

'You have already seen our years four and five. Let me show you round the other classrooms before you go,' said the principal.

The second room they walked into was for the year three students – the class that Vasu would join. A pupil was standing in front of the other pupils with his palm held out and tears streaking down his cheeks. The teacher, a middle-aged woman with a pinched, discontented look on her face, held a long bamboo switch.

'Four,' said the teacher and the cane whistled down in an arc. *Thwack.*

Pari winced and unconsciously rubbed her palm as the bamboo made loud contact with the boy's hand. 'Stop,' she cried out, unable to prevent herself.

Everybody looked at her, surprised.

'How can you hit a small boy so mercilessly?' Pari said to the teacher.

The teacher moved her hands behind her, so that the cane was hidden – like a schoolboy surprised in an act of petty theft. 'He didn't bring his homework. He claims that his little brother urinated on the book,' she said.

Several pupils giggled until the teacher glared at them. The boy being punished looked even more miserable.

'Don't . . .' Pari said weakly and turned on her heel.

'Madam, we believe in discipline,' said the principal, running behind her.

Pari increased her pace and left without looking back.

She blinked and saw Vasu sitting in front of her, his expression still disgruntled. She smiled and put her hand on his arm. 'You will be able to start at a good school soon.'

She had been wrong even to visit that school. How could a place of education that itself broke rules teach children anything?

Vasu started getting up from the table but Pari stopped him. 'Now, don't leave that last piece of idli. All the strength of the food is in the last morsel.'

'That's not true,' said Vasu.

'Of course it's true. My mother said so.'

'That's what you always say, but she must have been mistaken. I asked Rehman Uncle and he said that the last part of the food has the same amount of strength as the first one.' He looked at her with a smug smile.

'What does Rehman know?' she said.

'He knows everything.'

'Don't be cheeky. Nobody knows everything, except God. Go on, eat that last bit,' she said and stared at him, until he grumpily put it in his mouth. 'Put the plate away and wash your hands. Get your bag, we have to leave.'

She was eating the last of her breakfast when there was a loud crash. She turned quickly to see Vasu hopping on one leg, holding his foot. His face was screwed up in pain. She rushed over and sank to her knees, taking his foot in her hands.

'Are you all right?' she asked, feeling his toes.

'Yes,' he said after a while. 'I am sorry.'

There was a rolling pin on the floor, next to a broken teacup. Vasu had accidentally knocked both from the sideboard.

Pari sighed. The room was too small for both of them. She

had taken it when she had moved to the city from the village after her father died. It had been fine, if slightly cramped, for living in on her own but it was definitely too small to raise a child. Also, much as she loved Vasu, he was a boy and she needed her privacy sometimes. The entire place was one room, ten feet by twelve feet, plus a bathroom. She had set up one corner of the room as a kitchen and the rest was living room, bedroom, study and wardrobe combined. The only way they survived was by spending a lot of time with the Alis, who lived just across the road.

She had to find a bigger place. It was not as if she didn't have money. Her inherited capital was actually growing because her monthly expenses were less than her dead husband's pension added to her own salary from the call centre.

'There's too much stuff here,' said Vasu.

Pari gave the boy's foot a final rub and stood up. 'Don't worry. We'll soon move into a two-bedroom flat. We can afford it.'

# CHAPTER TWO

Pari had spent many months reading Shakespeare while nursing her father in his final illness and she remembered lines from the bard's plays on the odd occasion.

> I have seen a medicine
> That's able to breathe life into a stone,
> Quicken a rock, and make you dance canary
> With spritely fire and motion.

The potion that made one dance canary, whatever that was, had been Helena in *All's Well That Ends Well*. Rather unlike the government, thought Pari as she looked around. This office had done the opposite. It had found a way to squeeze the passion out of the most fundamental events of any life – birth and death, finding and losing a mate, gaining a home – and turned them into dull, stodgy prose on grey, curling paper.

The room was small and stiflingly hot. The press of people was overpowering. House buyers, brokers and bored civil servants jostled for space among piles of files under the patina of dust that overlay everything. The stuffy air made her feel faint. Squeezing her eyes shut, she tried to ignore the chatter and the press of the women on either side of her on the bench where she sat.

A hand on her shoulder shook her and she looked up with a jerk to find Rehman gazing at her, concern in his eyes. 'Are you all right?' he asked.

'Too hot,' she said, wiping her forehead with a tiny hand-kerchief.

'Then you will be glad to know that this office is for registering commercial transactions. *We* have to go round.'

There were far fewer people on the other side. They were ushered into an office by an attendant in a starched white shirt and trousers with a broad red sash across his upper body, who whispered to them to wait at the back until it was their turn.

A young couple were standing in front of the registrar and their family members formed the rest of the audience in the room. The young woman had elaborate henna patterns on her arms and glowed with the special radiance that only brides have. Her partner was dressed in a suit that seemed too large for his thin body.

Pari was surprised to see that not only were there two sets of parents but that everybody looked very pleased. If they were all happy, why were they having a civil ceremony rather than a religious one?

She watched the bride, who couldn't seem to stop smiling. Pari thought back to her own wedding. She had married young and it seemed like a long time ago now, though it had been only four years. Much had happened in the intervening period. The oh-so-short time that she had spent with her handsome, loving husband now seemed like a dream, a drop of morning dew that evaporated as soon as the sun touched it.

Her husband had died in an accident. Shortly afterwards, while she was still reeling from that awful blow, her father had suffered a stroke that had left him incontinent and prone to violent seizures. She had nursed him for a year on her own, until he too had passed away. It was then that Pari had decided to leave the village where she had grown up.

She took a deep breath. The past is another country – where had she read that? The registrar seemed to be in some confusion. The two fathers and the official were holding an urgent, whispered conference. She looked at her watch. It was almost eleven.

Should she marry Dilawar? The proposal had come out of the blue. Dilawar's family was so posh – a Nawwabi family with a rich lineage. On top of that, he was an executive with a multinational company, earning what to her seemed like an unreasonably large salary. What did they see in her? She was an orphan who did not know anything about her real parents except that they had been poor enough to give up their new-born daughter for a relatively small sum of money. She had been sold at birth – even now that thought had the power to hurt her in the dark reaches of the night.

Would Dilawar and his family expect her to give up Vasu? That's what widows normally had to do to get remarried. But she had sworn to look after him. Nothing would separate them, she told herself.

Rehman bent his head and whispered, 'What did you say?'

Perhaps she had muttered it out loud. Their eyes met. 'Did you say that you knew Dilawar?' she asked.

'Yes,' said Rehman. 'We were classmates and good friends at school. We went to different colleges and lost touch after that.'

Pari nodded and stared straight ahead. The rest of the witnesses had joined in the conference at the lectern. Only the bride and groom, gazing at each other and smiling, seemed to take no part in the discussion. Pari studied Rehman's profile out of the corner of her eye. She wondered what was going on in his mind as he watched the scene in front of him.

She and Rehman were Muslims, but his ex-fiancée, Usha, had been a Hindu. He had planned a registered wedding, just like this one. Was he imagining himself standing there with Usha? He was doing a remarkable job of hiding his heart-break, but he had become silent and stiff since his engagement was broken off. She suddenly realised what it must have cost Rehman to agree to come here with her today. She reached out and took his hand.

He looked at her, eyebrows raised in surprise.

'Thank you,' she said softly.

'What for?'

She shrugged. 'Everything,' she said.

'Pagli,' he said. 'Foolish girl.'

At that moment, as she looked intimately at Rehman, though specks of dust dancing in the beams of sun from the windows in an airless office full of hushed conversation, something extraordinary happened. A revelation burst on her like a bolt of lightning. She loved him. No! She was *in love* with him. The certainty of it staggered her and she dropped his arm as if it were a hot skillet. Where had that come from? And what was the point? He was still deeply emotionally involved with his ex-fiancée. And she was a widow who had just received a marriage proposal. Why did God play such cruel jokes on her? Hadn't He tested her enough?

She kept her attention resolutely focused on the knot of people before the registrar, conscious of Rehman's eyes on her for a long moment before he too looked ahead. The problem at the dais seemed to have been resolved and the bride and groom were pushed to the front again.

Marriage was fine, Pari thought. Nobody, not even Pari herself, could begrudge her that. Though she had come up with many reasons for not immediately accepting Mrs Bilqis's proposal, guilt had not been one of them. But falling in love . . . She shook her head slowly. Love was something else altogether. She could not betray her dead husband. Her heart did not belong to her any more. She had given it away to her husband a long time ago.

The registrar said, 'Do you, Sujata, accept Vijay as your husband?'

'I do.'

Less than five minutes later, the register was signed and the formalities complete. One of the women in the audience showered the couple with rose petals. The pink confetti softened the harsh office. As the pair went past, Pari called out, 'Congratulations!'

The bride turned towards her and gave her a wide smile. Before the young woman could say anything, one of the matrons in the family looked at Pari with horror and stepped in front of the bride, speaking to her but with her eyes on Pari. 'Don't say a word,' she said in a harsh whisper. 'It is bad luck. Don't begin your married life by talking to the witch. These office people should have more sense than to let inauspicious widows in when there's a wedding taking place.'

The other family members looked alarmed and speeded up their pace. The bride averted her eyes.

Pari flinched as if she had been slapped. This kind of reaction was not uncommon, though most people didn't realise quite this quickly that she was a widow. Was her widowhood tattooed on her forehead for all to see? Perhaps her dark clothes and lack of jewellery gave her away.

'How dare—' began Rehman, moving towards their receding backs.

Pari put a hand on his arm. 'It is OK, Rehman. Leave it.'

'No, it is not all right. I'll make them apologise for hurting you.'

His anger warmed her. She wanted to tell him that she loved him for taking it so personally, but instead she said, 'Let's just go to the registrar. He is free now.'

She took out the papers from her handbag and passed them over to the official.

'Who were those people?' said Rehman, indicating the previous group with a jerk of his thumb.

'They are two big landlord families,' the registrar said. 'The actual religious wedding is tomorrow but they wanted to apply for a US visa so they needed a wedding registration document.'

Before Rehman said anything more, Pari interrupted. 'What do we care who they are? I want to get back to Vasu.'

The registrar flipped through the papers. 'These documents have only the mother's name,' he said, and looked at Rehman. 'What about the father?'

'That's right,' said Pari. 'I am adopting him. There is no need for a father.'

The official seemed confused. 'I am not sure . . .' he began. He looked at Pari more carefully. 'You two are not married.'

'That's right. Is there a law that says that you have to be married to adopt?'

'Yes, there is,' said the registrar, surprisingly.

Pari was crushed. She had not anticipated this. 'Oh, what do we do now? What will Vasu say?' Without the adoption papers, his schooling would be delayed yet again.

Rehman took out a crumpled sheet from his trouser back pocket and smoothed it out in front of them. 'The law specifically states that an unmarried man may not adopt a child. Women are allowed to adopt whether they are married or not. There is no requirement for a father.'

Pari gave Rehman the same look that a thirsty traveller might give a working fountain. 'Are you sure?' she said.

'It's all here in black and white,' he said, pointing to the paper. It was a prominent lawyer's opinion citing article numbers and precedents.

'I'll have to check this, but I don't have the necessary books here,' the registrar said.

Rehman pointed to the telephone number on the letterhead. 'Give the lawyer a ring. He is expecting your call.'

'Give me a moment,' said the registrar, taking the paper and getting up from his chair.

'You are a godsend! But how did you happen to have a lawyer's opinion handy?' said Pari, as soon as the official left the room.

'I am always prepared,' he said, grinning.

'Come on, tell me. You obviously thought there might be a problem. But how . . . Actually, I don't care. I am just so happy that you are here.'

'There was a case recently that Ammi showed me in the papers. A Japanese couple had paid a poor woman in north India to be a surrogate mother. Unfortunately, the couple got divorced before the baby was born and the Japanese woman did not want anything to do with the baby. The husband was still keen but, as a single man, he was not allowed to adopt. The surrogate mother didn't want to rear a Japanese-looking baby that was technically not hers. That got me thinking. How would a simple official in a town like this be expected to know the law in these cases? So, I consulted the lawyer and had him prepare the document.'

'Thank you,' said Pari. After a moment, she asked, 'What happened to the poor infant?'

'The Japanese baby? The husband's widowed mother came

to India and adopted him. Mother and son then took him home to their own country.'

Pari hugged Rehman's arm tightly. 'You are great,' she said.

'I know,' said Rehman, grinning.

Pari gave him a punch on his arm. 'I don't want to give you a fat head, but I don't care. I feel like singing.'

Rehman looked apprehensive. 'You won't, will you?' he said.

Pari laughed – a clear, bright sound that seemed incongruous in the dusty room.

The registrar came back to his desk. 'It turns out you're right. So everything seems to be in order.'

He asked Pari to sign her documents in two places. Now that the moment was so close, Pari's fingers started shaking and she couldn't hold the pen properly. Rehman's hand felt warm as it closed over hers and held it steady. When the shaking stopped, Rehman stepped back. She signed the document and the registrar stamped it with an official seal.

'Congratulations, madam. You are now a mother.'

Tears welled up in her eyes. The shabby government office suddenly looked beautiful.

Aruna gave the blood-pressure pill to her father-in-law and handed him a glass of water. He swallowed the pill and washed it down, then smiled at her and went back to his television show.

Aruna put the glass away and went into her bedroom, closing the door behind her. Her neurosurgeon husband, Ramanujam, was already there, sitting at the table, looking through Cat-scan slides and making notes in preparation for the next day's cases.

'How is it going? Nearly finished?' she asked, hopefully.

Ramanujam shook his head. 'Difficult case,' he said, tapping the papers before him. 'It's a meningioma – a brain tumour – but it has grown so much that it will be tricky to remove.'

'You have been looking at those X-rays for a long time. The best thing you can do is to rest now and go into the operating theatre in a relaxed frame of mind.'

Ramanujam flicked his pen on to the table and massaged his fingers. 'As usual, you are right,' he said. 'There is nothing more to be learned from these slides. Right, let's talk about something else. Have amma and naanna gone to bed?'

'Your father is still watching television.'

'I've been thinking,' he said.

'That's a bit unusual, isn't it?' she said quickly.

'Ooh! The little bird is spreading its wings.'

Aruna flushed. She wouldn't have made that comment a few months before, but as time passed her confidence had been growing. Not more than a year ago, she was a poor girl who had despaired of ever getting married because of her family's financial circumstances. Now, she was the daughter-in-law of a wealthy family. Whenever she thought about the twists of fate that had brought her from there to here, she marvelled. She looked around the airy room – the marble floor, the rosewood bed with its sprung mattress, the teak table with its beautiful anglepoise table lamp, the painting of a Kuchipudi dancer standing on one leg, the en-suite bathroom . . .

Ramanujam stood up from the chair and stretched mightily. Aruna admired his bare chest and the muscles on his arms. She was certainly a lucky woman.

'No, seriously,' he said. 'Before we got married, you told me that you'd never been out of the state and we haven't ventured anywhere since then either. So, let's go on a holiday.'

'A holiday?'

That was a new concept for her. All her previous travels had been local, either to a temple town for a pilgrimage or to an uncle's house for a change of scenery, sometimes both at the same time, as her paternal uncle was a priest at a famous temple of Lord Venkateswara.

'We'll go to Mumbai and stay in a nice hotel.'

'A hotel?'

'Why do I hear an echo?' he said. 'Yes, from there we'll go to Goa. You can hit the beach in a nice pink bikini.'

'Bikini?'

'Echo! Echo! Echo . . .' he said, his voice dropping with each successive word.

'Don't be ridiculous,' said Aruna, ignoring her husband's interruption. 'I am not going anywhere in something like that. I don't even look at magazines with pictures of women dressed in such skimpy clothes.'

'All right,' her husband said seriously. 'You can come dressed in a nine-yard sari and keep your eyes on the sand. I will look at all the foreign women sunbathing, so I can describe them to you.'

Aruna frowned for a moment then gave a sudden grin and punched him on his upper arm. 'You will run a mile if one of them even speaks to you,' she said.

'You will be pleased to know, madam, that I didn't spend every night of my college in my hostel room.'

She rolled her eyes and said, 'Oh yes, didn't you tell me that you were a member of the astronomy club in college?'

She grinned when he became speechless, before sticking her tongue out at him and going into the bathroom to brush her teeth. Night-time teeth-cleaning was another of the rich people's habits that she had picked up since getting married, along with changing into a nightdress rather than sleeping in her sari. When she came out of the bathroom, Ramanujam was already in bed. She got in, snuggled up against him and put her head on his right shoulder.

'Won't the holiday cost a lot of money, especially staying in hotels and eating out every day?' she asked.

'Don't worry about that. We deserve a holiday.'

'I wonder . . .' said Aruna and then fell silent.

'What?'

'Oh, nothing – just a thought. What if I feel like eating rice and rasam with poppadum? I am sure that a place like Goa won't have any south Indian food.'

Ramanujan smiled, half turned and kissed her on the top of her head.

Aruna rubbed her hand over his chest and stroked the stubble on his cheek. 'I think that there should be places to stay with a kitchen, so you can cook your own food.'

'What kind of fun would that be? Going to the market, chopping, frying and cleaning – you might as well stay home. At least here, you have servants to help.'

'It will still be a change and fun to see bazaars in other places,' said Aruna. 'Sometimes you can go to restaurants and sometimes you can eat in.'

'Aruna's self-cooking cottages,' said Ramanujam, using his hands as if framing a banner in the air. 'I can see it now. It will be a national chain – in all tourist places from Kashmir in the North to Kerala in the South. Save money and enjoy.'

'Now you are making fun of me.'

He turned on his side and tightened his arms round her. His lips found hers and there was no talk for a while. Suddenly, she pushed him away and jumped out of the bed. He looked at her in surprise.

'In all this talk about holidays, I forgot to take my pill,' she said. She opened her wardrobe and took out a small box. 'I only wished to delay children so that I could continue to work and support my sister in college. But you've made me realise that there's another good reason: I want to travel with you and see all of India before we have kids.'

'That's a great plan,' said her husband.

# CHAPTER THREE

Pari put the phone down and looked around her. A long row of cubicles faced her, each occupied by a person wearing headphones. She took off her own set, massaged her ears to get the blood flowing through her earlobes again and got up.

Unaccountably, she felt nervous. Sailaja, her best friend in the place, caught her eye and gave her a thumbs-up sign. Pari smiled back at her and made her way to the personnel department. Today was the last day of their batch's probationary period. One by one they were being called into the HR manager's office and given their papers. So far, the results had gone according to expectations – everybody had passed except one young man who was patently unsuitable for the work and had botched even the simplest tasks.

As Pari walked past Sailaja, the seated girl patted her hand and said, 'Let's go to Green Park tonight to celebrate. They have a dosa festival with chefs from Madras.'

Pari nodded and continued on her way. Soon, she was rereading the letter in her hand in disbelief. The HR representative across the desk would not meet her eyes. Pari looked at the letter again:

```
. . . We regret to inform you that we are unable
to offer you a permanent position at this time.
Due to current economic circumstances, we have
had to take tough decisions. We will keep your
details on file and get in touch with you if a
suitable vacancy comes up. We wish you all the
best . . .
```

'I don't understand. I have done very well during my pro-bation.'

The young woman from HR stirred. 'We take a number of factors into account, not all of which are immediately obvi-ous,' she said. 'Anyway, this decision does not mean that you performed unsatisfactorily. You must know what is happening to financial institutions around the world. We simply do not need as many people as we originally estimated.'

'But I did better than most people who have been made permanent,' said Pari.

The HR representative's face froze. 'We made it clear at the start that being made permanent at the end of your probation was entirely at our discretion. We do not have to give any rea-sons for our decision either way. You have the right to write to the head of human resources and we will consider your appeal in the appropriate manner.'

Pari got the message. She could write but her letter would simply be filed away somewhere. All the same, what had she got to lose?

'Yes, I *will* write to your head about the lack of clarity in your selections,' she said, the words sounding hollow.

'As you wish,' said the young woman opposite her, pushing a pen and paper towards her.

Less than ten minutes later, Pari was out of the building. The harsh mid-morning sun made her blink and she suddenly felt lost. What was she going to do all day? Vasu wasn't expected back till the afternoon and Mrs Ali was visiting one of her sisters for lunch. All the friends she had made among her colleagues were busy working in the building behind her. They would be sitting in long rows in their cubicles, wearing headphones and waiting for the red light on the computer to indicate that a call had been patched in.

'Good morning, madam. This is your service representative Pari. How may I help you?'

She suddenly felt such a surge of visceral hatred towards her ex-colleagues that it was like a physical blow. A couple of people she knew by sight came out of the office and she hurried away, not wanting them to see her. A three-wheeled auto-rickshaw tuk-tukked down the road, belching smoke from its exhaust. She hailed it and got in quickly.

The driver turned and asked, 'Where do you want to go, madam?'

Her mind went blank and she just waved her hand as if to say, forward. The driver shrugged his shoulders and the auto-rickshaw started moving.

What had gone wrong? She had been sure of being offered the job and all the comments from her trainers and managers over the past months had done nothing to dispel her confidence. She knew, without false modesty, that she was better than many staff in the office who had been there much longer. Why had she been chosen for the chop rather than somebody else?

'Which way do I go, madam?' the driver's voice broke into her thoughts.

Out of the side of the auto-rickshaw she saw the blue of the sea. 'Stop here,' she said.

She paid the fare and made her way across the road, towards the beach. It was deserted at this time of day, except for a pack of dogs in the distance. The sun burned her face and she shaded her head with the dupatta that covered her shoulders and chest like a shawl.

Why had *she* been chosen to be kicked out? After a moment's reflection, she realised that this was a fruitless line of thought. If it wasn't her, who else did she think had to be let go? Sailaja? Bobby? No, that was wrong. While it was unfair for her to be singled out like this, she didn't wish it on somebody else. Except . . . Except that she actually did, in some corner of her mind. She didn't want to be the one to be standing idle in the middle of the day with nothing to do. She wanted to work; she wanted to be busy.

She sat on the low, wide wall that separated the beach from the road. The beach, a hundred feet or so wide, stretched out on either side of her for some distance. Waves rose and crashed tirelessly into the sand, rather like her thoughts. She remembered the most terrible night that she had ever endured – when her husband's body had been brought home from the hospital after the accident. The back of his head was bashed in, but from the front he looked as if he were asleep. His muscled arms, the broad chest of a born athlete, the sculpted face of a man who could have been a film star, looking so peaceful . . . She had expected him to rise at any moment and give her that crooked smile of his.

A seagull went screaming past her. She shook her head. Unfair as this day was, it did not, in any way, compare to that tragedy. And yet she had survived even that and found a modicum of happiness. Well, not quite happiness. A tiny bit of not-sadness. Life carried on, she knew that more than anybody else.

She thought about Bilqis Madam and her son. Should she accept the proposal to marry Dilawar? In the end, she didn't have anything to hold her back in Vizag now. Although she had been strong and independent for almost two years, she was tired. It would be good to let somebody else make all the decisions and just occupy herself in running a home.

The breeze from the sea ruffled the dupatta over her head. The soft cotton felt good against her cheeks. She had enjoyed a physically sensuous marriage with her husband. She had not thought about it since, but she could feel her senses wakening again, as if after a long slumber. The warm sun soaked into her and she regarded her body with dispassionate interest. Her husband had taught her to be comfortable within herself. Also, the year-long nursing of her father, helpless, drooling and incontinent after his massive stroke, had removed any vestiges of embarrassment over bodily functions. Nevertheless, she could not imagine being in bed with Dilawar. After all, she had seen only a photograph of him, though it was clear that he was handsome. She could imagine herself in Rehman's arms – his intense eyes drilling into her and his lanky body pressing powerfully against her. She squeezed her hands into tight fists and shied away from the thought. He was still in love with somebody else and she was sure that Mr and Mrs Ali had higher hopes for their son than a now-unemployed widow.

She wondered what would happen if she jumped off the wall on to the sand and started walking towards the blue horizon. Would she be scared when her feet got wet? When the water reached past her thighs? What about when it touched her chin? She didn't know how to swim but she didn't think she would turn back even then. Tears trickled down her cheeks. She was weary, worn out, fatigued – life was so difficult. Pari felt all alone in the world. She just did not feel like carrying on any more.

Suddenly, a hand gripped her shoulder. She turned, startled, and looked straight into the kindly eyes of Mrs Ali. She was shocked for a moment, confused by the unexpectedness of the older woman's sudden appearance. Mrs Ali sat down beside her on the parapet wall and hugged her. 'Oh, my dear. It's all right. Don't cry.'

Pari had not been aware that she had been weeping, but now she started sobbing even harder. 'I loved him, chaachi. I truly loved my husband. You believe me, don't you?'

Mrs Ali patted her gently on the back. 'Of course you did, my dear. Of course you did. We all know that.'

After a long time, she realised that Rehman was standing near by, speaking on his mobile phone.

'Thanks, Sailaja.' He was silent for a moment as he listened. 'No, no. I am really glad that you called. Your concerns were absolutely correct. Your directions were good too. We've found her now. I owe you a coffee.'

Pari realised that she was not alone after all. She had people, family and friends, who cared for her and looked out for her. She remembered her boy, Vasu. She, in turn, had somebody to look after, too. While she had been mired in her own dark thoughts, she had forgotten her adopted son. He had lost his father, then his mother and finally his grandfather, with whom he had been living. Yet, he was such a happy lad. It was not just children who learned from parents; it could work the other way round as well, she realised. A mother could also learn how to deal with life from her son.

Pari pushed herself out of Mrs Ali's arms and wiped the tears from her cheeks. Jumping up, she said, 'Come on, chaachi. Let's go and get some tea. That's enough moping around for one day.'

A well-dressed, handsome man in his late twenties strolled past the Gateway of India in Mumbai. It was Sunday afternoon. Tourists, mostly Indians from smaller towns and villages – they were all smaller than Mumbai – milled about under the shadow of the massive stone monument erected to commemorate the visit of King George V to Bombay before the Delhi Durbar of 1911. Like many Indians of his age, the young man had heard about this royal audience, and the fact that it was from this spot that the last British soldiers left these shores after India's independence, but as far as he was concerned it was all ancient history.

Hawkers sold everything from toys to snacks and drinks underneath the eight-storey-tall yellow basalt arches, built in a Muslim style with pointed doorways and carved trellises but decorated in Hindu fashion. It was originally conceived to be the end of a grand avenue that had never been laid out for lack of government funds and therefore stands at an angle to the streets leading up to it. Constructed by the British, paid for by the Indians, in an amalgam of styles and oddly aligned, the Gateway of India is even more representative of the country than its original designers ever intended.

For many in the crowd, this was their first visit to India's biggest city and they stared goggle-eyed at everything – from the crenellated top of the monument to the unceasing traffic on the roads, from the beautiful Taj Mahal Hotel in front of them to the jetty behind, leading to ferries for the nearby Elephanta caves, known for their thousand-year-old sculptures of handsome gods and voluptuous goddesses. Dustbins were dotted around the plaza – not always a common sight in India – in the shape of penguins.

A young boy asked his father, 'Why does that penguin have such a wide-open mouth?'

The father, carrying a smaller girl in his arms, replied, 'Look at his big belly; he is hungry and that's why he has opened his mouth wide.'

The handsome young man smiled and walked on, outwardly confident, although it wasn't long before his nervousness came back. He was surprised by how jittery he felt. His heart was beating fast and, in an attempt to calm down, he repeated to himself, 'My name is Ricky.'

The noises of the city surrounded him. He loved cosmopolitan Mumbai – here he could live the way he wanted to, without nosy neighbours interfering. Parts of Mumbai are among the most crowded areas in the world – with places where the population density touches a million people per square mile – and paradoxically, it was here, in the heart of this multitude, that he could be his true, individual self. But he was gradually admitting to himself that he was on the verge of a very big step and it was putting him on edge.

How had he come to this? A couple of weeks ago, he had gone to a café in the suburb of Bandra to catch up with a friend. He'd been stood up – the friend never made it. After nursing a couple of coffees he'd started to feel hungry and he had made his way to a nearby McDonald's.

'A McMaharaja, please.'

'Would you like to make it a meal?' the person behind the counter asked with a practised smile.

Ricky nodded. A minute later he carried his food to a table and unfurled his newspaper. He finished his burger and started on the fries, slowly reading the paper. A young woman in figure-hugging jeans and a cropped T-shirt walked past, talking on a mobile phone – all painted lips and nails. Ammi would have a fit if she saw a girl dressed like that, he thought idly.

Somebody cleared their throat next to him and he turned to see a guy in his early twenties standing next to his table. His first reaction was that it was a restaurant employee and he almost pushed his tray towards him, but a second look made him stop. The newcomer had a cleft chin, full lips and smooth cheeks; he was wearing a tight T-shirt that showed off his biceps and his rippling abs. A couple of giggling teenage girls walking past suddenly fell silent, both staring out of the corners of their eyes. Ricky could empathise with the girls. The youth was worth staring at.

'I knew you were one of us as soon as I saw you,' said the young man.

'One of us?' Ricky said, puzzled.

'There is no need to be shy. Why don't you come here on a Sunday, about five in the evening,' the young man said, tapping on a card and pushing it across the table towards him.

When Ricky automatically reached for the card, his new acquaintance had touched the back of his hand with his fingers. Physical contact between men is not uncommon in India and Ricky did not pay it much attention at first. But then the youth's fingers made a rubbing motion against his skin. The tiny movement felt very personal and an electric shock passed through him. Taken by surprise, Ricky jerked his head up to look at the youth. He was smiling and Ricky noticed how beautiful his eyes were. They seemed to be smiling too.

'I don't u–understand,' stammered Ricky.

The youth moved away but, as he did so, he gripped Ricky's shoulder and said, 'Be brave, be true.'

Ricky had left the McDonald's and rushed home to his flat, where he propped the business card up on his fridge. Over the next several days his stomach had flipped like a pancake every time he had seen it. The little card grew larger and larger in his imagination. Even at work, while locked in meetings about a new advertising campaign for an old detergent, his mind would suddenly go back to that scrap of white, standing oh so innocently on his refrigerator.

Sunday had come and gone but still Ricky had ignored the

card's silent call. However, he found himself having conversations with himself: 'I can just go for a lark. I don't have to do anything. Just curious . . .'

Another part of his brain would reply, 'Curiosity killed the cat.'

By the following Sunday, he had convinced himself that a visit would be all right. Come the afternoon, he slid into the driver's seat of his car but after a moment's thought got out and walked to a nearby taxi rank.

'Afternoon, saab,' said the driver, an old Muslim with a grey beard and a white lace cap hugging his head. Golden lettering on a green sticker along the bottom of the windscreen proclaimed in elaborate Arabic calligraphy, 'There is no god but God, and Mohammed is His prophet.'

Ricky's throat was dry as he said, 'Gateway of India.'

He thought that the pious driver would be able to make out his guilt from his face. But the driver calmly turned the flag down on the meter and set off. Along the way, they drove past the Haji Ali Dargah, the tomb of the fifteenth-century saint from Bukhara in the old Persian Empire. The tomb stood out at sea, a third of a mile from the mainland, and a line of pilgrims were walking on the narrow causeway linking the two. It must be low tide, thought Ricky. At high tide, the causeway was submerged, making the tomb an island. The driver bobbed his head in a prayerful gesture towards the white dome and minarets. Ricky's face reddened with guilt once again at the thought of going to the Gateway of India. But of course, the driver didn't see anything wrong in a young man visiting one of India's most popular tourist attractions. Gradually, Ricky had relaxed.

A crow, scavenging around the bins for scraps, suddenly flew past him, flapping its wings almost in his face. This brought Ricky back to the present. He would have to stop daydreaming and keep his wits about him.

He crossed the plaza and went down some steps. Several men stood in a small open area by the water. A few sat on broken concrete pillars. They were distributed in small groups and seemed to be deep in earnest conversation.

His legs suddenly felt heavy, as if he would need a forklift truck to move him forward. He didn't know what to do. He turned and looked back despairingly towards the solid mass of the Gateway of India, the world of normality where families congregated and fathers answered their children's questions. Ahead . . . Ahead was his destiny, maybe.

# CHAPTER FOUR

As bravely as he could, Ricky walked towards the group of men. One of them stopped him and said, 'Yes, what do you want?'

Ricky took out the business card and glanced at it, even though its contents were seared into his mind. 'I am looking for Shaan,' he said.

The man looked at him curiously and called out to one of the others, 'Hey, Rambo. Is Shaan coming today?'

The man called Rambo, who despite his name was short and slight, strolled over and looked at his watch. 'Yeah, but later,' he said. 'Why don't you come back in an hour's time?'

Ricky nodded. His mouth was dry. As he walked away, he felt reprieved. He was about to throw away the card but realised that would be littering. I have to be in the office early tomorrow, he thought. I need to go back home and it's for the best that Shaan wasn't here.

He passed the hungry penguins, but did not feed them.

All of a sudden, he changed his mind about going home. It was better to have dinner in town and avoid the evening traffic, he decided, and he crossed the road towards the Taj Mahal Hotel. As he approached its entrance, a magnificent, tall Sikh doorman, sporting a glorious handlebar moustache and a bright turban, opened the door. A cool, air-conditioned atmosphere enveloped Ricky as he walked in. The foyer was busy: with Arab men in white robes leading wives covered in black burqas, with Europeans and Americans in suits, and with rich Indians in a variety of clothes. He had been before and knew his way to the restaurant.

He lingered over the meal of Hyderabadi biryani washed down by a Kingfisher beer, thinking about the next day's work at the office: a presentation about the advertising campaign for his boss's boss. Briefly, the image of the young man, Shaan, came to his mind but he pushed it away. I've had a lucky escape, he reflected. I don't want to get involved in that scene. This biryani is really good, he thought. Each grain of rice separate and the lamb cooked to perfection, succulent and almost melting in the mouth, the spices precise and offset by the yoghurt raita.

When he emerged from the hotel, it was dark and the streetlights were on. The same moustachioed doorman who had welcomed him asked him whether he wanted a taxi. Ricky thought for a moment and shook his head. 'After that wonderful meal, I need a walk,' he said.

He crossed the road towards the sea and the Gateway of India. The crowds there had thinned out a little. He started walking aimlessly and before long he was hailed by the skinny and weedy man called Rambo.

'Welcome back,' said Rambo. 'Shaan should be here shortly.'

Ricky nodded, surprised by how he had ended up here again, despite his intention to go home. His stomach tightened and he wondered whether he should leave. Before he could make up his mind, a voice behind him said, 'Hello, darling. I haven't seen you here before.'

Ricky turned to see a man of indeterminate age standing in front of him. His lips were reddened and his long hair was slicked back. His black eyes were well defined with kohl. The man put his right hand on Ricky's shoulder with a languid movement. Although extremely nervous, Ricky was fascinated too.

The man patted Ricky's cheek, his long nails scraping over his skin, sending shivers through Ricky's body. 'Oh, what a plump cockerel you are. I am coming over all faint.' The man waved his left hand in front of him as if it were a fan and fluttered his eyelids with a simper.

Ricky felt hot and blushed.

'Oh, maa!' cried the man and moved closer to Ricky. 'You are sooo handsome,' he purred.

Ricky was frozen to the spot, like a fawn caught in the headlights of a rushing car.

'My name is Manek. People call me the Queen. What's your name, darling?'

Ricky didn't know how it had happened, but Manek, the Queen, was now so close to him that, as he said those words, Ricky could feel Manek's breath, warm and tingly on the side of his face. As Ricky started back, the Queen's lips brushed against his cheek.

'Hai rabba,' Manek said, before Ricky answered his question. 'Oh, God. We'll have such fun, darling.'

Suddenly, Ricky felt hands on his back, pulling him away from Manek. Ricky looked around, surprised. It was Shaan, the young man who had given him the business card in the café the other day. Ricky saw that his memory had not been false: Shaan was really handsome, with broad shoulders, an oval face, a perfect, long nose and thick, jet-black, shoulder-length hair. His lips didn't need to be painted; they were naturally pink.

Manek, the Queen, reacted with a screech. 'I saw him first, he's mine,' he shouted, waving his arms.

As Ricky gazed at the screeching man, it was as if the scales had fallen from his eyes. Manek was much older than he had first thought – well into his thirties or even forties. There were wrinkles around his eyes and the flesh on his upper arms was flabby.

'I—' Ricky began to say.

'He came for me,' interrupted Shaan. 'Go away and find somebody else.'

'And how are you going to make me go away, pretty boy?' said Manek. 'You won't be so attractive with a few scars down your cheeks.'

To Ricky's horror, Manek's long nails now looked like the claws of a raptor.

'That's enough,' said a voice. The thin and weedy Rambo was standing quietly near them.

Ricky was astonished when Manek lowered his hands and subsided. 'I saw him first,' he protested feebly.

'He came for Shaan more than an hour back. Go away now.'

Manek made a moue at Shaan and walked off, his head held high.

Shaan said, 'I am sorry about that. The Queen is a commercial – and a bad one at that. He will be nice and friendly for a couple of months and then he will start blackmailing you – threatening to tell your family and employers about what you do unless you pay him.'

Ricky felt faint at the words *commercial*, *blackmail*. He should have listened to his earlier instincts and stayed away.

Then Shaan gave him a brilliant smile. 'I am glad you came though,' he said and touched his arm lightly.

Some of Ricky's doubts vanished. 'Why did Manek go

away quietly when Rambo said so? Manek looked as if he could snap Rambo into two.'

Shaan laughed. 'His name should give you a clue. Rambo carries a wicked knife and can look after himself. He is a good guy, though. He doesn't like to see innocents exploited by the commercials too much.'

Ricky raised his eyebrows. He had a lot to learn.

Shaan held Ricky's elbow and pointed. 'Let's sit there.'

The next couple of hours were amazing for Ricky. He found Shaan an intelligent conversationalist. They talked about a number of topics ranging from clothes and fashion to politics and books. Even favourite movies.

'*Casablanca*,' said Ricky.

'For Humphrey Bogart, right?'

Ricky blushed. 'What about you?'

Shaan didn't have to think. 'Any of Almodovar's movies . . . *The Law of Desire*, for example.'

'I haven't seen that one,' said Ricky.

'It's an early Almodovar. Released in the late eighties, I think. Basically there is a love triangle between three gays. Antonio Banderas is to die for – he looks beautiful and the way he lusts after the older man, mmm . . .'

'I have seen a couple of the director's movies. Warm photography and all that, but I don't really like him that much,' said Ricky.

'Why not?'

'Well, I probably started off on the wrong movie. I saw *Talk to Her* first – you know the one in which this guy is in love with a girl in a coma and tells her father that he is gay so he can become her carer?'

Shaan nodded. 'He looks after her – bathing her, massaging her body every day and talking to her about what is happening in his life during the day. It's beautifully done.'

Ricky shook his head. 'The movie might have looked lovely, but I was not at all convinced. The guy, I don't remember his name, says – the last four years have been the richest of my life. That is rubbish. Looking after a bedridden person is just soulless work. There is nothing romantic about washing somebody's unresponsive body, turning it daily and looking after it. Bodily wastes don't become less disgusting just because the person is unable to help it.'

Shaan, surprised by the vehemence in Ricky's voice, shrugged his shoulders. 'What about Indian movies?'

'*Sholay*,' said Ricky confidently, naming India's biggest film hit of all time, a curry Western, set in the badlands of the Chambal Valley.

'Who doesn't? Do you think the two leading men, Jai and Veeru, were gay?'

Ricky looked shocked. 'They were just friends,' he said.

'Sorry, buddy. I don't buy that.'

Ricky laughed. 'I'll have to take out the DVD and watch it again, carefully.'

'Do you know about the court case in Delhi asking for the anti-homosexuality law to be struck down?' Shaan said, changing the subject.

'It has been going for a long time, hasn't it?'

Shaan nodded. 'Almost seven years. There are going to be more hearings soon and a few of us are planning to go to Delhi for them.'

'What will you do there?'

'We'll attend the court. Go on a procession outside, invite the media.'

Ricky shook his head. 'Not me,' he said. 'I can't afford to be anywhere like that. My friends and relatives might see me; I might lose my job.'

'You have to be brave, Ricky. Otherwise nothing will change.'

'Change? Whoever said that the wheels of justice grind slowly didn't know about Indian courts. Here they don't move at all – the wheels are jammed fast. Even if the case concluded tomorrow, society will not look at us differently. Let's talk about something else.'

To his surprise, Ricky found out that Shaan had gone to a college in London and now worked for a small non-governmental charity connected to Aids-related projects.

'But you can easily get a much higher-paying job in a multinational company,' Ricky said.

Shaan shrugged. 'I am very open about liking men rather than women,' he said. 'My employer is a European charity and they don't let my preference in partners override everything else about me.'

Ricky had always hidden his sexuality. His teenage years had been a secret torment while he tried to figure out why he couldn't understand, really truly understand, his friends' motivations when it came to girls. It had taken him a long time to admit to himself that he was gay. He had, of course, told nobody about it and frequently used humour to deflect any suspicion. He was sure that his family did not know, because they were constantly pestering him to get married.

'What do your parents say?' he asked.

'My mother still keeps in touch,' Shaan said. 'My father . . .' He shrugged.

'It must have taken guts to face up to them.'

Shaan shrugged. 'Be brave, be true. That's my motto. I am what I am. What's the point of hiding it?'

Before Ricky could reply, Rambo came rushing over. 'Run,' he said. 'Police raid.'

As Rambo disappeared into the gloom, Shaan jumped up, grabbing Ricky's hand. 'Come on, let's go.'

He led Ricky away from the Gateway of India towards

some construction material lying on the side of the road, guiding him between a stack of bricks and a mound of sand. They crouched behind a row of black drums that had once held tar but were now empty. Behind them lay the sea. No escape that way; they would just have to stay hidden until the police left. Whistles sounded and bright pinpricks of light flashed about, carried by unseen hands. There was a lot of confusion as people ran in all directions.

'Surround the area,' came a loud voice of authority. 'Don't let any queers escape.'

Another voice, 'I've got a couple here. Help me.'

Ricky's heart started thudding. Would he be found and arrested? What would happen if a journalist got hold of the news? How would he face his colleagues? He might lose his job!

The noises continued in the dark. 'I've got another one. Who's got the handcuffs? Aargh! The fairy's scratched me. Take that, you b—'

Biff . . . Thud . . .

Ricky closed his eyes and buried his head in his arms. What a stupid drama to get involved in.

Shaan reached out and gripped his arm. 'It's OK,' he said. 'Relax.'

Ricky shook his head. 'I have a bad feeling about this.'

'They won't find us here. We are past their cordon,' said Shaan.

Ricky hoped so and looked up again as the action unfolded. The confusion seemed to be resolving itself. Groups of men were dragged to one spot by police constables and made to sit on the dusty ground with their hands on their heads. A van with barricaded windows was driven close and its lights were switched on, illuminating the scene. One of the policemen was rubbing his arm and cuffed his prisoner, before shoving him roughly into the huddle of captives. Ricky saw that the prisoner was Manek, the Queen, looking ragged. His make-up was smeared and his hair hung wildly around his face. He couldn't see Rambo among the prisoners.

A stray dog with pendulous teats strolled up to Ricky and Shaan, baring her teeth in a snarl. That's all we need, thought Ricky. They were probably infringing on its territory. Ricky waved at it to go away but the dog stood her ground. Shaan scrabbled in the dust. Picking up a stone, he tossed it lightly in the air and caught it again in his hand. The dog backed away with her tail rigid. Ricky let out a sigh of relief.

When he looked in front of him again, the handcuffed Manek was standing in front of the inspector saying something. A few moments later, the officer, Manek and a constable marched straight towards their hiding place. The constable shone his torch and beat his lathi against one of the drums. The iron-banded bamboo stick boomed loudly against the black metal.

'Come out,' he shouted. 'We know you are there.'

Ricky and Shaan rose slowly. Instinctively, they held up their hands at shoulder height. Manek's face twisted with malice. Shaan looked sanguine but Ricky felt terrified of sharing a cell with Manek overnight. He was sure that Manek wouldn't leave him alone – there would be some incident.

Shaan lowered his hands. 'An interesting sight, Inspector,' he said. 'We were just watching you making the arrests and wondering what the hungama was.' Forcing himself to be calm, Ricky followed his example and brought his hands down as well.

'That's not true,' shouted Manek. 'They were both here before.' He pointed to Ricky and said, 'That man propositioned me and I refused him.'

A hot response came to Ricky's lips but he controlled

himself in time. Instead, he said softly, 'I don't know what he means, Inspector. I've never seen him before.'

Manek tried to say something but the inspector flicked him with his service baton. 'Shut up,' he said. 'I can recognise a queer when I see one.'

Ricky racked his brains. Opening his wallet, he took out a few hundred-rupee notes. 'Can't we come to some arrangement, sir?' he said.

The policeman waved the money away. 'Qeesay mein rakh,' he said. 'Leave it in your pocket.'

Ricky emptied his entire wallet. He had over five thousand rupees. 'Let's just settle it here,' he said. 'If we go to the station, more people will get involved and everybody will get less.'

The inspector looked a bit doubtful and seemed to be wavering. Seeing this, Manek screeched, 'You can't let him go. He's the same as all of us.'

The officer's face flushed red. 'Did I ask you to talk, you fag?' he shouted and gestured to his junior colleague. The constable raised his lathi and brought it down on Manek's buttocks.

'Oww!' screamed Manek and hopped up and down, clutching his behind. The stick was raised again, laying a second blow across Manek's lower legs. Another constable rushed up and the inspector turned to him.

'Take this . . . this fairy away and if he utters even one word, shove your lathi down his throat.'

'Don't worry, sir,' replied the constable. 'He won't talk if he knows what's good for him.'

Manek was taken away and roughly propelled to the ground among the other prisoners.

The inspector addressed Ricky, who was still holding the money. 'What shall we do with the two of you?' he said.

Ricky said, 'Superintendent Khan in Bandra is a family

friend but I don't want to involve him in a delicate matter like this unnecessarily.'

'Oh, you know Khansaab. Why didn't you say so right in the beginning?' He turned to the constable and made a sign.

The constable took the money from Ricky. Shaan reached over and extracted a five-hundred-rupee note from the policeman's hand. 'For a taxi home,' Shaan said.

The constable looked about to protest, but the inspector said, 'Take their details and let them go.'

The constable took out a small notebook and a pen. Having got Shaan's details, he turned to Ricky. 'Name?'

'Er . . . Ricky.'

The inspector tapped Ricky's shoulder with his baton. 'Sir, you might have friends in high places, but please don't insult our intelligence.'

Ricky gulped, feeling like a little schoolboy in front of a headmaster. 'Umm . . . Dilawar Beg.'

Father's name, address, date of birth. 'Mother's name?'

'Bilqis Bano.'

'Native place?'

'Vizag.'

By now, the police van had filled up with the prisoners. The constable got in and shut the door. The inspector stepped into the jeep. The vehicles made a three-point turn and sped away, leaving the two men alone.

'Ricky . . . or Dilawar?'

Dilawar blushed. 'Sorry. I was too scared at first to use my real name.'

Shaan gave him back the five-hundred-rupee note and said, 'You are so deep in the closet that you are actually standing in the next room.'

Dilawar's face sagged, sure that he would lose this new-found friend. He looked at Shaan anxiously, but to his surprise, Shaan was smiling. 'Be brave, my friend. By the way, do you really know Superintendant Khan of Bandra?'

'Of course not,' said Dilawar. 'I saw his name in a newspaper article I was reading when you gave me your card in McDonald's the other day. He had apparently given a speech at the local Rotary club about police courtesy and honesty.'

'Ha! That must have been a riot,' said Shaan.

Dilawar laughed with relief and clapped the beautiful youth on the shoulder.

Shaan said, 'Your place or mine?'

By eight-thirty in the morning, Mr Ali could not wait any more. He had finished his breakfast of vada – spicy lentil doughnuts – an hour earlier. In half an hour Aruna would join him and clients would start coming in. How was he expected to begin his day without a cup of tea? For forty years he had had his cuppa straight after breakfast. What was his wife doing that was more important than that?

He walked into the kitchen to find Mrs Ali squatting on the floor, holding a halved coconut shell against a metal scraper. As she turned the handle of the scraper with her other hand, tiny slivers of white copra fell in a pile on the fan-shaped, plaited-bamboo sieve underneath. Seeing him, she stopped scraping the coconut, dabbed the beads of sweat from her forehead with the end of her sari and looked up. 'What do you want?' she asked.

'Where is my tea?'

'I am busy,' she said.

'I can see that. But what is so urgent about scraping the coconut now? I have been waiting for my tea for almost an hour.'

'Who am I doing this for?' said Mrs Ali. 'Rehman's left for the village, so the coconut chutney is just for you. I bet there won't be any complaints about how much work I am doing when you sit down for lunch.'

'That's not what I am saying,' said Mr Ali. 'You just need to prioritise your tasks, that's all. Lunch is not for hours while I want to have my tea now, before clients start coming.'

'Don't talk to me as if this is your office – priorities and schedules and whatnot. I know perfectly well how to run the household without your help.'

She started turning the handle of the scraper rapidly. Its metal teeth must have run through the white flesh and into the shell because the snow-white pile was now dusted with brown shavings.

'Arre baba,' said Mr Ali in irritation. 'Why are you taking the wrong meaning for everything? I want tea and I want it now. And move the coconut around because I want to eat the flesh of the coconut and not its shell.'

Mrs Ali dropped the coconut and stood up. 'You will have to wait for your tea,' she said.

'Why?'

'You would know why if you paid any attention to what is happening around the house. You have your business, your clients and your post, and my voice is just background chatter to you. As long as your meals are regularly on the table and clean clothes are in your wardrobe, you don't listen to anything I say. You must be thinking: it's just the madwoman; if I ignore her, she will crawl back into her kitchen and I can get on with my work.' Mrs Ali started walking out of the door.

'My tea . . .'

'Forget your tea. Have you seen the sink?'

Mr Ali took a quick peek at it before following his wife. 'It looks normal to me. It's full of dishes.'

Mrs Ali's voice rose. 'It is *not* normal for the sink to be full of dishes at this time, as you would know if you paid *any* attention to what goes on in the house. They should have been washed ages ago.'

'So why—'

'It is because of that Swaroop woman on the second floor next door.'

Mr Ali almost said, 'I don't understand,' but stopped himself just in time, recognising that it was the wrong thing to say. He remained mute.

'Leela always came to our house first in the morning to clean the dishes and sweep our house. But now that witch insists that Leela go to her flat first. See, she still hasn't come. How can I make tea if the dishes are all dirty and the maid hasn't been?'

Mr Ali refrained from uttering the first thought that came to his mind – that his wife could wash the tea-kettle herself. He knew that was the wrong thing to say too.

'All right,' he said finally. 'I'll wait for my tea. It is not that urgent.'

Mrs Ali sighed. 'You go and do your work. I'll see what I can do.'

# CHAPTER FIVE

Rehman got off the bus by the teashop and slung his cotton bag over his shoulder. It was around eleven in the morning and the sun was hot on his back. A line of old men sat under the teashop's awning of thatched palm leaves, talking listlessly.

He had finally reached the village, having stayed a couple of extra days in town in case Pari needed any help. Unable at first to understand her moods – alternating between gloom and carefree giddiness – he had finally figured out that the loss of her job had been totally unexpected, leaving Pari feeling shocked and a little humiliated. His parents, and especially his mother, had taken Pari under their wing while he had taken charge of Vasu, arranging for the official copy of the adoption certificate to be issued and using it to enrol him in a school. On the day that they bought all the textbooks and exercise books, together with a rucksack with a picture of a cartoon character on it, Vasu had been so excited that Pari had to shout at the boy to make him go to bed.

Rehman had been taken aback by how much it all cost, but Pari insisted that money wasn't a problem at all, even though she had been sacked. 'My husband's pension and my father's money is enough to last my whole life even if I don't earn a rupee myself,' she said.

When Rehman mentioned the amount to his mother after Pari and Vasu had gone home, Mrs Ali wasn't so sure. 'I know that money is not an immediate issue for Pari, but I think she is taking it far too lightly,' she said.

Rehman himself never worried about money. 'What's the problem?' he said. 'Pari's told me how much she has and I think she's fine.'

'You know as much about money as a fish knows about spinach,' his father said, jumping into the conversation. 'When are you going to get back into a job yourself instead of wandering from village to village like a dervish?'

'We are talking about Pari, not about me.'

Mrs Ali said, 'You youngsters think that life will just continue on an even course. Pari doesn't yet understand exactly how expensive kids are. She's already spent thousands of rupees on the school fees, books and uniforms. This is just the start of the primary school. As he grows older, all these costs will go up and there will be many others. And, Pari, of all people, should know that things can go wrong at any time. She needs to set money aside for contingencies like illnesses and accidents.'

'Ammi, relax. Don't worry about it.'

'No,' his mother said. 'If you just sit and eat, even a mountain will be worn away. I am concerned.'

Rehman shook his head. His parents had lived too long counting every rupee for them to change their attitude now.

He started walking down the lane towards Mr Naidu's house. Vasu had lived in this village not that long ago. Now that it looked as if Pari might remarry, Rehman wondered what would happen if she became a mother. Would she love her natural-born child more than her adopted son? Would she resent Vasu and neglect him? He was sure that Pari would not do that, but what about her new husband? How would Dilawar treat an eight-year-old boy to whom he had no ties of affection?

Rehman looked around him, before setting off down the main road to the village. Stretching from the highway to the river, it was an old, grey concrete ribbon, thick with dust and cracked in places. Rehman passed the market, empty now but crowded on Wednesdays. Just past the temple and behind it lay the only multi-storey house in the village, belonging to a rich landlord who also happened to be the president of the village council. A mango tree with a twisted trunk stood just inside the temple yard, making the boundary wall bulge outwards. This early in the year, the blossom was just turning into small fruits that would become ready to eat at the height of summer, if the village boys didn't get to them first. Wild plants with purple and pink flowers abounded near a kink in the road where the sewer overflowed. Two young pigs were luxuriating in the resulting mud.

Rehman finally turned into Mr Naidu's lane. He could see Mr Naidu's house now – a one-room thatched hut. Next to it was a bigger, pukka building that belonged to Mr Naidu's cousin. The cousin – also called Mr Naidu, because that was their caste name – had refused to look after Vasu after Mr Naidu passed away because he believed that Vasu brought misfortune on his guardians.

Rehman remembered what the cousin had said at that time: 'Some people are just born at the wrong time, under a malevolent conjunction of planets, and misfortune stalks them all their lives. If they till a field, the rains will fail that year; if they need to cross a river, they'll find it in spate; their wife might be barren or, if not, then their sons turn out uxorious and ungrateful to their parents.'

He had warned Rehman to be careful because, he said, ill-luck could strike just as easily in a town as in a village. Could Pari losing her job be due to Vasu's influence? Could bad luck really dog a boy through his life, singling him out?

Rehman dismissed the thought as fanciful. He was an engineer, a rational man who believed in cause and effect. The idea that the stars that were visible in the sky at the birth of a person could influence what happened years later was surely ridiculous. But he knew that many people thought differently, preferring to believe in stars and astrology. It gave them some form of comfort, he supposed, though he didn't know what kind of consolation could be obtained from imagining that you were a puppet and had no control over what happened to you.

Aruna had been busy in the marriage bureau since first thing and by ten-thirty her throat was hoarse from all the talking to clients.

A young man who had come with his mother and sister was being exceptionally rude, refusing to look at the photos they tried to show him. As they were leaving after a fruitless half-hour, the young man said loudly for everybody to hear, 'I don't believe in arranged marriages anyway.'

Mr Ali looked at him and said mildly, 'However you find your bride, regrets are inevitable. At least if it is an arranged marriage, you can fault your parents, otherwise you will have only yourself to blame. And, believe me, it is always harder to bear something if you cannot blame somebody else for it.'

Aruna couldn't stop smiling and the young man flushed.

When the next family left, Aruna sighed and stretched. 'I thought they would stick to the sofa for ever,' she said.

Mr Ali smiled at her and said, 'You were so patient with

the other father. I wanted to tell him that his daughter would not get married to a rich executive from a wealthy family just because that's what he has planned.'

Aruna nodded. She knew about events not going to plan, though in her case it was the plans that had been pessimistic and the reality that had exceeded all expectations. Because her family had used up their savings when her father fell ill, her engagement had been broken off and she had been working as a shop girl in a department store – a job she disliked intensely. She had also joined a typing institute, aiming for an office-based job. Madam had seen her passing the house to her lessons each morning and one day had called out to her. To Aruna's surprise, she was offered a job in the marriage bureau.

She had grown to love it here – the gentle Mr Ali and his slightly intimidating wife, the many clients and their some-times peculiar requirements. And, of course, lovely, lovely Ram who had one day walked into the marriage bureau and her life. Her husband and his family were wealthy, so money was not an issue for her any more, but her parents remained poor and her sister was still in college. Many families, espe-cially, rich, landed families like her in-laws, expected the girl to give up her job on getting married, so before she accepted his proposal she had made Ram promise that she could con-tinue working and use her salary to help her family.

Mrs Ali came out on to the verandah with three glasses of lemonade on a tray. Aruna took a long sip of the cool drink and said, 'Thank you, madam. I needed that.'

Mrs Ali smiled. 'I could hear the two of you talking to those new clients. I wonder why it's so busy today.' She turned to her husband. 'Did you put more ads in yesterday's paper?'

Mr Ali shook his head. 'No more than normal.'

Aruna said, 'It is Punnami, madam. The moon will be full

tonight and many people think it is lucky to start new ventures today.'

Mrs Ali nodded. 'Of course,' she said. 'I had forgotten about that.'

Mr Ali read the newspaper, while Aruna put away the files. Soon, the only noise was the traffic on the road outside.

'How is Vasu doing in school, madam?' Aruna asked, after a while.

Pari's son, Vasu, had been tutored by Aruna's father, a retired teacher, until he had been admitted to school.

Mrs Ali said, 'It's just been a few days, everything is still new. Pari says that he's already made a friend, so I think it is going well.'

'My father is missing him,' Aruna said.

'Children have a way of doing that. They just enter your life and take over your heart,' said Mrs Ali.

'Not yet for me, madam,' said Aruna and laughed, embarrassed. 'I have to work for at least two more years until Vani's education is complete.'

'Yes, how is your sister?' asked Mrs Ali.

'She is well, madam. I keep telling her to enjoy her college days. They'll pass quickly and she will never be as carefree as she is now.'

Mrs Ali had never been to college herself, but she could guess what Aruna meant and she nodded.

A young man came by some minutes later. 'My sister is studying in America and I've come on her behalf.'

They took his details and were surprised to learn that he was a Tamil. 'We don't have any Tamilians on our books,' said Mr Ali. 'I don't think we can help you.'

'My sister and I were both born and brought up in Vizag, sir,' said the young man.

'Even if your family had settled here for the last three

generations and can speak Telugu perfectly, you will still be regarded as Tamils and it is unlikely that anybody will consider your sister for an arranged marriage,' said Mr Ali.

Tamils came from the neighbouring state to the south. While there were many similarities, they spoke a different language, a number of their dishes were different and they prayed to some gods that the Telugus considered minor deities.

'But we are Brahmins, sir.'

'It makes no difference. This is not about religion – this is about region. You should find a marriage bureau that specialises in your community.'

'I want to enrol my sister in your marriage bureau. Here is the fee.' He took out a five-hundred-rupee note from his shirt pocket.

'I am telling you that it will be a waste of money.'

'I don't care, sir. Just let my sister become a member.'

Mr Ali looked at Aruna, at a loss. She shrugged delicately. If somebody wanted to throw their money away, who were they to refuse?

'All right, young man. But don't complain to us later that we didn't warn you.'

'There is no danger of that, sir.'

The youth left and Aruna silently filed away his sister's details.

'It takes all sorts,' said Mr Ali and Aruna agreed with him. Apart from her salary, she got a commission for every member who joined, so she didn't mind.

The gate opened again to admit a grey-haired, elegant, long-nosed lady, her back straight as a bamboo. Mr Ali recognised her without any prompting from Aruna, which was unusual for him.

'Salaam A'laikum,' he said.

'Wa 'Laikum As'salaam,' replied Mrs Bilqis, taking a seat. 'I have come to talk about Pari.'

Mr Ali nodded and went into the house, returning with his wife.

Mrs Ali said, 'Please come inside. Don't sit on the verandah like an outsider.'

The three older people went into the house, leaving Aruna to mind the office. Mr Ali switched on the overhead fan.

'Please take a seat,' said Mrs Ali, indicating a long settee in the living room.

Looking up, she noticed a cobweb in the corner above the door and cringed inwardly. She had checked the room after their servant maid, Leela, had cleaned the place in the morning. How could she have missed something so evident? It was because Leela was not coming at her usual time, decided Mrs Ali. Everything was delayed and rushed – nothing was done properly any more. The web was almost circular and a small spider sat in the middle of it. The shimmering threads swayed slightly in the breeze from the fan but the web was fairly inconspicuous. To Mrs Ali's eyes, however, it seemed as obvious as the lighthouse beacon that flashed from the Dolphin's Nose Peak at night.

Mrs Bilqis was about to sit down, when Mrs Ali hurriedly pointed to a chair facing the other way and said, 'No, no. Not there. Please sit here.'

'There?' Mr Ali had just sat down in the designated chair.

Mrs Ali turned to her husband and said, 'Let Mrs Bilqis sit there.'

'It's all right,' said Mr Ali. 'The two of you can sit on the settee.'

Mrs Ali could see the spider's web from the corner of her eye. The spider was now moving down one of the threads. Her husband, of course, would be totally oblivious to it.

'Get up,' she said brusquely to him. 'Let our guest sit there.'

'Why?' he said.

Aargh! She could scream. Why were men so clueless? Instead, she glared at him. He couldn't figure out why, but he knew when to listen to her. He and Mrs Bilqis exchanged places.

'Would you prefer tea or lemonade?'

'No, no. I am fine. I don't need anything.'

'No, you must—'

The ritual of offer and counter-refusal ended, as it must, with Mrs Bilqis accepting a cup of tea. They all sat down and, after a moment or two of small talk, Mrs Bilqis said, 'I have come to ask for your help.'

'We will assist you in any way we can, madam,' said Mr Ali.

'Pari has refused the match with my son,' said Mrs Bilqis.

Mrs Ali nodded. 'She has told us.'

'My initial reaction to her rejection was to treat it as an insult and not speak to her again. However, I've given the matter some more thought and realised the wisdom of our elders in always using a mediator to follow up these proposals. So, I've come to ask you both: will you act as a go-between in this matter?'

Mr Ali shook his head. 'Pari has already refused. What's the point of a middleman now?'

Mrs Ali waved a hand at her husband. 'Please let the lady speak. I am sure she has something in mind.'

'Just because Pari is a widow and looks after a child, we keep forgetting that she is still a very young girl. Most women of her age are still in college and thinking about dresses and make-up,' said Mrs Bilqis.

'Do you want us to talk to Pari and convince her to agree to your proposal?' said Mrs Ali.

Mrs Bilqis smiled. 'They say that a raised eyebrow is enough to convey an entire message to an intelligent person and I think you understand what I mean. Pari is not able to think straight. My son is a handsome, kind man. He has a good job and earns a lot of money. He will keep his wife in great comfort. And our family is second to none. She will have respect in society.'

'I don't understand one thing,' said Mr Ali. 'As you say, yours is an aristocratic family and your son is in a good position. You can have any woman as your daughter-in-law. Why then are you so insistent on Pari? She is a lovely girl, but she is a widow and she is the mother of an eight-year-old. And she has already refused you. Why don't you find somebody else?'

Mrs Ali frowned at her husband. 'What are you trying to do?' she said. 'Are you trying to drive the lady away?'

Mrs Bilqis raised her hand. 'Bhai-saheb has raised a valid point. There are two reasons why I am persisting with the match. One, I think Pari is the most suitable girl I have seen so far and I don't want to lose her because of a misunderstanding. Two, I am not in the habit of giving up. I've started, so I'll finish this task, one way or another.'

'Like Hatim Tai,' said Mr Ali.

Mrs Bilqis smiled. 'Yes, like the legendary Hatim, who completed all those difficult labours for his king without ever admitting defeat.'

Mrs Ali said, 'We can try to change Pari's mind but I can tell you one thing now: she will not give up her son. There's no point in even trying to talk to her about it. And we don't think it is right, either.'

Mrs Bilqis took a deep breath. 'I am not saying that this is ideal. To be frank, I would have preferred it if the boy was not part of the package. However, it is what it is. In fact, if Pari was the kind of person who would give up her just-adopted son because it is in her convenience to do so, then she wouldn't be the woman for my son.'

'Are you saying—' said Mrs Ali.

'Yes,' interrupted Mrs Bilqis. 'Pari can keep her son with her even after marriage.'

'In that case, I think we can have a chat with Pari and try to talk her round. Did you know that she has lost her job at the call centre?' said Mrs Ali.

'Oh!' said Mrs Bilqis, a muscle in her face twitching slightly, as if under a sudden strain. 'I didn't know that. How is she managing financially?'

'She has money that she has inherited from her father and she also gets a widow's pension, so that's not an immediate problem,' said Mr Ali. 'She is also fortunate that she is the kind of person who doesn't need much money to be happy.'

Mrs Bilqis leaned forward, her back still straight. 'Even with my limited meetings with her, I can see that she has the right disdain for money, but has she thought about the future? She has a boy to look after. How is she going to cope on her own? If she marries my son, not only will money never be an issue but there will also be a man in the house to take care of her and the little one. Not many men will come forward to marry a widow with a child. If one does agree to marry her, he is likely to be much older, balding and with a paunch, and he will probably have children of his own. Is that the kind of man you want for her?'

Mrs Ali reached out and patted Mrs Bilqis's hand. 'You're right. This is a very good match. Her first husband was handsome and a fit athlete, and she will never be satisfied with somebody who is not good-looking. Once she gets over her initial resistance, Pari will be happy with your son. We will do our best to convince her to become your daughter-in-law.'

Mrs Bilqis got up. 'Thank you. Maybe the loss of her job is a sign from above that she shouldn't remain alone all her life.'

Mr Ali nodded. 'Leave it with us,' he said. 'Pari is a well-brought-up girl and I am sure that in the end she will not say no to us.'

As they all turned to the door, Mr Ali pointed to the corner. 'Oh, look,' he said. 'That spider has caught a mosquito in its web.'

'I don't see anything,' said Mrs Ali, glaring at her husband.

'There,' said Mr Ali, helpfully pointing. 'Just above the door, in the corner.'

'Good evening, sir,' said the watchman, lifting his hand in a salute.

Dilawar handed his car keys to the Gurkha, who was armed with a stick and a whistle. 'Evening, Bahadur. The wheels weren't scrubbed last week.'

The watchman nodded. 'I will make sure they are cleaned, sir. The other gentleman is already here,' the watchman said and followed Dilawar to the lift, leaning past him to press the button for the top floor before stepping back as the door slid shut.

Dilawar grinned; Shaan had arrived. In the days since they had met at the Gateway of India, Dilawar and Shaan had grown close. Shaan lived in a poky flat somewhere in the outer suburbs, so Dilawar had given him a set of keys to his own flat.

'What's the point of spending two hours each day in the rush-hour trains?' he had said.

The local trains in Mumbai are always crowded, but when they are at peak capacity, morning and evening, normal calculations are abandoned and the railway authorities use a measure called the Super-Dense Crush-Load Factor. Sardines in a can have more wiggle room than a Mumbai commuter on his long journey home.

Dilawar let himself into the spacious, airy flat that he was so proud of. Pale yellow walls glowed in the light of the setting sun, which was streaming through the west-facing French windows. Beyond them, a balcony overlooked a panoramic view of the city. Dotting the walls were paintings of rural Indian themes, mostly featuring rugged people and inanimate objects like doors and cartwheels in strong russets and reds. Two Mughal miniatures, depicting scenes from a Muslim emperor's court, took pride of place in the centre of the wall facing the entrance to the living room, highlighted by spot-lamps.

The aroma of Basmati rice and unfamiliar herbs tickled Dilawar's nostrils. The kitchen door opened and Shaan came out, wearing an apron and holding a ladle.

'Freshen up, Dee,' he said. 'Dinner will be served soon.'

Dilawar smiled with pleasure as he went into his bedroom. Even though he had spent the day in an air-conditioned office and travelled to and from the office in an air-conditioned car, the grime and humidity of Mumbai had still managed to find their way on to him. Just like God, a friend had told him once. You can hide, but the Mumbai dirt will find you. He took a quick shower, changed into comfortable cotton evening clothes and joined Shaan in the kitchen. The granite worktop was spotless. A plate held a bunch of chopped coriander, thinly sliced ginger and chillies in neat piles. Green liquid was boiling in a pot on the hob.

'You have a lovely kitchen here,' said Shaan. 'It seemed a shame not to use it.'

Dilawar had all the latest mod-cons but the only appliance that saw any use was the microwave. He either ate out or called a widow who lived near by and who, for a small fee, delivered one vegetable, one chicken or mutton curry, rice and phulkas, tortilla-like rotis – all freshly made.

Dilawar took one of the slices of ginger and tested it between his teeth. He frowned and said, 'That's funny. This ginger tastes lemony.'

Shaan snatched the plate away. 'Don't take anything from here. I need them for the dish. That's not ginger, by the way, it is galangal.'

'Galangal? Never heard of that,' said Dilawar. He examined the thin, fibrous slice closely. 'Looks just like ginger.'

'I was in town earlier today, so I went to Crawford Market and got all the ingredients for tonight's dinner.'

'It smells delicious,' said Dilawar, indicating the boiling pot with a jerk of his chin. 'The building looks impressive from outside, but I've never gone in.'

'Not been to the biggest vegetable and meat market in Mumbai? You are such a philistine, Dee. Did you know that it was the first building in India to be lit by electricity or that Rudyard Kipling's father designed its stone fountains? Now, out of here – I am almost done. Why don't you relax in the living room?'

'OK,' said Dilawar, going to the door. 'I'll crack open a bottle of wine. White or red?'

'White, definitely. A Riesling, if you have one.'

'A sweet Mosel?'

'Perfect!'

Dilawar unlocked an antique wooden cupboard in the living room. An electric wine cooler was hidden inside, holding several bottles. He took out a chilled bottle and picked up the corkscrew from its usual place next to the cellar.

'Where—' he started to say, before noticing that the small table on the balcony had been laid with a tablecloth and two places set. Some covered serving dishes stood on the table already.

By the time Dilawar poured the wine, Shaan was waiting

with a tureen. He went back into the kitchen, switched off all the lights in the flat and returned with a candle in a holder, having doffed his apron. The tropical sun sets quickly; it was dark now. Shaan struck a match and lit the candle.

They slipped into their seats. 'Thank you, Shaan,' said Dilawar. 'This is lovely.'

Shaan smiled, his beautiful face flickering in the glow of the candlelight. Dilawar's heart skipped a beat. They raised their wineglasses.

'To friendship and love,' said Shaan.

'Friendship and love,' acknowledged Dilawar.

Dilawar took a sip. Shaan slowly moved his glass in a circle and took a deep sniff of the wine. Taking a small sip, he held the liquid in his mouth, closing his eyes. Finally, he swallowed and looked at his companion.

'Riesling's such a transparent wine, Dee. You can smell the flowers and the clay soil. After leaving London, the one thing I've really missed is good wine.'

Dilawar smiled indulgently. The two men sat with their backs to the living room. A million lights had come on below them and a glowing red and yellow snake of vehicles moved along the Western Express Highway. Dilawar could make out the constellation Ursa Major, the Great Bear, in the sky above him. This was the tallest building around and the architect had done a good job. Each balcony was hidden from the view of all the others and the two friends were in complete privacy. A child's high-pitched voice carried in the dark from a balcony somewhere underneath them and to their right. The heat of the day had dropped with the setting of the sun and a teasing breeze wafted over them.

'Oh, I almost forgot,' said Shaan. He twisted round and pressed a button on the remote control in his hand.

I see trees of green, red roses too
I see them bloom for me and you
And I think to myself, what a wonderful world.
What a wonderful world . . .

The baritone voice of Louis Armstrong lingered around the two friends on the balcony and then faded into the Mumbai sky, like smoke from a campfire into clear air.

'I raided your music collection. Hope you don't mind,' said Shaan. He ladled a broth with king prawns, mushrooms and bamboo shoots into two bowls. 'Tom Yum soup.'

'That was good,' said Dilawar when they had finished. 'Quite spicy.'

'Thanks,' said Shaan. They cleared away the bowls and sat down at the table again. Shaan served steamed rice covered with Thai green curry. 'It's really supposed to be served with sticky rice, but I don't like it, so I've made Basmati rice,' he said.

Dilawar took a mouthful of rice, gravy and chicken. 'Lovely,' he said. 'It's just perfect.' With his eyes closed he breathed in the fragrant aroma and said, 'Mmm . . . Smells exquisite. Where did you learn to cook like this?'

Shaan actually blushed and grinned, showing his white, even teeth. 'In London,' he said. 'As a student.'

As his father was a rich industrialist, Shaan's college days had been very comfortable. When he returned home with a degree and a new knowledge about himself, he had gone straight to his parents and told them that he was gay. His father had ranted and raved that no son of his would insult him by being anything less than a man. Shaan was the youngest child and favourite son of his mother, and she shed many tears. When his father realised that Shaan would not change, he threw him out and told Shaan's two brothers and sister not to have any contact with their sibling.

'My mother called today,' said Shaan. 'She is going with Dad to Switzerland. They are accompanying the commerce minister to Davos for the economic forum.' His mother secretly kept in touch with him, from time to time.

Dilawar raised his eyebrows. 'Davos, with the minister? That's quite an honour.'

Shaan shrugged. 'Honour, shmonour,' he said. 'I've been thinking about why Dad was so angry with me. I think he is actually a closet gay.'

Dilawar choked and coughed. His eyes watered and he hit the back of his head with the palm of his hand to clear his airway. Shaan held out a glass of water to him and Dilawar took a sip.

'You are crazy,' he said weakly, when he got his voice back. 'It's your father you are talking about.'

'Oh, he would commit suicide before admitting it even to himself, but I am certain.'

Dilawar laughed. 'I wish you wouldn't spring such things on me when I am eating. I nearly choked.'

Having finished their meal, they dragged their chairs closer to one another. Stretching out their legs on the railing of the balcony, they sat in companionable silence, sipping the wine. Louis Armstrong's songs had long ended.

'When are you going to London?' Dilawar asked.

'Next week. Be good while I am gone.'

Dilawar looked at his friend and grinned. 'I should be saying that to you. I am sure you'll have more opportunity there than I'll have here.'

Shaan smiled. 'You are right. London's a great place. Let's plan a holiday there. I can take you round and show you so many places. We should go in July or August. There's probably no more pleasant a place on earth than England on a nice summer day.'

Dilawar nodded. 'I don't have a passport. Let me start with that.'

They lapsed into silence once more. Dilawar thought he agreed with the old crooner. It was indeed a wonderful world.

'Look,' said Dilawar, pointing into the starry sky.

A meteorite made its quick, fiery dash towards the earth. Shaan smiled at him. 'Thank you,' he said. 'That's the first time I've seen a shooting star.'

Dilawar shook his head and placed his hand on Shaan's knee. 'No, thank *you*. I have always been confused about what I am. All my previous encounters have been furtive and left me feeling unclean and guilty. You have shown me tonight that it need not be like that.'

Silence fell between them again. Dilawar drank in the younger man's profile and his heart started beating faster. The thought of Shaan being away for a whole week, among his old friends in London, was like a spear in his heart. The strength of his feeling surprised him. He bit his lower lip and looked away, towards the hills in the distance. Was this what love felt like?

# CHAPTER SIX

When Rehman woke up the next day, he couldn't figure out for a moment where he was. Roughly hewn beams of fibrous wood held up the thatched palm-leaf roof above him. Cobwebs stretched out in every corner. A cow's long moo came from outside. He remembered . . .

Vasu had lived here with his grandfather, after Vasu's parents – very good friends of Rehman – had died within a short time of each other. Then, a few months ago, Mr Naidu had taken his life after a disastrous harvest had left him in debt to a farming company that had supplied him with seeds, fertilizer and technical advice. None of Mr Naidu's relations in the village had been willing to take in the boy, because of a superstitious belief that Vasu brought bad luck to his guardians, as evidenced by the fact that his father, then his mother and finally his grandfather had all died while looking after him. Rehman had taken Vasu with him to the town of Vizag and Pari had adopted him.

Had Mr Naidu's fields really been sold off? Was there any money left from the sale after the debt was paid off? Who owned this house now? Whatever was left of all this belonged to Vasu and Rehman wanted to make sure that the boy was not short-changed. Also, Pari had told him to collect Vasu's birth certificate and any other papers he could find.

She had said, 'Who knows what we'll need in future? Just get everything you can lay your hands on that has a mention of Vasu or his parents or grandparents. It will also be good for him to have those details when he grows up.'

Rehman got out of the cot. His back felt as if it were criss-crossed with hot brands from the hemp rope with which the cot was strung. The thin sheet had done nothing to cushion him. He went into the courtyard at the back, drew water from the well and performed his ablutions, shivering from the cold water. He watered the mango tree that Mr Naidu had planted just before his death. It was small and hadn't yet rooted firmly into the ground. When he arrived yesterday it was looking very sorry indeed. Now its leaves were standing proud and shiny.

Rehman walked outside. A man in shirt and trousers went past him on the street – a commuter to the nearby town. A couple of women were carrying water in plastic vessels on their heads. Fresh cowpats lay on the dusty road and a girl ran over and started collecting them. The dung would be dried in the sun and used as fuel for cooking.

Rehman knocked on the open door of the neighbouring house. The previous evening, Mr Naidu's cousin had invited him over for breakfast. After they had eaten, the cousin, whose name was also Mr Naidu, accompanied Rehman to the panchayat office to see the village secretary.

'Without somebody from the village, the secretary won't do anything,' the cousin said.

The secretary was not in. An old man, the caretaker, said that the local Member of Parliament was visiting the nearby town and the secretary had gone to see him.

'The president is in, though,' the old man said. 'He belongs to the opposition party and won't visit the MP,' he clarified.

'Mr Reddy, BA,' said the nameplate on the door. Traditionally, the panchayat was the village council of five elders. In this democratic age, the five are elected by the villagers but the councils are still mostly dominated by the landowning castes.

The president, Mr Reddy, was a tall, bluff man with a bushy moustache. Rumour had it that he was angling for his party's nomination as the candidate for the state's legislature in the next election.

'Ha, Naidu,' he said, to the cousin. 'What can I do for you? And who is this foreigner?'

'Namaste, saar,' said Mr Naidu. 'This is Rehman, the man from the city who helped my cousin.'

'Please sit down,' the president said.

The caretaker came in and Mr Reddy asked him to get two teas. The caretaker nodded and left the room. Mr Reddy turned to Rehman.

'I've heard about you, young man. Any friend of one of my village people is a friend of mine. You not only helped the poor man before he died but also helped the whole Naidu caste afterwards by taking the boy away.'

Mr Naidu's cousin looked embarrassed. Rehman shrugged. 'I just did what I had to,' he said.

'Don't be modest, young man. Nobody here wanted to take the orphan into their family after his grandfather died. You did something brave.' He turned to Mr Naidu. 'I am not saying that you didn't have a very good reason. Anybody could see that boy was bad luck.'

The president must have realised that, while Rehman was an outsider and didn't have a vote, the Naidu caste were at least fifty strong in the village. Rehman suppressed a grin at the thought.

Mr Reddy turned to Rehman again. 'Is everything all

right with you? Have you had any misfortune since you took the boy into your family?' he asked.

Rehman reflected on the past few months. He had been engaged to be married to Usha and she had broken it off. While his immediate sense of despair had dissipated as the weeks went by, his heart still ached. Pari had adopted Vasu now, of course, and she had lost her job.

'No,' he said, brightly. 'Everything's fine. Vasu is doing well – he has just started school. No problems at all.'

Mr Reddy nodded. 'Good to hear that. But you didn't come here to listen to my speeches. What can I do for you?'

'The boy's grandfather owned three acres of land and the house in the village. I want to know what has happened to them and to make sure that Vasu inherits what's his.'

'The secretary is away. He has all the papers. But I know that the cotton company has placed a lien against the farm. I am pretty sure there is no charge on the house.'

'What does that mean? Does the land belong to Vasu or not?'

'In theory, yes. However, it cannot be sold or mortgaged without the charge being cleared. At some point, the company will ask for its money back and then it either has to be repaid or the land will be auctioned off.'

'When will that be?'

'I don't know,' said the president. 'To be frank, I don't like outsiders coming and forcing us farmers to sell our lands. And Mr Naidu has already paid the ultimate price. I will delay the matter as much as I can. Once these companies get the idea that they can ride roughshod over us, who knows where it will end?'

Rehman nodded. 'Thank you,' he said. 'We'll come back when the secretary is here.'

They took their leave and emerged into the bright sunshine.

'That reminds me,' said Rehman. 'We never got the tea that he ordered.'

Mr Naidu pointed to a buffalo with glossy black skin that was calmly tugging at a bundle of straw in the shade of a mud wall. 'You could have waited until that buffalo had finished chewing its cud and still not got your tea.'

'Why?' said Rehman. 'He told that old caretaker to get it.'

'That was just to make you feel good without that tightwad having to spend any money.'

'But what if we were really important visitors? How would the old man know when he was supposed to bring us tea?'

'Do you remember that he asked for two teas? If he had wanted three teas, including one for himself, the caretaker would have known to get them.'

Rehman laughed. 'I certainly got fooled.'

'The whole village knows he is a miser. What else can a moneylender do but hoard his gold, counting every sovereign?'

'Why do the villagers vote for him then?'

Mr Naidu shrugged. 'He has a web of contacts – many people depend on him for their livelihoods in one form or another. He can make their lives miserable if they don't support him. Don't get me wrong – it is not all intimidation. He can also be charming when he wants to be. He is like the jackal in the children's story that ingratiates itself with lions and fights with smaller animals to get what it wants.'

Rehman nodded. Even in a small village, there were wheels within wheels.

Later that afternoon, Rehman was sitting in the shade in front of the hut, going through a metal trunk that he had dragged outside. It looked as if Vasu's grandfather had not thrown out a single paper. The trunk held the adangal – the land ownership papers, Vasu's school books, Vasu's father's practical notes from college, old calendars with pictures of gods and goddesses, and simple tallies of the sacks of grain he had sold in the markets over the years. Vasu's grandfather had been illiterate. He knew how to read and write numbers, but not words.

It was probably easier for the old man to store all the papers than to risk throwing away anything important by mistake, thought Rehman. I should just take the whole trunk back to town. Vasu can decide what he wants to keep and what he wants to throw away when he grows up. It is not my place to choose.

A male voice said, 'The president is asking for you. He wants you to come to his house.'

Rehman looked up. A thin, wiry man in his thirties was standing in front of him. He was bare-chested and wore a panchi, a long cloth wrapped around his waist, like a typical villager. Rehman had never seen him before.

'All right,' said Rehman. 'Wait a moment.'

He started putting the papers and books back in the trunk. The man continued to stand there, making Rehman uncomfortable. 'Sit down,' he said. 'You don't need to stand.'

The man squatted on the ground.

'No, no,' said Rehman. He took some old engineering textbooks of Vasu's father from a three-legged stool and said, 'Sit here.'

The man shook his head. 'It is better if I stay where I am, sir,' he said. 'It won't look good if anybody sees me sitting on the same level as you.'

'Don't be silly,' said Rehman, but the man did not budge. Shrugging his shoulders, Rehman quickly packed everything away and locked the trunk. The man was from a lower caste and while it did not make a difference to Rehman where he sat, the villagers probably had a different opinion. As Rehman stood up, he saw the man's eyes fixed on the ground next to the trunk, staring intently, like a hungry tiger gazing at a tethered lamb. Rehman saw that he had left out the deeds to Mr Naidu's fields. The president's man was almost definitely illiterate, but it was clear that he had recognised the adangal – the official document on stamped paper, detailing the chain of ownership of land over at least one hundred years.

Rehman sighed in annoyance, unlocked the trunk and put the deeds away, before dragging the heavy trunk back into its place in the hut.

'Was Mr Naidu a relative of yours?' the man asked as they walked towards the president's house.

'No,' said Rehman. 'Did you know him?'

The man shrugged. 'I worked for him occasionally during harvest time,' he said. 'He wasn't bad for a landowner.'

Rehman nodded. A few seconds later, the man said, 'I heard that you are going to fight the company who lent the money to Mr Naidu.'

Rehman said, 'Where did you hear that? Anyway, the company did not lend the money. They supplied Mr Naidu with seeds and fertilizer.'

The man said, 'It comes to the same thing, doesn't it? If he was not family, why are you wasting so much effort in fighting for his cause?'

Rehman didn't answer immediately. They walked on in silence for a moment.

'Should we only look after ourselves?' Rehman said finally. 'Aren't humans better than animals who think only of their own hunger and thirst and feed just their own children?'

The man gave a short laugh – almost a grunt. 'Poor people don't have the luxury of such philosophy, sir. We can think only of our own needs.'

Rehman nodded silently, not knowing what to say. He noticed that the man's heels were cracked and callused after a lifetime of going barefoot.

As they reached the end of the street, the man guided them on to a narrow path between the temple wall and a ditch. They had to walk single file; the path was stony and dotted with thorny ground creepers, but the unshod man just walked stolidly on, as if the soles of his feet were made of tough leather.

Rehman asked, 'What's your name? What do you do?'

The man turned his head and spoke over his shoulder. 'My name is Sivudu. I am a labourer for the president. I work wherever he tells me – sometimes in the house, sometimes in his shop or in one of his farms at sowing and harvest time. If you have the energy to spare, why don't you help us poor people instead of taking on a rich man's problem?'

'What are you talking about? Mr Naidu wasn't rich. He barely had enough to survive from harvest to harvest.'

'A god has problems that only he sees and a dog has problems that only it feels. You insult our difficulties by referring to a landowner's issues in the same breath. I have work for only nine months of the year. The other three months, my family has to starve. How do you think I feel when my child cries with hunger and I can give her only thin gruel that swells her belly but doesn't fill her?'

'Can't you go to town and find work there?' asked Rehman.

'Do you think it's so easy? Some of us have chains that bind us here and won't let us leave.'

They turned at the end of the path and came to the president's house, fronted by a flower garden. Apart from the temple, it was the largest building in the village, three storeys tall. A car stood, covered by a tarpaulin, under a shed open on three sides. A large Alsatian dog stared at Rehman, panting with its tongue hanging out. Rehman was glad to see that not only did it look well fed, but it was also chained. The president sat in the garden, in the shade of a fragrant sampangi tree.

'What nonsense are you filling my guest's ears with?' he said to the labourer.

'Nothing, sir,' said Sivudu. He didn't stand straight any more – his shoulders were hunched and he kept his eyes on the ground. 'I was just saying that I am lucky to work for you, sir. I can eat almost all year round.'

'Quite right,' Mr Reddy said, twirling his moustache. 'You've wasted enough time. Go and dig the compost into the roses now.'

Sivudu glanced at Rehman with hooded eyes and moved away. Mr Reddy and Rehman went into the house.

'Why did you want to see me, sir?' said Rehman.

The big man ignored him and hollered into the interior, 'Get a tea for the visitor.'

Rehman gazed around him. A garlanded picture of Lord Venkateswara hung on one wall. The opposite wall was dominated by a floor-to-ceiling picture of the Gateway of India on a bright sunny day. The people milling around the foot of the massive monument looked tiny. A row of motorboats were moored along the jetty behind it.

Rehman's eyes left the picture and scanned the room. The floor was laid with marble and all the furniture was solidly made in what looked like teak. A display case at one end showed off a number of brightly coloured soft toys still in their plastic covers to ward off the dust.

Rehman was pleasantly surprised when a teenage girl, slightly better dressed than a servant maid, came in with a cup. Different rules apparently applied here where the offering of tea was concerned.

'What about you, uncle?' said the girl.

The president shook his head and she went out. 'That's my niece,' he told Rehman. 'My cousin's daughter. She lives with us.'

And works for her supper, thought Rehman, taking a sip.

'I heard that your father runs a marriage bureau,' the president said.

Rehman was astonished. 'How do you know?' he asked.

'We get the paper here too,' said the man. 'The Marriage Bureau for Rich People – that's your father's, isn't it?'

Rehman was never comfortable with his father's frank admission of wealth as a criterion for selecting his clients and he squirmed. 'Yes,' he said finally.

'Excellent,' said Mr Reddy. 'I've known about you coming and helping Naidu at the farm for years, but I never gave it much thought. I can see that scions of wealthy families have their own ways of thinking. I am really impressed with your dedication to a late friend.'

Rehman tried to shrug this off. Why was he being praised so much? What did the president want? Did he want to take over Mr Naidu's lands? His eyes roamed again over the large hall with the car outside and the gold rings on the president's fingers.

'We are not rich,' he said at last. 'Just middle class.'

The president tapped his nose with a finger as if sharing a secret. 'I understand,' he said.

Rehman sipped his tea and waited for the other man to speak.

'I am looking for a husband for my daughter, Roja.'

'I see,' said Rehman.

'I want Roja to marry my cousin's son, the brother of the girl who brought you the tea.'

Why are you telling me this, thought Rehman, but he kept silent and just nodded.

'The boy already helps me with the business. There won't be any money or property division issues, if Roja marries him. He will stay with us in this house, so my daughter won't have to move out. I have ambitious plans for my political career and when I move on to a bigger stage, I can make sure that my daughter's husband takes over my position on the village council.'

'Sounds ideal,' said Rehman diplomatically.

'Exactly,' said Mr Reddy. 'He takes my every wish as his command and never answers back. The boy would make the perfect son-in-law.'

'Women are strange creatures,' said Rehman. 'I don't understand why your daughter would refuse to marry such a paragon.'

Mr Reddy shook his head. 'If your son doesn't listen to you, you can beat him. What can you do with a daughter? Nothing, that's what. Take it from me, never have a daughter; always go for a son. That way you won't have to pull your hair out with frustration.'

Rehman nodded. 'Wise words, sir. I'll keep your advice in mind,' he said.

'Anyway, I am at my wits' end. I've suggested a few other men, but Roja just laughed them off. She wants a city boy.'

'Sir,' said a voice from the front door. Sivudu stood just outside and to one side, only half visible. 'I have finished.'

'What are you standing there for? Am I expected to shout for you now? Come here so I can talk softly,' said the president loudly.

The man wiped his feet on the mat and walked in hesitantly. 'Can I take a break, sir?'

'Did you interrupt me to ask that? Couldn't you have waited until I was free? Lazy workers, all the same, you will do anything to avoid your duties. No, you cannot take a break. Take the dog for a run now.'

Sivudu stood his ground for a couple of seconds, then turned away. The president shouted after him, 'And why have you entered the house with dirty feet, tracking manure in?'

Sivudu just continued walking away.

'You called him in, sir,' said Rehman.

'You have to be careful with workers. Never let them become complacent,' said Mr Reddy. 'Anyway, why are we talking about unimportant matters? We were discussing my daughter's wedding. She has a lot of gold jewellery and I have set aside a large sum of money for her dowry. Does your father have any Reddy caste matches? Their family has to be of similar status to our own.'

Like Naidu, Reddy was both a person's surname and his caste.

'I don't know,' said Rehman. 'He must have. There are lots of members from different castes.'

'If I give you all the details, will you ask your father to send me the names of any suitable bridegrooms for Roja?'

'Oh, no, sir. I don't get involved in my father's business. I will give you his phone number. It will be best if you contact him directly. In fact, you should probably go and visit the marriage bureau yourself. My father runs it from our house and you can easily go there in a few hours in your car.'

'All right,' said Mr Reddy. 'Give me your address. What time is he open?'

Rehman thought for a moment. 'Mornings before noon or before seven in the evenings,' he said. 'My father has a siesta in the afternoon and won't see anybody before four.'

Mr Reddy got to his feet. 'All right, young man,' he said.

Rehman wrote his father's details on a piece of paper, stood up and handed it to his host. 'I'll be off,' he said.

The big man escorted him out of the house. 'Why do you neglect your own father's business and waste your time looking after some other man's affairs? If you were my son, I wouldn't let you be footloose like this.'

Thank God you are not my father, thought Rehman. Your daughter is no fool, to try to get away from you. Rehman smiled as he took his leave, not trusting himself to speak.

# CHAPTER SEVEN

Pari closed the gate and walked past the guava tree on to the verandah. Mr Ali was talking to a young man who had the name of a courier company printed on his shirt and Aruna was typing something on the computer.

She waved to them both and went through into the living room. Mrs Ali was not there. The Alis' house was long and narrow with all the rooms in single file. Pari passed into the bedroom, then into the dining room and finally into the kitchen. Her aunt wasn't there either, but there was a pan bubbling away on the hob. As she watched, the water started boiling over the sides of the pan. Pari rushed to lower the flame.

Mrs Ali came in from the backyard with a pan full of prepared fish pieces ready for cooking. 'Thanks for taking care of the dhal,' Mrs Ali said. 'It took longer than I expected to clean and cut up the fish.'

'Why are you cooking lunch so early?' Pari asked.

'I am just getting some of the ingredients ready for later,' said Mrs Ali.

She scooped up a few lentil grains from the pan on the back of a wooden spoon and poked them with a finger. Satisfied, she switched off the gas and turned to Pari.

'Come on, let's sit under the fan in the living room. I'll finish it off later. What did you pack for Vasu's lunch?'

'Rice with tomato khatta and soya bean fry.'

Mrs Ali smiled. The chopped tomatoes cooked with onions, mustard seeds and curry leaves was a favourite of Rehman's and Vasu had taken it for his own.

Pari continued, 'I packed chicken curry the other day, which he loves, but the boy sitting next to him turned out to be a Brahmin and complained that it stank, so Vasu has told me to pack only vegetarian food.'

'Children are like that,' said Mrs Ali. 'They are so easily influenced by what other kids say – it is scary.'

They reached the living room. Mrs Ali switched on the fan and the two women sat down next to each other on the settee. Mrs Ali's eyes went automatically to the corner where she had noticed a cobweb some days earlier when Mrs Bilqis had visited them. The room was now spider-free but checking the corner had become almost a reflex for Mrs Ali.

They were silent for a while, listening to Aruna and Mr Ali's voices on the verandah. A motorcycle went past, its exhaust making a loud noise.

'Mrs Bilqis came to see us,' said Mrs Ali.

Pari's body went still. 'What did she say?'

'You know what she wants.'

'That woman is unbelievable. I've already refused her – very clearly. Why did she come to you?'

'Forget the woman and why she came here. Do you not want to remarry at all?'

'I . . . er . . . don't know,' said Pari slowly.

Mrs Ali remembered finding Pari alone on the beach when she had lost her job. 'Is it because you still love your husband? Do you think marrying again is wrong?'

'Yes . . . No . . . I am confused. Why do I have to make

such difficult choices? Why can't my life be simple?' said Pari, her voice rising at the end.

Mrs Ali reached out and held Pari's hand. 'Into each life, a little rain will fall,' she said. 'But everyone must suffer the sun burning down too. That's just the way it is. You loved your husband dearly and losing him was a terrible tragedy. They say that those whom Allah loves, He gathers back into His embrace more quickly than others and that's obviously what happened to your wonderful husband. The question is, what do we do now?'

'Are you telling me to forget my husband?' asked Pari, withdrawing her hand from the older woman's.

'Would you forget him if I asked you to?'

'No,' said Pari, shortly.

'Then why do you think I am saying that? You are taking this the wrong way. Perhaps I am not expressing myself properly. You *will* remember your husband for ever. In your mind, he will always be young and handsome, the perfect mate. I pity the poor man who comes into your life next. The reality of him will never match up to the memory of your first husband.'

Pari jumped up from the settee. 'I don't understand what you are saying, chaachi. Anyway I have to go to the market. I'll see you in the evening.'

Mrs Ali got up slowly, wincing at the twinge in her knee. 'Come with me into the kitchen. Help me make lunch,' she said.

Pari looked undecided for a moment, but gave in.

'Mash the dhal,' said Mrs Ali.

Pari nodded and picked up a round-headed wooden mallet. Mrs Ali started peeling an onion.

'Pari, do you want to live in that small room all your life?'

'Of course not,' Pari said. 'You know that I am looking for a two-bedroom flat.'

'How can you afford it? You cannot just spend every rupee you get from your pension and savings each month. Your expenses will grow.'

'I'll get another job,' said Pari.

'It's not that easy,' said Mrs Ali. 'Oh, you will get some job. But it will pay a pittance and you will have to work really long hours. Ask Aruna. Before she became an assistant here, she was working as a salesgirl in a big store. She had to work until eleven at night and do a full shift every alternate Sunday. You can't even do that because you have Vasu to look after. What's the fun of working all hours and missing out on caring for your child?'

Pari used the mallet to give the glutinous yellow dhal an extra-hard shove against the sides of the vessel. 'Something will turn up,' she said.

'You are talking like the man who got lost in a forest and started praying for help. Later when he came back home and people asked him whether the prayers had worked, the man replied that God did not have a chance because a guide turned up just then to lead him out of the forest. Don't be silly, Pari. Something has turned up. I remember having a very similar conversation with Aruna before she got married. You think . . .' Mrs Ali shook her head. 'I will tell you what I told her then: the seasons don't wait for young women to make up their minds. As you get older, it will become more difficult to make a good match. From the photos I have seen, Dilawar is a handsome man with a good job and Rehman says he knows him from when he was a boy. I don't think you can get a better match if you wait.'

Mrs Ali put a tiny pan, just a few inches across, on the hob and added a teaspoon of ghee. The white fat turned into clear, yellow oil and its rich fragrance filled the kitchen. Once it was hot, she reached for the spice container for some mustard seeds, catching Pari's eye as she did so. The young woman's beautiful face was so crumpled and forlorn that Mrs Ali's heart melted like the ghee.

'Don't be so sad. I am sorry to speak like this, Pari. You are right. Everything will be fine. Listen to me wittering away; that's what arthritis does to you. The doctor says there is no remedy for it and you begin to think that all problems in the world are like that – no cure, no cure.'

'What you are saying makes sense, chaachi. It wasn't that. I just remembered – the smell reminded me – my husband used to love adding ghee to his food. I stopped him because I read somewhere that it raises cholesterol and can cause heart attacks . . .' Pari's gaze took on a faraway look and Mrs Ali couldn't make out what she was thinking. Then Pari said softly, almost inaudibly, 'What a silly woman I was, thinking I could plan for the future.'

Unexpectedly, Mrs Ali's eyes filled with tears. 'Oh, my poor darling. Maybe you are right too. Your uncle and I spent all our youth slaving away on a meagre income but still putting aside what we could. We made enormous sacrifices at that time for those savings, but now the amounts look laughably small. It wasn't just us – most of the people round us did the same. Were we correct? Some people, like chhote bhaabhi, your youngest aunt, weren't that careful. They bought the latest saris and visited out-of-town friends and relatives at the smallest excuse. The years passed for them, just as they passed for us. Who can say who was right?'

Pari smiled at Mrs Ali and gave her a sudden hug. 'You are a dear,' she said. 'Don't change your whole life philosophy because of me. I am just a confused woman who cannot make up her mind.'

'What's burning?' said Mr Ali, coming into the kitchen and looking at the two women in surprise. 'What are the two of you doing here, standing right by the stove and acting like kids ignoring their homework?'

Mrs Ali hurriedly lowered the flame. 'Nothing,' she said. She gave the onions in the pan a quick twirl with a wooden spatula. 'The cooking's going well.'

Mr Ali turned to Pari and said, 'Didn't you say you wanted to go to the market? A new grocery store, the kind where you go round the aisles with a trolley and pick up whatever you want, has opened in the next street. Let's go.'

Pari nodded and, a few minutes later, she and Mr Ali were out of the house.

They walked along the dusty edge of the road. 'Mrs Bilqis came to the house,' said Mr Ali.

'Not you too, chaacha,' said Pari. 'Chaachi was just talking about it.'

'We promised Mrs Bilqis that we would talk to you about the match,' said Mr Ali.

Pari regaled him with big eyes. 'Oh!' was all she said.

'Don't feel that we are putting you under any pressure,' said Mr Ali.

A three-wheeled auto-rickshaw went past with a banana plant sticking out of its open side, almost brushing them off the road and into the gutter of dirty water.

'Well, we are putting you under pressure,' conceded Mr Ali. 'But it's all in a good cause.'

Pari remained silent.

'You are a young girl, younger than most of my clients in the marriage bureau. You've got your whole life ahead of you and you cannot live it alone.'

'I am not alone,' said Pari finally. 'I have all of you to look out for me.'

'You can have the whole world looking out for you, Pari,

but it is not a substitute for that one special person to share your life with.'

'Why, chaacha,' said Pari, looking at her uncle in surprise. 'That's a beautiful thing to say.'

Mr Ali grinned at her, suddenly looking much younger than his sixty-odd years. 'But you know all about it. You had it, not that long ago.'

Pari sighed, holding her head stiffly at an odd angle.

Mr Ali continued, 'It might seem to you that the universe has come to an end. But remember, as long as there is life, the world still exists and you should not give up hope of happiness. You will not get back exactly what you enjoyed with your first husband, but there is no reason why you cannot recapture most of that love and romance if you marry again. In fact, you never know, it might be even better the second time round.'

Pari shook her head slightly.

Mr Ali said, 'They say that if He-Who-Gives wishes to make you rich, He can tear open the sky to fill your house with gold. You have to believe that, Pari. You will always have a sweet spot in your mind for that short time with my nephew, but a few years down the line you could be looking upon that time as part of growing up and becoming ready for the real story of your life.'

'Why are you and chaachi so keen on this match?' asked Pari.

'There are two different things you need to sort out in your head. First, should you marry again or remain single for the rest of your life, and second, is Dilawar the right man? We can talk about the pros and cons of Dilawar, but in answer to the first question, I really think you must marry again. I came to your father's house once when he was bedridden. Do you remember?'

Pari, puzzled at the sudden change of topic, nodded. Her father had suffered a stroke and she had been looking after him, completely housebound, with no respite. Three months into this confined existence, Mr and Mrs Ali had come to the village. Mr Ali had said that he would look after his cousin for the day to allow Mrs Ali to take Pari to Rajahmundry, the nearby town. The two women had gone round the shops there and bought saris, little accessories like hairpins and bands, slippers for her feet and, she remembered, a clock with a red dial. The salesman who had sold it to her had been smarmy, making comments about her looks. Mrs Ali and Pari had eaten out – a vegetarian thali in the Café Godavari. For those few hours, a load had lifted from her shoulders and she had really enjoyed herself.

Mr Ali said, 'While you were out, your father wanted me to kill him.'

'What?' said Pari loudly.

A fat man, with plump, hairy arms poking out a short-sleeved shirt, stared at her curiously. Pari ignored him and said more softly, 'What are you saying, chaacha? Anyway, he couldn't speak. Nobody except me understood the sounds he made.'

'We knew each other since we were boys. We used to play together. It was difficult, but he managed to communicate with me. You see, even with his mind so destroyed, he knew how you were trapped in looking after him and felt very guilty.'

'What did you say?'

'I told him that I couldn't do it. Allah gives us life and He should be the one to take it away. But I could understand why my cousin was asking me for such a big favour and I told him that I would look after you. I promised him that I would make you happy again.'

'I didn't know,' said Pari slowly.

'There was no need for you to be told,' said Mr Ali. 'Anyway, that's why I cannot keep silent if I think you are making a wrong decision. Your aunt and I have to speak out.'

'OK,' said Pari. 'I will think seriously about what you said. Please let Mrs Bilqis know that I need some more time to consider her proposal.'

Mr Ali smiled at her. 'Good.'

They reached the shop – set in what had once been two houses side by side. It looked well-lit and welcoming, with clean tiled flooring and neat shelves down long aisles. A watchman in brown clothes stood outside with a whistle and a notebook. A beggar woman, in rags, came up to them and asked for money. The watchman shooed her away, telling her not to disturb their customers. The guard smiled as he accompanied Mr Ali and Pari to the door, where he gave them a wire shopping basket.

They went inside. 'I wonder how a big shop like this can make any money with so few customers,' said Mr Ali.

Pari shrugged lightly. 'It's still early days, isn't it? I am sure clients will turn up. These big businesses must know what they are doing. They wouldn't just pour money down the drain.'

'I suppose so,' said Mr Ali, though he wasn't sure that big necessarily meant brainy.

Pari picked up a bar of soap and toothpaste. When she turned around, she found that Mr Ali had vanished. She found him in a different aisle, examining a packet of dried fruit.

'It's funny,' she said.

'What's funny?' asked Mr Ali.

'Chaachi and you are both asking me to marry again, but your reasons are so different. Chaachi was telling me all about security and money, while your reasons were all about love and finding a partner. It's the exact opposite of what I would have expected. If anything, I thought you would give me all the practical reasons while chaachi would go all emotional on me.'

'That's where you are mistaken,' he said. 'I've always thought that men are more romantic than women.'

Pari laughed, a gay sound that filled the place and caused the woman sitting by the checkout counter to glance at them. Pari put a hand to her mouth and stopped laughing. 'How can you say that, chaacha? That's ridiculous.'

Mr Ali looked at her seriously. 'It's true,' he said. 'Romance isn't just about pink balloons and heart-shaped cards, you know. It is something much deeper.' He put a hand to his heart. 'Here, where it matters, men are more caring. Ask any young woman what kind of man she wants to marry and the answer will be a prince or a millionaire. Ask the same question of a hundred men, and very few will say that they want a princess or a rich girl. They want somebody beautiful and kind.'

'Yes, *beautiful*,' said Pari, raising her eyebrows delicately.

'Boys want a girl for herself – for what she is and has within herself. Girls, on the other hand, look for things external – money, status and so on. Tell me, which is more romantic?'

Pari shook her head widely. 'Chaacha, let us just agree to disagree on this one.'

She couldn't stop smiling for hours, however.

# CHAPTER EIGHT

The following day, Mr Ali and Aruna were going through the morning's post when a middle-aged stranger walked in. Looking uncomfortable, he let his eyes wander round the verandah that had been converted into an office.

'Namaste, sir. How can we help you?' said Mr Ali finally.

The newcomer had a broad face and a bulbous nose, wore khaki trousers and a brown short-sleeved shirt with two pens clipped inside its top pocket.

'My name is Chandra. I've come regarding a match for my daughter,' he said, taking out a handkerchief and wiping his forehead. After the showers of the previous week, the mercury was now climbing back into the mid-thirties.

'Please sit down,' said Mr Ali. 'Would you like a glass of water?'

Soon, they were down to business.

'My daughter looks a bit like you,' said Mr Chandra, pointing to Aruna. 'She is only a twelfth-class pass – never went to college. She was just not interested in studies. She can run a household, though. As my mother used to say, why does a woman need more education than to read the *Ramayana* and keep the washerman's tally? We have properties, an oil mill and a car-hire business that's flourishing. How was I to know . . .' The man spread his arms out. 'Anyway, we belong to the Baliga Kapu caste. How does your marriage bureau work?'

Mr Ali frowned. Usually, they did not accept people as members unless they had a college degree. But the man's distress was patently obvious – and he was rich. Mr Ali glanced at Aruna, who bit her lip and gave him a slight nod. Mr Ali leaned forward.

'We advertise on your behalf in newspapers and forward you any letters we get in response. You can go through them and contact anybody who you think is suitable. We give you details of all eligible boys we have on our books. At the same time, we also send your details to our members, so you can get called by other people too. The membership fee for a year is five hundred rupees.'

Aruna took out a list of Baliga Kapu grooms and handed it to Mr Chandra. 'Have a look at these matches, sir,' she said.

The man smiled at her and started going through the list. Taking out one of his pens, he circled a couple of entries. 'Interesting. There are some good candidates here,' he said, looking up.

Aruna took the list from him and handed him another piece of paper. 'Please fill in this application form.'

Mr Chandra went through it, writing in the answers. He finally put the cap back on the pen, took out a five-hundred-rupee note and handed it along with the form to Mr Ali. Aruna extracted several papers from the wardrobe that served as their filing cabinet and put them all in a long brown envelope. Taking the filled-in form from Mr Ali, she added it to a pad with a bulldog clip holding more forms, then wrote a number on both the form and the envelope.

Aruna handed the envelope to Mr Chandra and said,

'That's your membership number, sir. Please bring this number with you when you come back so we can easily track down your details. Do you have a photograph of your daughter?'

'No, should I have brought it with me?'

'It's not necessary,' said Mr Ali. 'But if you can bring it with you the next time, we will keep it on our files. Also, we have photos of young men from your caste and in your daughter's age bracket. Do you want to see them?'

Mr Chandra shook his head. 'I don't have time now. I'll come back with my daughter.'

For a man who said he had no time, Mr Chandra didn't seem to be in a hurry. He sat quietly, staring at the collage of letters and photos on the opposite wall, then gave a big sigh and turned to Mr Ali. 'I didn't think I would ever have to do this,' he said.

'Do what, sir?' asked Mr Ali.

'Start looking for a groom for my daughter all over again. My daughter's marriage was decided years ago. We'd even got as far as gathering the trousseau and planning the wedding . . .' His voice trailed off.

Mr Ali said, 'Life is a game of snakes and ladders, sir. You are steadily progressing across the board, rolling sixes on the dice and thinking you are going to win – and suddenly you land on a long snake and slide several rows down, far away from the destination again.'

Mr Chandra looked at Mr Ali in surprise. 'You are right,' he said, trying to smile, but ending up with a grimace.

Aruna said, 'There's nothing to be embarrassed about using a marriage bureau, sir. We get many clients here – doctors, engineers, even senior officials in the government for their sons and daughters.'

Mr Ali nodded. 'That's true. The world has changed. The

old certainties are no more. We have to move with the times and this is just another small thing. Unless we are prepared to change our methods slightly, the traditions would break down completely. In which case we might not be able to find a suitable match for our children, which would mean they would have to go out into the world and find their own partners.'

Horrified, Mr Chandra stuck his tongue out a fraction and touched both his cheeks with his arms crossed as if to ward off evil. 'Ayyo,' he said. 'That would be totally shameless. Don't talk about such things, sir. You are right, it is better for us to compromise in small things, so we can preserve the more important matters.' He stood up. 'I don't know what I was expecting from a marriage bureau, but I am happy with what I've seen. I'll come back with my daughter in a day or two and we will go through those photographs then.'

Vasu jumped off the motorcycle from behind Rehman.

'Bye, Vasu. See you this evening,' said Rehman.

'Bye,' said Vasu, waving hurriedly. He had a heavy rucksack of books on his back, a tiffin carrier of food in his right hand and a water bottle in his left. He greeted a friend in the milling crowd of children and soon the two boys walked away through the school gates, oblivious to the adults dropping them off.

Rehman returned home to find Pari chatting to Mrs Ali in the living room. He had been summoned back to Vizag by his mother. Although he had protested that he still had not met the village secretary regarding Mr Naidu's land records, his mother had told him that it was more important that he come back to the city. Infuriatingly, she had not told him what was so urgent until he had returned. It turned out to be that he had to talk to Pari and convince her to marry Dilawar.

Rehman sat with the ladies for a few minutes, hearing in

the background his father and Aruna talking to a client on the verandah. Eventually his mother stood up and headed for the kitchen.

'I want to discuss something with you,' he said to Pari.

'All right, what did you want to talk about?' said Pari.

'Not here,' said Rehman. 'Let's go up on the terrace. We'll have more privacy.'

They walked through the verandah on to the front yard and took the stairs by the side of the house. The roof was one long concrete slab encircled by a waist-high parapet wall, with a water tank occupying one corner. Several short concrete pillars with iron rods sticking out of them stood a few feet inside the perimeter. If they ever needed more room, these stubs would be built upon to form the skeleton of the next storey.

The blocks of flats on either side were so much taller that the windows overlooked the Alis' roof terrace. While they could hear voices and the sounds of radios and televisions, Rehman and Pari could not see anybody. High up as they were, there was a light wind from the east, but there was no protection from the sun on the flat roof. Pari covered her head with the ends of the dupatta.

'I've never been up here before,' she said, leaning over the parapet and looking down to the front of the house. The height gave her a different perspective on a scene she was used to seeing every day. Across the street, her room was visible behind the trees that lined the other side of the eighty-foot-wide road. Telephone and electrical cables criss-crossed from one side to the other as if trying to tie the two together.

'What did you want to talk about to me about?' she asked, finally turning around and facing him. She was smiling.

'It's about Dilawar,' he said. 'Ammi tells me that you don't want to marry him. I think you should give it more thought.'

Pari's smile faltered. When he had told her that he wanted to talk to her in private, where they could not be overheard, she had not been able to help wondering . . . No, that was silly. Rehman was still in love with his ex-fiancée and she shouldn't forget that. She shook her head.

'You are as subtle as a the music of a wedding band,' she said. 'At least your parents were more delicate.'

Rehman shrugged. 'Blunt or not, the matter's the same. When I talk to ammi and abba, it is clear that you are confused. Dilawar's a great guy – I know him from my school days and you could not find a kinder boy. People don't change that much, you know. All of us boys were envious of his body, like a bodybuilder but not with extreme muscles like the men you see on TV. And all the girls in the school loved him.' Then he added quickly, 'Not that he showed any interest in them or them or anything. He was a well-behaved boy.'

Pari remained silent, staring past Rehman at the coconut trees swaying between the buildings behind him.

Rehman said, 'I really think you shouldn't reject the match.'

Pari's frustration at how dense Rehman was being about her and the situation she found herself in, unable to articulate her feelings, suddenly boiled over.

'Oh, you think I should accept the match, do you? Why don't you just hold a gun to my head and marry me off to the first man to come walking down the road?' She turned and pointed at an old man shuffling slowly along below them. 'Hey, old man,' she shouted.

The man looked around, startled, but didn't see her until she shouted again.

'Old man, do you want to marry me? I am a widow but I promise I will be a good wife.'

The man looked shocked and touched both his cheeks

with his right hand. 'Ram, Ram,' he muttered and scuttled away, shaking his head as if wondering what the world was coming to.

Rehman pulled her away from the edge of the roof. 'What are you doing, Pari?' he said, frowning.

Pari turned on him in fury. 'Is this a marriage or a tamasha, a play? Do I get any say in the matter or is it a case of, oh, the poor widow – she doesn't know what's good for her; let us run her life for her as if she is some puppet who will dance the way we want when we pull the strings?'

The dupatta slipped off her head and a few strands of hair waved in the breeze. Rehman was struck dumb.

Pari continued, 'Well, what do you say? Do you think I am just saying no for the fun of it? I am not a shy maiden blushing away from thoughts of marriage. I have brains and I have thought this through. Do I want to move to a flat in Mumbai? Will Vasu be happy in a big city far away from all of you?'

'I can look after him—' began Rehman.

'Vasu is not a parcel to be passed from hand to hand. He is my son and he will stay with me. As a mother, I cannot just think of myself. I have to consider what's best for my boy too.'

Pari's glare was so fierce that Rehman involuntarily took a step back. He remembered what Vasu's grandfather, Mr Naidu, had told him once. Panthers sometimes hid in sugarcane fields to give birth. The animals could usually be driven off by loud noises but woe betide a farmer if he ever unwittingly came between the panther and her cubs. Forget running away, the mother would savage the interloper. He held up his hands.

'Sorry, that was a mistake,' he said. 'I was only saying that because I wanted you to consider the matter without the burden of thinking about Vasu.'

'There you go again,' she said. 'A child is not a burden to its mother.'

'But that's not quite what I meant—'

'Aargh!' she screamed suddenly, and started beating him on the chest with her fists. 'Don't talk to me about a man I've never met and have no feelings for. Give me my husband back, smiling in that crooked way of his. Allow me to cook his favourite khatti-dhal and salted-fish curry served the way he wanted with warm rice and dollops of ghee. Let him lift me up in the air as if I were a doll and feel his strong hands around my waist. I want to sit pillion behind him on our motorbike with one hand on his strong shoulder, leaning against his body to whisper into his ear. Return my father whole and hearty, indulging my every whim – not distressed and lying in his own waste, longing for death. I want to be in bed with my husband, knowing that neither of us had slept with another; that we didn't need to be ashamed of our bodies in any way because neither of us had any other body to compare ourselves with. Can you give me that?' Her voice had been steadily getting louder until she was almost scream-ing at the end. 'Can. You. Give. Me. That?' she repeated, in a voice made harsh by emotion.

Rehman listened to her in agony. What she really wanted, of course, was to turn the clock back to when she was a simple housewife in a village – married to a good man of reg-ular habits, following a path smoothed by tradition and the feet of millions of women before her.

An extra-hard blow drove the breath from his lungs and he grunted, becoming aware that she was still hitting him and not gently either. Rehman seized her wrists, one in each hand and held them inches away from his chest. He was sur-prised by how much strength it took.

Incongruously, an image of his dry stick-insect-like college physics teacher came to his mind, adjusting his thick glasses and intoning the second law of thermodynamics in his high voice, 'The entropy of an isolated system always tends to increase when it moves from one state of equilibrium to the next.' The implication of this law is that the arrow of time only travels forwards and cannot be turned back.

Their bodies were very close now and he looked into her unblinking eyes. Her arms had gone slack and he didn't need much force to hold them in place, though he didn't let go. He decided that she would not appreciate a science lesson, so instead, he quoted something else that he had come across in his teenage years.

> The Moving Finger writes; and, having writ,
> Moves on: nor all your Piety nor Wit
> Shall lure it back to cancel half a Line,
> Nor all your Tears wash out a Word of it.

They heard a window rattle in the building next door and looked up. A housewife was looking at them curiously from one of the second-floor flats. Pari twisted her arms free and jumped back. Red in the face, she turned away from Rehman and the onlooker, whipping her dupatta back over her head.

Rehman glanced up again to see that the woman had withdrawn back into her flat. He rubbed his chest and said, 'Have you considered a career in boxing? I reckon you could give Muhammad Ali a lesson in sparring.'

Pari turned back and smiled at him. 'That was a beautiful verse,' she said. 'It's not yours, surely.'

'Much as I'd like to claim it, no. Have you heard of Omar Khayyam?'

'Of course,' she said. 'Wasn't he a mendicant who wandered in the desert singing songs about wine and women?'

'Well, he was actually a scholar and philosopher. The poem I quoted is one of his ruba'iyah, a quatrain – probably his most famous.'

'I hadn't heard it before,' said Pari.

Rehman realised just how limited Pari's education had been. Her fluency and knowledge made him forget that she had started studying English only four years ago and, much as she'd read, there must be even more gaps.

Pari continued, 'I am sorry about shouting at you like that and hitting you, Rehman. I don't know what came over me.'

'Don't feel bad, you are right. You've had abba and ammi and me all talking about it and felt you were under pressure. That's not the intention – not mine, anyway. I won't speak of this again, after this one last time. So you haven't actually met Dilawar?'

'No,' said Pari. 'I've seen his photo, of course. He is a handsome man.'

Rehman shrugged. 'Looks aren't everything. Why don't you meet him? Have a chat with him – tell him about your fear of moving to a faraway city and your concerns regarding Vasu. See how he reacts, what he says. Then you can decide whether you should marry him or not.'

'That's—' Pari shook her head. 'That's not how my first marriage was fixed.'

'That marriage was within the family. We all knew one another. This is different. Meeting your fiancé is not something the elders would ever suggest, but . . .'

Pari turned away and stood straight as a slender reed, gazing towards the horizon, her dupatta fluttering behind her like a banner in the wind. Rehman couldn't see her face. As he looked at her slim but shapely body, admiration for her crept up on him. What a brave girl she was. She faced so many problems and this was the first time that she had shown any evidence of the stress she must be under. He wished he could do something, anything, to lighten her load and make her happier. He rubbed his chest again with a rueful grin. She was a mean boxer, though. He hoped Dilawar could stand up to her.

Pari faced him once more. 'For a man who knows nothing about girls, you have come up with a sensible idea. I will meet your friend and we'll see what happens after.'

Now that she had agreed to his suggestion, Rehman wondered why, despite the bright fireball of a sun in the clear, blue sky, the day suddenly seemed to have lost its brightness.

'What a bother it was,' said Mrs Ali. 'Honestly, it would have been less trouble to arrange a daughter's wedding than it was to buy the phone. Ration card, voting card, this certificate, that proof. Does anybody even check all those documents once they collect them?'

'Oh yes, madam,' said Aruna. 'Ever since mobile phones started being used by terrorists, the government is pretty serious about identifying who owns which SIM card. If the documents are even slightly out of order, your phone will be cut off within forty-eight hours.'

Mrs Ali was now the proud possessor of her first mobile phone. If she was really candid, she didn't actually need the phone, but everybody seemed to have one nowadays. She had read in the paper that fifteen million phones were being purchased every month, and surely so many consumers couldn't all be wrong. The same article had said that more people in India now owned mobile phones than in America. She had felt a moment's pride in that statistic until her husband pointed out that India had a population three times the size of the USA's and surely there were not three times more phones in India. She had shrugged irritably at him, thinking that was not the point, but being unable to articulate what the point was, she had asked for a phone of her own, prepared to argue that if Aruna and Pari – and even the tailor who had come to measure their windows for the curtains – had a phone, then she ought to have one too. To her surprise, Mr Ali had agreed immediately.

She still remembered the time when they had first applied for a phone – a proper black one that had a dial with little holes showing the numbers into which you put a finger and turned in a circle to make a call. It had a loud brash ring that was instantly recognisable, so that you did not have to wonder whether the tinny tune, seemingly coming from nowhere and everywhere, was somebody calling you, or a car reversing, or a visitor with his fat finger pressed to the doorbell. They had been advised that the waiting list for a phone was seven years. According to the dismissive clerk at the post office, they were lucky that it was only seven. The government had just sanctioned a new exchange as previously the waiting list had been twelve years. She knew men who had died disappointed and phoneless, and whose children had fallen out with one another over who would inherit the father's position on the waiting list.

Yesterday evening, she and her husband had gone to an air-conditioned, though terribly crowded, shop, been waited on by an attentive salesgirl and come back home, triumphant, with a phone. Actually, it had been a little bit more complicated than that. They first had to negotiate strange names like Nokia, Motorola and Samsung, then terms like pre-paid, post-paid, calling plans, SIM, GSM and SMS. After that they were given a box of sealed envelopes, each with a phone number written on it, and the salesgirl had told them to choose one. Mrs Ali selected a number with a repeating pattern that would be easy to remember. At that moment, the man standing next to them, waiting for his turn to be served, said, 'Madam, that's a bad number.'

Mrs Ali stared at the speaker in surprise. He looked like a daily-wage labourer – his clothes were serviceable but old, and his feet were shod in tattered rubber slippers. She remembered an old maxim about a man who could not afford to feed his family but always bought wax for his moustache. The saying has to be updated, thought Mrs Ali, to refer to people who can't afford shoes but bought mobile phones.

'Why is it a bad number?' asked Mr Ali.

'If you add up all the digits, it comes to sixty-one, whose sum is seven,' he said. 'Everybody knows that seven is not a good number.'

The word for seven in Telugu sounds just like the word to cry and is considered inauspicious.

'We don't believe—' Mr Ali started saying.

Mrs Ali interrupted him. 'We are Muslims,' she said. 'In our language, Urdu, the word for seven sounds like that for friendship. We don't consider it a bad number.'

The man nodded and went back to choosing a phone model.

'Why—' began Mr Ali in a whisper.

'Shh,' said Mrs Ali in Urdu so the labourer wouldn't understand. 'I know what you were going to say and I don't want a discussion on the merits of numerology.'

The girl took the envelope from them and said, 'Do you have two forms of ID, one with a photo and one with your address on it?'

Mrs Ali stared at her husband in consternation. 'No,' she said.

Wherever they went, whether to the local grocery shop, their bank branch or even the goldsmith, their faces were their identification.

'Why do we need papers to prove who we are?' said Mrs Ali. Then a thought struck her. 'We are not paying with those new-fangled, what do you call them . . . credit cards. We will pay in cash.'

'Sorry, madam. It's not about money. It's a government regulation.'

The salesgirl was smiling but inflexible. No paperwork – no phone.

As they turned away in disappointment, the girl said, 'Why don't you call somebody at home to bring the papers?'

'That's why we need the phone,' said Mr Ali. 'To call people.'

The girl didn't see the irony of the situation, but eventually offered them the use of the shop's phone to make the call. Rehman brought them the papers and after that they were out in half an hour. Rehman had taken the transaction for granted but Mr and Mrs Ali were impressed that one could walk into a shop with a little money (and some documents) and come out with a phone, connected to the world.

Mrs Ali looked at Aruna. 'I don't like these long numbers,' she said. 'The land phone numbers are so much easier to remember.'

'But you don't need to memorise them, madam,' said Aruna. 'Your phone will keep track of them for you. You select the person by name. Here, let me show you.' She came out from behind the table and sat next to Mrs Ali. 'Whom do you call most often?'

Mrs Ali took out a battered, old address book and pointed out a few of the numbers. Aruna entered them.

'Do you want my number?' Aruna asked.

Her husband had bought her the phone as a present during the festival of Sankranti, the three-day celebration of the main harvest being brought in. Aruna now took it out of her handbag and showed it to Mrs Ali.

'Oh, that looks nice,' said Mrs Ali, holding the sleek instrument. 'Was it expensive?'

'I think so, but Ram won't tell me. To be quite honest, I would have loved it even if it was the cheapest toy, because he bought it for me without my even asking for it.'

Mrs Ali smiled. 'Yes, it is nice when our men do that, isn't it? It is so easy to please a woman – just some unexpected flowers or a sari or even a bit of help in the house when we are not well – but somehow men never seem to understand that.' She looked at Aruna's phone more closely. 'What are all those pictures on the screen?'

'They are different apps, madam. This one, for example, shows our exact location.' Aruna tapped the icon and the phone displayed their co-ordinates.

'What's the point of that?' said Mrs Ali. 'You know where you are – you don't need the phone to tell you! All gadgets have become complicated now. Last month, we went to buy a TV.'

Aruna nodded. The Alis' TV was almost as old as the television in her parents' house.

'Well, the salesman showed us so many TVs and they all had such complicated remote controls with lots of tiny buttons, just like a mobile phone, that we gave up and decided to stick with our old TV.'

Aruna laughed.

After a moment, Mrs Ali said, 'Your parents don't have a phone, do they?'

Aruna shook her head. 'No, madam. Vani has been asking for a mobile phone, though. I've told her that I might get her one for Dusserah.'

Dusserah was the other main Telugu festival, to celebrate the killing of the demon, Mahishasurah, by the goddess Durga – and the autumn harvest.

Mrs Ali said, 'Yes, your sister goes to college. I am sure it will be useful for her.'

Aruna showed Mrs Ali how to bring up the list of names on the phone and called her own number. When Aruna's phone rang, she immediately hung up and fiddled with the keys. 'I have stored your number now,' she said.

'Thanks, said Mrs Ali, frowning with concentration. 'It doesn't seem too difficult. So whom do you call on the phone? Your husband?'

Aruna blushed. 'Yes, I call him at the hospital to find out when he's coming back. I also call Peter, our driver, when I have finished shopping, so he can come and pick me up. I've only had the phone for a couple of months, but already I wonder how I used to manage without it.'

Mrs Ali said, 'Does Ramanujam ever call you or is it always you calling him?'

'Oh, no, madam. He keeps calling me too. Last Monday I went to my parents' place for the afternoon and he called me three times. Vani started teasing me and it was very embarrassing.'

Mrs Ali smiled at Aruna's earnest expression and said, 'That's all we need. Whatever little chance we have of escaping from our husbands by visiting our birth families is gone. They will be tracking us down and asking us to come back home as soon as we have reached somewhere. How unlucky we are not to have even this tiny amount of freedom that our grandmothers enjoyed.'

Aruna laughed and Mrs Ali joined her. 'Yes, madam. You are right. We should tell our men to be more patient and not keep calling us all the time.'

A rattle came from the iron gate of the verandah, making the two women look up and their mirth instantly was expunged. Pari stood there, her slim frame silhouetted against the bright light, her dupatta trailing behind her and her hair windblown. She stared at them intently and something about her face made Aruna shiver. Before they could say anything, Pari turned on the spot and left. The two leaves of the gate slammed against each other loudly.

Pari crossed the road blindly, making for her room and crashing into a passing pedestrian. He almost swore at the unexpected bump, then fell silent at the despair on her face.

Pari tried to tell herself that Mrs Ali and Aruna were not being deliberately malicious. They had surely not even been thinking about her. If she and her husband had had mobile phones, he would probably have called her every ten minutes. She would never have complained. Never.

# CHAPTER NINE

Even though it was four in the morning, the arrivals area outside Sahar airport in Mumbai was crowded. Neatly dressed limousine chauffeurs from posh hotels held up placards for businessmen; Muslim women in all-enveloping burqas looked ardently for their Gulf-returned husbands; family members, young and old, all jostled in the pre-dawn hours. International air travel is still relatively uncommon in India; there are often several excited people looking out for each disembarking passenger, so the assembly was quite large. As each trolley turned the corner and hove into sight, those waiting stared anxiously to see if it was *the* one.

'The flight from Muscat landed fifteen minutes ago,' announced a burly Sikh and the news spread through the throng.

Suited and booted businessmen were the first out, walking purposefully towards the placards that bore their names and handing their luggage over to the drivers, their movements slick with practice. After that came couples carrying babes in arms, sometimes with older toddlers in pushchairs. They gazed around, confused at the large numbers of people and the sauna-like heat, even at this early hour. A whole family rushed over when a young husband and wife emerged with a small baby. The matriarch of the family hugged her son, noting how thin he had become, then turned to her daughter-in-law – or, rather, to the baby with the daughter-in-law.

From eavesdropping on the family's conversation before the plane had landed, Dilawar knew that the young couple had been married for almost two years and this tiny male baby had been as eagerly awaited as any heir to the throne of England. He saw with a grim smile that the baby had been plucked out of its mother's hands and was engulfed by the whole family, pushing the poor mother to the outskirts. The baby, naturally, started howling at being surrounded by a whole bunch of strangers pulling funny faces at it. Oh well, I am sure that the young woman's standing will rise as the mother of the family's first grandson, thought Dilawar.

He waited another five minutes before Shaan finally appeared. Dilawar waved until his friend caught sight of him and came over. Dilawar smiled broadly and moved to shake his hand, but Shaan brushed it aside and hugged him. Dilawar hurriedly pushed Shaan away and said, 'Not here, people are looking. They might get suspicious.'

Shaan laughed. 'This is India, my dear. As a former prime minister once said, we don't have any homosexuals in this country. The folks round here will just think that we are long-lost brothers reuniting after many years. Loosen up.'

But Dilawar couldn't relax and held Shaan at arm's length. 'Let's go,' he said, pointing. 'My car is over there.'

They started walking in the direction of the car parking area, Dilawar taking over the trolley. Many long-haul flights had just landed and the place was busy. As they crossed the road and manoeuvred the wonky trolley through a small gap in the line of low boundary stones separating the road from the car park, Shaan said, 'I missed you, Dee. It's good of you to come. I wasn't sure whether you would or not.'

Dilawar shrugged. 'It was Sunday, so I decided I might as well save you a taxi fare.'

Shaan laughed. 'You can't fool me, Dee. You couldn't wait to see me either.'

Dilawar glanced towards Shaan and their eyes met. For some unaccountable reason, Dilawar blushed. The effect was even more pronounced in the orange glow of the sodium vapour lamps. Shaan placed a hand over Dilawar's, on the push-handle of the trolley. Dilawar jerked his hand away, as if touched with a hot brand.

'Be brave, Dee,' said Shaan.

Dilawar shook his head. 'I am sorry, Shaan, but I keep thinking about what happened at the Gateway of India when we met. All those police . . .' Dilawar shuddered. 'What we are doing is still illegal in this country.'

Shaan said, 'Well, society will never change unless we fight against it. If people like us, educated and relatively well off, are afraid to show our love, what hope is there for the poor boy born in a village who dares to be a little different? First, we have to change the law of the land and then we can work openly for people to change their minds. There is a Gay Pride march tomorrow afternoon from Flora Fountain to the Vidhan Sabha, the state legislature. I am planning to attend. Why don't you come too? The more people who come on the march, the more likely we are to be successful.'

They walked in silence for a moment or two. Then Dilawar shook his head.

'Call me a coward if you want, Shaan. But I'm not ready and, if you want to know the truth, I don't think the country is ready for such a radical step either. I prefer the American military policy on these matters: won't ask, don't tell.'

They reached the car and stowed Shaan's luggage into the boot. 'Did you enjoy London?' Dilawar asked.

'I love London,' said Shaan. 'I have many friends there and always have a wonderful time. The flight back was horrible, though. Two stops in the Gulf and we were delayed getting out of Heathrow, so we missed the connection at Muscat.'

'I don't understand why you used that airline,' said Dilawar.

It was lucky that he had checked the arrival time of the plane before setting off for the airport, otherwise he would have been waiting for hours.

'A small factor called money,' said Shaan. 'My employers are great, but don't pay as much as detergent manufacturers.'

Dilawar laughed. 'We'll go to London next year and I'll pay the airfare,' he said. 'And we'll fly direct.'

Shaan smiled at him. 'I knew I didn't fall in love with you just for your pretty face,' he said. 'It's good to be back home again.'


Later that evening, after dinner, Dilawar and Shaan sat down with cups of coffee in Dilawar's living room.

'Come over here,' Shaan said, patting the seat next to him on the sofa. 'I've got a video of the wedding to show you.'

Dilawar rolled his eyes. 'Why would I want to spend the first evening you are back looking at the wedding of people I don't know?'

'You will find this interesting, trust me,' said Shaan, taking his laptop out of its case and switching it on. From another pocket in his rucksack, he fished out a DVD.

Dilawar watched his boyfriend's lovely face crinkle with concentration as he typed in a password. Shaan's tongue flashed pink as it darted over his lips and Dilawar's stomach tightened with desire.

'Hang on. If we're going to watch them on screen I've got just the thing.'

Taking the disk from Shaan, he went to a side cabinet, popped it in and pressed a button on a black remote control. A small motor whined and a white screen lowered from the ceiling, hiding the Mughal miniature painting. The picture of an old-fashioned album was projected, several feet high and the same width across, on to the screen. The image became sharper and more vivid as Dilawar switched off most of the lights in the room.

'Wow,' said Shaan. 'When did you get it?'

Dilawar shrugged. 'I felt lonely last weekend and went shopping. I said I would take their top-of-the-range kit if they could install it within a couple of days.'

'Perfect,' said Shaan. 'The show will be really amazing now.'

Dilawar sat down next to Shaan, putting an arm round his shoulder. Shaan gave him a quick peck on the cheek. 'Ready?'

'Go for it.'

Shaan clicked a button and the image started moving. The book opened slowly and a young woman, in her late twenties, appeared, getting dressed in a flowing ivory-coloured wedding gown. She was in three-quarters profile, her shoulders bare and her blonde, curly hair piled high. She had coquettishly pulled up her frock so that the hem was well above her knee, revealing high heels, a trim ankle and the top of a stocking. The ring finger on the hand holding up the skirt bore a large solitaire diamond.

Unlike most men, Dilawar was able to coolly dissect her appearance without being overwhelmed by her beauty. She could easily have been a model, tall and slim with a creamy complexion. A hint of cleavage could be seen and her smile would have transfixed any heterosexual male. Dilawar merely noted that the smile gave her cheeks dimples and that her eyes were remarkably clear and a deep blue.

'That's Lisa. Many girls in London want a gay man-friend and I was hers. We went out to many places where either of us needed an opposite-sex partner.'

'Why do girls want a gay friend?' asked Dilawar.

'Apparently we are more sensitive.' Shaan shrugged. 'Different way of talking. Different way of communicating with women.'

'You mean we are not emotionally retarded,' said Dilawar.

'Exactly,' said Shaan.

As other people came in front of the camera, Shaan pointed out friends of his. All the women were in hats and the men wore suits and bow ties – some even had top hats. Dilawar thought the men looked very smart.

The wedding party had now reached a proud building with a classical look. Wide steps, flanked by stone lions, led up to the entrance. Ten tall columns in five pairs supported the front elevation like a Greek temple.

'Nice,' said Dilawar.

Shaan nodded. 'That's the old town hall in Westminster. As you can see, it was a lovely, sunny day. I know that means nothing to us here in India where we are used to ten months of blue skies a year, but the weather that day in London really lifted everybody's spirits.'

The group was joined by others, posing for a photograph on a grand marble staircase. Another woman stood next to Lisa, wearing a matching ivory-coloured bridal dress. They both held identical bouquets of flowers.

The other lady was older, probably in her mid to late thirties, and pretty in a severe, school-marmish way. She had dark hair and was more flat-chested than Lisa. Dilawar was confused.

'Did you meet up with another wedding party?' he asked.

'No,' said Shaan, laughing. 'Lisa and Gail are getting married to each other.'

'What?' said Dilawar, turning to look at Shaan. He swivelled his head back to the screen and turned back again to Shaan. 'You mean they are . . .' His voice trailed off.

Shaan laughed at his friend's thunderstruck expression. 'Yes, they are lesbians.'

'Wow!' said Dilawar. 'Are such marriages really allowed over there?'

'Strictly speaking, they are called civil partnership ceremonies, though everybody just refers to them as gay and lesbian weddings. Things have changed dramatically in Britain. Just over fifty years ago, Alan Turing, the father of computer science and the one man more responsible than any other for winning the Second World War, agreed to be chemically castrated in lieu of going to prison and committed suicide because he became ineligible for security clearance to continue his work when it became known that he was gay.'

Dilawar gave Shaan an odd look. 'Indeed . . .' he said.

Shaan continued, 'While gay relationships were illegal, lesbianism was never technically banned in England.'

'How come?'

'The story is that when the Labouchère amendment banning gross indecency between same-sex couples came to Queen Victoria for signature, she crossed out the phrase about lesbians because she refused to believe that women would ever do such a thing.'

'That's weird. I bet the current queen doesn't have the same power,' Dilawar said.

'What does Gail do? She looks like the headmistress of a school.'

Shaan shook his head. 'She works in the City, in a bank. I don't know exactly what she does, but I heard that she manages more than a billion pounds in assets.'

The screen now showed a room with an elegant fireplace with a brass guard and a white mantelpiece on which stood a big vase of flowers. Tall windows framed with yellow curtains let in the light. Lisa and Gail stood in front of the fireplace facing an official. To one side the audience sat on yellow-upholstered chairs. A handsome older woman had a fixed smile on her face while the man next to her had his arms folded across his chest and stared straight ahead.

'Who are they?' asked Dilawar, pointing.

'Lisa's parents,' said Shaan. 'Lisa told me that the day before the wedding they had a couple and parents' supper.'

'Oh!' said Dilawar. 'That's an interesting custom. I don't think that will ever catch on in India, especially among Muslims. The bride and groom, or, er . . . bride and bride, I guess, wouldn't be allowed to meet up before the wedding.'

'Yes, that will be the day . . .' Shaan laughed. 'Anyway, at the supper, Lisa's father accused Gail of corrupting his daughter.'

'Oh, *dear*!'

'Exactly. Highly embarrassing as Gail's mum and aunt – her father is no more – were also there.'

'What happened then?'

'Lisa stepped in and warned her dad not to say such things to Gail. She told him to accept her for what she was and let her lead her life in the way she wanted.'

Dilawar's eyes widened. It had been a long time since he had spoken to his father, but he doubted that he could ever have said something like that to him.

'Apparently, it got a bit sticky after that. Lisa's mother waded into the conversation, telling Lisa to watch her tongue and show some respect to her father, and announcing that this whole ceremony was a perversion of a proper wedding.'

'So how did it end?'

Shaan shrugged. 'Lisa used the nuclear option: her parents had to accept what was going on or not come to the wedding at all. It was her special day, she said, and she asked them not to spoil everything and make her regret inviting them.'

'Wow!' said Dilawar. 'If that had been an Indian wedding, the drama and fights and tears would have come out at the ceremony, while here everything is going smoothly – looking rather civilised,' said Dilawar.

Shaan laughed again. 'We are an emotional people,' he said. 'But, in England, manners are about keeping a stiff upper lip and being polite, saying please and thank you.'

On the screen, the registrar, a large black lady, said, 'Lisa and Gail wish to affirm their relationship and to offer to each other the security that comes from vows sincerely made and faithfully kept. If any person here present knows of any lawful impediment to this civil partnership, then he or she should declare it now.'

The camera moved to a radiant Lisa and an intensely concentrating Gail, then panned to the other people in the room, who all seemed to be holding their breath, before moving back to the registrar.

'Lisa, repeat after me . . .'

'Gail, I pledge to share my life openly with you. I promise to cherish and tenderly care for you, to honour and encourage you. I will respect you as an individual and be true to you through all the good times and bad.'

After Gail said the same words – with Lisa's name – the registrar continued, 'We now come to the exchange of rings . . .'

The audience burst into applause as the couple slipped the rings on to each other's fingers.

'How come there were so few people for the wedding? There can't be more than about twenty in that room,' said Dilawar.

'This was just the registration ceremony. After this, all of us, except Lisa's parents, went to the reception.'

The party had been held in a manor house that had been converted to a hotel. Ivy covered the walls and framed its leaded windows. Chimneys punctuated the pitched roof like soldiers on a march. Lisa and Gail, looking similar from the back except for their hair and their heights, walked hand in hand, staring into each other's eyes, up three old-brick, semi-circular stairs to a patio, the wedding party following behind. As they reached the top, the rest of the guests already assembled there burst into cheers. Lisa's smile made her face bloom like a pink peony and even Gail looked less forbidding.

The couple of hundred or so guests formed two long rows in front of the entrance to a wing of the hotel, leaving an aisle-like gap down the middle. Lisa and Gail walked between the two rows, arm in arm, each holding a bouquet of white roses. Confetti was showered on them and four small girls, dressed in blue frocks, stumbled behind the brides, grinning and looking important.

Dilawar was shocked. 'The children,' he said. 'What were they told about the wedding?'

Shaan shrugged. 'Young people find it easier to accept. If the parents don't make a song and dance about how strange it is for two women to marry, their children will take it in their stride,' he said.

Dilawar shook his head, unconvinced.

When Lisa and Gail reached the head of the queue, they

looked over their shoulders. The moment was captured perfectly on the screen – their dresses matching, their hair contrasting, their smiles identical.

Energetically, both tossed their bouquets over their heads, the flowers tumbling several times before coming down again. Lisa's bouquet was caught by a woman who jumped high in the air, so that others standing near by had no chance. As soon as she landed, clutching her trophy, she turned and hugged her boyfriend, squealing in delight. He looked shell-shocked.

Two men lunged for Gail's bouquet. One of them, with the advantage of a few inches of height over his rival, caught it. The two men then fell in each other's arms and danced an impromptu jig, laughing and whooping.

'Are they . . .' asked Dilawar.

'Yes, there are lots of gays among the guests,' said Shaan.

Once Shaan pointed it out, Dilawar wondered how he had missed the signs. It was clear that some of the men, in formal suits, waistcoats and bow ties, were clearly partners.

Waiters circulated with flutes of champagne and drinks. The party slowly lost its formal edge and people became more boisterous as the alcohol took its toll. Dilawar shook his head – this was something else that would not happen in a Muslim, or even in a Hindu, wedding, really.

On the edge of the screen, a woman with a sleeping baby in her arms was talking to a man. He touched the woman on her cheek with easy familiarity and said something to her, making her laugh. Another woman came up to the couple, slipped her arm around the first woman's waist and kissed her on the neck.

Dilawar was confused. 'Who?' he said, pointing to them.

Shaan froze the picture and looked at where Dilawar's

finger was pointed. 'Oh, that's Marie and Nicola. The man is Mark and he is Marie's ex-husband. They got divorced after Marie and Nicola got together.'

'The baby?'

Shaan shook his head and restarted the DVD. 'Not Mark's. Marie had the baby after moving in with Nicola.'

'How?'

'Artificial insemination,' said Shaan.

On the screen, another woman, hugely pregnant, joined the trio. 'That is Mark's latest wife, his third, and that bump, hopefully, is his baby.'

Abruptly, Dilawar stood up, knocking down a small table. Kicking it out of the way, he left the room abruptly. Shaan looked up in surprise and paused the video. When Dilawar did not return after a few minutes, he went in search of him and found him on the bedroom balcony, looking out over the low-lying buildings and slums.

'What is it, Dee?' he asked softly.

Dilawar took a long time to answer. 'Do you remember the movie *Four Weddings and a Funeral*?' he said.

'Of course,' said Shaan. 'Who doesn't?'

'At the funeral of the bearded man, his boyfriend says that his partner preferred funerals to weddings on the principle that he was more likely to be involved in one at some point.'

'I remember,' said Shaan. 'Just before he recited that lovely W. H. Auden poem that completely broke me down. I was bawling at the end of that scene.'

'Me too,' said Dilawar. 'Anyway, I am like that man. What's the point of watching this event that we have no hope of ever replicating here? That ceremony, those understanding guests, the little bridesmaids, the mix-and-match partners – all those things could be happening on Neptune, for all we care. We live in India and here if you even tried to hire a hall for a wedding like that, you would be hounded away by barefoot people throwing their sandals at you. For a long time, the government's response was that there was no Aids problem in India because there were no homosexuals here. That is the level of denial that exists in our society.'

'That was years ago, Dee. Since then the government has kicked off a campaign to educate people about Aids. Attitudes can change. That's why I am going to Delhi to attend the court case against the law banning homosexuality, and you should come too.'

Dilawar shook his head. 'I am sorry, partner. Nothing will change. That case has been going on for seven years and will probably go on for another seventy. And anyway, attitudes will not change. I cannot shove my views down my parents' throats. They will be humiliated by everybody around them.'

'Do you think they are unaware of your attraction?' said Shaan, softly.

'They may be, they may not be. But as long as I keep it ambiguous, they can fool themselves and hold their heads high in society. Ignorance is bliss, as they say.'

'That's a ridiculous attitude to take,' said Shaan. 'You are saying that it is better to be hypocritical than to be honest.'

'Do you know what happened the other day? As I was coming back from the office, the watchman downstairs told me that it was good that you were not coming here any more. I was surprised and asked him why.'

Shaan looked at him intently.

Dilawar continued, 'The watchman said that a couple of other residents in the building had told him to warn me that this was a family-friendly place. They would not tolerate misbehaviour and said that you should be banned from coming here. If not, my case would be discussed at the next residents' meeting and they would boycott me and get me kicked out.'

'How can they do that? You own this flat and you have as much right as they have to live in it.'

'It's not just about rights, Shaan. I don't want to live in a place where everybody's face is turned against me and where people refuse to talk to me. I cannot lead that kind of life.'

'What did you say when the watchman told you that I would be banned from entering the building?' Shaan looked at Dilawar's face for a moment and shook his head. 'You didn't protest against that, did you?' Shaan's eyes widened as another thought struck him. '*That's* why you came to airport to pick me up. Yes! You didn't come there to meet me at all. You only came because you didn't want to be embarrassed by my turning up at the gates of your precious flats.'

Shaan went back into the living room, took out the DVD and started packing it away.

'What are you doing?' asked Dilawar.

'What do you think? I am leaving you here with your family-friendly neighbours so you can say hi to them when you bump into them by the lifts. I don't want to disturb your tranquil haven, after all.'

Dilawar made an ineffectual gesture with his hand but said nothing.

Shaan turned at the door and said, 'To love is to be brave. You obviously don't know the meaning of either word. I have a word of advice for you. Don't fall in love. Be promiscuous. Get a new boy every week. That way nobody will suspect you.'

Dilawar stayed rooted to the spot for a long time after Shaan left. I love you, Shaan, he thought. But I am also a coward. I don't deserve somebody like you. A fat tear rolled slowly down each cheek, but Shaan did not come back.

# CHAPTER TEN

'The porcelain cups and saucers need to be washed today,' the second-floor madam said.

'All right, amma,' said Leela, sighing.

The extra money from serving one more household was welcome for the servant maid, but she was getting older and did not have the same energy that she had ten or even five years ago. What can't be changed must be borne, she thought. It was just her karma that her grandson's treatment had sucked away all their savings and that she had an alcoholic husband who didn't bring a penny into the household.

The second-floor madam – her name was Swaroop – came out with a teapot and a plastic tray and added them to the pile of dirty dishes already waiting.

'Haven't you started yet?' she said to Leela. 'I don't have all day to wait for you. My guests will be coming soon.'

Leela picked up a mixture of sand and detergent with a piece of coconut coir and started scrubbing the cups.

'Does the widow live with the old couple and their son?' Swaroop asked.

'Who?' said Leela, looking up. 'Oh, Pari-amma. She

comes over a lot, but she lives with her son in the upstairs room in the ticket inspector's wife's house.'

'Yes, I have seen her with that boy. He can't be her son, surely. He is so dark and scrawny, like an undernourished crow. Also, I heard that he came to town with the neighbour's son, the one who keeps going off to villages for weeks at a time – who knows what he gets up to? Maybe he had a relationship with some village woman and that boy is the result. And why should the widow look after his child? Do you think there's something going on between them?' Swaroop obviously did not expect an answer from the servant maid, because she continued, 'It's dangerous for an unmarried man and a woman to spend so much time together. I would have thought that a respectable lady like Mrs Ali would realise it.'

Leela bridled at the woman's comments. She had been working in Mrs Ali's house for a long time, while she had only started here a few months ago. Also, Mrs Ali had always been fair with her and had even helped her when her grandson had been diagnosed with a brain tumour that needed to be operated on. In fact, the doctor who had cured her grandson was the husband of that nice Brahmin girl who worked on the verandah of their house.

'Nothing like that, amma. Both the youngsters are very sensible people. I am sure that there is nothing wrong. Muslims are even more strict about these matters than we are. And as for that boy, he is an orphan who doesn't have anybody else, so Babu brought him home. But how can a man look after a child? That's why Pari-amma adopted him. The boy will be company for her as well.'

The doorbell rang soon after Leela left.

'Hello, Sonia. Muaah! Come in, what a lovely sari . . . Where did you buy it?'

Soon, all the guests had arrived and snacks like samosas and spring rolls were circulating.

'You won't believe what I saw the other day,' Swaroop said.

'What?' chorused four women. The other three raised their eyebrows.

Swaroop leaned over confidentially and said in a dramatic whisper, 'I saw the Alis' son and that widow woman from the opposite house hugging each other.'

'Ooh!' said some of the women, craning forward.

'Are you sure?' said Manju, one of the guests, who lived in the same building as Swaroop but on the other side. 'They are a good family and their son is always involved in some social movement. Pari is a relative of theirs.'

Swaroop straightened her back and looked haughtily at the woman who had dared question her. 'I know what I saw with my own eyes, Manju. They had sneaked up on to the terrace but forgot that our windows overlook their roof. He was reciting some romantic poetry to her and they were immersed in each other. As soon as they noticed me, they sprang apart like guilty teenagers.'

'Pari wants to rent my neighbour's flat when they move out. They were a bit dubious about renting to a widow but Mrs Ali spoke to them and they didn't want to refuse a respectable lady like her,' said Manju.

Swaroop said, 'I will warn your neighbours. After all, we don't want our building to become the centre of some illicit activities, do we?'

'When is your mother-in-law coming?' asked Sonia, after some time.

Swaroop scowled. Her father-in-law had died recently of a heart attack. As a consequence, her husband and his brother had decided that their mother should now live with them rather than on her own. Swaroop had fought long and hard with her husband to prevent her mother-in-law coming to stay with them, but to no avail. Usually so compliant, her husband had become adamant and insisted that he had a duty to look after his mother. As if he would. She knew that all the real work would fall to her. Her mother-in-law was still active, however, so she would get her to take over the kitchen, decided Swaroop. After all, who better than a mother to cook for a son, she thought, temporarily ignoring the fact that she too had a ten-year-old son. She had managed to convince her husband that her mother-in-law would shuttle between her sons every six months rather than every year. More than six months with that old biddy in the small flat would surely drive her mad.

She looked up to see Sonia smiling sweetly at her. Swaroop's lips tightened.

'What's the latest in the Dilawar–Pari love kahani?' said Nadira.

'Hardly a story. Go on, have one more doodh-peda,' Mrs Bilqis said to her friend, pointing to a small china plate with round white coins made of milk and sugar, covered with finely beaten silver foil.

'I will,' said Nadira. 'They are lovely, almost melting in the mouth. So what's happening?'

'Pari wants to see Dilawar before making up her mind. She would like to talk to him face to face, so I've asked Dilawar to come down to Vizag.'

Nadira raised her eyebrows. 'Oh, so the young lady is becoming quite modern, isn't she? Did she see her first husband before marrying him?'

'That was different. She says she has a son now and wants to make sure that Dilawar is all right about it. I can sympathise with that.'

Nadira shook her head. 'I don't understand you, darling. Where is my old friend who would stand no nonsense from anybody – especially a little slip of a girl who is puffed up with her own importance? Let's look at her negative points, shall we? She is pretty, I grant you, but she is a widow, not a fresh-faced maiden. She has a son and doesn't want to give him up, yet she expects Dilawar to raise a boy who is not his own child. She has no family who will pay a dowry. She—'

'Stop it, Nadira,' said Mrs Bilqis. 'I am aware of all these things, but you know Dilawar's condition. That's why I have to go along with whatever Pari says for the time being.'

'So what about Dilawar's condition? Nobody knows about it and nobody can even guess it. He is a handsome boy who can attract any girl. In fact, the other day Ashraf's cousin came to our house. He talked in a very roundabout way, but basically he wanted to know whether you would consider his daughter for Dilawar, now that your original deadline has passed without any wedding. I told him the match hadn't fallen through – just delayed. But if you want, I can go back to him and settle the matter.'

'It's not that easy, Nadira. I am sure that Dilawar will not want to marry any girl by deceiving her. He's a genuinely good boy. You know he won't do it. And anyway, let's say he somehow did agree. What then? Can you imagine the scandal? The girl will go back and tell her parents and they will be extremely angry that we tricked them – and rightfully so, don't you think? That's why Pari, without a family, is ideal.'

'But what about Dilawar? Won't he tell all to Pari and will she then agree to marry him?'

'No, he won't. I have a plan. I will talk to him and convince him not to say anything. And I am also confident that once he starts living with a beautiful girl like Pari, he will be cured and everything will be fine. I hope that in time they will have their own children too.'

'What about this boy of hers then?'

'Any child of Pari and Dilawar will definitely be more beautiful than that mongrel kid she has adopted and I expect that the attraction between Pari and the boy will then naturally reduce. But I am not a cruel woman – he can grow up with Pari and Dilawar and help around the house. I am sure they will educate him and find him some sort of adequate living, as a clerk or something. After that, what happens to him is whatever is written in his book.'

Nadira said, 'I always said that you were the most intelligent woman I've ever known, darling.' She popped another peda into her mouth. 'You didn't tell me where you got these sweets.'

Half an hour later, Nadira left. The maid came in and cleared the table but Mrs Bilqis continued sitting on the sofa, staring at nothing. Was she really intelligent? She didn't know. She heard a noise like a wild animal grunting from one of the inner rooms and she was tempted to ignore it, but got up slowly. Duty first; always, duty first.

The ornate, hand-carved bed had been part of the trousseau that she had brought with her as a young bride from her father's house. It was now her prison – no, that was not correct. It was the stake in the ground to which she was tied with ropes of duty and tradition. Her husband lay on the bed, immobile except for his eyes, which tracked her.

She bent under the bed and, taking out a chamberpot, she helped him relieve himself, then adjusted his clothes. In the en suite bathroom, she emptied the pot before returning it to its place. Seated on the chair next to the bed, she mused on the withered body of the once-handsome man. His eyes never left her. Was he afraid that she would come in one day and smother him? Who knows what he thought any more. He had been confined to that bed, unable to speak or move any part of his body, for the last twenty years. When she had found out that Pari had done a similar service to her father, she had realised that she had been right in her choice. Any woman who had looked after a bedridden man would have all disgust of bodily functions squeezed out of her. When Pari learned Dilawar's true inclinations, she might be unhappy, but she wouldn't find it repugnant. Mrs Bilqis was sure about this.

Dilawar had been kind and sensitive even as a child. She remembered how he used to bring home stray puppies from the street. He had always been a mummy's boy but he also adored his father.

She recalled the terrible weekend that had destroyed her happy life. Dilawar had been less than ten years old. Her husband had gone out hunting. They had an ancestral estate several miles out of town, bordered by a forest and with a lodge in the middle of it. Those were the days when the forest department was much more lax about rich people killing a black buck or a wild boar, though even then the animals were becoming scarcer and it was common for her husband to return empty-handed. She had just put the children to bed and was telling the cook what to prepare for breakfast the next day when a frantic voice had called on the phone: 'The Nawab-saab has fallen off a horse. He is not able to move.'

Her husband had been bedridden ever since, but that wasn't the most terrible thing. Her husband had not actually gone hunting. In fact, he had never left town. He had spent the day at the house of a friend whose husband was away on business. The friend's husband had returned unexpectedly and it was Mrs Bilqis' husband who had jumped out of the bedroom on to a ledge, wearing almost nothing. He had tripped while trying to pull up his trousers and fallen to the ground twenty feet below.

How many times before had her husband been with his mistress when he had supposedly gone hunting? What about when he was away on business? The four of them – Mrs Bilqis, her friend and the two men – had spent many happy days together. Her friend had become particularly close, visiting her very often. Were her friend's smiles in those days just happiness at seeing her? Or was there another meaning behind them? That is the terrible thing about infidelity: it brings into doubt all that has gone before, so that even the happy memories are cast in a more sinister light – stealing not only the future, but the past too.

A few months after her husband had been settled permanently in the bedroom, her patience had finally run out. She had screamed at him as he lay staring at her, 'This is what happens when you go chasing after girls, you idiot. I hope that strumpet was worth spending the rest of your life in bed, lying in your own waste. We had a golden life and you've destroyed it with your lust for women. You foolish, foolish man.'

A noise at the door had disturbed her and she had turned back to see the boy Dilawar, his eyes round and wide. She had shut up immediately and taken him back to bed.

Had that outburst had a long-lasting impact on her son? She didn't know. All she cared about was finding a solution to the problem.

She sighed and left the room, switching off the light behind her. The bedridden man's eyes tracked her all the way out.

Ramanujam upturned the Pages Bookshop bag on to the bed. Aruna stared in surprise at the books.

*Lonely Planet, Rough Guide, Goa Tourism Department, Museums of Mumbai*, she read, running her hand over the glossy covers. 'Why did you get so many books?' she asked. 'The holiday hasn't even started and you are already spending money on it.'

Ramanujam shrugged. 'We don't go on holidays very often. In fact, this is our first! We might as well do it properly. Babur was telling me that he is taking his family on a ten-day tour of Thailand, Malaysia and Singapore. We should do that too.'

'Go to a foreign country? No, baba,' said Aruna. 'There is so much we haven't seen in our own country. What's the point of going elsewhere?'

'Don't fret,' said Ramanujam. 'That's for next time. Let's talk about this holiday first.'

'What clothes should I pack?' said Aruna.

'Jeans for Mumbai and a bikini for Goa,' said Ramanujam.

'Back to that same old mantra again? Are you sure you want me to come with you? You might enjoy ogling the girls more if I stayed at home.' Aruna was frowning.

'What's the fun of looking at the girls if you are not next to me?'

'Why? Do you want me to protect you from the slaps and sandals that will come your way when you drool over them?'

'No, darling. It's to remind me that you are the most beautiful woman around and nobody else can match up,' he said.

'Hmm . . .' said Aruna, mollified. 'You are good with words anyway.'

She started taking off her sari, unrolling the long cloth from around her waist and legs, ready to change into a night-dress.

Ramanujam picked up one of the guidebooks and started leafing through it. 'Did you know that Bombay was originally part of the dowry of the Portuguese princess Catherine de Braganza when she married Charles II of England?'

'Part of a dowry? How ridiculous!' said Aruna.

'Mumbai wasn't a big city at that time. It was actually seven separate islands inhabited by a few fishermen.'

There was a knock on the door and Aruna, half undressed, looked at her husband in panic. He pointed to the en suite bathroom and Aruna staggered into it, hobbled by the loose sari enveloping her feet.

'Who is it?' he called out.

'Me,' said Ramanujam's father.

Ramanujam checked that the bathroom door was closed and let his father in.

'What is it, naanna?' he asked. 'Is everything all right?'

His father came into the room and waved his hand dismissively. 'Yes, yes, everything's fine. Your uncle called from Kakinada. He's received a wedding proposal for Chitti and he wants me to go there immediately.'

Chitti was his father's younger brother's daughter.

'That's great news, naanna. Do you want me to come too? Our flight to Mumbai is not until the day after tomorrow.'

His father shook his head. 'I will leave first thing in the morning, before you are even awake.'

Aruna came out of the bathroom, her sari back in place. Pulling up a chair from the study table that Ramanujam used, she urged her father-in-law to sit down.

'I heard the news. So Chitti has finally agreed to a match?'

Ramanujam's father smiled at her. 'Yes, that's why there is no time to lose. Unfortunately, it means a bit of bad news for you.'

'Oh!' said Ramanujam. 'What's that?'

'I will be away for several days because we are all gathering at your uncle's place in Kakinada and then going to the boy's

family in Yanam to finalise the details. And the farmer next to
our land near Kottavalasa has made up his mind to sell. You
need to go there for the registration.'

'So what's the problem?' said Ramanujam. 'I can go to the
farmer tomorrow and be back by the evening. As I said, we
are not leaving for Mumbai until the day after.'

His father shook his head. 'It's not that simple. The farmer
said the documents are mortgaged with the State Bank. It will
take him a few days to get the papers back and only then we
can get it registered in our name.' He turned to Aruna. 'Sorry,
child,' he said. 'I know you have been really looking forward
to this holiday, but you will have to postpone it for a week or
so.'

Aruna just nodded mutely. Her husband said, 'All the tick-
ets and hotels are booked, naanna. We won't be able to
organise them all again at such short notice. Why can't we
register the land either when you come back from Chitti's
engagement or when we are back from our holiday?'

'Sorry, Ramu,' said his father. 'I've already paid the money
to the farmer to redeem his mortgage. It's not good to delay
the registration. Transactions are like milk – the longer they
are out in the open, the greater the chances of spoilage.'

'But, naanna,' said Ramanujam, before falling silent. He
sounded to his own ears as if he was ten years old again. He
sat down heavily on the bed with what was almost a flounce.

'Maava-gaaru – father-in-law – is right,' said Aruna. 'That
land business is worth lakhs of rupees. We can't risk delaying
it just to go on holiday.'

'Millions of rupees, dear, not just hundreds of thousands,'
said Ramanujam's father. 'I've been after that farm for a long
time because it bridges two of our other holdings. I couldn't
risk it going to anybody else and losing it for ever so I had to
give the farmer the money when he approached me.'

'But the holiday . . .' began Ramanujam, in a last-ditch effort that even he knew was doomed to failure.

'Wherever we go, it will be a holiday,' said Aruna. 'I'll come with you and we can spend an extra few days there. We can go to Mumbai and Goa some other time.'

'It's a really small town. There'll be nowhere to stay,' said Ramanujam, sighing. 'It's OK; I'll just go on my own and sort it out.'

'Nonsense. Aruna is correct,' said his father-in-law. 'I know the revenue officer there. I'll get him to arrange a room for the two of you in the government guest house. I'll ask Peter to sort out a four-wheel-drive vehicle with a driver and you can explore the nearby villages. It will be enjoyable.'

Ramanujam looked dubious, but gave in. 'All right. How will we know when to go?'

'As soon as the farmer has redeemed his documents, he will call me and I will ring you. The branch manager of the bank is a friend of mine and he will call me as well, so we'll know if the farmer uses our money to pay off the loan and then tries to renege on the deal.'

Aruna marvelled at how many people her father-in-law could call on for help.

'All right,' said Ramanujam. 'What do I check the documents for?'

Ramanujam's father smacked his forehead. 'When our elders said that too much education turns brains into mush, they must have been thinking about you. Check the adangal – I know that field has been with the farmer's family for generations, but make sure the document refers to the right piece of land. It should be 4.7 acres. Why am I telling you simple facts that you should already know? You've been coming with me on these occasions since you were a teenager.'

'I never paid much attention,' Ramanujam confessed. 'You

know I am not interested in all this dealing-wheeling, naanna.'

'Not interested? Do you think your income from being a doctor supports all this?' his father said, waving his hand in a circle, as if to encompass the house, the garden and everything else around them.

'We don't need to keep buying and selling lands and houses, naanna. We have enough money to support the next four generations even if we didn't earn a single extra naya paisa. And my doctor's salary is not exactly small. Why don't you take it easy and stop running around?'

The older man stood up abruptly. 'Is this what I should be listening to? Money is like water in a pond. If there is no stream flowing in, the pond will dry up. Nabobs, far richer than us, have become paupers when their income didn't keep pace with their expenses. You've had an easy life so far; grow up now and start taking your responsibilities seriously. You will be told when you have to go to the village. Just make sure you do and try not to mess it up.' He turned to go.

Ramanujam stared with a frozen expression on his face. Aruna rushed forward and stopped her father-in-law.

'My father always says that one should not leave for a journey on an angry note. Please, sir, come and sit down. You know your son better than anybody else, so you must be sure that he never meant to insult you. He was only looking out for your health.' She turned to her husband. 'Weren't you?' she said. 'Weren't you?' she repeated more loudly, when he didn't reply.

Ramanujam looked at Aruna as if startled and stood up. 'Yes, naanna, sorry. Of course, I didn't mean any offence.'

His father turned back and sat down on the chair. 'Isn't it said that one single act of taking a dip in the River Ganga is enough to wipe out a lifetime of sins?'

Ramanujam nodded slowly.

'In the same way, even if you acted foolishly every single day of your existence, you will still not be a fool.'

Ramanujam gazed at his father in silence.

'Ask me why.'

'Why?' said Ramanujam reluctantly, knowing that his father was not about to flatter him.

'Because you married this wise girl,' said his father. 'That balances everything else out.'

Aruna blushed. Ramanujam suddenly smiled and pulled Aruna down next to him. 'You are right,' he said. 'I am sorry, naanna. I will try to pay more attention in future.'

His father shook his head. 'I was wrong. There is no point in trying to teach a cow to act like a guard dog. It's just not in its nature. You are a good doctor and that's where your mind should be – on your patients, not on the next deal.'

'So what's the way forward, maava-gaaru?' asked Aruna.

Ramanujam's father thought for a moment and then broke into a smile. 'I've got it. Why does Ramu have to do it when I've got a daughter?'

'Of course, Mani,' said Ramanujam. Mani was Ramanujam's married sister and mother of two. She had not initially been happy with her brother marrying a poor girl like Aruna, but was now friendly with her sister-in-law.

'I told you that you were a fool and I was not wrong,' said his father happily. 'How can we put anything in her name? If we do, it will belong to her husband and in-laws. I am not doing all this work to give away our wealth. No, I meant Aruna.'

'But . . .' protested Aruna. 'I don't think . . .'

Her father-in-law waved her down. 'You have a good head on your shoulders and you will be perfect. Register the land in your name. I will tell the revenue officer to check all the paperwork for you and make sure there are no problems.

When I come back, I will show you all the different properties we have and you can slowly start taking over from me. You are both right, I do need to start taking it easy at my age.'

Unexpectedly, tears filled Aruna's eyes. The idea that a girl like her from a poor family would be the mistress of a large property portfolio was overwhelming. Her father-in-law was also being very progressive. Ownership of land was strictly passed down from father to son and transferring it into a daughter-in-law's name was almost unheard of. Why, she might get ideas above her station and start feeling independent!

Aruna got up, bent and touched her father-in-law's feet with her hands. 'I will try my best to justify the confidence you are showing in me,' she said.

The old man blessed her in Sanskrit with a hand over her head. 'Chiranjeevi soubhagyavati bhava,' he said. May you for ever remain a married woman. 'I am sure you will not let me down.'

'After tomorrow, I have the rest of the week off,' said Aruna, straightening up. 'I hope that Sir won't mind if I turn up having told him that I am going to be away on holiday.'

'Of course he won't. No employer will,' said her father-in-law. 'How is Mr Ali, by the way? I haven't met him since your wedding.'

Like his daughter, her father-in-law too had initially been against their marriage; he had even gone to Mr Ali's house to threaten him for encouraging the unsuitable match. Aruna didn't know what exactly Mr Ali had said, but her father-in-law had been convinced enough to go ahead with the wedding.

'He is doing well,' said Aruna. 'Madam says that's because he doesn't let anything worry him.'

'So many people have asked me why I am sending my

daughter-in-law out to work,' Ramanujam's father said. 'As if I am forcing you to go out.'

'Oh,' whispered Aruna.

It had been one of her conditions before agreeing to marry Ramanujam that she should be allowed to continue working after the wedding and use her wages to help her parents and sister.

'Don't look so worried,' said Ramanujam's father, smiling. 'They are just jealous that I have such a good daughter-in-law. Your parents don't have a son, so I don't see anything wrong in your supporting them in their old age. And I trust Mr Ali and his wife. They are good people.' He stood up.

'Naanna, who is going with you and amma?' said Ramanujam.

'Well, Peter is driving us,' said his father.

'Peter's leg gives him difficulty, naanna. Also, in a wedding house, there will always be work. Why don't you also take Kaka and his sister with you?' said Ramanujam.

'If we take them all, who will help you here?' said his father.

'We are both on holiday from the day after tomorrow anyway. We can manage easily.'

'There is no need for that. There are servants in your uncle's house too.'

'I insist,' said Ramanujam. 'They will be able to help in Kakinada and in Yanam too.'

His father looked doubtful. Aruna glanced at her father-in-law and then turned to stare at her husband, puzzled. Why was Ram being so insistent? Suddenly it felt as if a light had been switched on in her mind and she understood.

'Yes, maava-gaaru,' she said. 'We'll just be here for a few days until the farmer gets his papers ready. What will the servants do after that on their own? It's better if you take them with you. At least they'll be some use to you there.'

Her father-in-law nodded and stood up. 'That makes sense, I suppose. All right, we'll do that. I'd better go and tell them to pack and be ready for the morning.'

He left and Ramanujam closed the door behind him. Aruna hugged him tightly. 'I love you,' she said, her eyes shining. She was smiling.

'Come home early tomorrow,' he said. 'I'll be back as soon as I hand over the patients.'

Aruna nodded enthusiastically, her face against his chest, her smile refusing to leave her. Several days on their own in the house with nobody else around, not even servants. She could cook for her husband whatever food he liked and they could lounge around the whole time, letting their hair down, playing silly games, being free with each other. When she gazed up at him, his stare was intense and her mouth was slightly open, her lips feeling full and moist. Aruna and Ram had never experienced such privacy before. It would be better than any holiday.

# CHAPTER ELEVEN

'What was so urgent that I had to drop work and come to Vizag?' Dilawar said to his mother.

They were on NH-5, the highway leading home from the airport. He had caught an early-morning flight and now it was just past 9 a.m.

'I am hungry. The airline food was like plastic. I couldn't stomach it at all.'

'By the time we reach home, the maid will have puri halwa ready. Your favourite. What do you eat for breakfast in Bombay?' she asked. His mother still called Mumbai by its original name, even though it was now many years since its name had changed.

'If it's a weekday, I just have toast with jam.'

'How can you eat bread, like an unwell person? Can't you get a proper cooked breakfast of idli sambhar or roti sabzi in Bombay?'

'Who has time in the mornings, ammi-jaan?'

'That's why you need a wife to look after you,' she said.

'Ammi-jaan! Not again. How many times do we have to talk about this matter? I don't want to marry just so I can have a cooked breakfast every morning.'

His mother was silent for a moment and then said, 'And what do you do at weekends?'

'Oh, I get up late and have a brunch. Before Shaan left, he used to cook something.'

'Who is Shaan?' said his mother sharply.

Dilawar's face froze in horror and he went quite pale as the blood drained from it. He stared at her, goggle-eyed. 'Umm . . .' he said, his mouth opening and closing like a goldfish that has jumped out of its bowl.

His mother fixed him steadily with the same laser-sharp look that he remembered from when he was a boy and had broken a window with a cricket ball.

'Umm . . . a friend,' he said. 'Just a friend,' he repeated, more firmly. An ex-friend.

They both sat back, each looking out of their side-window, while the driver negotiated the four-lane road into town, slowing only where the traffic police had constructed chicanes with makeshift barriers to cut speed and reduce traffic accidents.

An hour later, Dilawar was in the living room watching a Test match between Australia and India. Having eaten, he had sat with his father until the bedridden man had fallen asleep. Dilawar was now fulminating against the umpire who had not given the Australian batsman out.

'Don't you have eyes, you blind idiot,' he said. 'The batsman was miles out. You could have fitted the entire Great Barrier Reef between him and the crease.'

The umpires halfway round the world totally ignored Dilawar's shouts and the Indian bowler started his run-up for the next ball. Disgusted, Dilawar threw the small cushion in his hands down on the floor.

His mother came in with Nadira Aunty. 'Why are you making such a racket? You will disturb your father.'

Dilawar took his eyes off the TV and turned to his mother. 'I don't remember abba-jaan taking a nap so early in the day,' he said.

His mother sighed and sat down next to him. Nadira Aunty sat opposite. 'He had a chest infection a few weeks ago and that took a lot out of him. Since then, he has been getting tired very easily and sleeping much more.'

Dilawar bent down and picked the cushion up off the floor. He had vague recollections of his father as an active man who played cricket with him and took him swimming, but in reality those memories had been largely blotted out by a lifetime of watching his father lie in bed, silent and immobile, moving only when turned by others to prevent bedsores. Apart from a retainer who came twice a week to help give his father a wash, his mother pretty much looked after him on her own.

Much of their family wealth had been frittered away in a fruitless attempt to find a cure. Finally his grandparents' death, and an honest doctor's opinion that the damage was incurable, had put a stop to the money gushing out to charlatans and fake herbalists. More had been lost in a court case – he wasn't clear what it was, nobody ever talked about it – but it involved old family friends-cum-business partners who had fallen out with his parents. Dilawar remembered that there had been angry recriminations and talk of betrayal between his grandfather and the other man, but it was all ancient history now.

They had never actually become poor – there were too many parcels of land, pieces of art and antique jewellery and silverware for that – but his mother felt humiliated having to bargain endlessly for a few extra rupees with the smarmy brokers who bought these heirlooms. The family had slowly begun living on less and less, shedding celebrations, retainers and expenses each year, like a star that, after going nova, contracts on itself and dims slowly. Once Dilawar started earning, he had asked his mother to hire more servants and a nurse for his father, but his mother had gotten used to caring for her husband on her own and she refused. She had, however, upgraded to a full-time maid and a part-time cook, so she could leave the house for a couple of hours every now and then.

His mother, unaccountably, seemed nervous. He looked at Nadira Aunty. The two friends definitely had something more than their arms up their sleeves.

'Why did you call me so urgently from Mumbai?' he asked.

Before his mother could say anything, Nadira Aunty said, 'We have found a bride for you.'

Dilawar realised that he should have suspected something like this. When the original date that his mother had given him for his wedding had passed, he had been happy – thinking that the whole matter would blow over. But it obviously hadn't.

'Not again,' he groaned.

Out of the corner of his eye, on the TV screen, he saw a ball catch the top edge of the bat. The ball skied upwards, like a bullet ricocheting, and two Indian fielders ran forwards, adjusting their position below it with minute crablike steps, their hands cupped in front of their chests, like devotees expecting a gift from heaven. Dilawar held his breath. Was this the breakthrough that the Indians had been toiling for all day? Just as the ball came into view at the top of the screen, the two fielders collided and looked momentarily startled. Dilawar leaned forward, watching intently, in an agony of tension. The ball hurtled towards the waiting men and . . .

. . . the image on the television seemed to be sucked into a black hole, reducing to a bright spot in the centre of the screen that then winked out. Dilawar stared at the TV for half a second longer, his mouth open.

'I don't believe it,' he said fiercely, throwing the cushion back on the floor. The electricity supply in Mumbai was very reliable and he had forgotten how frequently they had power-cuts in Vizag. Had the ball been caught or not?

'What has the poor cushion done to be treated so badly?' said his mother.

He turned to her and saw that she was holding the remote control of the TV in her hand. Suddenly, he realised that the fan was still running. 'What . . . Why did you switch it off?' he said.

'Forget the silly game,' she said. 'They'll show it again. Listen to what we are saying.'

'Show it again? That was a live broadcast.' He stared at his mother for a moment, then sat back. 'All right,' he said sulkily. 'What do you want?'

His mother put the remote away. 'Marriage,' she said.

'No, ammi-jaan. Not the same old broken record again.'

'You are the one going round and round in a loop, repeating yourself. I have found a girl who we think is perfect for you. We want you to marry her.'

'But I don't want to marry a girl,' he said.

'Who will you marry if not a girl? A mare?'

Dilawar clamped his mouth shut. That was the second time he had made a mistake since returning home. His mother was an intelligent woman – he would have to be more careful.

Nadira Aunty said to Mrs Bilqis, 'Didn't you say that you needed to buy some toiletries? Why don't you go to the shops? I want to talk to your son.'

'But—' began his mother.

'Alone,' said Nadira Aunty.

A look passed between the two women that Dilawar couldn't decipher, but his mother walked over to Nadira Aunty, hugged her and left the room. Nadira Aunty turned to him and said, 'Come and sit here. I am too old to shout across the room.' She patted the place next to her on the sofa.

He joined her and said, 'You are not old, aunty. You look as if you are twenty-five. Why don't you leave your husband and we'll elope to Mumbai?'

'You are such a flatterer,' she said, patting his cheek, but looking pleased nonetheless. She sounded breathless as she said, 'You are so handsome that I would do it but I am afraid that my husband would track us down and shoot us.'

'I don't care,' said Dilawar. He declaimed dramatically, 'For one second with you, I'll suffer the agonies of infinity.'

'Wah, wah!' Nadira Aunty said. 'Now I want you to say the same thing to this girl.' She was holding a photograph of a young woman, her face turned three-quarters of the way towards the camera, laughing.

She could be considered pretty, he supposed. 'Who is she?' he asked aloud.

'Your would-be. This is the girl your mother has found for you. This photo has not been touched up in some studio. She really is that beautiful, if not more.'

Dilawar shook his head. 'I am talking about marrying you and you are promoting a rival,' he said.

Nadira Aunty said, 'Don't joke, Dilawar. Is there a girl in Mumbai that you want to marry? If there is, tell us and your mother will happily—'

'There is no one,' said Dilawar shortly. Shaan's image came briefly to his mind, but he pushed it aside. 'There is no girl.'

'Do you know why I asked your mother to leave?'

'So we could make arrangements for running away?' he said.

'Chup,' she said, frowning. 'Don't talk nonsense. You don't want to marry any girl, do you? Ever.'

Dilawar was taken by surprise. The smiling aunt that he had always joked with had disappeared and in her place was a formidable Amazon.

'You were always my favourite, since you were a boy who used to steal my make-up. I like you much more than your brother, who has no sense of humour.'

Dilawar said, 'You are my favourite too.'

'The question now is, what are we going to do with you?'

Dilawar shrugged. 'Leave me alone. Maybe it is not in my destiny to get married.'

'Look at me,' she said.

His eyes met hers. He noticed how her skin, glowing in its youth, was now parchment-thin. She was still handsome, and her grey hair had been dyed with henna for so long that her orange hair no longer provoked comment.

She locked her eyes on his and said, 'Do you have someone in Mumbai?'

'I . . .'

His gaze faltered. She calmly put a finger under his chin and adjusted it until their eyes met again. It dawned on him with a sudden conviction that she *knew*. Yet, there was no anger or disgust in her expression. Instead, he sensed a vast well of sympathy. The issue of his sexuality suddenly seemed selfish and he was ashamed of himself. What was that quote that his high-school English teacher loved so much? 'No man is an island, entire of itself. Each is a piece of the continent, a part of the main.' John Donne. His actions had consequences, he realised.

'What do you want me to do?' he asked.

She tapped on the photograph. 'The girl's name is Pari. Your mother has been chasing her for weeks, months, and

Pari has been dragging her feet. First she said maybe; then she said no. Then she said . . . Anyway, I was outraged. How dare this slip of a girl demur at marrying my friend's son? I wanted your mother to ignore this girl and look for somebody else. Do you know what I am saying?'

Dilawar nodded.

'Then I realised why your mother was being so single-minded. She has found absolutely the best possible match for you.'

'It's impossible,' said Dilawar. 'I am not marrying her and ruining a young woman's life.'

'That's because you are a good boy,' she said, approvingly. After a short silence, she continued, 'Did you know that Pari is a widow?'

'What?' said Dilawar. 'She looks so happy. Are you sure?'

'How selfish you men are . . . Does a woman forsake the right to even a moment's happiness once she loses her husband?'

Dilawar reddened. 'No, that's not what I meant,' he protested. 'I—'

Nadira Aunty raised her hand. 'Pari is a delightful girl, full of life. But I had a long chat with her and, underneath those smiles, she is very lonely. Did you know that she's not only a widow but also an orphan? Her mother died when she was young and her father died a little while ago. He suffered a massive stroke and was bedridden for a year. She looked after him all on her own.'

'You mean like mother . . .' said Dilawar, glancing towards his father's bedroom.

'Nobody can compare to your mother. She's been caring for your father for over twenty years. But Pari is definitely made in the same mould as Bilqis. You know how widows are treated in traditional towns like this – she is looked down

upon in small things, not invited to weddings or engage-
ments and other female-only ceremonies. If she marries a
second time, she will be spared all these problems. She can
play a full part in life once more.'

'So why doesn't she get married again? It's not as if Muslim
women are not allowed to remarry.'

'You have been away for too long,' said Nadira Aunty.
'Have you forgotten how things work here? She doesn't have
parents. Her uncle and aunt are helping her, but it's not the
same, is it? Also, because she was feeling lonely, she adopted
a poor village orphan. Now, you tell me, who is going to
agree to take on an eight-year-old boy?'

Dilawar nodded slowly.

Nadira Aunty took his hands in hers and leaned forward.
'Pari is a poor, oppressed village girl who lives in a single
room with no modern comforts. She has to come down two
floors every morning for her drinking and bathing water,
carrying the heavy buckets upstairs. She has just lost her job
and is looking after an adopted son on a widow's pension and
the savings her father left her. You will be doing a good deed
by marrying her.'

'But—'

'It is not all one way, Dilawar. You need to get married too.
All this fun you are having is fine now because you are young.
Society will look on you differently as you go into your thir-
ties and forties without a partner, even in Mumbai.'

Dilawar thought of Shaan and the wedding ceremony that
his friend had attended in London. What wouldn't he have
given for their relationship to be formalised like those women
in England? But that was not possible. He just wasn't brave
enough to face down the entire world. No wonder Shaan had
left him when he was such a spineless jellyfish.

Suddenly, the image of Manek, the ageing queen, came to

Dilawar's mind. He saw himself like that, his looks crumpled past their best, still going to the Gateway of India to meet men, and the thought terrified him.

He looked at Nadira Aunty.

She said, 'Pari is ideal for you. All she wants from the marriage is security. She doesn't want more children – she already has a son. Marry her and you can continue your life as you want. She will give you respectability, she will give you a ready-made son; she will look after you in good health and ill. You will give her back the status of being a married woman and her son a far better future than she can on her own. You will take her away from a daily round of drudgery and into a comfortable, modern life. God knows that it is not ideal, but you have the basis for an arrangement here. It will also make your mother happy and stop some of the comments that people make to her.'

'I am not sure—' began Dilawar.

'Your mother never complains but think about the kind of life she has had for the last twenty years.'

'Yes . . .' said Dilawar hesitantly. He wasn't sure where the conversation was going now.

'Do you think she would appreciate any help in looking after your father?'

'I've told her so many times to hire a nurse, but she won't listen to me,' said Dilawar.

Nadira Aunty sighed. 'Your mother is old-fashioned that way. For her, duty is the biggest virtue in life. After a brief outburst right at the beginning, she has never once uttered a word against your father or the work that has been forced upon her, not even to me. But if you married Pari, she could help your mother.'

'What?' said Dilawar. 'How? Won't she be in Mumbai with me if we get married?'

'Eventually, yes. But think about it. I've talked to Pari and the biggest objection she has to this wedding is uprooting her boy away from everything he knows and taking him away to Mumbai. She's probably scared herself, though she won't admit it. She is still in love with her husband and I am sure that she feels guilty about marrying another man. Why don't you leave her here after marrying her?'

'I don't understand,' said Dilawar. 'What's the point of that?'

'You will take her out of that cramped room and bring her here. Lovely as it is, God knows that this house needs the patter of a child's feet to brighten it up. Pari will lose the mark of being a widow. Her boy will get a father. You can continue your life in Mumbai as normal for now. Your mother will get a companion and helpmate. After all, Pari has experience in looking after a bedridden man. Over time, she can convince your mother to hire nurses and in a couple of years, as and when you both feel ready, you can move her to Mumbai.' Nadira Aunty's eyes were shining. 'I think it's the perfect solution.'

'Did ammi-jaan say this to you?' Dilawar asked. Nadira Aunty looked askance at him and Dilawar mumbled, 'Sorry, of course not.'

'I thought of it just now as I was talking to you. Am I a genius or what?'

'Or what,' said Dilawar, smiling.

Nadira Aunty let go of his hands forcefully in mock anger. 'Pari wants to meet you and talk to you about her son. She is scared that if she marries you, she will have to give up her boy. Allay her fears. You can also take the opportunity to study her. Look beneath her façade of bright chat and smiles and see whether I am speaking the truth or not. One always dreams of a marriage filled with romance and adoration, but in both yours and Pari's cases, that is just not possible and this is the best that can be done. But there are many kinds of love, Dilawar. Once you decorate a house together, host parties, deal with boring guests, stay up late, worry about a sick child and share the joy of a son getting into a good school, it is impossible not to feel something for each other. This love will bring happiness and solace and that's not to be sniffed at.' Nadira Aunty got up. 'I will tell your mother that you have agreed to meet Pari.'

Dilawar pondered for a moment, wondering when he had indeed agreed to this. 'I didn't say . . .' he said, looking up, but his mother's friend had already turned away.

'What did I do to deserve an aunt like you?'

Nadira turned back and smiled at him. 'You are a kind man and a good son and that is what matters most, not anything else. To me, anyway.'

After she left, he sat staring at the blank TV for several minutes, his mind numb. Finally he picked up the remote. There was a soap on the screen, showing the usual mother-in-law, daughter-in-law tussles. The day's cricket was over and he still didn't know whether the batsman had been caught out or not. He sighed and slid forward, leaning his head against the back of the sofa, looking straight up at the ceiling. Shaan . . . That was the one thought reverberating round and round his brain. Why did I have to lose you?

He thought about the wedding that his friend had attended in London. It was beautiful, but even there Lisa's parents had not accepted their daughter's wedding to another woman. Over here, it was simply impossible. John Donne came to his mind again: 'No man is an island.' He could not just ignore his family and act as if his deeds in Mumbai would have no repercussions in Vizag. His mother deserved some happiness, surely, after more than twenty years living like a widow –

worse than a widow, if the truth be told, because his father had not *actually* died. And if he could bring some cheer into her life, he should, shouldn't he?

And what was the point of thinking about Shaan? He had been dumped for being a coward. He would just have to get over it.

What had Nadira Aunty said? Pari was still grieving for her husband and was not looking for love. He thought about the orphan boy, Pari's son, whom he had never met. He could make sure the boy got a good education. He could play cricket with him, teach him to bat and bowl, take him to matches in Mumbai and see the world's best players in action. He had thought that he would never have children and did not realise until now what a pang that had always been. A slow smile crept over his face, like a thief stealing into a shadow. He felt a thrill at the thought of raising a son and being the best father that any man could possibly be.

# CHAPTER TWELVE

By ten in the morning, the sun was sharp and the heat lay like a blanket over the verandah. The ceiling fan and the smaller table fan were both running at full speed, but Pari still felt hot. Until now, she hadn't fully appreciated how good the working conditions in the call centre had been. But there was no point thinking about that. Aruna had gone on holiday, and Pari was helping out in the marriage bureau.

The gate opened, admitting a family – a couple in their late forties and their daughter. They came on to the verandah and introduced themselves. After a fumble, Pari looked up their details on the computer. They were Vaidiki Brahmins, the priestly caste – the same as Aruna, though she had married into a Niyogi, or a more secular, Brahmin family – and were already members, having joined by post.

'We want to see more information about these people,' said the father, handing Mr Ali some names and addresses of existing members.

Mr Ali pulled out the requested forms and photographs and handed them over. The family started poring over them. Gopal, the postman, brought the day's mail. Mr Ali showed Pari how to sort the letters into different categories – requests

for new lists, application forms with fees, and requests for
information about some bride or groom they had advertised
for. Mrs Ali carried out to them a tray with glasses of cold
water. Pari jumped up and served everybody.

The father and daughter thanked her and took deep gulps.
The mother smiled nervously at Pari and just held the glass.
Pari wondered whether it was because she was a widow that
the woman hesitated to drink water taken from her hand.
Then she realised that she was being paranoid. The family
were Brahmins and it was natural that the lady should hesitate
about drinking water in a Muslim household. In fact, the
woman might not drink water in any non-Brahmin house,
even if it was Hindu.

Stillness, broken only by the sound of quiet conversation
between the couple and their daughter, descended on the
verandah-turned-office and several minutes passed.

'No, naanna. Not that one,' said the girl, her voice suddenly raised.

Pari glanced up from the table at the family. It was obvious
that the discussion had been ongoing for a while. The father
seemed upset, the girl adamant and the mother torn, looking
first one way and then the other. Realising that they now had
an audience, the mother touched her husband's sleeve. He
looked at her with irritation, as if he was about to snap at her,
before seeing her pointing finger.

'How things have changed, sir,' he said to Mr Ali. 'If my
father ever said jump, I would only ask how high on the way
up. Nowadays even girls have such strong opinions. It makes
me wonder what they go to college for. Do you think the
professors lay out lectures on how to be obstinate and be
rude to parents?'

'I am not being rude, naanna,' the girl said.

'See,' said the man, with the air of a mathematician who

has just proved an axiom. 'Would I have ever contradicted my father in front of outsiders?'

Mr Ali smiled sympathetically. 'Do you want to go home and continue this discussion there?' he said.

The father, a Mr Bhaskar according to the application form, sighed and leaned back. 'What is there to hide, sir? I want her to marry one man and my daughter prefers another. It's an age-old story.'

The girl, Anu, said, 'See, even you admit that it has been going on for ever. You were unnecessarily maligning my college and my generation.'

Mr Bhaskar shook his head. 'Why did you go into literature? You should have been a lawyer. Your opponents would have raised their hands in surrender as soon as you walked into court.'

Pari smiled. While their differences of opinion appeared genuine and deep, it was also clear that they were both trying to convince the other and neither had brought up the ultimate option of overriding the other's wishes. She turned to the mother. 'What do you say, madam?' she asked.

The mother shook her head. 'Who will listen to what I say? Their arguments began when this girl started saying no as a toddler and they will continue long past the time I go to Vaikuntham – the Lord's abode.'

Mr Bhaskar fanned out a couple of photographs like playing cards and said, 'It's a straight choice between these two. We've eliminated everybody else.'

Mr Ali took the photographs and showed them to Pari. She pulled out their details and stared at them in surprise. 'They are such opposites,' she said.

'That's why we are unable to agree,' said Anu.

Both the men in the photos were good-looking, but one was a priest and the other was an officer in an American bank.

Mr Ali said, 'According to this boy's father, he doesn't just work in a bank, he works in an *investment* bank. They don't take deposits and give out loans, he said.' Mr Ali shrugged. 'To be very honest with you, I don't understand what the point of a bank is, if it doesn't let people save and borrow.'

Mr Bhaskar grinned. 'These strange banks seem to pay well, though. If we go with the banker, he earns a good salary and travels the world in luxury. The priest, on the other hand, will never become rich but will be respected by everybody in society and can live anywhere, not just in big cities.'

'Why do you want to force your daughter to marry a religious man if she is not interested?' said Mr Ali. 'The life of a priest's wife will be somewhat restricting, even dull.'

Mr Bhaskar looked confused for a moment and then laughed uproariously, slapping his thighs, tears rolling down his cheeks. His wife and daughter started smiling too. Mr Ali and Pari stared at each other in amazement. Surely Mr Ali's comment hadn't been funny?

'I am sorry,' said Mr Bhaskar finally, calming down, but unable to stop chuckling. 'If only life was that simple. You see, I want my daughter to marry the banker. It is she who prefers the priest.'

Mr Ali's mouth opened and closed again without a word. He was speechless, a rather rare event. The girl coloured, but met his gaze steadily.

'I don't want to move from Mumbai to New York to London like a nomad just to earn a living. If times are good, these bankers are on a roll and when the economy turns, as it always does, they get fired. Who wants to live with such insecurity? And you are wrong if you think that just because the other man is a priest, he is old-fashioned.'

Anu must have seen the puzzlement on their faces because

she continued. 'You are probably wondering how I know whether he is modern or a stick-in-the-mud.'

Mr Ali scanned the priest's details. His name was Dharam Kumar. He had written 'Call me DK' on his form. He thought Anu was probably right, but it seemed a small detail to hang a lot of faith upon.

Anu said, 'Even though we saw the details here, we know him from before. It is a slightly complicated relationship to explain, but he is effectively a distant cousin of mine, yet in a line that allows us to get married.'

Mr Ali nodded. 'I see,' he said.

Anu went on, 'He wears trousers instead of tying a panchi round his waist and drives around on a motorcycle.'

Her father broke into the conversation. 'He wears *trousers*. That explains it. He must be modern!'

'Don't be sarcastic, naanna. You know what I mean.'

Mr Bhaskar said, 'It's true that priests don't starve, but they lead an austere existence. I grew up in an agraharam – land granted to Brahmins by ancient kings – and I know how priests live. Lots of cleanliness, education and culture, but a very threadbare life ruled by customs and traditions. You've never seen it because I moved away from our forefathers' vocation. I came to town after high school to your maternal grandfather's house. I had only two things in my pocket – an introductory letter from my headmaster and twenty-five rupees that my mother had got by pawning her silver anklets. I don't know what your grandfather saw in me, but he took me under his wing and started me off as a messenger in his printing business. He gave me more and more responsibilities and eventually his daughter's hand in marriage.'

Anu's mother nodded vigorously and blushed when everybody's gaze turned to her.

Anu's father continued, 'Poverty is like a deep hole in the

ground: the horizons of a person stuck inside it are limited and he can see only a little bit of the sky. When a man tries to climb out of it, the sides keep giving way and dumping him back at the bottom.'

'Well said,' replied Mr Ali. 'I couldn't have come up with a better analogy.'

Mr Bhaskar nodded and smiled. 'I did not leap Hanuman-like out of that hole just to see my daughter slide down its sides again.' He was referring to the monkey-god who had leapt across the ocean in the epic Ramayana.

Anu said, 'You never told me all this, naanna.'

Mr Bhaskar shrugged and spread his hands. 'You never asked me. But in this place, it just feels so comfortable. It is not like an office – it feels more like visiting family friends that you've known all your life and somehow your tongue just loosens up.'

'Thank you,' said Mr Ali. 'You could be describing a wine bar where the alcohol gets rid of your inhibitions.'

Mr Bhaskar laughed.

'So I am told,' added Mr Ali. 'Not that I personally know anything about wine and bars.'

'Of course you don't,' said Mr Bhaskar and laughed some more, before becoming serious again. 'Sir, please tell this silly girl that being poor is not a joke. It will affect not only her but also any children that she will have.'

Before Mr Ali could say anything, Anu answered. 'I know that poverty is not fun, naanna. But there is a big difference between being poor and not being rich. Things have moved on since you were a boy. As the country has become wealth-ier, so have priests. They are not limited to a small temple and the few houses they can walk to. They ride on bikes extend-ing their catchment area to the whole town. They use computers to build horoscopes. We will never be hugely affluent, but I reckon that we can have a comfortable life. I'll be happier here with all my family and friends around me than I will in Mumbai with more money and bigger expenses.'

Mr Bhaskar looked at Mr Ali. 'She just won't listen, sir. She has a ready reply for anything I say. What can I do?'

Mr Ali smiled. 'Your daughter has a very sound head on her shoulders,' he said. 'There is nothing that you or I need say to her. You should be proud of Anu. I think that the man who marries her is lucky indeed. Why do you think that only the man determines a couple's fortunes? Your girl has a bright future and her husband will be a part of it. If I were you, I would concentrate my attentions on your other daughter and let Anu make her own choice.'

Mr Bhaskar looked silently at everybody on the verandah and then gave a big sigh. 'My younger daughter, Ankita, is eighteen, going on thirty-five. She is ten times more intelligent than Anu and a hundred times more stubborn. What am I going to do?'

Mr Ali shook his head and said softly, 'You have my sympathies, sir.'

After the family left, Pari helped Mr Ali put the files away. The girl, Anu, is right, thought Pari. To avoid being poor, you don't have to become rich. I have enough money and can earn some more, even if not as much as in the call centre. Vasu and I can manage perfectly well here. I just need to move into a bigger flat and life will become more comfortable. There is no need to marry Mrs Bilqis's son just for the sake of security.

Later that afternoon, Rehman and Pari got off the auto-rickshaw in front of the hotel gates and walked through to the air-conditioned lobby of the five-star hotel. A handsome young man was the only occupant of a sofa. His long legs were crossed at the ankle and he was reading a business magazine. Rehman took the lead and went up to him. Pari fell behind, suddenly nervous. The man glanced up and broke into a smile when he saw Rehman. He stood and the two friends hugged each other while the woman, for whose sake the meeting had been arranged, looked on, bemused.

'How long has it been?' asked Rehman.

Dilawar counted on his fingers and said, 'Nine, no, ten . . . years.'

'That's right,' said Rehman.

He turned to Pari and introduced them to each other. They moved to the restaurant whose large glass windows overlooked lawns on all sides. Rehman remembered his tryst here with his ex-fiancée. He and Usha had been so much in love with each other. It was a shock to realise that this was the first time he'd thought of Usha today. The sense of loss, which had been devastating at first, had attenuated to a dull throb.

Pari studied the two men. Both were good-looking in different ways. Dilawar was slightly taller, with broad shoulders and perfect hair, and he was clean-shaven. His lips were sensuous, thought Pari suddenly, watching him enunciate his words. His clothes were well pressed and he wore cufflinks in his shirt sleeves. Her eyes were fixed on him as he unfolded the white linen napkin with a snap and laid it on his lap, as if he totally belonged in this posh place. He looks like a fruit, thought Pari. A ripe, perfectly formed apple, juicy and crunchy, with no blemishes – like the kind you get in those new-fangled grocery stores with trolleys and open shelves.

Rehman's shirt was clean, but the crease on the sleeves was muddled as if it had been ironed sometimes one way and sometimes another. Pari knew that it was his 'best' shirt that Mrs Ali had made him change into, from a rough cotton kurta. There was a cut on his cheek where he had nicked himself shaving. His hair was just on the borderline of being unkempt, his barber's visit probably overdue by a week. She doubted that Dilawar patronised a mere barber. He probably went to one of those air-conditioned hairdressing *salons*. Her husband had visited a salon like that once – and had come back scandalised.

'They charged me three hundred rupees!' he had said. 'I was very lucky to have the money on me. Otherwise they might have set me sweeping the floor or something.'

How she had laughed then. His usual haircut used to cost about thirty rupees. Why was she thinking of her husband now?

Pari doubted whether Rehman even visited one of those humble hairdressing shops that her husband had gone to. There was a barber on the street behind their house. He had a medium-sized, slightly tarnished mirror propped against a tree and was usually found sitting on a wooden stool, sharpening his knife against a leather strop. She had seen him once with a client. The customer sat on the stool facing the mirror and, in the absence of a revolving chair, the barber walked backwards and forwards around the man with a pair of scissors and a comb. That was more Rehman's style.

Rehman is like a mango that you buy from a street-side hawker, she thought. The golden-yellow skin was just a bit wrinkled, with a long smear down the side where the acidic sap had trickled out, causing a few pieces of straw to stick to it, while the bottom tip is still a little green, which might mean that the fruit was not yet as sweet as it could be.

She made an effort to listen to their conversation but they were talking about some old classmates of theirs, so she tuned them out again and fell back to studying the two men. It was a couple of minutes before it occurred to her that she preferred homely mangoes to exotic apples. Her expression became stern and she silently told herself that mangoes were not on the menu.

'We are boring the good lady,' said Dilawar finally.

'No, no,' said Pari, unconvincingly.

'Of course we are,' said Dilawar. 'I can tell by the look on your face. My colleagues have exactly the same expression when I am making a presentation about the effect of the latest ad campaign on the quarterly sales. But not as beautiful, obviously.'

Pari blushed.

Dilawar continued, 'I would be fed up too if the two of you ignored me and started talking about people I didn't know.' He smiled at her, showing his even teeth.

She couldn't help smiling back at him.

Rehman said to Dilawar, 'I didn't come here to be an unwanted bone in a kebab. Ammi asked me to—'

'Say no more,' said Dilawar, holding up his manicured hands. 'I haven't been away from Vizag so long that I have forgotten how things are done here. You make a lovely chaperone. Sooo strong . . .' They all laughed at the camp tone of his last sentence. Dilawar turned to Pari. 'Thank you for meeting me away from the house.'

'That's not a problem,' said Pari. 'I requested the meeting, after all.'

'But you were probably expecting to have this conversation with all our relatives in the next room, if not actually sitting beside you. Don't worry – your chaperone will protect you if I turn out to be an axe murderer.'

Pari nodded, smiling. She wondered whether people living in big cities like Mumbai automatically developed this skill of making others feel comfortable. Would Vasu grow up to be an extrovert if they moved to Mumbai?

The conversation went into a lull for a moment before Dilawar started speaking again.

'Shall I kick off by telling you a bit about myself?' He didn't wait for an answer. 'I've been living in Mumbai for the last seven years. I stay in Worli, do you know the city?'

Pari shook her head.

'It's a nice area,' Dilawar said. 'I won't go into all the details of my job and salary; I am sure my mother has already told you all that. I love jazz and movies. My favourite film is *Casablanca*. "Of all the gin joints in all the towns in the world, she walks into mine." Humphrey Bogart is just masterly in it.'

Pari looked blank and Rehman said, 'She hasn't seen that film.'

Dilawar appeared shocked for a moment, then recovered. 'Haven't seen *Casablanca*? I really envy you. To see it for the first time when you are old enough to appreciate all the nuances . . . What else do I like? Oh yes, I love Bade Mia's in Colaba. You have to sit on a bench on the footpath outside crumbling buildings, but the food is simply outstanding. The baida roti is to die for.'

Pari was tongue-tied. This was going too fast for her. It had taken her more than a week after her wedding to discover half as much about her husband as she had found out about Dilawar in a few minutes. Also, what did she know about strange music and foreign movies? Dilawar's world was so different from hers. Would he think that she was a rustic simpleton?

Rehman said, 'Pari is a great cook too. You should try her prawn curry sometime. And she may not know much about Hollywood movies, but she is an expert on Shakespeare.'

'Shakespeare?' said Dilawar.

'The bard himself. Go on, ask her about any of his plays.'

'To be or not to be . . .' he began. Rehman slowly shook his head and Dilawar stopped. 'You guys are putting me on the spot,' said Dilawar and thought for a moment. 'A plague on both your houses . . .'

'Mercutio in *Romeo and Juliet*,' said Pari.

Rehman said, 'Come on; that was easy. Even I knew that. Something harder.'

'The course of true love never did run smooth.'

'Lysander in *A Midsummer Night's Dream*.'

Rehman smiled proudly as if he had personally coached her in English literature. Pari gazed back at him gratefully. She didn't feel so much out of her depth now. 'Why did you choose that quote?' she asked. 'Is there some reason for it?'

Dilawar was struck dumb for a moment as he remembered Shaan. 'Oh, it just popped into my head. I don't have any girlfriends in Mumbai, honest.'

Rehman and Pari laughed. 'Of course you don't,' said Rehman.

'What does that mean?' said Dilawar loudly. A passing waiter glanced at them and Dilawar said more softly, 'Sorry.'

Rehman said, 'I was just saying that, of course, you don't have any girlfriends. You wouldn't be here with me and Pari if you loved somebody else in Mumbai.'

Dilawar nodded. 'Enough about me,' he said. He turned to Pari. 'Let's talk about someone more interesting – you.'

Pari looked at both of them for a moment and bit her lower lip.

Rehman said, 'Do you want me to leave you both alone for some time?'

'Just for ten minutes?' she said.

Rehman nodded. 'I'll take a walk along the beach. Give me a call on my mobile when you are done.'

As soon as Rehman left, Dilawar said, 'That's a great

technique to leave without paying the bill. I should try that next time.'

Pari smiled, some of her nervousness dissipating. 'Did you know that I am a widow?' she said.

Dilawar nodded. 'Ammi-jaan told me. I have no problem with that.'

Pari gazed into his eyes briefly and looked away. 'Do you know that I was an orphan?'

'Yes, I heard that your father died recently. I am sorry.'

Pari shook her head. 'I am not just an orphan now. I always *was* an orphan.'

Dilawar regarded her quizzically, his neatly groomed eyebrows coming together in perfect unison.

'Your mother has this notion that just because I have a long nose I must belong to some aristocratic family. But the truth is that I don't even know who my birth-parents were. When I was a baby they sold me to ammi and abbu.'

'They must have had their reasons. And technically, you weren't an orphan, because your parents were alive. They might still be alive, you know.'

'As far as I am concerned, they are dead,' she snapped. Taking a deep breath, Pari met his eyes. 'Lots of poor people have children. They don't sell them off.' She fell silent for a moment and then grinned at him. 'I don't know why it bothers me so much. After all, if they hadn't done that, ammi and abbu wouldn't have become my parents and I cannot imagine how I would have grown up without them.'

'Matters of the heart don't have to make sense,' Dilawar said.

'True,' she said. 'Anyway, I wanted you to know before you made up your mind.'

'Did you really think it would influence my decision one way or another?' said Dilawar.

Pari bit her lower lip again. She had been sure that it would, but the idea now seemed ridiculous. 'There is more. I have a son.'

She took a photograph out of her handbag and showed it to Dilawar. A young boy with dark-chocolate skin and one of his front teeth missing was squinting into the sun and smiling widely.

'He's cute,' said Dilawar. 'But you don't look old enough to have such a big boy.'

'His name is Vasu. He is an orphan too. I adopted him.'

'I was just kidding. I already know about him.'

'You do? He is the most important thing in my life right now. We come as a package. I will only marry a man who will treat him kindly and look after him like a father should.'

'I respect that,' said Dilawar. 'If we get married, he will be our son, totally. You don't need to have any worries over that.'

'Thank you,' said Pari. 'You are a good man.' She smiled at him quickly and looked away.

'Tell me about your husband,' said Dilawar.

'What?' she said quickly.

Dilawar returned her gaze steadily and covered her hand with his. 'You loved him. You miss him. Talk to me about him.'

His hand on hers did not feel uncomfortable. It was almost brotherly, somehow. Tears welled up in her eyes. 'Nobody has ever asked me that. It is as if they are too scared to jog any memory of him. Even Rehman, normally so unafraid of everything, never mentions him. Do they think that if I don't talk about him, I won't think about him?'

Dilawar squeezed her hand gently.

She continued, 'I loved my husband. He was everything a

wife could ask for – handsome, funny, kind, loving. We were both very young when we got married and setting up house was almost like playing a game. I already had experience of running a kitchen, of course, since my mother had died, but somehow doing it in my own house . . . it was different. He always said he would take me to visit the Taj Mahal, but we never went.' She shook her head. 'Sorry, I don't want to burden you with my baggage.'

Dilawar withdrew his hand. 'Don't be sorry,' he said. 'It is fascinating. So what do you think about moving to Mumbai?'

'To be honest, that is my biggest worry. Vasu has already suffered a lot of change in his short life. I have just got him admitted into a school and he is slowly making friends. If we go to Mumbai, the language will be different, so not only will he have to move schools, he also won't be able to understand any of the boys or teachers there.'

'You don't need to know the local language, Marathi, to get by in Mumbai. English and Hindi are sufficient.'

'He knows only Telugu. He has just started learning Hindi and English. I am concerned about that.'

Dilawar said, 'Don't take this the wrong way, but I have a proposal. My mother here is very lonely. What would you say if I asked you to continue living in Vizag for a year or two after we got married?'

'And look after your father?' she asked, fixing him shrewdly with her eyes.

Dilawar flushed. 'Of course not. I was going to tell you about that next, but I can see that ammi-jaan has already spoken to you about my father.'

Pari nodded.

'My mother refuses any help to look after him. She thinks it is her duty. Look, I won't beat about the bush. I want you to convince my mother to hire servants to nurse my father.

Meanwhile, teach Vasu English and Hindi. We can be visiting and getting to know each other. We can then move to Mumbai and live together.'

Pari considered for a moment. 'It's not a bad idea,' she said finally. 'I don't mind helping your mother care for your father. I am sure she will be more open to accepting my assistance rather than that of some servants. It will give me time to get accustomed to being married again and also for Vasu to prepare for a move to the big city.'

Dilawar nodded. 'Have you asked Vasu what he thinks about you marrying again?'

She looked at him, startled. 'No . . .' she said slowly. 'I didn't want to say anything until it was all finalised. Do you think he will mind?'

'I am not sure. It is worth preparing the ground before springing it on him, though.'

'You are right,' she said. 'I think you'll make a great father.'

How had they slipped into an agreement that they would get married?

He smiled.

'Do you like cricket?'

The conversation flowed on smoothly without any awkward pauses. After almost an hour, Pari said, 'Shall I call Rehman? He must be wearing out the leather of his chappals wandering up and down the Beach Road.'

Dilawar nodded and she took out her mobile phone.

While they were waiting for Rehman to return, she heard for the first time the song playing in the background.

> One, two, three, four . . .
> My love will open the door,
> Five, six, seven . . .
> And show you heaven.

'What rubbish lyrics!'

Dilawar grinned. 'It's not Shakespeare, that's for sure.'

Pari laughed. Dilawar made her feel so comfortable. All her earlier worries seemed silly now.

# CHAPTER THIRTEEN

Aruna and Ram finally went to bed at the end of their first day alone in the house. 'I thought they would never go,' said Ram.

Her in-laws and the servants were supposed to have left early in the morning. In the event, it was well into the afternoon before they departed.

Aruna laughed. 'Your mother was shouting instructions to me even after the car turned the corner,' she said. 'Close all the windows, lock the doors, leave a light on . . .'

Aruna had not gone in to work after all and Ram had come home by lunchtime, surprised to find his parents still there.

'Well, let's have a lie-in tomorrow.'

'Lie-in?'

'Wake up late,' he said. 'Say after ten in the morning.'

Aruna looked shocked. 'I've never done that,' she said. 'How can you sleep after the sun comes up?'

'Never woken up late? You, my darling, have missed out on some of life's greatest pleasures. It's very easy – you just pull the sheet over your head, hug me tight and keep your eyes closed.'

Aruna laughed. 'Sounds very decadent. But I suppose that's what holidays are for.'

She woke up at six in the morning as usual. The silence in the house was unfamiliar – by this time people would be about and things would be happening. She almost got out of bed before remembering what Ram had told her the previous night. She turned towards him. He had such a boyish look on his face when he slept – despite his stubble.

The buffalo's moos trickled through her consciousness some time later. She ignored them at first, but the bellows became louder until she couldn't sleep any more. Ram tried to grab her, but she extricated herself from his embrace, quickly changed into a sari and went outside. A plump buffalo stood at the gate, mooing. Dried bits of straw were sticking to its rough pelt and its shiny nose was a darker black than the rest of its body.

'Shoo,' said Aruna, waving her hands. 'Go away. Don't stand there. You'll probably do your business and foul up the street in front of the house.'

The buffalo extended its neck and mooed again.

Aruna looked into its soft eyes and was puzzled. What did the buffalo want? Then she noticed a bundle of straw behind a tree by the gate.

'Ah! Is this what you are looking for?' she said and held it out to the buffalo, which immediately pulled it from her and started chewing on it.

This must be their milk delivery. The buffalo, knowing its rounds, would go from house to house where it was needed, with the milkman following later. Sure enough, a man in a loincloth and a torn vest soon appeared, with a round vessel in one hand and a straw-filled effigy of a calf under his other arm. Walking up to the buffalo, he hit it on its haunches with the bottom of the container.

'You know you are not supposed to stand in front of the gate,' he admonished the animal. Another buffalo that he had milked at the end of the street made its way past them to its next destination. The milkman turned to Aruna and said, 'Where is Kaka?'

'He is out,' she replied.

Leaving him at the gate for a moment, she returned with a copper pan, half filled with water. In the meantime, the man had put the stiff-legged imitation calf by the side of the buffalo where it could see it out of the corner of one eye. Aruna handed the pan with the water to the milkman, which he used to wash his vessel and the buffalo's teats. He gave the pan back to her, showed her that there was no water in his vessel, and squatted by the buffalo's rear legs, clamping the vessel between his knees. Squeezing and pulling the buffalo's teats, he expertly directed the stream of milk into the container. Aruna knew that it was actually more difficult than it looked. If he was too gentle, no milk would come and if he was too rough, the buffalo would kick the man and overturn the vessel.

She suddenly remembered and asked, 'How much milk do we normally take?'

'Three litres, madam.'

'We don't need that much today,' she replied. 'Half a litre will do. And we don't need any from tomorrow for four days.'

'Why, madam?' he said, turning his head to look at her while his fingers carried on milking. 'Has everybody gone out?'

'Yes,' said Aruna, then bit her tongue. This was exactly what her mother-in-law had warned her not to say. 'No . . .' She gave up.

When she came back into the house with the milk, Ram

was already up. 'Why did you get up so early?' he said. 'I thought we were having a lie-in.'

'Somebody forgot to tell the buffalo and it arrived at its usual time,' she said.

'Let's go back to bed,' he said.

'I can't. I have to boil the milk, otherwise it will get spoiled. Since we are up, I might as well make breakfast. Do you want to eat poha?' she asked.

The boiled flattened rice, sautéed with spices, diced potatoes and onions, was an unusual breakfast in south India but Mrs Ali had described it to her the other day and she wanted to try it out.

An hour later, Ram smacked his lips and said, 'That was wonderful, darling. Are you trying to make me feel guilty about the holiday?'

'Why do you say that?' said Aruna, frowning.

'This is what they eat in Mumbai for breakfast.'

'Oh, I didn't know that!'

'Right,' he said. 'What shall we do now? Do you fancy a long drive along the Beach Road? We could go to Yarada Park, on the top of the Dolphin's Nose Peak.'

Before she could reply, the phone rang. It was his boss. An important politician and his entourage had been ambushed by Naxalites – Maoist guerrillas – and the survivors, including the politician, had been brought back to the hospital. Ram was needed immediately for surgery.

The rest of the day passed slowly for Aruna, who had never been by herself in such a big house. She felt like a seed rattling about inside a ridged gourd that has been dried to make a loofah. She made dinner but that didn't take long for just two people. It was almost six in the evening before she heard the car coming in through the front gate and rushed to the door.

Ram looked tired and she took his briefcase from him. He gave her a lopsided smile.

'Sorry, baby,' he said. 'It just took longer than we thought. One of the patients had a blood clot in the brain that needed to be removed.' He flung himself on to a sofa. 'I don't know what the world is coming to. There were big crowds of people chanting slogans in support of the politician and lots of policemen trying to hold them back. It was like a political rally. We tried to tell them that patients need peace and quiet, but who cares what doctors say?

'Let me take a quick bath,' he continued after a moment. 'Then we can go out for dinner.'

She shook her head. 'I've already made dinner. You've had a long day. Let's relax at home, just the two of us.'

He disappeared in the direction of their bedroom and its en suite bathroom. Aruna went into the kitchen to serve their meal. Just as they were sitting down to eat, the bell rang. They looked at each other in surprise. Ram went to the door, coming back with her parents and her sister Vani. Her mother was carrying a big shopping bag with a tiffin carrier in it.

'Vani told me that all the servants had gone, so I got dinner. We can all eat together,' said her mother.

Aruna glared accusingly at Vani. Her sister shrugged, as if to say that it wasn't her idea. There went their plans for a quiet dinner for two. Oh well, she thought. They were going away to the village soon and they would have a peaceful holiday there . . .

'Of course, amma,' she said dutifully. Vani and Ram started giggling.

The next day Pari was again helping Mr Ali in the marriage bureau. He had asked her to pick out all the people who had written more than a month ago but had not yet become members. She was slowly gathering the information. The sun was bright outside and, as usual, the fan was going full blast.

The middle-aged man who walked in had a broad face and a bulbous nose. Two pens were clipped inside his shirt pocket. His confident manner suddenly evaporated when he saw her.

'Namaste,' Pari said, courteously.

He acknowledged her greeting with a nod of his head and said, 'You are not the girl who was here when I came in last time.'

Pari smiled. 'No, sir. Our regular assistant, Aruna, is on leave. I am just filling in temporarily.'

A young woman, about the same age as Pari, appeared behind the man. Mr Ali came out on to the verandah just then and looked at the man quizzically.

'You have been here before . . .' he said.

The man nodded and gave his membership number to Pari, who pulled the details out and handed them to Mr Ali.

Mr Ali skimmed through them and looked up.

'Now I remember you, Mr Chandra. You must forgive me. My memory isn't what it used to be and I usually rely on Aruna to tell me who's who. Have you come to look at some photographs? Isn't that what you said you would do?'

Mr Chandra nodded. 'That's why I have come with my daughter.'

Mr Ali turned to Pari and said, 'Please give them the Baliga Kapu bridegrooms album.'

Mr Chandra's daughter, Mani, had stopped her studies after year twelve and had never attended college. One of the conditions for joining the marriage bureau was that both bride and groom had to be college graduates, but Mr Ali had made an exception and allowed Mani to join because Mr Chandra had looked desperate.

He regarded them carefully. Mr Chandra was slowly turning

the pages of the album. His daughter Mani was looking every-where except at the photographs. She caught Mr Ali's eye, flushed and turned away, facing the wall. Mr Ali couldn't figure out why Mr Chandra had been so keen to join the bureau. Mani was still quite young and there was no need to start wor-rying about her marriage for several more years yet.

'What do you think of him?' said Mr Chandra, showing his daughter a picture.

She twisted her mouth into a disagreeable moue and ignored him.

'Have a look, dear,' said her father.

Mani turned in a sudden fury, grabbed the album from her father and threw it on the ground. Pari stared in horror, first at the fallen book and then at the sullen girl.

'How dare you?' said her father and half raised his hand to strike her, before dropping it. His shoulders drooped and he bent to the floor to pick the book up. His hand touched his daughter's feet and she automatically jerked her legs away. She pointed her hands down and then touched them to her forehead.

So the girl had not totally lost her manners, thought Pari. She still hasn't forgotten that an older person touching a younger person's feet is disrespectful and a sin.

Pari looked more closely at Mani and realised that what she had mistaken for sullenness was actually misery. Pari rushed out from behind the table and sank to her knees in front of the girl. Taking Mani's hands in her own, she said, 'What is the problem, Mani?'

Mani silently shook her head, tears rolling down like big pearls down her cheeks. Pari turned to Mr Chandra in baf-flement.

He gave a big sigh and told her, 'Sit up, my dear. It's not good for a lady like you to be on her knees in front of my worthless daughter.' When Pari hesitated, he continued, 'Please get up. I will tell you the story of why my Mani is so sad.'

Pari sat on the chair opposite them and Mr Ali took the chair next to her.

'When I was a boy, we were rich and owned many cattle and fertile lands by the River Godavari. But one day, my father came under the influence of an evil temptress in the nearby market town. My mother fought with my father to no avail, then became morose and took to her bed. As the atmosphere at home became darker, I started spending more time with my best friend, Surya. He was the son of a family very similar to ours and the same caste as us. We swam in the river and flew kites; we teased the girls by pulling their pigtails; we played with marbles and climbed trees; we even studied sometimes.'

Mrs Ali came out with a tray of glasses. Mr Chandra thanked her and took a gulp of the cool water.

'If you are wondering why I am so openly airing the family's dirty linen, there is nothing secret about any of this. Everybody in our village knows what happened to our house. The harlot sank her fangs deep and started extracting gold, gems, silk saris and God knows what else from my father. Soon, her brother became the manager of our lands. Over the next few years, while the fields groaned under the weight of golden sheaves of rice and the harvests were bountiful, our income kept falling. Eventually the manager suggested to my father that he sell some land. Selling land, like smoking cigarettes or drinking alcohol, is habit forming – the first time, it is shocking, but it becomes progressively easier and soon you cannot do without it. Our fields, so fertile and well watered, were parcelled off for the same price as less productive farms halfway up a hill and away from the road. I don't know why the manager bothered to fleece us, because all that money would have gone to his sister anyway. But that's how the world is – once people know that you are a sheep who can be cheated, they will ravage you from all sides like ravenous jackals.'

Mr Ali got an inkling of how Mr Chandra had become the successful businessman that he now was.

'My friend and I grew up and we both got married. Surya had a boy and, soon after, Mani graced our house. I tried to reason with my father but was unsuccessful. After my mother passed away, I left home and moved to Vizag with my wife and Mani. I got a small job in a car dealership that barely paid enough to survive on. And so life continued for a few more years until, one rainy evening, my father was involved in an accident when returning home from the harlot's house and he died. We rushed to the village as soon as we got the news. The Jezebel and her brother were nowhere to be seen.'

Mr Chandra looked up at the ceiling for a moment and closed his eyes.

'When I went through the papers and discovered just how much of our wealth had been drained away, I felt physically sick. I cursed my father for being a besotted fool and robbing me of my patrimony. Even our house was pawned to the rafters and did not belong to me.'

Mr Ali nodded sympathetically. 'It must have been a bad time for you,' he said.

'Yes,' said Mr Chandra, sighing at the memory. 'A couple of days later, while we were still at the village, my friend Surya came to our house with his son. Mani and the boy started running around and playing but I sat there on my haunches, staring miserably at the ground.

'"Are you all right?" he asked, after some time.

'I looked up at my friend. "How could he do this, Surya?

How could my father betray us so badly? What am I going to do now? How can I look after my family on the pittance that I am bringing in?"

'I started sobbing and Surya hugged me. "God will provide," he said.

'I pushed him away. "What will God do? Make brinjal sour curry, that's what He will do. How can I save for Mani's future on what I am earning? Who is going to marry a penniless girl?"

'Surya looked at me and my wife and said, "That, at least, is a problem I can solve." He turned and called the children over. "Do you kids like each other?" he asked.

'"Yes," said the boy. "She is all right for a girl. She knows how to play marbles."

'Mani just nodded.

'"Do you two want to get married?" Surya asked.

'"What? Now?" asked the boy, looking startled.

'"No, silly," said his father, and laughed. "When you are grown up."

'"That's all right then," said the boy and the two children ran away, giggling.

'"I don't understand," I said.

'"It's simple," said Surya. "I propose an engagement to tie our families together."

'Surya was a true friend. I broke down again. "I will remain forever in your debt," I said, bringing my hands together in a salutation.

'After the tenth-day death ceremony for my father, I packed up and left the village for probably the last time. Now, I had no ancestral house to go back to.

'About a month later, when cleaning his car, I found a wallet belonging to the owner of the dealership. It was stuffed with money and papers and he was very happy when

I handed it back without stealing anything from it. After that I got promoted to a more responsible job and saved up enough money to buy a beat-up mini-van that had been involved in an accident. I got it repaired by one of the mechanics in the workshop, took it to my village and hired one of my father's old farmworkers' sons as a driver. The van became a shuttle taxi between the village and the market town. The fare was cheap but the taxi was always overflowing and soon paid for itself. I bought another taxi and then another. Business boomed and I left my job to set up on my own.

'One evening, my old friend, Surya, visited us with his son. I was shocked to learn that my friend's entire extended family had been wiped out by Naxalites in a night-time raid. The Maoist guerrillas had burned down their house, in which I had spent so many happy hours, as well. He and his son had escaped only because they had been away for the night. He was now destitute.

'"What are you going to do?" I asked him.

'"I have heard that the Gulf is booming. Even ordinary workers are earning vast sums. I want to go there and try my fortune. I know an agent who can organise a visa and a job but I need money to pay his fees."

'I agreed to help him. I mean, money wasn't such an issue for me any more.

'"I have one more favour to ask," he said. "Can I leave my son in your house while I am in the Gulf?"

'"Of course. He is going to be my son-in-law anyway. I'll be glad to bring him up in my house. Don't worry about your son. Go in peace and concentrate on making your fortune."

'Did my friend have a premonition of the future? Who knows? He said, "If anything happens to me, will you continue to look after my son?"

'I said, "In the name of the Lord, your son will receive a good education. He will never lack for love or care."

'He, in turn, promised, "In the name of the Lord, you will not have to look elsewhere for a son-in-law. When they come of age, my son and your daughter will get married."'

Mr Chandra drained the glass of water and looked up at Mr Ali and Pari. 'Sorry for taking so much of your time.'

'Your story is fascinating,' said Mr Ali. 'What happened after your friend left?'

'He died in that faraway land within weeks of his arrival. The police there didn't care. To them, he was just a number on a passport – not a father with a son. They said it was an accident and closed the case.'

'I see,' said Mr Ali. 'And your friend's son continued living with you? What was his name?'

'Yes,' said Mr Chandra's daughter, Mani. 'His name is Kiran. We went to school together. I was never very good at studies and after twelfth grade I just gave up, but Kiran went on to do bigger things.'

Mr Chandra spoke again. 'He now comes back and says that he has fallen in love with another girl from his medical college and doesn't want to marry Mani. After his father died and he became a penniless orphan, I could have used him as a servant, but I didn't. I raised him as if he were family, spent lots of money on his education. Becoming a doctor is not cheap. I did all this because of my word to his father and also with the understanding that he would marry my daughter. There was nothing secret about that. Everybody, including him, knew and agreed to the pact. He claims to be an educated man, but how can he be when he makes his father a liar by breaking his promise?'

'Don't say that, naanna,' said Mani. 'He has fallen in love

with another girl. It is just my karma that I am in love with *him.*'

Mr Chandra turned to Mr Ali. 'Even now she won't hear anything against that boy. But tell me, sir, shouldn't a father's word carry greater weight than this . . . this *love?*'

Mr Ali said, 'The world is changing, Mr Chandra, and the old certainties are no more. But I think your daughter has the right attitude. He has grown up for many years in your house like a son. Why curse him now? He has made his decision. It is best to see how we can move forward.'

'That's why I am here,' said Mr Chandra. 'To look for other matches.'

'No,' said Mani. 'I know I cannot have Kiran, but I will never get married. I have grown up expecting to marry him and I cannot imagine anyone else as my husband. I feel as if caterpillars are crawling on my body even to think of any other man.' She shuddered, and her eyes filled with tears.

Mr Chandra gave a sigh and slumped in the sofa, like a balloon deflating. 'This is what she keeps saying. What can I do, sir?'

Before Mr Ali could reply, Pari turned to Mani. 'You have shared the story of your life. Now, listen to me. Do you know that I am a widow?'

Mani shook her head.

'Yes, I guessed,' said Mr Chandra.

'Do you think this is the life I chose for myself?' Pari kept her eyes on Mani until she was forced to respond in the negative.

Pari said, 'My husband and I loved each other. We got married young, set up house and enjoyed life – going to movies, eating pakoras on the ghat, having picnics by the riverside with friends and throwing dinner parties on Saturdays. We talked about the future as if we were standing at the head of a long river, like the Godavari or the Ganges. Our days stretched out in front of us, in a never-ending stream. When shall we have children? Not right now. When should we go to the saint's anniversary festival, in Ajmer Sharif, on a pilgrimage? In a year or two. Let's visit the Taj Mahal – but not this season . . .'

A bus went past on the road outside, its horn blaring loudly.

Pari continued, 'One afternoon, my husband went out on some silly errand and our dreams all ended, just like that. What I am saying, Mani, is that life does not go as we plan. That's what your father's life should teach you as well. If you had asked him as a boy whether he would have been happy to lose his father's lands and leave his village, he would have definitely been horrified. But today, he is a far more success-ful man than he would have been if he had stayed in the village. I wanted to kill myself on the night that my husband died. But today, if I am not exactly happy, I am not unhappy either. I have a son and I have received a marriage proposal from a man who seems quite nice. You don't have to get married right now when your heart has not yet mended. You are still young. But don't say never and give up entirely on life either.'

Pari turned to Mani's father. 'I know that you are just worrying about your daughter, sir. But don't hurry her. She is still hurting. Support her through this difficulty and in time she will start to live fully again.'

Mani nodded slowly.

Mr Chandra exhaled loudly, his body sagging. 'You are right,' he said finally. 'Wisdom is not dependent upon age. You've proved that today, my girl.'

After they left, Mr Ali turned to Pari and said, 'That was lovely. The girl now has space to recover from her heartbreak while at the same time the father is more hopeful and less anxious. It was lucky that he didn't ask for his fees back, though. Too many more of these good deeds and I'll be left without a business.'

Pari looked at her uncle apprehensively, until she saw the twinkle in his eye and laughed.

# CHAPTER FOURTEEN

Mrs Ali closed the iron gate of the verandah noisily and stormed in. With her face set, she did not even glance at her husband, who was working at the table. Seeing her expression, he said, 'What happened? Where is Pari? She said she would come back to help.'

When she did not deign to reply, he got up and followed her into the house. Mrs Ali went into the bedroom and slammed the door behind her. In the corridor just outside stood Rehman, who had returned from visiting friends about fifteen minutes ago and had been taking a quick bath. He was bare-chested, with a long towel round his waist. Father and son looked at each other, mystified.

Rehman said silently, with exaggerated lip movement, 'What?'

Mr Ali shrugged his shoulders. 'I don't know,' he replied in the same silent-movie mode.

Mrs Ali and Pari had gone to put down the deposit on the two-bedroom flat in the building next door and take possession of the keys. Pari and Vasu had packed everything up in their room across the road. Rehman had agreed to help them and they reckoned that they could shift all their belongings in less than an hour.

'It will be such a relief to be able to move freely again without banging into something,' Pari had said. She had promised Vasu that he could have a room for himself with his own bed.

As Rehman's fresh clothes were inside the bedroom that was now inaccessible, he went back to the bathroom to put on what he had been wearing, hoping they hadn't got wet during his bath.

Ten minutes later, Mrs Ali joined her husband and son in the living room, having changed into an old, faded cotton sari.

'What happened?' said Mr Ali.

'I tried calling Pari but she is not answering her mobile,' said Rehman.

Mrs Ali glared at him. 'She has some sense, at least,' she said. She took a deep breath and said, slowly and deliberately, 'I have . . . never . . . been so insulted in my life.'

'What?' said Mr Ali. 'What are you talking about?'

Mrs Ali turned on her husband. 'Do you know what the neighbours are saying about us? Do you have any interest in what is going on around you, apart from that stupid marriage bureau of yours?'

'You are not making any sense,' said Mr Ali. 'Tell me exactly what happened.'

'As you know, Pari has been really looking forward to moving into a bigger flat. Everything was agreed with the landlord and he said that today after two in the afternoon was an auspicious time to take the deposit and formally give us the keys. So, Pari and I went there with the money.'

Mr Ali nodded. He was aware of all that, but he knew better than to interrupt his wife. She seemed calmer now but it wouldn't take much to upset her again.

'The landlord ushered us into the flat. His wife and the

woman, Swaroop, from one of the other flats on the same floor, were waiting for us. "Do you want tea?" said the land-lord's wife.

"'No, no. We are fine," I said.

"'I insist.'

'Soon we were all sipping tea. "Did Leela come to your house on time today?" asked Swaroop. "I ask her to come early and she always delays in the morning. I don't like to have a dirty flat until lunchtime."

'Swaroop knows that Leela works in her flat before she comes to our house, because Swaroop insisted on it. She has put Leela in a difficult position and upset all my morning rou-tines, and now that woman sits there, as if a kulfi won't melt in her mouth, making comments like this. I was angry, but just nodded.

'After a minute or so, Swaroop said to Pari, "Vasu is not your real son, is he?"

'Pari said, "Do you think he is imaginary?"

'Swaroop flushed and I smiled at Pari. "You know what I mean," Swaroop said.

"'No," said Pari, quite seriously. "What exactly do you mean?"

"'Haven't you adopted him?" she said, almost tri-umphantly, which was a bit puzzling.

"'Yes," said Pari. "But that doesn't make him any less real. He is my son."

"'Adopt, shadopt," Swaroop said, dismissively waving her hand like someone brushing off a fly. "That's just a piece of paper. A woman cannot really claim that a child is hers until she has carried him in her womb for nine months."

'Pari went dumb and bit her lip. I knew that the vile woman had landed a mean blow.

"'I thought you Hindus had more respect for adoption than

that," I said. "After all, wasn't one of your gods, Krishna, raised by his aunt, Yashoda? And before he went to meet his biological mother, didn't he tell Yashoda that she was his real mother, forever ahead of the woman who had given him birth?"

'They were all silent, perhaps surprised by my knowledge of Hindu mythology. I didn't tell them that I knew about Krishna and Yashoda because I had watched the TV serial a few years ago.

'I drank some more tea and looked around. It was a nice flat. Pari would be very comfortable here. The windows faced east, so the morning sun would shine into the house and in the afternoon a cooling breeze would blow in. The side of the flat wasn't so ideal because it was very close to the building next door, but you cannot have everything. Why was this Swaroop woman sticking to the flat owners like a gecko to a wall? If she leaves, we can conclude our business and go on our way, I thought.

'"Leela tells me that your son brought that boy from the village," Swaroop said.

'"Yes. Vasu is the son of his best friend who died, so Rehman brought him home," I said. I doubted very much that Leela had volunteered the information. All servants gossiped, of course; that was only to be expected, but Leela was more discreet than most.

'After some more time, it was clear that the woman had no intention of leaving and the landlord and his wife didn't seem to be saying anything, so I signalled to Pari. She took out a bundle of notes from her handbag. "The deposit for the flat," she said.

'The landlord's wife shrank from the money as if it was the root of all evil. The landlord licked his lips and shook his head. "I am sorry," he said to Pari. "We have already given the flat to somebody else." He wouldn't look at me.

'"What?" said Pari. "But you promised . . . I have packed up everything, just ready to move."

'The landlord and his wife just stared ahead with stony expressions on their faces. Swaroop, the dai'n, was smiling like a witch. I am sure she had something to do with this.

'"It is not good to go back on your word like this," I said to the landlord. "What is the matter? Have you been offered a higher rent?"

'"No, nothing like that," said the landlord, finally looking at me. "Umm . . . we've just decided against it."

'"But how can you change your mind like that?" said Pari. "My son is looking forward to moving into a bigger flat; he will be disappointed so much. I have packed; I have arranged with Mrs Ali's son to help me with the luggage. It is not fair to tell me at the last minute that I cannot have the flat. I thought we had agreed everything and today was just a formality. Why are you saying no now?"

'After a moment's silence, Swaroop said, "How can they tell you? They are decent people and they feel ashamed even to bring matters like this to their lips. They only want to rent their flat to people of good character. Not to loose women like you." She looked straight at Pari.

'I was livid. "How dare you say that about my niece? Maybe you so-called high-class ladies talk like that at your kitty parties or whatever it is you call your get-togethers. We think a hundred times before saying a word against a woman's character. Anyway, what is it to you? You are not even a flat-owner here, you are just a tenant."

'"It is everybody's responsibility to make sure that bad behaviour is driven out of the neighbourhood, not just the landlord's," Swaroop said. "You will, of course, speak out in her favour because you want to protect your son's reputation." She pointed a finger at Pari. "Did you not have a secret tête-à-tête with Mrs Ali's son? Don't deny it, because I saw you both in each other's arms."

"'I . . ." said Pari. She was speechless and I had the horrible feeling that Swaroop, the witch, was speaking the truth. That much was clear from Pari's eyes.

'Swaroop hadn't finished. "And the boy that your son brought from the village – I don't believe that he is some best friend's son. He looks like a servant from the middle of nowhere. Are you sure that your son hasn't had a tumble with some rustic girl? He disappears off to the villages often enough . . ."

'That was the problem with reputations, I thought. Once one allowed even a tiny bit of mud to stick, every action becomes suspect. Suspicion kills faith, the Prophet had said and, of course, he had been right.

'I turned to the landlord and his wife. "Have you called me into your house to insult me? If you don't want to rent your flat to us, that's your privilege, even though you are breaking your promise. But then, have the courage to just say so, rather than insult invited guests under your own roof. That is not seemly."

'Pari and I swept out of the flat without a backward glance.'

Mrs Ali looked at her son, sitting on the sofa and said to him, 'How could you do this, Rehman? What were you thinking?' Words failed her and she shook her head.

'I don't know what you are talking about,' said Rehman. 'There is nothing going on between Pari and me; that woman was talking rubbish.'

'I know there is nothing going on between you and Pari. But I could also see the truth of that woman's accusation in Pari's face. You have to observe proprieties – this is not America or England where men and women can go round hugging each other in public. No person has ever had the chance to say one word against me until now. I had to sit there and listen to that two-bit woman spouting off.' Mrs Ali's voice dropped into a low growl that the men could barely catch. 'How dare she cast a slur on me?' Then she looked straight at Rehman and her voice rose again. 'There is no use in pointing fingers at outsiders if our own family members are foolish enough to give people a chance to talk.'

Before Rehman could utter a word, his father said, 'What a stupid thing to do, Rehman. We are responsible for Pari. If news of this gets back to Mrs Bilqis, what will happen? This is the one chance for Pari's happiness and you are jeopardising it.'

Rehman was quite used to his father jumping to conclusions regarding his actions, but he was hurt by his mother's words. She had always supported him, even when she couldn't go against his father.

'Ammi,' he said. 'Please listen to me. Pari and I haven't done anything to be ashamed of.'

'Did you or did you not go on the roof terrace with Pari?' she asked.

'Yes, but—'

'But nothing, Rehman,' interrupted Mrs Ali. 'Don't you see that is enough to set tongues wagging? We live in a small town and reputation is everything. If our lives are comfortable and easygoing, it is because everybody around respects us and comes to our aid if we ever need anything. Once we lose that, life here can be hell.'

'Yes,' said Mr Ali. 'Aruna was just talking about the same thing the other day. The only reason she is able to work in our house is because Ramanujam's father trusts us and believes that we are good people. If tongues start wagging, he will not allow his daughter-in-law to come here every day.

Everything we have achieved can disappear in a puff of smoke if ugly rumours start to fly around.'

'You are both being ridiculous,' said Rehman. 'You are paying far too much attention to silly hearsay and not listening to me.' He turned to his mother. 'Have you asked Pari?'

'I did not have to ask her,' said Mrs Ali. 'Her face showed the truth of the gossip very clearly. She looked so shocked that I doubt if she will ever come back here again.'

'What?' said Rehman. 'And are you just going to leave it like that? Let us go and bring her back, show her that she is welcome here as always.'

'We can try, but I doubt if she will come. If she does, people will say that the rumours are indeed true, and her reputation will be in tatters. Have you ever seen ducks and hens in a shower? The rain is the same, but while the ducks can completely ignore the water, the hens get wet and stand there miserably with their feathers dripping and their heads tucked into their chests. It is exactly like that with you and Pari. A man can disregard talk like this, but a woman simply cannot.'

'But . . .' said Rehman. 'How is she going to manage if she doesn't accept our help? How will she look after Vasu and find another job?'

'You should have thought of that before, Rehman,' said Mr Ali. 'Why start worrying about it now?'

'Fine,' snapped Rehman. 'If you think it has to be a choice between me and Pari, then I will move out. She needs your help more than I do. The friend I just met wants to rent out a room in his flat and I'll go there.' He stood up, took out his mobile phone and started dialling.

Less than half an hour later, he was dragging a suitcase on to the verandah. His father had a stony expression on his face, but his mother looked wretched.

'Right, I am off,' he said.

His mother held out a hand as if to stop him but his father said, 'Let him go. What's the point of a boy who doesn't even understand the damage his behaviour is causing.'

'Please . . . not again,' said Mrs Ali. 'I thought you two had gone past fights like these. There must be some other solution.'

Rehman shook his head. 'For now there is no other way out. But don't worry so much, ammi. I am off to Vasu's village with Dilawar tomorrow, anyway. And Pari will get married to him soon and then all these silly rumours will die a natural death.'

Mrs Ali did not quite smile, but her face lightened up. 'All right,' she said. 'Take care of yourself. I will talk to Pari and make sure she doesn't feel abandoned.'

Dilawar shook his head. 'How can you have so much confidence? Powerful people have preyed upon peasants since ancient times. This kind of exploitation is normal human behaviour. Isn't it presumptuous to think that one man like you can change it?'

Rehman said, 'It probably is conceited of me . . . All I can say is, if you don't even leave the house for fear of the journey, how will you ever reach your destination? And I am not alone, you know. I have been in touch with a few non-governmental organisations. Most of them don't want to get involved because they prefer to deal with problems like Aids or, nowadays, green issues, for which they can get funding from abroad. But a couple have shown an interest.'

It was just after four in the afternoon and the pair of them were walking down a narrow lane in the village to the now-abandoned hut in which Vasu and his grandfather had once lived.

Vasu's grandfather, Mr Naidu, had cultivated a small field that had been in his family for generations. Rice had been his main crop, though in the borders he had grown gongura – red spinach – and vegetables like brinjals and okra to supplement his income. Tired of living from harvest to harvest and worried about how to provide for Vasu's future when he was growing weaker each year, Mr Naidu had signed a contract with an agricultural company to grow cotton. The agreement was that the company would provide special genetically modified seeds, fertilizer and technical assistance. In return, Mr Naidu would sell all his cotton to the company, hoping that this would fetch him more money than the rice he normally grew.

Over the years, Mr Naidu had lost many crops – mostly due to the baking sun that shrivelled all plant life when the monsoon rains failed. Ironically, the cotton failed because it rained too much at the wrong time. The field had become waterlogged and the buds bearing the soft white fibre had rotted. The company had then told Mr Naidu that he still had to pay them for the seeds and other supplies. When he protested that he had no money to do so, they suggested that he sell off the land and had themselves taken a lien on it. Unable to contemplate the loss of his beloved land, Mr Naidu had committed suicide.

'It is a big problem,' admitted Rehman. 'And I think the company has been applying pressure to the farmers since I last came here. Nobody wants to talk about the contracts any more. But we cannot give up. The point is that the two signatories to the contract are unequal and all the risk is being pushed on to weaker party – the farmer. That needs to be changed.'

'I hear what you are saying,' Dilawar said. 'But it feels so hopeless. There are so many farmers and, from what I gather from the few I talked to, they are beset by a number of problems, not just these unfair contracts. Who cares about these little people? Certainly not the government, especially when faced with rich businesses with cash to spare for lobbying.'

'We have to make them care,' said Rehman.

Dilawar was reminded of Shaan and his insistence on going to Delhi to attend the court case, when everybody knew that the anti-homosexuality law was a hundred and fifty years old and that there was no support for its repeal in a conservative and religious country like India. What enabled men like Rehman and Shaan to fight against impossible odds? Why didn't they see themselves as Don Quixotes, pointlessly tilting their lances at windmills?

Dilawar's own attitude was that some things could not be changed and just had to be endured. His grandfather had been a man like his friends. When Dilawar's father had been brought home from hospital, bedridden and unable to move, his grandfather had gone from doctors to quacks to so-called holy men. There was nothing wrong with that, of course, but his grandfather had never given up. The old man just went on for years and years. It was only when he had finally died that his mother had obtained a measure of peace by being allowed to accept her husband's fate. Dilawar remembered being shocked by just how much of their family wealth had been wasted on his father's treatments. Sometimes impossible odds were just that – impossible. Struggling against them got one nowhere. His own policy was clear: if at first you don't succeed, try again. If you still fail, give up. There's no point in being a bloody fool about it.

He did not notice a thin, winged insect land on the side of his exposed neck.

'Oww!' said Dilawar, scratching the bite, thoughts about his father, and the nature of men who never gave up, temporarily interrupted. 'What were we talking about?'

'Farmers . . . and fairness,' said Rehman.

'Yes,' said Dilawar. 'When I was in the town, it all sounded so plausible. We would go into the village, find the men who have been cheated, get their evidence and start building a campaign for justice. I thought that with my degree in law and my experience in running marketing programmes, I would be able to help you. But now I can see the reality. This is not a task for one or two men.'

'So you think we should not even attempt it?' said Rehman, disappointed.

'No, I am not saying that . . . Well . . . actually . . . damn it, you are right. That is what I am saying, I suppose.'

Dilawar felt miserable. He was letting down his old class-mate, just as he had his wonderful Shaan. What a pain in the backside these men on a mission were. Why couldn't he have fallen in love with a nice, quiet boy who wouldn't rock the boat?

He kicked irritably at the dark shell of a palm fruit on the road. Then he looked at his soft-leather moccasins and despaired to see them thickly caked with mud. They had been especially hand-sewn for him by Mr Chang, the elderly Chinese shoemaker in Bandra, and had cost him enough to keep any of the households in this village in comfort for two or three months. The shoes were ruined – he doubted whether they would ever be wearable again. He had better not show these shoes to Mr Chang. The master cobbler had a temper and he would probably refuse to make him another pair.

Rehman stopped to greet an old woman. Dilawar stood a little distance away, gazing around at the small houses with their whitewashed walls red with dust to waist height. A couple of buffaloes ambled along – one of them using the road as a latrine and the other eating some paper lying on the ground. It was all so still that it took him a moment to realise that his ears had been straining for the sound of an engine or a motor, a burst of music or some other sign of civilisation, of people and culture. The silence felt unnatural to him.

'Are there any creature comforts in this hut we are going to?' Dilawar asked when Rehman rejoined him.

'Yes, I've organised a table fan just for you. You'll be fine.'

# CHAPTER FIFTEEN

The lights in the guest house looked welcoming through the windows, but the whiskered man who answered the door wasn't so hospitable. He shook his head.

'Sorry, sirs. I cannot give you a room without an official letter.'

He was thin and stooped, and his hair grew in all directions, like weeds on government land.

'I can get the letter but it is too late now,' said Dilawar. 'We just want to stay one night. We will be gone early tomorrow and nobody will be the wiser.'

Earlier in the day they had reached Mr Naidu's hut, but numberless mosquitoes had come out of their hiding places with the dusk and driven them out. Apparently, Maoists had blown up a transformer and there was no power in the village, rendering useless the fan that Rehman had borrowed. Finally, on Mr Naidu's cousin's advice, they had made their way to the government guest house on the edge of the nearby market town.

Rehman bit his lip. He didn't mind going back to the village even though the mosquito swarm had been pretty thick. But he could see the angry lesions on all exposed areas of

Dilawar's skin and felt sorry for him. Besides, he didn't want to face Pari and tell her that he was responsible for her fiancé turning into Elephant Man.

The lights in the guest house shone bright. Power wasn't a problem here. Dilawar took out a fifty-rupee note from his pocket and slipped it to the caretaker.

'It's just for one night. I'll give you some more before we leave tomorrow.'

The caretaker still appeared doubtful. Rehman looked away, embarrassed, unwilling to be party to bribing a government employee. Hearing footsteps, he saw a couple walk on to the verandah from outside and recognised them with surprise.

'Hello.'

'Namaskaaram,' said Aruna.

Ramanujam and Rehman smiled and nodded to each other. 'My friend and I are trying to get a room for the night,' Rehman said.

'Do you know these people, sir?' asked the caretaker to Ramanujam.

'Yes, these are our people only,' said Ramanujam, indicating that he knew them quite well.

'Why didn't you say so in the first place, sir?' the whiskered man said to Dilawar. 'The gentleman and lady have come with the highest recommendation and any friend of theirs is welcome to stay here.' He moved back from the door, allowing them entrance.

Dilawar leaned towards Rehman and whispered, 'He has not returned my money though.' Rehman laughed and introduced Dilawar to the couple.

The caretaker led Rehman and Dilawar into a basic, but clean, room, dominated by a large double bed formed by jamming two single beds together and veiled by a nylon mosquito net. There was an en suite bathroom and a fan hung from the ceiling. Dilawar looked around in satisfaction.

'We'll be safe here tonight,' he said. He turned to the caretaker. 'Where is my room?' he asked.

'Sorry, sir. This is the only room available. This place has just two bedrooms and the other one is being used by the doctor gentleman and his wife.'

Dilawar stared glumly at the net-caged bed for several seconds, then turned to Rehman. 'What do we do?'

Rehman shrugged. 'It's no big deal. We can share the bed. It looks wide enough.'

Dilawar laughed nervously. 'Do you know what one strawberry said to the other?'

Rehman shook his head.

'We wouldn't be in this jam today if we hadn't been in the same bed.'

Rehman smiled and Dilawar felt a bit foolish. He wished it was Shaan who was here. *He* would have appreciated the joke a lot more.

Half an hour later, the four of them were sitting at the dining table in the living room eating rice, dhal and an indeterminate vegetable curry cooked by the caretaker's niece. Aruna had brought a bottle of home-made mango pickle, which she shared with Rehman and Dilawar, making the food a little less boring.

Ramanujam told them about the land that they had purchased from the farmer. Aruna mentioned that there was a lake near by that was worth a visit, even though it was now much shrunk because it was summer. When Dilawar found out that the couple had cancelled their holiday to come here, he started talking to Aruna about Mumbai – the crowds, the buildings, the local trains, the clothes that the Goan secretaries wore, about Fashion Street and Chor Bazaar, a market for

second-hand items, reputedly used by burglars to fence their
ill-gotten goods. He did not mention Mumbai's most popular tourist attraction, the Gateway of India.

After dinner, they moved to the settees and switched on
the television for the news. Aruna was reminded of her parents' house. This was what her father did too – watch the
news straight after the meal. Having cleared the table, the
caretaker announced that he was retiring for the night and to
knock on the door to his room if they needed anything.

On the television, a journalist outside an imposing-looking
building was saying, 'The Delhi High Court has ruled that
Section 377 of the Indian Penal Code is unconstitutional and
violates the fundamental right to equality before the law.'

'Wow!' shouted Dilawar and, scrambling for the remote,
raised the volume. The others looked at him curiously.

'What—' began Rehman.

'Shh!' said Dilawar, laying a finger across his lips and leaning forward in rapt attention.

Many men and women, most of them dressed in flamboy-
ant colours, were dancing in the street. Others were banging
traditional drums with curved sticks and blowing whistles.

'It is difficult to say who are the men and who are the
women,' said Aruna. 'What is happening?'

'They are gays,' said Ramanujam. Aruna looked confused.

'Not just gays,' said Dilawar. 'The full spectrum of LGBT
community is there.' Seeing the uncomprehending looks on
the faces round him, he explained, 'Lesbian, gay, bisexual and
transgender – LGBT.' A handsome young man came on the
screen. 'Shaan!' cried Dilawar, then added in a softer voice,
'Sorry, I know him quite well, so I was just surprised to see
him so suddenly on TV.'

'Do you have any comment?' asked the journalist.

'I am very emotional at the moment,' said Shaan. 'We have

been fighting to overthrow this relic of the British Raj for a long time. Do people know that the law against homosexuality was created by Lord Macaulay in 1861? Now that the Delhi High Court has shown us the way, we can move forward to get laws for safety, security in marriage and jobs for the gay community. Today is a wonderful day for everybody who believes in equality in our great country.'

The reporter moved on to another man. 'What do you think of the High Court's decision, sir?'

'This is the last thing we need,' the man said. 'We already have a big problem with Aids. Legalising this behaviour will only make it worse.'

'No, you idiot,' said Dilawar, drowning out the news footage. 'What fans Aids in our country is not homosexuality but ignorance. Section 377 is actually obstructing those, like the Naz Foundation, who are trying to raise awareness of HIV to prevent its spread.'

'You seem to know a lot about this case,' said Ramanujam, raising his eyebrows.

'People in big cities like Mumbai are probably all aware of issues like this,' said Aruna.

Dilawar laughed. 'People in big cities are not that different to people elsewhere,' he said. 'It's just that Shaan has been telling me about it.'

'You do realise that it was not the Supreme Court that made that judgment but the Delhi High Court,' said Rehman.

'Maybe all the gay people will migrate to Delhi,' said Ramanujam.

'It could become the gay capital of the country!' said Dilawar.

'My old classmate from medical college lives in Delhi. I'd better warn him about the danger,' said Ramanujam and chuckled.

'Would that be a warning or a tip-off?' said Dilawar.

Everybody was smiling now, but then Aruna frowned. 'The rest of the country might see even less of this behaviour then,' said Aruna. She pointed to the screen. 'But do they have to hug and kiss in public? I know people do that in foreign countries, but here even married men and women don't act like that – it is against our culture.'

'They are just happy today, I guess,' said Dilawar. He turned to the others and said, 'That reminds me of a story. This conductor used to see a young couple get on to his bus at the terminus every day. They would always sit in the same seat and were very jolly and touchy-feely, laughing and talking the entire journey. After this had gone on a long time, they disappeared. He didn't see them for almost a month. Then one day, they were back in his bus and sat in their usual seat. But now there was no chit-chat between the couple, no touching each other, just silence. After a week or so of this changed behaviour, the conductor couldn't resist any more. He went up and said to the couple, "Excuse me, I don't mean to pry but is everything all right between you?"

'"What do you mean?" asked the man.

'"I have been seeing you on my bus for almost a year now. You used to brighten up my day with your smiles and good cheer. But since you've come back from your break, you have changed. You don't talk to each other any more. You avoid each other's touch, you both look miserable. What happened?"

'"Oh!" said the man. "We got married."'

They all laughed. Ramanujam said to Aruna, 'We are not like that, are we?'

She smiled at him and said nothing. Things had been bad for a few months after they had got married. Ramanujam's sister had been very mean to Aruna and she had felt that her husband was not supporting her. Aruna had even left home and gone back to her parents, but it had all ended well. And the last few days with just her husband and nobody else around had been blissful.

The news moved on to other topics and they switched off the TV. Aruna took out sapota fruit – chikus – that she and Ramanujam had bought earlier in the day from a village market and passed round a plate of the brown, thin-skinned fruit. The chikus smelled lovely and the golden flesh under the unprepossessing brown skin was firm and sweet.

Outside, a goatherd, delayed past his normal time by a straying ewe, hurried silently past on the dark path with his mixed flock of goats and lambs. The owner of the animals would be unhappy with him for not having them locked up before nightfall. The young man hoped that the landlord would not hit him because of that. A goat got distracted by a bush and the man clicked through his cleft palate. The goat fell back in line. Animals understood the broken sounds he made better than any human except his mother.

As the years passed, he had found more and more solace in the company of his flock. His mother was growing old and couldn't work as hard as before. He gave everything he earned to her, but he still felt bad that he couldn't help her more. At least, he had this job, even if it didn't pay very much. Following the animals in the forest every day, away from people, suited him. He had visited the town once as a teenager, and some kids had made fun of his disfigured face. He had never gone back.

As he passed the guest house, he looked at the puddle of warm light spilling out of the windows; he heard genial conversation and a sudden burst of laughter. The poor goatherd wondered who the lucky people were who sounded so happy and secure from all problems. A wandering holy man had once told him that everybody got the life they deserved because of the karma they had built up in their previous lives. He wondered what he had done in a previous incarnation to deserve his disability. In the next life, I will be like those people in the house, he thought. My mother tells me that I haven't harmed a single soul in this life, so I am bound to be reborn as a rich man.

Just after midnight, the door to the backyard of the largest house in the village was opened from the inside. There was no moon, and the stars shone down brilliantly. The yard was silent, the chickens were roosting in their coop, the buffaloes had stopped chewing the cud. Even the dog was asleep and did not make a sound. The hinges had been oiled just the day before and did not squeak as they usually did.

Several young men, their heads covered by sheets that also obscured their faces, rushed in, almost knocking down the man who had opened the door. He tried to run away but he was swiftly caught and thrown to the ground. A rope was produced to tie him up like a lamb being taken to market.

'What are you doing?' he said softly. 'Not so tight.'

'We have to make it look realistic,' said one of the intruders and laughed, pulling once more on the rope. The last man in relatched the door. The leader of the gang pointed and signed for him to stay where he was. The man nodded and slid to the ground.

The leader went to the trussed-up man and bent over him. 'Shall I kill the dog?'

'No,' said the man on the ground. 'I drugged the dog and it will be asleep for hours. Leave it alone.'

The leader nodded and gave the signal. The men spread out in pairs, making their way across the yard towards the house that still slumbered peacefully. Room by room, the terrified occupants of the house were brought into the hall. A servant maid screamed, 'Dacoits, help!'

The leader moved forward quickly and stopped her mouth with his hand. 'Shut up, you idiot. We are not robbers. We are Naxalites; nothing will happen to you if you do as we say.'

The woman fell silent, except for some low moans. The leader pushed her to the ground in the centre of the hall where the others also lay. A young girl, about eight years old, dark and small for her age, who also worked in the house, moved to the woman's side and started crying silently. Big tears rolled down her cheeks. The servant maid hugged the girl tightly.

'Amma, why do they have guns?'

'Shh . . . my daughter. It's nothing. We'll be all right. Just listen to what I say and follow what I do.'

The leader surveyed the motley group, consisting of family members as well as servants.

'Where is the landlord?' he asked one of his men.

'He has locked his door. We are looking for a crowbar to break it down.'

'Make sure that there is no other exit from the room.'

'Yes, comrade,' the man said and started to make for the master bedroom.

'No, wait. He might have a mobile phone. We can't take the time to break down the door.' He turned towards his hostages and looked at them carefully. 'You!' he said, pointing to a young woman in an expensive nightdress. 'Come here.'

The young woman hesitated. The leader stepped in among the hostages and pulled her up by the arm. His fingers dug into her soft skin and she flinched, but said nothing. He dragged her to her father's bedroom and shouted through the door, 'We have your daughter with us. If you do not come out this instant, I'll start disrobing her.'

There was silence from the other side of the door. The leader waited a couple of seconds, then pulled the girl's head back by her hair. 'What's your name?' he asked, pushing his face close to hers, his teeth bared.

'Roja.'

There was silence inside the room. The man's grip on Roja's hair tightened. She raised her arms to her head ineffectually but didn't utter a sound.

The leader raised his other hand towards the front of her nightdress, but before he could do anything more, the door opened and a tall, fat man with a luxuriant moustache emerged.

'Let her go, you brutes,' he said.

The leader abruptly released the girl and she almost fell. Stepping forward, he drove a hard fist into the fat man's stomach, like a piledriver into soft ground. The struck man groaned and sank to the floor.

'Naanna,' cried the daughter and ran to her father, kneeling down and hugging him.

Soon, everybody was in the living room, seated in one half of the room. Apart from the landlord's daughter, the group comprised his wife, his niece and nephew, his old mother and the servants. The young intruders stood around the perimeter of the room, holding guns and wickedly curved machetes.

The landlord was wheezing on the floor, on his knees near the front, away from the rest of the household. One of the Naxalites stood by him, holding a piece of paper, while the leader of the squad sat on a chair. On the wall to one side, the picture of Lord Venkateswara looked silently down on the entire tableau.

'Let us commence proceedings,' said the leader, raising a hand. 'Comrades, the sixth squad of the People's Revolutionary Struggle have received allegations that this bourgeois reactionary has committed crimes against the working class. Let us hear his crimes and pronounce judgment.'

The landlord and his family moaned. The man standing next to the landlord unrolled the paper in his hands. 'Mr Reddy, age forty-nine, of Vizag district – is that you?'

The landlord remained silent until the man gave him a kick. He nodded. Another kick. 'Yes,' he said sullenly.

'What do you do?'

'I am the village president. I have received my party's nomination to stand as a member of the state's legislative assembly at the next elections.' Mr Reddy looked squarely at the man seated in front of him. 'You won't get away with this, you scoundrel. I have the police in the palm of my hand. We will root you out and kill your entire group for this outrage.'

The leader leaned forward in his chair. 'My name is Adi. I am the commander of this dalam. Make sure you tell that to the police so they know whom to look for.' He laughed and sat back. 'Delhi is far away and I am here in the room with you. Fear me; don't try to make me afraid, you fool.' He waved negligently to the man standing by the landlord. 'Go on, Leninkumar. We have one more operation after this tonight. Let's not waste any time.'

Leninkumar – meaning son of Lenin – read from the paper. 'The first allegation: Reddy employs young children in his house and farms and makes them work long hours.'

He beckoned to the small girl sitting with the servant maid. The child looked terrified and clung to her mother. Leninkumar went over to the prisoners and smiled at the girl.

'It's OK, dear. I just want to ask you a couple of questions. We won't harm you.'

The mother nodded to the child and she reluctantly stepped forward.

'Good girl,' said Leninkumar, patting her on the head.

She stood slightly behind the landlord. Leninkumar got down on his knees so that his head was level with hers.

'Where do you work?' he asked.

'Here, of course,' she said.

Leninkumar struck his forehead and said, 'Doh! Of course you work here. What a clever girl you are. What time do you start in the morning?'

'As soon as I wake up.'

'And what time is that?'

'I don't know. As soon as the cock crows.'

'Oh, that is early. Do you mind starting work before the sun has come up properly?'

'No. I have been doing that since I was small.'

Leninkumar looked at the eight-year-old and smiled sadly. 'I see,' he said.

The child suddenly leaned forward and said, in a little-girl voice that was meant to be a secret but carried, 'Actually, in winter, I don't want to get up. But amma tells me that we are poor and cannot sleep until the sun rises.'

Leninkumar gulped and looked away for a moment, before turning back to the girl and giving her a too-bright smile. 'What work do you have to do so early in the morning?'

'I have to heat up the water for Roja-amma.' She turned and pointed to the daughter of the house. 'My mother carries the water from the well in a big, black vessel and puts it on the three stones in the back of the house. She lights the fire with the kindling and I have to make sure that the dried cowpats catch fire properly. I blow air through the tube. Sometimes, I stir up the ash and it gets into my eyes and makes them water, but I am getting better. Once the water is heating up, I soak all the soiled clothes in the big tub, so that my mother can wash them later.'

'Do you go to school?'

'No. We cannot afford books. Also, I have more work to do. I help amma collect cow dung so she can pat them into discs and dry them for fuel.' The girl spread her fingers out and moved her hands as if she was flattening dough into shape.

Leninkumar made a face. 'Isn't that a bit icky?'

The girl laughed. 'Yes, it is. It stinks, but I am used to it now.'

'Do you get paid any money for your work?' he asked.

The girl looked at her mother. Leninkumar turned to the servant maid. 'Does your daughter get paid for the work she does?'

The woman stayed silent.

'Yes, or no? Simple answer.'

The woman shook her head. 'She gets food to eat,' she mumbled.

Leninkumar kicked the landlord in the side. 'How much food does a small child eat, you bastard?' he shouted. When the landlord did not reply, the young man cuffed him on the head.

A squeak from the group of prisoners drew Leninkumar's attention. Roja, the landlord's daughter, was staring at him, covering her mouth with the back of her hand. Her cousin was hugging her. Roja met his gaze for a moment and then dropped her eyes, looking ashamed. So she should, thought Leninkumar, hotly. He was sure that it was the first time she had thought about how her comfortable life was achieved.

The leader said, 'Let us move on; are there any another allegations?'

'Yes, comrade,' said Leninkumar. He turned to the child, scooped her up in his arms and carried her back to her mother. 'Good girl,' he said. 'You were very brave.' He walked back to the landlord. 'Does a man called Sivudu work for you?'

The landlord nodded, after a prompt.

'Sivudu . . .' Leninkumar called out loudly. 'Are you here?'

There was silence. After a couple of minutes, the man who had opened the door to the Naxalites was brought in by two of the young men. His legs had been freed, but his upper body was still tied up with ropes.

'Free him,' said Adi. 'He is a working-class man, our witness; not a prisoner.'

The ropes were rapidly cast off and the servant stood next to his kneeling master. Sivudu gazed around and his eyes settled on Leninkumar, holding a paper. He looked vaguely familiar, as if Sivudu had seen him somewhere before. It took Sivudu a moment to remember – this fighter looked like that other young man, Rehman, who was battling on behalf of the dead farmer. Sivudu peered at him closely and realised that, though they were both the same height and their noses and chins looked a bit alike, their eyes were completely different. This man's face had a hardened look that he had not seen in Rehman.

The man tapped the paper in his hand. 'Sivudu, how long have you worked in this house?'

'Five years, ayya.'

'You don't need to address me with respect. You are older than me,' said Leninkumar. 'Did you want to work here for all those years?'

'No, ayy—' Sivudu shook his head and straightened his shoulders, casting off the habitual subservient stoop that he adopted in his employer's presence. He said, more strongly, 'No. I do not want to work here, but I have no choice.' He pointed rudely to the landlord. 'He claims that I owe him money and I have to work for him until I repay the loan fully.'

'And do you owe him money?'

'No! I borrowed two thousand rupees for my wife's treatment when she was unwell. I repaid that a long time ago, but he says that it is still outstanding.'

'What about the work that you have been doing here for all these years? Surely that should be enough to pay off the loan?'

'I don't understand these matters, ayya,' Sivudu said. 'I am a simple man. I keep paying every month, but the debt never seems to reduce.'

'If you think you have paid it off, why don't you leave? If you cannot stay in the village, then just go to the town. The landlord cannot trace you there.'

'I am afraid of the police. My master is a big man; he has friends among the officers. They come here for festivals and feasts. Even if I run away, my whole clan is in this village – my brothers and cousins and uncles and aunts, nephews and nieces. Who knows what will happen to them if I run away and leave my loan papers behind?'

Leninkumar turned to the landlord. 'Big man,' he said. Some of the young men in the Naxalite group sniggered. 'Where is the loan document? Show it to this court. Let us see if Sivudu is telling the truth.'

After some not-so-gentle persuasion, the landlord produced two long keys to the safe in the bedroom. Three of the men were dispatched to empty its contents and bring them in front of the judge.

Leninkumar looked around the room while they were waiting. Why was money so important to some people that they would do anything to get it? By forcing the young girl to work all day, the cruel landlord was not only stealing her childhood, he was robbing her future too. He stole a glance at the landlord's daughter. He knew that she was a rich bourgeois brat, spoiled and unaware of the cruelty that her class was perpetrating on the proletariat. She had probably never wondered how the water for her bath warmed itself or the clothes that she changed out of were magically washed and pressed.

Their eyes met and, to his annoyance, it was Leninkumar who turned away first. Why was he getting flustered by a woman – especially a rich woman, who represented everything that was wrong with the world? He was a soldier of Marx and Mao, fighting for the revolution. She was a parasite on society. He had nothing to be ashamed of. He looked at her again and she stared back at him.

Leninkumar's eyes moved to the little servant girl sitting with her mother. Roja's gaze followed Leninkumar's and her face flushed. In Roja's defence, he thought, now that she had come face to face with the reality of the situation, she appeared remorseful. He decided, for her sake, to be less violent with her father. There was no need to hit him, really.

The insurgents came back, heaving in a bed sheet by its corners. When they let go of the sheet, spilling its contents on the floor, everybody gaped in amazement. There were gasps from the servants and the insurgents alike. Kilos of gold jewellery, much of it set with sapphires, emeralds, diamonds and other precious stones, bundles of one-hundred and five-hundred-rupee notes, and pages and pages of official documents representing acres of land, loans and, Leninkumar thought, people's lives lay spread out in front of them.

Sivudu suddenly pointed to a small booklet and said, 'There, that's mine.'

Leninkumar bent down and picked it up. 'How do you know?' he asked.

'I recognise it,' said the illiterate villager.

Leninkumar examined the booklet in his hand. It had a red

vermilion mark halfway down the front cover, as if asking for the Lord's blessing. Truly, Marx was right, he thought. Religion *is* the opium of the masses. He opened the book and saw Sivudu's name on it. He glanced at the older man and nodded.

Holding it aloft in his hand, he said, 'Let it be recognised that this book was found in the defendant's safe.' He turned to the landlord. 'Is this a true record of your dealings with Sivudu over the matter of the loan?'

The landlord nodded.

Leninkumar leafed through the book until he came to the last entry, made two weeks ago. 'It says here that Sivudu owes Reddy three thousand and two hundred rupees.'

'That is a lie,' screamed Sivudu. 'I only borrowed two thousand rupees and I have paid far more than that over the years.'

Leninkumar said, 'I see a thumbprint here against the figure. Is it yours?'

Sivudu peered at the book and said, 'Yes, that is mine. I put the mark there.'

'Then how can you say that this is a lie?' said Leninkumar. 'If you put your thumbprint in a document, we have to assume that you agree to what is in the document.'

'I am illiterate. I don't know how to read what is in the book. The landlord or his agent tell me to put my thumbprint every month in that book and I do it. They give me a little money and tell me that the rest is going to pay the loan. I know that I am being paid less than what I can earn outside, but the landlord told me that, until I clear the debt, my whole family can work only for him. We are not allowed to work anywhere else.'

Leninkumar's heart tightened painfully in his chest. He pointed to the servant maid and her little girl. 'Are they your wife and child?' he asked.

'Yes,' said the man, nodding. 'There were complications when she was pregnant with our second child and I borrowed the money to pay for her treatment. It was all in vain, however. We lost the baby anyway, and we are still trapped here.'

Leninkumar felt as if his blood was boiling. He shook the landlord's shoulders violently and gave him a blow on his back. 'How do you face yourself in the morning, you rascal? Aren't you ashamed to make a little child work to repay a loan that doesn't exist?'

He raised his hand before remembering Roja and lowered it slowly. His eyes flicked towards her. She had her face in her hands and she was sobbing in her cousin's arms.

Leninkumar stepped back and went through the book more carefully.

'According to the records maintained by Reddy himself, over the years Sivudu has paid back more than four thousand and five hundred rupees and still owes more than the original amount of two thousand rupees. I don't think I need to waste the court's time with any more evidence. This Reddy is a counter-revolutionary of the highest order. He is a parasite, a leech who sucks the working class dry to further his own ambitions. I ask that he be declared a class enemy and punished accordingly.'

The leader of the Naxalite squad, Adi, stood up.

'Do you deny any of the evidence that has been presented tonight?'

He waited a moment and when the landlord did not say anything, Adi took Sivudu's loan book from Leninkumar and handed it to the landlord along with a pen.

'Write on it: paid in full. And sign it.'

The landlord did as he was told. The writing and the signature were shaky but legible. Adi handed to Sivudu the book and thirty thousand rupees from the pile on the sheet. 'That's ten thousand rupees in wages for each of you for the time you have worked here. The debt has been officially cleared fair and square. You can go wherever you want.'

Sivudu took the money and the document, tears rolling down his craggy cheeks. 'Thank you, kind sirs. You have given my life back to me. I will leave the village straight away.'

Adi nodded. 'You do that,' he said. 'It is probably for the best. But if anybody dares to hassle you or any member of your family over what happened today, they will have me to deal with. Is that clear?'

He looked around the room like a bull elephant trumpeting a challenge. Nobody responded. He turned back to the landlord.

'I declare you a class enemy. All your gold and money is forfeit to the People's Struggle to help us fund the revolution. And I sentence you to death.' Adi raised his gun.

The women moaned and Roja's sobbing became louder. Leninkumar moved forward and put a hand on Adi's arm. 'Let's take him hostage,' he said. 'He has much more money and properties in the town. He can be more valuable to us alive than dead.'

Adi's finger tightened on the trigger and the hammer on the gun drew back a few millimetres. The bloodlust in Adi's eyes was clear but Leninkumar regarded his commander steadily. Finally Adi relented, the trigger moved back to its position and the gun was put away in its holster. Leninkumar released the breath that he had not realised he was holding and turned back to the group of prisoners. He said to Roja, 'You!'

She lifted her eyes to his, her face ravaged by tears.

'You are responsible for paying a ransom for your father.

We will be in touch with you soon about where to deliver it and how much to pay, but, rest assured, it will be steep. You had better start collecting the money straight away.'

The landlord was blindfolded with a heavy gunny sack placed over his head and shoulders. A loop of rope was tied around him, effectively putting him in a straitjacket, and a length of it was used to lead him out like a cow on a leash. Some of the young men gathered up the gold and cash, ignoring the documents and books lying on the floor, while others in the group emptied cans of kerosene throughout the house. Finally, everybody was driven out and the building was set on fire. The chickens squawked in their coop. One of the servants raised its vertical door and they rushed out. Leninkumar saw Sivudu lifting the heavy dog in his arms and carrying it away from the yard.

The insurgents left with the landlord, leaving the household silhouetted by the inferno. Leninkumar wondered what Roja and the others would do. Would they try to extinguish the flames? The way the house had been doused in fuel, it would be impossible for them to even approach the fire, let alone to put it out. The nearest fire station was more than ten miles away, in the town, and by the time the firemen arrived, if they ever did, the house would be a cinder block.

# CHAPTER SIXTEEN

Rehman woke up suddenly, disoriented. It was dark and a ghostly veil seemed to be covering the bed. To one side he saw the obscure shape of a loose-limbed man sleeping next to him, before realising where he was. Pulling the mosquito net out from under the edge of the mattress, he got out of bed, tucking the net back so that Dilawar would remain protected, and left the room.

He walked into the living room, stubbing his toe against a chair, before making for the clay jar that held cool water. After a long drink, he found his way on to the verandah. It was difficult to make out anything, not even the faintest pinprick of light – either from distant stars or from neighbours' lamps, but there was a strange, flickering luminescence that he didn't understand. The branches of the surrounding trees wavered broodingly over him, like a witch's claws reaching for their victim, even though it was windless. Rehman felt breathless in the stillness and an unexplained sense of foreboding filled him. He had stayed in villages many times before, but well within their perimeters, surrounded by other houses, and there was always the sound of somebody coughing, a buffalo lowing or a dog barking. This was the first time he had slept in an isolated house like this, remote from other human habitation.

He padded softly along the verandah round the side of the house and was shocked to see a bright orange glow looming through the darkness. A fire – somewhere in the direction of Mr Naidu's village. Rehman stared open-mouthed for a moment before turning back for his mobile phone. His heart gave a leap and almost stopped when he saw a man standing in front of him. 'What—'

Something heavy hit Rehman on the back of his head and his legs buckled.

His body hurt. Vaguely, he heard a voice say, 'If he is not ready to walk in five minutes, shoot him. We don't have time to waste.'

He was too dazed to be afraid. His mind seemed to be moving like treacle. He drifted off again.

Suddenly, Rehman felt as if he was drowning. He spluttered and shook his head violently. A heavy kick landed on the side of his stomach, below his ribs, and he groaned, curling into a ball. He heard a feminine gasp and then a rough, baritone voice saying, 'Get up now. We don't have all night.'

He struggled into a sitting position and found himself face to face with a man about to empty a pot of water over his head. He squinted, thinking that the pitcher was familiar. 'Thatsh ze shame one I drank from,' he said, wondering why his tongue felt so thick and unwieldy. It was obviously important to listen to what the man was saying, but Rehman found his mind wandering. What an artful dodger the tongue is, he thought. He tried to articulate the thought, but his tongue kept getting in the way, somehow. He felt like laughing. Not so dodgy, after all, he thought, and this time he did laugh.

A few drops of water were sprinkled on his face and soft hands patted his cheeks.

'Rehman, wake up. These people are in a hurry and you have to recover soon.'

He peered at the woman kneeling in front of him. 'Pari, when did you come here?' he asked, smiling dreamily. 'You are sho beautiful. But what happened to your noshe? Why hash it become shorter?'

The woman stood and tried to pull him up by one arm, but he was too heavy for her and she sank back to the ground next to him. 'Come on, Rehman.' She seemed desperate.

'Pari, will you marry me?' he asked.

'Yes,' she said. 'But only if you get up and walk.'

Rehman beamed beatifically. 'There are many conditions of love,' he said. 'But that's a funny one. For you, Pari, I will do anything.' He pushed himself off the ground and stood up groggily.

'He's up – good,' said a man. 'Tie him to the others and let's start moving.'

Rehman continued smiling widely for a long time while the struggling train stumbled through the darkness, feeling the effects of every stone and projecting branch. Only the woman was free, darting along the length of the line, lending a hand to the men to keep their balance or to help them rise when they did fall, until eventually she too faltered. She was reduced then to plodding miserably along, her entire universe shrunk to the simple act of dragging one foot in front of the other.

After several hours, when the horizon was no longer black and the trees around them had started taking on a definite shape, the leader of the kidnappers called a halt. The prisoners sank to the ground, their legs too cramped even to feel relief. They fell asleep where they lay in the open.

When Rehman woke up, his neck was burning under the scorching sun. He tried to move his hands to feel it and found that they wouldn't budge. He looked down to see that his wrists had been tied in front of him and that the rope was attached to Dilawar, who was tied up in a similar way. Beyond him, the leash was also connected to Ramanujam and a tall, fat man who seemed familiar. Rehman squinted at him and realised that this last was Mr Reddy, the president of Mr Naidu's village council.

He twisted his head and gazed around. They were in a clearing in a forest; the sun had risen above the trees and was shining down on the entire group. Aruna was sleeping next to Ramanujam, even though she wasn't tied up like the men. She opened her eyes and stared back at him – the poor woman looked exhausted.

'Are you all right?' she asked.

Rehman opened his mouth to answer but his mouth felt as if it was filled with sand from Vizag beach. It took him a couple of tries before he could say anything. 'Yes,' he said. 'Was Pari with us?' he asked.

'She is in town, thank God,' she said. He thought she blushed, but it was difficult to say, because her skin was already red from the sun.

Rehman had a horrible suspicion. 'What exactly did I say last night?' he asked.

'Don't worry about it, my friend,' said Dilawar, who had woken up in the meantime. 'You had a pretty serious knock to your head. You looked like Baloo, the bear, in *Jungle Book* after the monkeys had finished with him.'

The previous night was a blur to Rehman. The last thing he remembered clearly was the heart-stopping moment when the man had appeared in front of him at the guest house; the endless plod through the forest was a confused jumble.

'Hey!' shouted Dilawar. 'Untie us, you bastards.' A mynah flew away, its wings flapping loudly, at the sudden noise.

After several minutes of shouting, a couple of men came into the clearing and approached them slowly. 'My name is Adi,' said the burlier of the two. 'I am the leader of this dalam, this squad. A number of my men think that it is too risky to take you with us. Leninkumar here thinks that you can be held for ransom, so I am making him responsible for looking after you. Don't give him – or any of us – trouble and you can crawl back to your miserable, parasitic lives soon. If you become a nuisance, you will be shot and your bodies left for vultures and jackals. Is that clear?' He looked at each of them in turn and they nodded. 'Good,' he said, and turned away.

Dalam, Leninkumar, parasites – Rehman was horrified. They had fallen into the hands of left-wing insurgents. He looked at Dilawar and mouthed, 'Naxalites. Sorry!' Why had he brought his old friend – and Pari's fiancé – to the village?

Dilawar's eyes widened. He struggled to remember what he knew about them. The movement had started in the sixties – the late sixties, he was sure – in a small village near Darjeeling called Naxalbari. A poor tribal man had been granted ownership of the land he farmed by the courts and had been attacked by upper-class villagers. The tribals counter-attacked and claimed the land and from this 'Naxalbari uprising' had come the word Naxalite.

He was sure that Rehman knew a lot more about them than he did. He wouldn't be surprised if Rehman had flirted with the Naxalites during his college days. It was students like him, highly intelligent and socially conscious, who were the most attracted to their left-wing ideology. Dilawar shook his head. Rehman would never be attracted by a movement that believed in violence to achieve their ends, he thought. And, over the years, much of the original vision of the Naxalite movement had been lost and they had split and splintered, and they had become another violent movement, preying on mid-level landlords and extorting mining companies – which invariably had to operated in remote forests – in the name of the revolution, prompting the Prime Minister to call them the most serious internal threat to India's national security.

'I need to go to the toilet desperately,' said Aruna to Leninkumar. 'Where?'

Ramanujam coughed and tried to signal his wife to stop, but she ignored him.

'Please?' she said, with a pleading look on her face.

Relenting, their captor called out and a few young men came into the clearing. 'Look after these people,' he told them and nodded to Aruna.

She stood up, her legs trembling from the strain, and almost collapsed. Leninkumar's hand shot out and Aruna had no choice but to hold on to it. After a moment, she let go of him and was able to walk.

One of the young men said, 'It is great to be a boss. While we are stuck with the men, he gets to escort the woman.'

They must have seen Ramanujam's face, because the same man continued, 'You, sit back. Is she your wife? Well, don't worry about it – our comrade will take *good* care of your woman.'

There was rude laughter and Aruna flushed. Digging her nails into her palms, she did not turn back. She really had to go to the toilet.

When she came back, several minutes later, the men were being taken one by one for their own ablutions. Again, Aruna was left untied. She was given a sloshing jerry-can and a small tumbler and asked to give everyone a drink. Once they were all watered and Aruna had used the last of the liquid to wash her face, Leninkumar and his men retired into the trees once more, leaving the group on their own.

Aruna sat next to her husband again.

'Why did you bring attention to yourself like that?' he said fiercely.

'What?' said Aruna, surprised by his anger.

'For the toilet,' he said. 'One of us would have asked. What was the need for you to do it?'

'Sorry,' she said.

'You are in greater danger than all of us,' Ramanujam said. 'You have to be careful.'

Aruna flushed again and looked away. Silence fell over the group. Mr Reddy's belly rumbled loudly and they all looked at one another. There had been no food all morning. As Dilawar was discovering, hunger pangs feel worse when one doesn't know when the next meal will come.

As the day passed, they all laboured under the weight of combined boredom and apprehension. Then there were the mosquitoes – it was worse for the men, because their hands were still tied. Aruna helped where she could by brushing the insects away.

'Go on,' said Dilawar to Aruna suddenly. 'Slap your husband. God knows when you'll get an opportunity like this again.'

Ramanujam glared at his fellow captive angrily.

'Ah!' said Dilawar. 'You've lost your chance now, you silly girl.'

Ramanujam scowled, but Aruna put her hand on his arm. 'It's OK. There was a mosquito on your cheek, but it's flown away now.' She leaned close to her husband and said quietly, 'When the men burst into our room last night, I managed to pick up my mobile phone and bring it with me.'

Everybody in the group heard her whisper. The landlord looked at her suspiciously and said, 'Where is it?'

It was a valid question. The men had all been frisked last

night but nobody had checked Aruna. Everybody knew that
saris didn't have pockets. Aruna shrugged.

'I've got it,' she said.

'Why didn't you tell us until now?' said the landlord; his
voice had risen.

'Shh . . .' said Rehman. 'Be quiet.'

Aruna said very softly, 'When I asked to go to the toilet, I
managed to send out a quick message.'

Ramanujam still looked worried. 'Was there a signal? Did
the SMS go out?'

Aruna nodded. 'I checked. Luckily there was one bar of
signal.'

'Your phone has GPS,' said Ramanujam.

'I know,' said Aruna. 'I sent our exact co-ordinates in the
message.'

'Wow! You are a star,' said Dilawar. 'Chand Bibi, Rani of
Jhansi, Joan of Arc, Margaret Thatcher and then you – what
a heroine you are.'

Aruna blushed.

'Whom did you send the message to?'

'To the first name in the address book – Ali madam.'

'Ammi?' said Rehman, and Aruna nodded. Rehman wondered – but didn't say out loud – whether his mother had a
clue how to read text messages.


Mrs Ali was sitting on the verandah when Pari arrived. It was
just before nine in the morning and the sun was shining down
on the front yard.

'Salaam, chaachi,' Pari said. 'You seem to be waiting for
somebody. Who is it?'

'Is it that obvious?' Mrs Ali replied. 'I am waiting for Leela.
Ever since that woman, Swaroop, in the next building has
taken her on as a maid, my whole morning routine has

become a mess. But today is the worst. She's never been this late before. And today of all days too! I wanted to dry the mangoes for achaar today.'

'Oh, what pickle are you going to make?' Pari asked.

'Aavakaai,' said Mrs Ali. Mango pieces with mustard and red chillies.

'Mmm,' said Pari, then her face fell as she remembered that her husband had loved to eat freshly steamed rice mixed with ghee and the red-hot aavakaai – something she had always stopped him from doing. 'Do you think they have ghee and aavakaai in heaven?' she asked.

Mr Ali, who arrived just then, answered before Mrs Ali could speak. 'What is the point of heaven if it doesn't have simple pleasures? It might as well be Dozaqh.'

Hell, indeed, if you cannot enjoy yourself.

Mr Ali continued, 'But what makes heaven different from this world is that the things that give us pleasure won't be bad for us. So, I'll be able to eat all the halva I want without worrying about diabetes—'

'And buy handbags without thinking about the cost,' said Pari.

'Or purchase cookpots even though there is no space in the kitchen to store them,' said Mrs Ali.

Pari moved behind the table and switched on the computer. Leela appeared just then, putting a stop to their conversation.

'Why are you so late, Leela?' asked Mrs Ali. 'I told you that we have to take down the jars and clean them for the pickle.'

Leela was a tall, gangly woman with a habitually toothy smile, but she wasn't smiling now.

'What can I do, amma? That second-floor madam's mother-in-law arrived last night and I don't know who is worse – her or the mother-in-law. Everything has to be scrubbed twice. No amount of dusting is ever enough. The younger madam tells me to clean the dishes first, but the older one insists that I should sweep her room before doing anything. If I didn't need the money, I would just leave, but what can I do?'

Mrs Ali was embarrassed. It was unlike Leela to complain about one employer in front of another.

'OK, OK,' she said. 'You are here now at least. Let's get to work.'

Mrs Ali and Leela walked to the back of the house where the kitchen was located. As they passed through the corridor that opened into the bedroom, Mrs Ali's mobile phone, which was resting in a letter-holder decorated with gold thread, chirped. Mrs Ali stopped and peered at the long cotton sling hanging from the nail, but the phone had gone silent.

'That's funny,' muttered Mrs Ali.

She reached for the phone but, just then, Leela called out from the kitchen, 'Which jar, madam?'

Mrs Ali left the phone to its own devices and joined her maid. The impatient soul who did not even have the manners to let the phone ring long enough would have to wait.


On the verandah, Pari slit open an envelope. 'What do I do with this card?' she asked.

Mr Ali looked at the wedding invitation with interest. 'This was an unusual case,' he said.

'It must be, if you remember it,' teased Pari.

Mr Ali laughed. 'Don't be cheeky,' he said. 'A boy and a girl, both attending the same American university, met through us. It shows you what a small world this is. They would never have got married unless they had come to us. They are both Brahmins, but the girl's family is not Telugu; they are Tamils, though they have been settled in Vizag for over thirty years.'

They were natives of the neighbouring state of Tamil Nadu and while there were many similarities between the peoples of the two states, there were also many differences – in language, food and gods.

He opened the turmeric-edged card. Below the standard phrases invoking the blessings of deities, grandparents and elders, the date, time and venue of the wedding were printed. Across the other, plain side, the bride's father had scrawled in green ink, 'Sorry for sending this to you by post, instead of delivering it personally.'

Mr Ali said, 'Take out both the bride and groom's forms and photos and put them in the drawer with the invitation card. Aruna might want to put it up on the wall over there when she comes back.' He pointed to the collage of photos and invitation cards that represented the marriage bureau's successes.

Pari nodded.

'Palm frooot . . . Cooool palm frooot . . .' came the shout from outside.

Seeing an old man going past with a basket on his head, Mr Ali went out to stop him and buy some of the fruit.

Just before eleven, two men, father and son, came into the office. Mr Ali was surprised to see them.

'Hello, Mr Rao,' he said to the older man. 'What a coincidence. We've just got a card from your viyyankudu. Your son's father-in-law has sent us an invitation.'

Pari looked at the younger man with interest and compared him to the photo she had seen of him in the album. He was tall and a bit plump. He had obviously put on weight since going to America. He had shaved off his moustache too.

Mr Rao said, 'Forget that card that you got in the post. I am inviting you personally. Anyway, it is more fun to attend a wedding as part of the bridegroom's party. You can throw your weight around.'

Mr Ali laughed. 'Please sit down. You do us honour by inviting us. Most people would rather forget about us as soon as the wedding is finalised.'

'How can we forget . . .'

Mrs Ali came out with chaai for everybody and sat down for the conversation; a card was produced for Aruna; Pari was included in the invitation; the wedding venue was discussed, before Mr Rao finally got up to leave, saying, 'We have relatives in the building next to yours. We should be going. After your neighbours, we have another thirty-two cards to deliver.'

Mrs Ali said, 'Who in the next building?'

'My daughter's brother-in-law – his name is Ravi and his wife's name is Swaroop.' Mr Rao took out a card from his cotton satchel and examined it. 'They live on the second floor.'

'I know them,' said Mrs Ali. 'Or at least, I know of them. We have the same servant maid. Did you know that the man's mother is staying with them now?'

Mr Rao said, 'I didn't know that. Thanks for telling me. I had better give her a card too.' He sat down and dug back into his bag. Taking out a blank card, he wrote the old lady's name on it. 'Right,' he said to his son. 'Let's go.'

'I am not coming there with you. That old witch is a menace. She buttonholed me at akka's wedding and wouldn't let me go for fifteen minutes.'

'Come on,' said his father. 'We'll be in and out. She might even be sleeping at this hour. Who knows?'

The young man shook his head. 'You go. I don't need to come. They are not that close relatives.'

Mr Rao sighed. 'All right, you stay here. I'll be back as soon as I can.' He turned to Mr Ali to ask courteously, 'Is that all right with you, sir?'

'No problem at all,' said Mr Ali.

Mr Rao left the verandah and Mrs Ali went back inside.

Mr Ali turned to the young man and said, 'Isn't it funny that you had to travel eight thousand miles to meet somebody who lives not eight hundred yards away from your house?'

The youngster looked shiftily around and then, leaning forward, said softly to Mr Ali, 'It is not that much of a coincidence. Do you remember what happened when Sowmya's brother came to join your marriage bureau?'

Sowmya was this young man's bride-to-be. Mr Ali thought back.

'Yes,' he said suddenly. 'I told her brother that we did not have any Tamil Brahmins on our rolls and it would just be a waste of money. But her brother wouldn't listen to me. He insisted on becoming a member.'

The young man nodded. 'I first noticed Sowmya in the departmental barbecue that was given for all us freshmen. I knew from her surname that she was Tamil, but I was surprised to hear her speak perfect Telugu. We then bumped into each other in the library, in the labs and on the campus. We gradually started talking to each other and I was amazed to find out that this girl whom I had never met before, was not only from Vizag, not only from MVP Colony, but also lived along the same road as us. We had the same taste in music, we both liked Telugu movies starring Venkatesh, we both laughed at Brahmanandam's jokes. We fell in love but we did not reveal our feelings to each other until my wisdom tooth got infected. I put off going to the dentist because I couldn't afford it.'

'Oh, I thought that in rich countries people did not have to worry about such things, unlike here.'

The young man looked at Mr Ali and Pari.

'That may be true in some other countries, but not in America. Medical insurance in USA is very expensive and the cover I had as a student was not very good. I would have had to pay a lot myself so I ignored the toothache for some time, hoping it would go away. But the pain just got worse until one day when I was in Sowmya's room, eating the mixed vegetable avial she had made for dinner, the pain went shooting through my jaw, down here.'

He drew a line with his finger along his neck, shoulder and arm.

'I fainted. Sowmya was frantic and dialled the emergency number. I was in hospital for two weeks and went heavily into debt. I didn't tell my family because I didn't want them to worry. Sowmya looked after me – without her, I don't know what I would have done. She even offered to sell the gold jewellery that her grandmother had insisted that she bring with her to America, but I refused.'

Mr Ali said, 'So you and Sowmya met and fell in love at the university. How do Sowmya's brother and this marriage bureau fit into your story?'

'We fell in love and became inseparable, but Sowmya was very scared of her grandfather. You haven't met him but I can tell you that he is a tyrant. He rules their entire household with an iron rod. Even Sowmya's father and uncles shiver when they hear his voice. We could have just ignored our families back home and got married in America, of course. But we didn't want to do that, if we could avoid it. We confided in Sowmya's brother and made this plan. He joined your marriage bureau on behalf of Sowmya and I convinced my parents to do the same for me. Step, by step, we manipulated the discussion. *It would be good if the partner is also studying for a Master's degree. Wouldn't it be great if he is already in the States – they will be able to understand each other. Oh look, this boy is in the same university as my sister. This girl is so perfect; what a pity she is Tamilian. They are Brahmins too, you know. She speaks Telugu fluently . . .'*

The young man gazed back at them, as innocent as a new-born calf asking its mother for milk.

Mr Ali said faintly, 'Go on.'

'There is not much else to say. We got there in the end: with patience, I might add, and without confronting people or challenging anybody.'

Mr Ali nodded. 'We have a saying in Urdu,' he said. 'A needle can sometimes achieve what a sword cannot. You and Sowmya have proved it.'

Later, when they were at lunch, they discussed the tale.

Pari said, 'They got what they wanted without breaking their family's hearts. What's wrong with that?'

'I am getting old,' said Mr Ali. 'I am shocked by the story. I don't know what to say.'

Mrs Ali said, 'Today, they can puff up in delight like puris in hot oil. But what goes around, comes around too. Their children will be ten times more devious than they are and will manipulate them in such a way that they won't even know when they have been twisted round like string on a spool.'

# CHAPTER SEVENTEEN

'The prime minister has asked the home minister, the health minister and the law minister to convene a commission and achieve a cross-party agreement on how to respond to the Delhi High Court's ruling on homosexuality. Listeners will remember that . . .'

One of the guerrillas reached out and switched off the radio. 'That's disgusting behaviour,' he said. 'The Chakkas should all be shot, not allowed to practise their deviancy.'

'And that's your answer to everything, is it?' said Dilawar. 'Shoot and kill?'

The kidnapped group had taken shelter from the hot sun under some trees and were resting against a large rock, along-side Leninkumar and a comrade, who had made them promise that they would not try to escape. Their hands had been untied and they had all been given rice and watery dhal to eat.

'If any of you runs away, we will shoot the others. You had better watch one another,' Adi had told them.

The forest was silent, except for a cricket somewhere and the song of some unseen birds. The other guerrillas were hidden from view, possibly enjoying a post-lunch siesta in some rough shelters.

Rehman said, 'This doesn't look like a permanent camp. What are you waiting here for?'

Leninkumar shrugged and said, 'If we go any deeper into the forest, we don't get a mobile phone signal, so Comrade Adi likes to spend time here when possible.'

Everybody's eyes flicked to Aruna. To distract the guerrilla's attention, Ramanujam quickly said, 'So you guys intend to create a revolution, but you still want to listen to the radio and use the infrastructure created by society.'

Leninkumar leaned forward, looking intense. 'We have many poor people in our country. That will never change as long as the oppression of the working class by the bourgeois continues. All religions, all advances of technology only serve to deepen the social control over the poor and continue the tyranny of feudalism and imperialism, and that's why our comrades started this fight. Our path is the Chinese path that Chairman Mao himself followed – a protracted people's war, an armed agrarian revolution to set up base areas in the backward regions, and slowly spread these throughout the country, encircling the cities and finally capturing them.'

'How can you even think that something like that will work?' said Rehman.

'It worked in Nepal,' said Leninkumar. 'There, the Maoists took over the rural areas, dragged the government to the negotiating table and forced the king out.'

'India is much bigger,' said Dilawar.

Leninkumar shrugged. 'It simply means we have a bigger area to hide in, and a bigger pool of poor, dispossessed people to recruit from. Our comrades have an ambitious dream – nothing less than to see the Red Flag fly from the ramparts of the Red Fort in Delhi.'

'India has faced many enemies throughout history and yet

endured,' said Ramanujam. 'And we will outlive your insurgency too.'

Leninkumar laughed. 'That's exactly where you are wrong. All its other enemies hit India where it is strongest: in its religious tolerance, its thriving cities and its democracy. We are different. We strike India where it is weakest – among its poor and dispossessed, its aboriginal tribals and landless labourers. We operate where the government is non-existent; where there are no schools, doctors, roads or electricity. Where a policeman does not mean law and order but, rather, a demand for a bribe. People come to us for protection and to settle disputes. Here, in our own state of Andhra Pradesh, agricultural workers used to be bonded to one landlord and paid a pittance. They were born in debt, they lived in debt and they died in debt. Since we've started fighting, workers are paid the minimum wage and are free to move jobs if they wish. That's why the people love us and we will eventually succeed regardless of the atrocities of the police.'

Rehman said, 'I agree with you that this is not a law and order problem to be solved by police action alone. But if you are so confident that the people love you, then why don't you fight in the elections? India is a democracy, after all. We have elections – too many, if anything. You can then address the problems from inside the system much more successfully than by creating all this mayhem and violence.'

'That is not possible,' said Leninkumar. 'Politicians are just puppets in the hands of capitalists and their lobbyists. How can you talk about democracy when votes are bought for cash or alcohol, and when those in power boast of their ethnic, religious and caste loyalties? Our armed struggle will unleash the huge, latent, revolutionary potential of the oppressed people of India and create a wave of mass political struggles in the country. That is the only way to change our society.'

'I disagree,' said Rehman. 'Governments are generally vulnerable to mass movements because they don't know how to handle them. But a modern state has several different options in which to counter insurgencies. They can use overwhelming police or paramilitary force, or they can create armed vigilantes like Salwa Judum, or they can round people up into guarded camps or . . . Whatever they do, the ones who'll suffer the most are the very people whom you claim to fight for. Gandhi realised this, which is why he stuck rigidly to non-violence and did not support revolutionaries like Bhagat Singh or Chandrashekhar Azad when fighting the British.'

'Gandhi!' The sneer in Leninkumar's voice was clear. 'My father, Mohan Babu, was a Gandhian all his life. He believed in non-violence and turning the other cheek. Fat lot of good it did him. He was shot dead by the police when leading a procession for a separate Telangana state. The system is too corrupt. Nothing can be achieved without a revolution.'

'That's not true, you know,' said Dilawar, who had been listening intently to the conversation. 'Look at the gays, they've struggled against even greater odds, entirely within the law, and they've succeeded. You heard the prime minister on the radio.'

The second guerrilla broke in, 'You mean those queers. They are weaklings, not even proper men. We are not like them. We are strong.'

Dilawar said, 'The gays are the ones who are celebrating on the streets of Delhi at the moment while you are skulking out of sight like cockroaches scared of the light.'

'Why you—' said the guerrilla, jumping on Dilawar and smashing his face with clenched fists.

Taken by surprise, Dilawar went down like a pole-axed steer, but after a couple of moments he started fighting back, twisting his body and landing a punch to the side of the guerrilla's stomach.

'Aah!' grunted the guerrilla, his mouth opening and his eyes closing with pain. Suddenly, Dilawar felt the other man's weight lift from his chest and he scrambled to a sitting position, not taking his eyes off his assailant.

'Enough,' said Leninkumar forcefully.

All conversation stopped as the captives held themselves tensely, wondering what was going to happen next. The only sound was the heavy breathing of Dilawar and the guerrilla. Dilawar's lip was split and he felt gingerly along the base of one tooth that seemed a bit loose. But he took grim satisfaction from seeing the twinge on his attacker's face as he gripped his stomach.

Dilawar heard the tinny tune playing in the distance for a moment before he recognised it as the ringing of a mobile phone – the sound was so out of place in the natural surroundings of the forest around them. But then, so were the green camouflage clothes and the firearms carried by the Naxalites. The ringing stopped but he couldn't hear the actual phone conversation.

The leader of the squad, Adi, came striding towards them with three of his men behind him, looking grim. Dilawar had the sinking feeling that it wasn't good news.

'Who among you has a mobile phone?' Adi asked.

They all stared at Adi, mute. Dilawar struggled mightily not to sneak a look at Aruna.

Adi glared at each of them in turn, then pulled up the landlord by the front of his shirt. Terrified, Mr Reddy closed his eyes and moaned incoherently. Adi gently patted the landlord's cheek and said softly, 'You tell me, my friend. Who among the people here used a mobile phone?'

'She,' said the landlord, gesticulating wildly at Aruna. 'She said that she had a phone.'

Adi let go of Mr Reddy, who crumpled in a heap, sobbing.

Adi's glittering eyes turned on Aruna. She shrank away from him, leaning into Ramanujam, whose arms encircled her.

'Well, well, well,' said Adi. 'The doe has a voice.' He extended his hand towards her, palm open, as if expecting a gift.

'I don't . . .' began Aruna and looked into Adi's eyes, like a mouse staring at a cobra. Her throat dried up. Mutely, she reached into the blouse that she wore under her sari and handed him the phone.

Adi caressed the sleek instrument, still warm from being against her skin. 'What else have you got there?' he asked, reaching forward and touching her breasts through her clothes.

Aruna gave a squeak and Ramanujam swung her away from Adi.

'How dare you touch my wife, you son of a widow!' he shouted and rushed at Adi.

Adi took one step back and drove a punch into Ramanujam's stomach. Adi's fist hadn't travelled far but it stopped Ramanujam as if he were a railway carriage hitting a buffer. Before Rehman and Dilawar could react, they were staring down the barrel of a revolver. To Dilawar's eyes, the small gun looked crude, as if it had been home-made, but the hand holding it was steady and Dilawar had no doubt that it was just as capable of killing him as one made in a modern factory. The two friends froze.

Ramanujam fell, retching, to the ground. Aruna screamed, 'Raaam—' and flung herself over his body, trying to cover and protect her husband from further blows.

Adi eyed the prone man. 'You are not even a capitalist worm to waste my energy on. It is your wife who has registered the land in her name – she is the class enemy.'

Adi dropped Aruna's phone on the dry, red soil of the

forest floor and crushed it with the heel of his shoe. The screen cracked in a crazy pattern and the keyboard shattered. When Adi was satisfied that it would never work again, he turned to his men. 'Tie them up. We are leaving in five minutes.'

The sun had already reached its zenith and it burned Aruna's back as they walked east.

The house was steeped in gloom, its inhabitants rendered mostly silent. The computer in the verandah was off. Everybody had gathered in the living room.

Mrs Ali said, 'The newspapers have been full of stories about Naxalites kidnapping people. I told you the last time that Rehman was taking a big risk in going to all those villages. But when did you listen to me?'

Before Mr Ali could reply, Azhar, Mrs Ali's brother, raised his hand and stopped him, then turned to his sister.

'What has happened has happened. Nothing will be achieved by throwing accusations at each other. And anyway, you are talking as if bhai-jaan pushed Rehman to visit those places. The truth is that Rehman is a grown man who followed his own heart. Let us concentrate on what happens next.'

Mrs Ali sighed. Her cheeks were streaked with tears, her hair hanging lifelessly down to her shoulders. Each one of her sixty years was clearly visible on her lined face. She looked at Pari and said, 'Shouldn't you go and collect Vasu?'

Pari stared at her in horror for a moment, before wildly checking her watch. It took her a couple of seconds to realise that she should have been at the school gates five minutes ago. She fumbled through the address book of her mobile phone and called the mother of one of her son's classmates, asking her to take Vasu home with her for the evening.

'Oh!' Pari cried, after hanging up. 'I am a bad, bad mother. How could I forget?'

Mrs Ali closed her eyes. 'It's all right,' she said. 'All women go through this at least once. And you have more excuse than most. You must have been so worried about Dilawar.'

Pari shook her head. In truth, she had not given much thought to Dilawar. She had been worried only about Rehman and as a result she now felt guilty. What kind of woman was she? She had forgotten her son *and* her fiancé. I will be a good mother to Vasu and a good wife to Dilawar, she thought, making a resolution.

Silence reclaimed the room. Pari thought back to the lunch they had eaten, just a few hours earlier. It had been such a happy occasion. After clearing the table, she had been walking towards the living room when she had heard Mrs Ali's phone beep. Mrs Ali was still in the kitchen, putting the leftover curries in the fridge.

'Chaachi,' said Pari, raising her voice, 'I think you've missed a call.'

'Yes,' said Mrs Ali. 'But it was strange; the phone gave just one chirp instead of the normal tune.'

Pari took the phone out of its cotton holder and flicked it open. 'You got a text message, chaachi.' She pressed a button. 'From Aruna.'

'Aruna?' said Mrs Ali and joined Pari. 'Why would she send me a text message? What's wrong with talking?'

Pari shrugged and opened the message. As she read it, the blood drained from her face and her legs almost buckled.

'What is it?' said Mrs Ali. 'Is everything all right?'

Something about her voice had attracted Mr Ali from the living room. Pari had looked at the elderly couple. 'Kidnapped . . .' she managed to croak.

After several minutes of confusion, things moved rapidly.

They had called Mrs Ali's brother, Azhar, who had phoned a police inspector friend of his. Together they had all rushed to the nearest police station. Azhar's friend was already there, even though he worked at a different station.

On being assured that this could not be a hoax message, Aruna's text had been copied down word for word and a First Information Report filed. They had discussed calling Aruna back, but Pari said that might put the prisoners in danger, if Aruna had not set the phone on silent. That was exactly what had happened in a movie she had seen some time ago. The heroine had hidden herself in a closet while a murderer searched her flat for her. He had almost given up and was about to leave when the hero called the heroine on her mobile and the murderer had found her. The police agreed with Pari and they decided not to call back.

'Your Aruna is such a clever girl,' said the police inspector admiringly. 'She has even included the latitude and longitude in her message.' He turned to a constable standing near by. 'See what maps we've got.'

The case was shifted to the main police station, near the barracks. Ramanujam's father had also been informed and had added his weight to the proceedings over the phone, telling them that he was rushing back to town. Soon the most senior police officials were involved. Even without Ramanujam's father's influence, the police had been galvanised by the precision of the information they had received from Aruna and their communication channels started buzzing.

In half an hour, Azhar's friend joined them in the small windowless room and said, 'The Greyhounds have been informed but they are currently on operations in the Nallamalai forests and it will take them some time to get here. Meanwhile, Inspector Verma has volunteered to lead a posse of police and we are organising it at the moment.'

The Greyhounds were a special force of commandos trained to fight the Naxalites.

Mrs Ali and the others nodded – not knowing what to say. The inspector looked directly at Azhar and sighed. 'You are my friend; I won't hide it from you. We'll get the men to head out there but we don't have the right vehicles.'

'I don't understand,' said Azhar.

Mr and Mrs Ali looked at each other with concern. What was the problem now?

'The location pinpointed by Aruna is in the forest and there are no driveable roads near by. We need several four-wheel-drive vehicles to take the men as close to the area as possible but the jeeps are all out in use.'

'Can't you call them back?'

'The ruling party is holding its convention in the next district and they have all been deployed there. We have made the request but it will take time. The commissioner has sent a strongly worded message so I am sure it will be taken seriously.'

Mr Ali spoke up. 'In a case like this, time is very important, isn't it?'

The inspector nodded. 'Yes,' he said.

'I might be able to help you with the vehicles. Get me a directory and a phone.'

Mr Ali was soon making his call. 'I need to speak to your boss urgently . . . Tell him it is Mr Ali from the marriage bureau.'

A few seconds later, Mr Ali continued, 'Mr Chandra . . . I need a favour.' He outlined the situation.

Mr Chandra said, 'Of course, sir. My whole fleet is at your disposal. You know my entire story; how can I refuse you? After what the Naxalites did to the family of my friend Surya, killing them all, and indirectly causing both his death and my daughter's unhappiness, I'll even drive the police myself if that's necessary. However, I have some drivers from the villages near by who know the area very well. They'll be with you in ten minutes.'

The Alis' doorbell rang and Pari went to answer it.

After the police posse had left, the family had returned home. Aruna's parents and her sister, Vani, were standing outside the verandah gate. Pari silently led them into the living room. Aruna's mother took one look at Mrs Ali and burst into tears. Aruna's father and sister stood awkwardly by her side, looking grim. Mrs Ali went up to Aruna's mother and the two ladies hugged. Tears started flowing down Mrs Ali's cheeks too. Slowly, they all sat down.

'I did not really believe it until I saw you,' said Aruna's mother. 'Oh, what a cruel day this has been. What harm have our children done anybody?'

Mrs Ali made no reply.

Pari turned to Vani and asked her in a soft voice, 'How did you know?'

'Aruna's father-in-law sent us a message,' Vani whispered back.

Pari nodded. 'Come on,' she said to the young woman. 'Let's make tea.' They went ino the kitchen.

'We must not lose hope,' said Mr Ali. 'Because of Aruna's courage and intelligence, the police and the Greyhounds know exactly where they are being held. Men are already heading for the spot and, God willing, our children will be free any moment now.'

While he was putting on a brave front, Mr Ali too was very worried. The Naxalites had recently declared that anyone owning more than five acres of land was a class enemy who needed to be punished. He was sure that Aruna's father-in-law had far more than that, and that Aruna and Ramanujam had gone to the village to buy even more land.

He wondered how Rehman and Dilawar had got caught up with the insurgents. He was just glad that the young people had been kidnapped and not summarily executed. While there is life, there is hope, he thought to himself.

Mrs Ali said to Aruna's mother. 'It is the first time you have come to our house and it is for such a dreadful reason.'

'What do the Naxalites hope to achieve by kidnapping people like us?' said Aruna's mother. 'We are not politicians. We don't have the power to change any policies.'

Everybody fell silent again. Finally, Aruna's father got up heavily and said, 'We will go to the Hanuman temple and pray. We believe that all travellers are under his care.'

Mrs Ali said, 'We will go to the dargah of St Ishak Madina on the hill.' She turned to Mr Ali and said, 'You are coming too.'

Mr Ali, who rarely visited saints' tombs, nodded in agreement.

Azhar said, 'I'll come with you as well, aapa.'

Pari declined. 'I have to look after Vasu,' she said. 'But my prayers will be with everybody.'

'Yes, let's pray,' said Aruna's mother, sounding bitter. 'What else can ordinary people like us do?'


'Nobody here, sir,' said the constable to the inspector, merely declaring what everybody could see with their own eyes. There were signs of a camp, but it was deserted. Inspector Verma gazed around him. What should he do now?

'Sir,' came a shout. 'Look at this.'

The inspector hurried over. Fragments of a mobile phone lay on the ground. He looked at them and sighed. 'Pick up all the pieces carefully. We may get a fingerprint or two when we take them back to town.'

He called to some of his men and said to them, 'Check the area methodically and see if you can find out which way the Naxalites have gone.' Clambering on to a large rock in the shade, he found the remnants of a meal. There was no doubt that they had been here and not that long ago. He whacked an overhanging branch with his service baton in frustration.

Inspector Verma was still young and wanted to get ahead in the service, unlike many of his colleagues who wanted only a safe posting in the commercial part of the city where they could get the maximum amount of bribes. People flung accusations at the police for beating prisoners to extract confessions, and for killing Naxalites and organised criminals by faking armed encounters. But, really, what choice did the service have? They were inadequately trained and woefully ill-equipped. And the number of policemen was nowhere sufficient for the task. There were less than one and a half policemen for every thousand people when the country probably needed double that. Moreover, policing was a state responsibility under the Indian constitution and the different states rarely coordinated their anti-Naxalite operations, allowing the insurgents to move from state to state when threatened.

Verma had volunteered for this mission even though it was dangerous. The rebels had better weapons than their own old service rifles. They also knew the jungles and the villagers much more intimately than the force.

The Naxalites cannot be far away, he thought. It had been only a few hours since the text message was sent and there were only dirt tracks to be seen. No vehicles could have taken their route; they must have been on foot. He watched his men poking under the rocks cautiously with the bamboo sticks, the lathis, they all carried, because Naxalites had been known to leave booby traps behind.

Everybody blamed the police, Verma thought, but nobody

increased their salaries, reduced the hours they worked, or gave them better barracks and proper equipment. And anyway, what could the police do on their own? The whole system was a shambles; the courts were jammed, the politicians corrupt; the divide between the rich and poor was increasing day by day. The wonder was not that the country had problems, but that it ran at all.

A group of constables came towards him, dragging a young man with them. As they drew closer, he realised that their prisoner had a cleft palate. Great, he thought. We now have to interrogate somebody who can't speak.

A constable propped the young man in front of the inspector, who could see that his men had already roughed him up. His right cheek bore the imprint of a lathi blow and his dusty old clothes appeared freshly torn. The inspector put on a stern face. 'Did you see a group of people walking away from here?'

'Un ock we sca . . . sh. My owsh we be angsh.'

The inspector turned to his men. 'Didn't you find anybody else? How will this fool answer any questions?'

The young man started to weep, desperate to get away. He repeated what he had just said, 'The flock will scatter. My owner will be angry.' The words were clear as they left his brain, but he could see that the police didn't understand him. He pulled free from the man holding him and tried to flee. Before he had taken two steps, he was pulled to the ground. A couple of men held his arms and legs while another two beat his back with their lathis.

'Amma, amma,' shouted the poor boy, trying to roll away from his tormentors, but only his mother would have understood his cries.

The officer raised his hand and the thrashing stopped. He walked over to the young man and squatted in front of him.

The witness dropped his face to the ground but a constable pulled his head up by the hair. The inspector spoke slowly.

'Did you see the Naxalites leaving this place?'

The man nodded, against the pull on his hair.

'Good,' said the inspector. 'Which way did they go?'

The man remained silent. The constable tugged on his hair, making his victim grimace in pain. Blinking, he tried to twist his head away.

The inspector nodded and stepped back. He signalled to his men, who set him free.

The goatherd scrambled up and pointed into the setting sun. 'Axasite shas ay.'

The inspector, a clever man, was expert at interrogating prisoners who could not talk properly, usually after they had been processed by his men.

'Naxalites that way?' he said, looking in the direction of the man's finger, towards the setting sun.

The man nodded.

Before the inspector could say anything further, the man waved his hands and made a bleating noise. 'Meh . . . Meh . . .'

The inspector considered him for a moment.

'All right,' he said. 'Let him go to his goats, men. We don't want to deprive him of his livelihood. We are policemen, after all.'

The man hurried away, despite his limp from the blows to his hips that had made them sore.

People assume that herding is a simple job. Take a closer look, however, and it is clear that an ocean of knowledge is required to do it. Normally, the herdsman becomes one with his flock, never far away from his animals, while leading them to the freshest green growth and keeping them safe from foxes and wild dogs. He had only ever lost one animal in his charge – a silly goat kid that had tried to jump a ravine that was too broad and deep. He prayed he wouldn't lose any today. The goatherd knew each animal individually – he had even named them. He had to find the Bearded One and the Spinach Lover first, he thought. They were the ones most likely to wander off.

The poor goatherd's heart now burned like a blacksmith's furnace with the wish that the Naxalites would kill the rich people they had kidnapped and he did not feel guilty that he had misdirected the police. Once he gathered his animals, he would go in the opposite direction, in the footsteps of the Naxalites, wiping out traces of their passage with a hundred hoof prints.

# CHAPTER EIGHTEEN

When she woke up the next morning, Aruna felt completely shattered. Her back was tender from sunburn, her legs were aching from the hours of marching and her heart was sick with hopelessness after her phone had been discovered. And she was now scared of Adi, the squadron leader, and his hot eyes.

She lifted her head cautiously and looked around. They were all piled into a hut, with the Naxalites nowhere to be seen. The door framed a low rectangle of light. The carefree sounds of the birds as they chattered and quarrelled about their daily lives indicated that they were still in the middle of the forest. Her bladder and her tongue both felt heavy – she simultaneously needed to relieve herself and drink some water, but she didn't want to venture out on her own. She would wait for her husband to wake up.

Some time later, the prisoners were sitting on a log. Aruna had been right: they were in the middle of a forest, though it gave her little satisfaction to be correct. A row of huts stood near by, under the trees. Adi and Leninkumar came towards them with a few of their men and a young couple who were obviously captives too.

Adi said, 'We will start contacting your people for ransom. Your hope is that your families love you enough to pay it quickly. If the police or your people try to be funny and the matter is not settled quickly, I will start killing you one by one. Pray for your lives or draw lots about the order in which you want to die.'

The prisoners were all too shocked to say anything.

'One more thing . . .' Adi said.

He flicked his head towards his men. Rehman, Dilawar, Ramanujam and Mr Reddy, the landlord, were each pulled up forcibly by a guerrilla and frisked, roughly but thoroughly, from head to toe. Once the search had finished, the four men sat mutely down again.

'Now you,' Adi said to Aruna.

'What?' said Aruna, her voice pitched high with fear, wrapping her arms around herself.

Leninkumar pointed to the young woman prisoner and said to Aruna, 'This girl will search you.'

The girl appeared to be no more than eighteen or nineteen and was a couple of inches over five feet. She wore a sari and a mangalasutram, two gold discs on a yellow thread, which marked her as a married woman. From the way she was standing close to the young man, Aruna guessed that he was her husband. The woman was neither fair nor dark and had what, in the marriage bureau, would be described as a wheatish complexion.

Aruna felt a pang when she thought of sir and the verandah shaded by the guava tree, with madam sitting in the chair opposite, reading a newspaper. Was that haven only a few hours' drive away? She wondered whether she would ever be back in that office again, dealing with the post and typing up lists of brides and grooms.

'Come, akka,' the girl said in a soft voice, taking on the role of younger sister to Aruna. 'These rakshasas won't give up until it is done.'

Aruna got up slowly. Rakshasas were demons of Hindu mythology who were particularly strong and active at night. Aruna thought the girl's use of the word was particularly apposite, given what had happened to them. The girl was also quite brave to talk about them so derogatorily in front of them. Or stupid.

'My name is Gita. What is yours?' the young woman said, leading Aruna behind the log.

She must have already been given instructions because she was methodical in her search. Leninkumar looked away but Adi and some of the men stared as Gita patted Aruna from her shoulders, over her chest, down her stomach and across her thighs. Aruna closed her eyes, willing the humiliation to end.

'Sorry, akka,' said Gita, when the Naxalites had left the prisoners alone once more. 'They told me to do it, and I am too scared of them to disobey.'

Aruna smiled at the girl and said, 'It is all right. How did you get here anyway?'

Gita started sobbing. 'These demons came to our village and abducted us from our marriage altar. Adi told us that until both our families pay a big ransom, they will not let us go. I am so frightened. Sometimes I think that we'll die in this forest.'

Aruna patted her on the shoulder. 'You mustn't think like that,' she said. 'Of course we'll all return to our families again.'

Gita shook her head. 'My parents took out loans for the wedding. Until the harvest comes in, they won't be able to repay those loans and borrow still more to pay the ransom.'

Srinu moved next to his wife and put his arm around her. It was clear that captivity had drawn the young couple closer together. Aruna suddenly remembered that she had read about Gita and Srinu's abduction in the papers. That had been weeks and weeks ago! A heavy weight, like a grindstone, settled on her heart when she thought that they too could be held in captivity for as long.

Gita looked up at Aruna and smiled. 'I am really glad you are here,' she said. Then, she clapped her hands to her mouth and blushed. 'Sorry. I didn't mean that it was good for you to be captured, but . . .'

Everybody smiled at the girl's confusion, their circumstances temporarily forgotten.

Aruna said, 'I know what you mean. Don't worry about it . . .'

Dilawar said, 'You don't seem very closely guarded. I am sure you could slip away easily if you wanted.'

'Don't be fooled,' said Srinu. 'There are lookouts posted around. We did try to escape in the beginning but we were caught and brought back. Adi said that if we try to run away again, it won't be very good for Gita. He also warned us that if we do get away, they will come to our village and massacre our entire families.'

'Remember what Adi told us. If one of us leaves, they will shoot all the others.'

'What should we do?' asked Aruna.

'Adi has told us that a ransom demand has already been sent out. I think we should all sit tight, until we see what's happening. It would be too dangerous to try anything rash at this stage.'

It was Dilawar who spoke those words, but there was unanimous agreement.

The day passed with the same mix of boredom and anxiety. The insurgents occasionally walked past. Leninkumar was nowhere to be seen but Adi made his rounds three times.

Dilawar turned to Rehman and said, 'How long have you known Pari?'

'You know something – I've actually known her since she was a child. Pari is not only my cousin's wife, she is also a second cousin on my father's side. Her father and my father were cousins. I didn't see that much of her when we were growing up because they lived in a different village. I only really started meeting her regularly when she got married.'

Rehman's eyes took on a faraway look.

'She was quite naive and demure in those days. Too young, really, to be running her own household. It could have gone badly, but Niaz and Pari loved each other. He was good for her as well – he drew her out socially and encouraged her to study further. They were a couple who were really made for each other.'

Rehman snapped back to reality and smiled at Dilawar.

'Sorry, you probably don't want to hear me talk about how good your fiancée and her ex-husband were together.'

'I want to know more about Pari. Her marriage was part of her and will always be important to her. I know that and I am not going to be jealous of somebody who is no more.'

Rehman clapped his friend on the shoulder. 'You are a good man. I am glad for Pari. She is a lovely woman: smiling, funny, open-hearted and generous to a fault. She deserves the best.'

Dilawar looked at Rehman oddly. 'You are right,' he said. 'She deserves the best.'

They fell silent as Adi walked past, carrying an AK-47. He didn't say a word, but under his gaze Aruna felt as if she was being stripped bare. She clung to her husband for comfort.

As the sun rose in the sky, the heat enveloped them like a suffocating blanket. The trees became still and no breeze disturbed the leaves. Big, black ants scurried about their duties in the red dust of the forest floor. Dilawar spent a long time drawing patterns on the ground with a twig, trying to distract the ants.

Finally, just as his eyes were drooping with torpor, two insurgents brought them a pot of steaming rice and a watery dhal. A third man followed them with a pitcher of water and some steel tumblers. They all stirred themselves, even though the menu at every meal was unvarying. Aruna wondered whether she should offer to cook, but she didn't want to draw any more attention to herself than she absolutely needed to. And what would happen if they decided that her cooking boosted the comrades' morale and made her crucial to the struggle?

'Where is Leninkumar?' asked Rehman.

'The comrade had to leave the camp on business.'

Mr Reddy winced as he tried to reach for the food, prompting Aruna to ask, 'Are you all right, sir?'

He nodded without speaking. She served the food on one of the disposable plates made from stitched leaves and handed it to him. He grunted, barely meeting her eyes. He did not apologise for betraying her mobile phone to Adi.

Mr Reddy looked at Rehman and said, 'I joined your father's marriage bureau. I spoke to somebody called Aruna and she sent me a list of Reddy-caste bridegrooms.'

Aruna's ears perked up when she heard her name. 'That's me, sir,' she said.

Mr Reddy eyed her in surprise for a moment and then turned his gaze pointedly towards Rehman. 'I even liked the details of a couple of names on the list. But what's the point? It's all lost now.'

'Lost?' said Aruna.

Mr Reddy refused to look at her or answer her.

Puzzled, Rehman met Aruna's eye and shrugged slightly.

Aruna couldn't figure out for a moment why Mr Reddy's manner towards her had suddenly changed and then it dawned on her. She had gone from being a rich man's wife to paid help.

A few seconds later, Mr Reddy said loudly, 'The bastards burned my house down. May their mouths fill with gravel and thirst for water. As soon as I am free again, I am going to make sure that the police chase down these sons of jackals, shoot them all and drag their bodies through the villages as an example to everybody.'

Aruna glanced around nervously. It didn't seem to be a good plan to broadcast to their captors – not if they wanted to stay healthy. She was inclined to ignore the rude landlord, but then decided that, just because he was discourteous, it wasn't a good enough reason to forget her own manners. After all, he was older than her and her parents had brought her up to be respectful of her elders.

'Was your family all right when the house was burned?' she asked.

'We were all outside. But I lost all my loan notes and my land registry documents. And they stole all the cash and gold I had in the house. Thieves, that's what these people are. The government has to take a strong line against them. Only then will the country prosper.'

'Why did the Naxalites target you, sir?' asked Rehman.

'It's that servant, Sivudu, in my house. He was acting all innocent, but I am not a fool. I can see that he is behind the raid. He must have tipped them off.'

Rehman remembered the barefooted labourer who had led him to Mr Reddy's house on his last visit to the village.

'Tipped them off?' said Dilawar. 'What secrets did he tell them?'

'Secrets . . .' Mr Reddy laughed. 'He must have told them about the money and gold I keep in my strongbox.'

'I see,' said Dilawar, looking sceptical. 'But whom would he have talked to? I mean, if I wanted to send a message to Naxalites, where would I go? I mean, not *now*. I can just shout from here, obviously. But before I got caught up in all this, I wouldn't know a Naxalite if he was under my bed with a machine-gun in his hands and the word Maoist tattooed on his forehead.'

'These poor people have their own network that respectable people like you and I don't know about. That's how they spread these false rumours.'

Aruna, born into a poor family, said, 'That's ridiculous, sir. If anything, it's the wealthy who have connections that the poor lack.'

Mr Reddy retorted, 'You are a girl. You don't understand these things. You cannot be too careful when there are riff-raff around; they will rob you blind if you give them half a chance. The poor are a big problem in this country and, unfortunately, our government is too weak to control them because the poor people have votes. We need more police to keep a strict lid on their activities.'

Aruna stared at him, open-mouthed. Finally, she said, 'Not all poor people are thieves. If they were, no number of police could save this country.'

Rehman said, 'I agree with Aruna. The problem we have is that our poor people are too easily controlled in the name of tradition, religion and caste. They don't demand their rights. They don't even know that they have rights to demand. But, sir, you must have always had money and gold in your safe. Why did they attack you now?'

'That Sivudu took a loan from me. Rather than repay it, he called in the Naxalites.'

Something in the landlord's reply triggered a memory in Rehman. What had the poor man said when Rehman had asked him why he didn't leave the village to earn more money if that's what he wanted to do? Oh yes. *Some of us have chains that bind us here and won't let us leave.*

Rehman mentally kicked himself. The man had been making a plea, and he had completely ignored him. He should have dug deeper and found out more.

He glared at Mr Reddy in anger. 'You were holding him in bonded labour, weren't you? And you were paying him too little for him to pay off his loan and you prevented him from working elsewhere. He could not have freed himself even if he had struggled all his life.'

Mr Reddy gazed back at them all coolly and said, 'Don't stare at me like that. It was a purely commercial transaction. He knew what he was getting into from the beginning. I didn't force him to take the loan from me. He was happy enough to agree to all my conditions when he needed the money.'

'Can't you even see what you are doing wrong?' said Rehman, banging his fist on the ground and dislodging two ants from a nearby twig. 'India has been held back for centuries, no, millennia, because of people like you and what you've been practising for generations. For your information, bonded labour is illegal. It was banned years ago. You are the president of the village council. You want to become a member of the legislature. If *you* don't follow the rules the government has made, what hope is there for the country? That's why people feel that they have to take the law into their hands and why you, and all of us, are stuck here in this dangerous situation.'

He turned away, shaking his head and closing his eyes.


Pari stirred the ridged-gourd and lentil curry with a wooden spatula and tasted it. She mixed in a quarter-teaspoon of salt and gave the curry another swirl.

'What homework did the teacher give you?' she said over her shoulder. She was back in her room with Vasu, making dinner for them both.

The rice on the other hob started boiling over just at that moment and she hurriedly reduced the gas. She wasn't quite in time, however, and a little starchy water spilled over the side. The blue flame flashed red. She took an old cotton cloth that she used to hold hot dishes and wiped the pan. The bottom of the cloth swung lower than she intended and it caught fire.

'Oww!' she cried. Her hand had been singed and she urgently beat the cloth against the table to stop it burning.

'Get the plates, Vasu,' she said. 'Dinner will be ready in a few minutes and we can eat.'

She turned off the gas to both burners and patted her forehead with the edge of her sari.

'Why don't you answer me, Vasu?' she said, raising her voice slightly, when she realised that the boy hadn't responded to anything she'd said. She turned to find the room empty.

'Vasu?' she said.

The living quarters were so small that from where she stood the whole could be taken in in one glance.

'Vasu?' she said again.

He must have sneaked out on to the terrace. She couldn't really blame him – it would be cooler outside than in the stuffy room. She went up the stairs, to find her landlady sitting on a cot on the roof.

'Did Vasu come here?'

'No,' said the old woman.

Where could he have gone? Pari's heart lurched. The streets could be dangerous, especially in the dark.

She ran down the two flights of stairs to the ground floor and on to the footpath. The washerman who pressed the clothes on the cart by the roadside had finished for the day and was just emptying the coals from his iron into the gutter. He looked at her and said, 'The boy went that way, madam. I shouted out to him but when he did not reply, I thought you must have sent him to get something from the market.'

She stared at him wildly for a moment before nodding and running in the direction he had pointed. Vizag has a population of one million and it seemed to Pari that almost every resident was out on the streets that evening. How was she going to find one small boy in this crowd?

A sob caught at her throat and she slowed down. Panic wasn't going to help. She walked slowly down the street, searching this way and that. A sharp stone pricked her foot and she winced. Looking down, she realised that she was barefoot. Vehicles rushed past, honking their horns and polluting the air with their smoke, almost brushing against the throng of pedestrians. She passed a dark patch of road where the fronts of the houses had not been converted to shops. When it became light again at the next stretch of shops, she thought her eyes were deceiving her. Vasu was sitting on a wooden stool, in front of a shop across the road, calmly eating an ice lolly.

She hesitated for just a moment before shouting out, 'Vaasoo!' and launching herself into the traffic.

An old man riding a bicycle, whose eyesight was failing and who was planning to give up cycling for ever, swore at the sudden apparition that jumped in front of him, swerving into the path of a teenage girl on a scooter. The girl had started driving only a couple of months earlier and was still unsure on a vehicle that weighed half as much as herself. She braked hard and wobbled into the path of a white Ambassador car, whose driver had been involved in two accidents in the previous month and who had been told by his master that he would lose his job if he was involved in any more crashes. The car driver honked and jabbed at the brake pedal, but wasn't quick enough to stop going gently into the back of the scooter. His reflexes were, however, too quick for the bus behind him. The bus driver had been thinking about the argument he had had with his wife that morning over her decision to invite his mother-in-law to stay with them for three months. Only now, when it was too late, did he see exactly how to demolish his wife's arguments, point for point. As his mind was busy revelling in his imaginary triumph, the red brake lights of the car in front of him flashed angrily and despite his desperate attempt, he crunched into the back of the car.

Behind the driver, in the bus, a teenage boy had been holding forth to a beautiful classmate for the last fifteen minutes about how to solve polynomial equations using the Newton–Raphson method. The cute girl had been smiling at him all the time and the boy had fallen deeply in love with her. When the bus stopped suddenly, the boy went barrelling into a skinny old woman and ended up in her bony lap. The ugly harridan called him names and twisted his ear until the tears came.

One look at the pretty girl's face as she tried to cover up her laughter caused the scales of love to drop from the intelligent boy's eyes. Spurred by that humiliation, the boy would give up trying to work out the inner workings of the opposite sex, and go on to win the Nobel Prize for Physics for decoding the inner structure of black holes. The girl, meanwhile, would marry her cousin, get divorced soon after and become a lecturer, ending up as the principal of the college she was now attending and a terror to any of her students who showed the slightest romantic inclination on campus. But all that lay in the future.

Vasu looked up from his lolly at the noise of the traffic snarling up and did not, at first, notice the madwoman running straight at him. When he finally saw his mother, it was too late to escape. Pari enveloped him in her arms, crying and laughing at the same time.

'Where did you go, Vasu? Why did you leave the house?' She mussed his hair and kissed him on the cheeks, embarrassing him terribly.

'I saw him walking down the street, madam. I called him over and gave him the ice lolly,' said the shopkeeper, smiling at her.

Pari looked at him in surprise and said, 'You've saved my life today. I don't know what I would have done if I hadn't found him. But how did you know he wasn't just a boy like any other, walking down the street?'

'He comes here with the old gentleman who buys rubber bands and paper clips,' the shopkeeper said. 'I knew he shouldn't have been out on the street on his own at this time.'

The shopkeeper must be referring to Mr Ali. 'Oh, that's my uncle,' she said. 'Thank you! Thank you very much. What does the ice lolly cost?'

The man waved his hand. 'No, no, madam. Don't worry about it. I just did my duty as any man should.'

Pari brought her hands together in front of her in a salutation. 'You are—'

'Hey!' shouted the man, flinging his hand up.

She turned and saw Vasu jump across the gutter and run down the street. 'Stop!' she shouted. 'Stop the boy.'

Some pedestrians, seeing a dark-skinned boy running away from a fair-complexioned woman, jumped to the obvious conclusion, caught Vasu and started raining blows on his head and shoulders.

'Stop, stop,' shouted Pari as she ran up to them. Her chest heaving, she asked, 'What are you doing? Don't hit him.'

'That's the only punishment these street urchins under-stand, madam,' said one man and gave Vasu another smack on the side of his head. 'Give back what you stole from the madam.'

'Don't you dare hit my son,' said Pari angrily, eyes flashing, and snatched Vasu away.

'Your son?' said the man, looking confused. 'But . . .' He looked at the snub-nosed, dark-eyed boy and the fair-skinned widow before him and shook his head.

Pari held on to Vasu's wrist like an udumu, the Bengal monitor lizard that has a grip so tight that enemy soldiers are said to have used it to scale the walls of fortresses.

'You are hurting me,' cried Vasu, trying to extract himself with his other hand.

She ignored his cries and dragged him all the way back to their room. Pushing him inside, she latched the doors behind her. She stood with her back against the door, panting.

'You hurt me. I hate you,' cried Vasu and flung himself face down on the cot.

When she recovered her breath, she slowly walked over and sat down next to him. Placing a hand on his head, she said, 'What happened, my son? Why did you run away?'

'I am not your son,' shouted the boy. 'My mother is dead.'

Pari didn't speak, just stroked his hair for several minutes. Finally, she said, 'Let's eat dinner.'

'Not hungry,' he said. At least he was not shouting any more.

'I'll feed you.'

'No, go away. I don't want you.'

What had gotten into him? Why was he behaving like this? She was already upset about Rehman and the others get-ting kidnapped and she didn't need this additional worry at this time. A thought struck her.

'Is this about Rehman Uncle?' she asked.

Vasu turned and burrowed his face into her stomach, his arms around her waist. He was sobbing.

'It will be all right, Vasu. You know Rehman Uncle – he will be fine.'

'No, no,' cried Vasu. 'He will die just like all the others and then you will die too, if you don't leave me.'

In his short life, Vasu had lost his father to an accident, his mother and then his grandfather to suicide. Rehman had brought him from the village to Vizag and Pari had adopted him.

'None of it is your fault, Vasu. Rehman will come back and I am definitely not leaving you for a long time. You cannot escape from me that easily.'

Vasu looked up from her lap. 'Promise?' he said.

'God promise,' she said. She could not stop herself thinking, Insha' Allah, God willing.

He gazed into her eyes for a long moment and then jumped up.

'What's for dinner?' he said. 'I'm starving.'

# CHAPTER NINETEEN

The shadows of the trees lengthened and a deep stillness took hold in the forest as the birds retired to their roosts for the night. Dilawar felt the silence as a physical weight. He had only ever known urban India, where there is never true quietness. And Mumbai, where he had been living for the past several years, really was a city that never slept.

Adi and a group of his men came over to them and before Dilawar and his friends realised what was happening, their hands were pulled behind their backs and tied up tight with rough coconut-fibre rope.

'Hey,' said Dilawar. 'Why are you tying us up now? Do we have to march again tonight?'

'Shut up,' said the man behind him, driving a fist into Dilawar's side.

Dilawar groaned and tried to wriggle his hands free, but they didn't move.

The man behind him squatted on the ground and put a rope round his legs. As the rope tightened round his ankles, Dilawar lost his balance and, unable to break his fall with his hands, landed heavily on his face. Blood spurted into his eyes and he moaned. An old cotton cloth was tied as a gag round his mouth.

'Why are you doing this?' cried Srinu, who had been tied hand and foot but not yet gagged. His wife, Gita, had already been tied and gagged, as was Aruna. The edge of Aruna's sari had slipped and the shape of her chest was clearly visible under her blouse.

Dilawar watched, his eyes moving frantically, as Adi slowly drew even closer to them.

'I don't have to tell you this, but I will anyway. We are going on a mission and will be a bit short-handed here. We will release you tomorrow morning, so don't make any trouble. Goodnight.'

As Adi turned away, Dilawar saw the leader's eyes lingering on Aruna. His disquiet increased when the men were taken to one hut and the women to another.

Tired after the day's tensions, and their rollercoaster emotions after getting the text message – first optimism, boosted by the police confidence, then despair, feeling crushed by the news that the kidnappers had moved on and could not be found – Mr and Mrs Ali had retired to bed early.

Mr Ali was soon snoring lightly – his wife had always been envious of his ability to fall asleep in any position, anywhere, and at any time. In contrast, she tossed and turned. She must have fallen asleep at some point, because she suddenly screamed and sat up. She looked around in confusion and it took her befuddled mind some time to realise that she was in her own bed and not in a forest.

'What is it?' mumbled Mr Ali, also woken by the scream. Appearing irritated, rather than concerned, he glanced at the clock and said, 'It's only been a couple of hours since we went to bed. Go back to sleep.'

'Nightmare,' gasped Mrs Ali. 'I saw them bound and gagged. A man with big eyes was coming to cut their throats.'

'Nonsense,' said Mr Ali briskly. 'We need to keep our

strength up and we can't do that if you keep waking up with your fanciful stories. It's probably just something you ate that's disagreed with you. Go, drink a glass of water and come back to bed.'

'What do you mean, something I ate?' said Mrs Ali. 'We only ate what I cooked. Are you saying that there is something wrong with my cooking?'

'No, that's not what I—'

'In the forty years that we've been married, when did you fall sick after eating my food?'

'I just—'

'The only times that you've ever had an upset stomach were when you ate out in restaurants. You get taken in by their shiny tables and well-dressed waiters but have you ever seen a restaurant kitchen? And the cooks? How do you know whether they wash their hands properly?'

'But—'

'Don't talk to me about food from outside. You eat from the same plate that has been used twenty-five times before by unknown people. They probably reuse the same dirty water to wash it each time.'

'I didn't—'

'I scrub each vegetable and peel it before cooking it. You sit at the table scoffing piping-hot food straight from the cooker and you have the nerve to tell me that there is something wrong with my cooking. Have you seen chhote bhaabhi's kitchen? I shouldn't say this but your sister-in-law doesn't know how to handle meat. She moves it from one place on the worktop to another and who knows what germs she is spreading? You don't say anything to her. You sit down quietly and eat whatever she serves. Why do you point the finger at my kitchen?'

'Listen—'

'And how can you sleep while your son has been kidnapped and Aruna, the girl you say is like your daughter, is at the mercy of ruthless ruffians and Pari is in danger of becoming a widow all over again even before she remarries? What kind of heart do you have in that chest of yours?'

Mr Ali stopped trying to remonstrate with his wife, got up and went out.

'Yes, disturb the peace and then leave the room. I will stay awake on my own,' shouted Mrs Ali after him.

He came back with a glass of cool water and silently handed it to his wife. She took it from him, almost snatching it, and emptied it in two gulps, then handed the tumbler back to him. By the time he had put it on the dining table and returned to the bedroom, Mrs Ali's eyes were closed.

He got into bed cautiously and was relieved to find that his wife was fast asleep. He stared at the revolving blades of the fan above him and listened to the tick-tock of the alarm clock on the dressing table for a long time before sleep claimed him.

Aruna found it difficult to sleep too. She was lying on her side and her left shoulder was cramped. The rough ropes chafed her wrists and, worst of all, an itch had developed on her chin just below where her gag ended and she could do nothing to relieve it. Over the past hour, the itch had got worse and it now dominated her thinking. She had tried to rub her head against the floor but that part of her chin remained out of reach. She squirmed once again, trying to think of something else, anything else, but her mind refused to budge from the pesky itch. In addition, a smell of roasting meat wafted over the air. As she was a Brahmin, and a vegetarian, the smell nauseated her.

She heard a noise at the entrance to the hut and twisted her head up to see a silhouette against the grey of the night sky.

The man looked oddly furtive as his head swivelled from side to side like a pedestrian waiting to cross a busy road. When he stepped inside, Aruna was horrified to see a long knife in his hand. As he came closer, Aruna realised it was Adi. She started squirming, trying to get away from him. When he held the point of the knife against her windpipe, she froze.

He put his hand, quite gently on her right shoulder and ran it softly down her arm. It felt worse than if he had been rough. She shuddered at the intimacy. He transferred his touch to her bare midriff, between her blouse and the knot of sari at her waist. The end of his index finger scraped her smooth skin and she wondered whether the callus was due to the constant fingering of the trigger of a gun. How many men had this rakshasa killed with the hand that was roaming over her body?

His hand changed direction, moving up to cup her breast. There was no change in his expression or in the steady pressure of the knife against her throat. She finally closed her eyes and whimpered behind her gag. She had always been taught that if a man other than her husband even touched her, she would bring shame on the family and its honour. Her mother used to say, 'Whether a thorn falls on a banana leaf, or a banana leaf falls on a thorn, it is the leaf that gets torn.' And so she had lived – dressing modestly, behaving demurely, never ostentatious, doing her best not to attract the attention of the opposite sex. If news of what was happening to her ever came out, she would be a *spoiled* woman and the slur would remain on her for ever.

At that moment, rage washed over her. How dare this man act as if her body was a mere object for his pleasure? Prudery, culture and religion might make her feel horrified and ashamed of what he was doing or trying to do to her. But that was not what Aruna now felt. Her body belonged to her alone. *She* would decide whom to share it with – who could touch her and who should keep away. This hooligan had no right to take this choice from her any more than a thief had a right to take money that did not belong to him. She opened her eyes fully and glared at him, in an effort to show the scorn she felt. She coiled her body like a spring, drawing her legs close to her chest and trying to move away from him, staring at him all the while. Adi finally looked away, unable to face her. Aruna felt triumphant, but the knife lay steady against her throat and Adi's left hand was now undoing the knot of the sari at her waist.

And then she kicked him, straightening out her legs with as much strength as she could muster. He had been squatting next to her on the balls of his feet, with his weight on his toes. Her feet caught hit him on his right knee and he went spinning, landing heavily on his bottom. The sharp knife dragged against her skin and left a line across her throat that swelled crimson. It stung like fire.

Adi swore and started getting to his feet. When he was halfway up, his legs still not fully straight, the other girl in the room, Gita, hit him behind the knees with her two bound legs. Adi fell forward and the knife flew from his hand. Aruna's eyes met Gita's. She was blinking and pointing with her chin. Aruna twisted around. Seeing that the knife was close to her, she started rolling towards it. Gita tried to kick Adi again but couldn't move her legs enough; he turned and gave her a backhanded slap. Gita fell back with a muffled groan, but in the meantime Aruna had managed to cover the knife with her body.

'Aargh!' snarled Adi and jumped on Aruna. He fastened his hand on her neck, making the cut smart even worse than before and bringing tears to Aruna's eyes. Like a wild animal now, Adi roared and pulled down the top of Aruna's sari.

Aruna's hands touched the knife's hilt and she frantically gripped it, but because her hands were tied, it wasn't much use. Adi straddled her waist and sat up with a triumphant look on his face as he prepared for her final humiliation. Aruna attempted to shake him off but his thighs on either side of her were too strong.

Suddenly, there was a loud crunch. Adi's eyes glazed over and he fell on top of her, chest to chest, his lips on hers. Aruna made a disgusted sound and tried to roll out from under him, but his dead weight made it difficult. Unconscious, Adi was finally pulled off her and dumped in a heap on the floor. Aruna was appalled to make out in the darkness a man leaning over her with a heavy branch for a cudgel.

Her body sagged in relief when she recognised Ramanujam. He quickly cut her hands and feet free with a small knife that Aruna was surprised to see. Her hands flew to the itch on her chin that she was finally able to reach and she scratched luxuriously.

'What took you so long?' she asked her husband, trying to act calm, despite her loudly beating heart and shaking legs.

'Your throat, it's been cut,' he said. His chest was heaving as if he had run a marathon.

'You are the doctor. Can't you see that it's just a scratch?' she said, staring into her husband's shining eyes.

They heard the muffled sound of a voice behind them and Aruna moved away from Ramanujam.

'Oh, sorry! We forgot Gita.'

They quickly untied her and the two girls hugged each other, laughing and crying.

'Thank you for helping me,' said Aruna.

Ramanujam used the ropes that had bound the girls to tie up Adi.

'Listen, we can't spend any more time here. When you leave the hut, don't stand up or someone might see you. Remain close to the ground, turn right and crawl over to the first hut that you see. The other men are there.'

Before any of them could reach the door of the hut, however, a man carrying an AK-47 burst in and the three of them froze. He gestured with his gun and Ramanujam raised his hands, while Aruna and Gita tried to hide behind him. Noticing Adi on the floor, he rushed forward.

'Comrade, come quickly,' he called out.

His cry brought Leninkumar, who appeared tired. Dust coated his clothes as if he had been on the road for a long time. He glanced at Adi's body and raised his eyebrows questioningly at Ramanujam.

'The . . . the son of a widow was molesting my wife,' said Ramanujam in answer.

Leninkumar sighed and looked even wearier than before.

'What do we do, comrade?' asked Leninkumar's man.

'Let me think . . .' said Leninkumar.

Silence fell. Ramanujam could hardly breathe. To come so close to escape and then be thwarted at the last minute was extremely frustrating.

His arms started aching and he lowered them a little. The junior Naxalite thrust his gun at him and Ramanujam held his arms up again. He tried to tell himself that it was just lactic acid building up in the muscles but the fire in them did not abate.

Finally, Leninkumar stirred. Looking straight at them, he said, 'First, I apologise for Adi's behaviour. We are fighters for a cause, not men out to get whatever we want by force. I want the three of you to leave now, before Adi regains consciousness.'

'What about the others?' said Ramanujam. 'We can't just go off by ourselves.'

Leninkumar shook his head. 'I can't let all of you go. My comrade here will listen to what I say, but most of the men in the group follow only Adi. If all of you go, you will be missed within the hour and it will just be worse for you.'

'Then I'll stay too,' said Gita. 'I am not going anywhere without Srinu.'

Leninkumar said, 'The matter is not open for negotiation. I should actually keep all of you here, and I am taking a considerable risk by releasing any of you. But while I am fairly certain that I can keep the others safe, I cannot say the same about Aruna. It is best that she leaves the camp as soon as possible.'

Aruna clutched her husband's waist and moved even closer to him.

Leninkumar said to Ramanujam, 'You and your wife will leave now. Gita will go to the other hut and stay with her husband.'

Ramanujam still hesitated, not willing to leave his friends in the clutches of the kidnappers, but seeing too, the opportunity that had come his way. The gun jabbed his stomach and Leninkumar's man growled, 'You heard the comrade. Now move. Don't be seen by anybody else.'

Ramanujam started towards the door of the hut, Aruna following behind him. Gita caught her hand and said, 'Akka . . .'

Aruna turned and hugged the younger woman, whispering into her ear, 'Don't despair. I am sure we'll see each other again very soon.'

Gita nodded and her miserable expression reminded Aruna of her younger sister, Vani.

'We are in trouble, aren't we, dora?' came the voice of the younger insurgent. Leninkumar had been promoted from comrade to chief.

'Yes,' said Leninkumar. 'Ahead of us is a deep trench and behind us a well.'

Ramanujam and Aruna slipped out of the camp and heard no more of the conversation.

Hours later, Aruna was past caring. The jungle was endless. The trees were monsters whose evil fingers stretched out to scratch her from all sides. She had no shoes and the ground, with its rocks and nettles, was rough on her feet. There was also the ever-present danger of stepping on an unseen snake or scorpion. When they broke cover she could occasionally see stars, but most of the time, the canopy of the forest made her feel as if she was in a tunnel.

After the fourth time she had stumbled in as many minutes, Ramanujam stopped and looked at her anxiously. 'I think we've come far enough. Let's stop here until day breaks.'

He moved them deeper into the trees and cut several long-leafed branches with his small knife. He arranged them like a bed and Aruna sank on to them gratefully.

They sat side by side, resting against the trunk of a tree. Aruna asked, 'How were you able to come to our hut at the right time?'

'When they threw us all into the one room, Dilawar was very distressed. He kept banging his head and feet on the floor. Finally, Rehman crawled over until he was behind Dilawar and managed to undo his gag with his fingers. As soon as he could talk, Dilawar told us that you were in danger and needed to be rescued. I became frantic when I heard this, of course, so we set about ungagging each other. Dilawar said that he was afraid because he had overheard Adi making a comment about how it was time for capitalist parasites to serve Marxist soldiers while looking at you. I started trying to free myself but nothing happened beyond chafing my wrists. Rehman tried to help me but the knots were too tight and we couldn't get enough purchase.'

Aruna lifted his hands and peered at them in the gloom. She couldn't make out much, but she kissed them lightly.

Ramanujam continued, 'Then, Srinu started making sounds behind his gag, so Dilawar untied the cloth round *his* mouth. Srinu told us that he had managed to get hold of a knife but he hadn't had the courage to make use of it yet. He said that if the girls were in danger, we should take it. The knife was tied loosely to the calf on his right leg and, with its help, I managed to get free. I was about to come out of the hut, but we heard a man coming towards us. I quickly gagged everybody, tied myself loosely and lay down behind Rehman and Dilawar. Mr Reddy, the landlord, started moaning behind his gag and trying to say something to the guerrilla. I was really afraid that he might spill the beans and ruin everything, but the insurgent just kicked Mr Reddy on his behind and told him to remain silent. As soon as the man went away, I untied myself and started freeing Rehman, but the moment his mouth was free, he said it was too dangerous for all of us to leave the hut, in case the men came up, and told me to hurry to you.'

'Oh!' said Aruna. 'I owe every one of you a debt.'

The mattress of leaves felt softer than the comfortable bed she normally slept in. Ramanujam settled down beside her and they stretched out, holding each other.

'I promised to look after you,' said Ramanujam. 'And I failed. I let you be kidnapped and face that monster on your own.'

'It's not your fault,' said Aruna. 'And you did save me in the end.'

Ramanujam's hand moved softly down her back and settled on the bare skin of her waist. For a brief moment, Aruna remembered Adi doing the same thing and she stiffened.

'Are you all right?' asked Ramanujam, withdrawing his hand immediately.

'Of course,' she whispered.

She moved even closer to him, flattening her body tightly against his. Taking his hand in hers, she replaced it on her waist. Suddenly all the weariness ebbed out of her body and she felt a new strength singing and surging through her. It was not the same thing at all, she thought. I want my husband to touch me.

She raised her hand to his cheek and its two-day-old stubble. 'I love you,' she said. Before Ramanujam could reply, she covered his lips with hers.

Minutes later, she was under him and he started undoing her blouse.

'No, wait!' she panted. '*I* want to make love to you.'

She rolled over and now their positions were reversed, with his back on the leaves and her straddling him. She raised his hands above his head and pinned them with one of her own. 'Kiss me,' she commanded fiercely, bending her face to his.

# CHAPTER TWENTY

Aruna woke up to a chorus of what sounded like a hundred tiny bells. The sharp, sweet sounds warbled all around her. She opened her eyes and came face to face with a large bull-frog the size of a side plate, which made her squeak. Ramanujam stirred beside her, sat up quickly and looked at her with concern.

'What is it?' he asked, scanning the area.

'I just saw a huge frog. Is it lucky to see a frog the first thing in the morning?'

'It must be,' he said. 'You wake up next to me every day, don't you?'

Aruna hit him gently on the arm. 'Don't be silly,' she said. 'You are a prince, not a frog.'

'I feel more like a tigress's prey after last night,' he said.

Aruna blushed. 'I am sorry. I don't know what came over me.'

Ramanujam tickled her under the chin. 'That particular tigress can come and visit me any time,' he said. 'And, yes, it is good luck to see a frog in the morning. It means there is water near by.'

They found the stream within a few minutes and quickly

splashed their faces, washed out their mouths using their fingers for toothbrushes and took a refreshing drink. He pulled out the knife and made a mark on a huge banyan tree.

'What are you doing?' said Aruna. 'This is not the time for graffiti.'

'Let's follow the stream,' said Ramanujam, ignoring her question. 'We are bound to come to a village soon and it will be better than blundering round in circles in the jungle.'

The stream seemed to go straight into a big mass of rock and they had some difficulty in keeping alongside it, but after that it became easier. The sun came up as they were walking, making the forest look very different in the daytime. Paradoxically, they didn't travel much faster than they had the previous night because, now, they could watch where they put their unshod feet. Seeing a wild boar drinking from the stream ahead of them, they slowed down. The animal looked up at them and vanished into the scrub. Aruna shuddered when she realised just how much of a risk they had taken in their mad nocturnal dash.

They continued following the stream, but soon the unaccustomed exercise of the previous few days took its toll. The muscles in Aruna's legs started complaining, then her already-blistered feet began bleeding. Sweat worked into the cut on her neck and its fiery burn vied with her feet and legs for attention.

'I can't go any further,' she said, sinking to the forest floor.

Nadira swept into the room briskly. 'Why aren't you ready yet?' she asked her friend.

Mrs Bilqis was still in the long, loose kaftan that she wore at night. Her face appeared blotchy and puffed up. Her hair was not brushed . . .

'And why are you looking so scruffy? You are the daughter-in-law of Sir Jehangir Talwar Beg, not some commoner from the town. I saw your maid when she let me in and she is looking a lot smarter than you. Come on now, buck up. We don't have much time.'

'What is the point, Nadira? I keep thinking of my poor son in those cruel men's hands and I don't feel like doing anything.'

'I don't believe it. Your ancestors led armies, for God's sake. Did your mother lie with a merchant while your father was away on a campaign? Is your true blood coming out now?'

Mrs Bilqis's hand shot out to slap Nadira. At the last moment, Nadira caught and held her friend's arm. 'There's still some fire in the old woman yet. Maybe your mother slept with a returning soldier instead of a wandering pedlar.'

'If it had been anybody else, I would have thrown them out for even thinking such things,' said Mrs Bilqis, glaring at her friend.

Nadira patted Mrs Bilqis's cheek. 'Get ready, darling,' she said softly. 'We are going to meet the Baba.'

'I lost all faith in holy men a long time ago,' said Mrs Bilqis. 'They are all just out to fleece you.'

'Baba is different. He has helped many people and never asks for money. And he won't carry out any elaborate rituals or anything. He simply writes out what you want in beautiful calligraphy on a small slip of paper, reads a dua, a prayer, over it and puts the paper in an amulet for you to wear. That's it. Many, many people swear by him.'

'If he doesn't take any money, why does he do it?'

'To help people, silly. Also, I never said that he doesn't take money. I said that he doesn't *ask* for it. If his intervention resolves your problem and you want to give him a gift, the Baba will not be so rude as to refuse you. Come on. Get ready. It will be good for you to breathe some fresh air anyway.'

Mrs Bilqis went into her bedroom to get changed. She knew from past experience that Nadira would not give up. She could be such a pain sometimes.

Mrs Bilqis had to admit that she felt better once she had changed and brushed her hair. She finished off her toilette by perfuming herself with attar of roses, then went into her husband's room. She moved him on to his back, plumped his pillow and told him, 'I am going out with Nadira to pray for Dilawar. I will be back in a couple of hours.'

Her husband's eyes followed her silently and seemed to gleam with a sudden intelligence when she mentioned Dilawar. How much did her husband actually understand? It was so frustrating not to know.

She switched on the television and flipped through the channels. A fashion parade was being shown on one station and she paused on it. A tall, young woman strode down the catwalk in high heels, wearing a dress that ended at mid-thigh and swished dangerously high as her legs moved. The model reached the end of the ramp and turned smartly, coming to a stop with one hand on her jutting hip. By some unseen magic, her dress flashed open, revealing the woman's bra and knickers.

Mrs Bilqis shook her head, telling her husband, 'I'll leave the TV on this channel. You might enjoy it.'

She left the room.


When Aruna's parents and her sister, Vani, reached the Hanuman temple, a pretty woman journalist was interviewing a priest in front of a TV camera. A brushlike microphone dangled at the end of a long pole above them, just out of the camera frame.

'Don't you find it ironic that a good man like Rehman who has fought on behalf of poor farmers should be endangered by Naxalites?' asked the interviewer.

'That is the nature of Kaliyugam – the age of evil that we live in,' said the priest.

He wore a white dhoti around his waist, leaving his chest bare except for the sacred thread that ran over one shoulder and round his upper body. The teenage Vani gazed appreciatively at this well-built, handsome, articulate man, who defied her image of priests as spindly older men with weak bodies.

The priest was continuing his answer. 'As Hindus, we believe that the world has seen nine ages already and we are now living in the tenth age. In this age, falsehoods flourish, truth gets into trouble and evil seems to have an easy ride. In this era, good intentions are perverted and Naxalites, who claim to fight on behalf of the poor and oppressed, cause much misery themselves. But evil doesn't have it all its own way. There is a God and he is watching the earth. We believe that prayer can help and that's why we are gathered here.'

The interviewer nodded and said, 'Thank you, Dharamgaaru.'

'My pleasure, and please call me DK.'

The interviewer said, 'This is Usha Malladi, getting reactions to the kidnapping by Naxalites of Rehman, the hero of Royyapalem, and his friends.'

As soon as the TV cameras stopped rolling, the priest came forward and greeted Aruna's parents, then led them towards the temple. Vani saw Usha following them.

'You can't come inside,' the teenager said to her. 'This is a temple.'

Usha looked surprised for a moment and then said, 'I want to pray too.'

Vani peered more closely at the journalist. Lines of stress

were etched around the glamorous woman's eyes. She might almost have been crying. Vani couldn't understand it at all.

When they walked into the courtyard of the temple, Aruna's father looked around, baffled. 'Is today an auspicious day? I've never seen the temple so busy at a normal time like this.'

'They are all here to pray for your daughter and son-in-law, sir. The news has spread everywhere and the people of the town are very concerned for the safety of all the captives. It is one thing for villagers to get kidnapped, but local people are a different matter,' said the priest who called himself DK.

Usha leaned towards Vani and whispered, 'DK rallied them all here by phone calls and personal appeals.'

They threaded their way through the throng to the front, where a large idol of Hanuman, the monkey god, presided over the sanctum sanctorum. Mr Somayajulu made a deep obeisance to the deity and stood sideways to face the audience without turning his back to the idol. At the sight of the hundreds of people gazing expectantly at him, sudden tears sprang to his eyes.

DK said in a voice that carried, 'Friends, Mr Somayajulu is deeply touched by your concern. Let us all pray to Hanuman, the god of travellers, the devotee who helped Ram and his brother in their quest to rescue Sita. Surely, the prayers of so many people will not go unanswered.'

DK's eyes flicked to a girl in the third row. Anu looked back at him adoringly. Her father had thrown in the towel about getting her wed to an American banker and their families had formally exchanged betel leaves and the couple were now engaged to be married. It was she who had brought DK's attention to the kidnapping and her would-be fiancé had swung into action with his customary efficiency.

★

On her return to the house, Mrs Bilqis put a hand on Nadira's arm. 'Thank you. I do feel better for having said the prayers and recited the ninety-nine names of Allah.'

The silver amulet on a black string was in her handbag. She wasn't convinced enough to wear it yet.

'I have to go,' said Nadira. 'I have been out since first thing in the morning.'

'Stay . . . just half an hour, please,' said Mrs Bilqis.

Nadira looked at her for a moment, then agreed. 'All right,' she said, seating herself on the sofa.

The maid came in and Mrs Bilqis said to her, 'Get tea for us.' Mrs Bilqis turned to Nadira. 'Give me a moment. I will check on *him* and come back.'

Mrs Bilqis went into her husband's bedroom and looked in. For once, his eyes didn't track her. They were fixed on the television, which, she was surprised to see, was tuned to a news channel. It was normally kept on entertainment channels. Then she remembered that she had left it running the fashion show. That was probably the 'news' at that time.

She went to the remote to change it, when the newscaster said, 'There is still no news on the four local people who have been kidnapped by Naxalites. This follows a spate of kidnappings of prominent landowners in villages and attacks on politicians. The police commissioner said that a search-and-destroy mission was in progress but that he could not give any more details. Earlier, our reporter, Usha Malladi, managed to speak to the state home minister regarding this issue. The minister said: "Our government is taking the matter seriously. We are pursuing a two-pronged approach. Strong police action on the one hand and an offer of amnesty and rehabilitation for any insurgents who give up their arms and surrender." Usha also spoke to the leader of the opposition, who said that the offer of amnesty for insurgents was misguided and would only encourage . . .'

Mrs Bilqis switched off the television. The channel repeated the same news every half an hour or so. How many times had her husband seen this item? She had not told him that Dilawar had been kidnapped, because she didn't want to worry him, even though she was never sure how much he really took in.

Putting the remote on the bedside cabinet, she looked at her husband. He was still gazing unblinkingly at the now-dark television. Something about his posture caught her attention.

A scream brought Nadira running into the room. Her friend was staring and pointing at the unmoving figure on the bed. One touch was enough to tell Nadira that her friend's husband had been dead for at least half an hour.

'I killed him,' said Mrs Bilqis. 'After years of wanting to end it all by holding a pillow over him, I finally did it.'

'What are you talking about?' said Nadira. 'I saw you walk in here just a minute ago. You didn't do it.'

Mrs Bilqis laughed manically. 'I killed him, just as surely as if I physically stopped his breath. I left the TV on the news channel and they were talking about Dilawar being kidnapped.'

Nadira looked puzzled. 'So?'

Mrs Bilqis said, 'Don't you see? For twenty years I wondered just how much he understood of what was going on around him. His eyes used to follow me, but there was never any other response. I did not tell him about Dilawar's trouble, just in case he understood, but when I left this morning, I left the TV on the news channel by mistake. You know how these channels are – they keep repeating the same news again and again if they don't have anything fresh to talk about. I wonder how many times he saw the news before it killed him.'

'We don't know that . . .' said Nadira.

'I am sure,' said Mrs Bilqis. 'I killed him.'

Nadira turned to her friend and shook her by the shoulders. 'Listen to me. You will never, ever repeat that in front of anybody else. Do you understand? You are not a husband-killer. I will not have people forget about the years of dedicated service to your disabled husband because of a false rumour that you somehow caused his death.'

Mrs Bilqis looked at her friend strangely and said, 'I don't care what people think about me any more.'

'But I do,' said Nadira fiercely. 'I care about my friend's reputation.'

Aruna lay on the hard earth with tears in her eyes. She had asked Ramanujam to go on alone, but he had refused to leave her. She felt that she was letting everybody down, but her bleeding feet would not let her stand up on the hard ground.

After almost an hour in which they had gone less than a hundred yards, a tribe of monkeys moved into the trees around them, talking in squeaks and obviously on their daily feeding round. A hundred pairs of eyes stared in surprise at the unexpected sight of the human couple. An old monkey, its grey fur coming off in clumps, leaving patches of bare skin, held a leaf in one of its paws. It calmly tore the leaf in two, stuffed one half into its mouth and dropped the other half. Before the falling leaf fluttered to the ground, the monkeys moved away – their chattering silenced.

Aruna closed her eyes, until she heard a smack. She opened them to see her husband striking his forehead.

'I am supposed to be a doctor,' he said. 'I am actually an imbecile.'

He stood up and started plucking leaves from nearby trees, high off the ground. When he had collected a whole bunch, he took out the small knife and approached her with an intent look.

'What . . .' she said faintly.

Soon, they were up and moving again. Ramanujam had cut off part of her sari, slit it into strips and used them as bandages to bind the clean leaves to make bootees for her feet. They made much better progress with Ramanujam supporting her, until abruptly they walked straight into a tented camp. Aruna felt a cold chill of shock at the sight of men armed with rifles and machine-guns.

'You are police, aren't you?' said Ramanujam, addressing a senior man who came out of one of the tents to stand before them.

'No,' he said.

Aruna and Ramanujam exchanged glances and Aruna's grip tightened on his fingers.

'We are the Greyhounds.'

Ramanujam's body sagged in relief. It was only then that Aruna realised how tense he had been – how tense they both had been.

'My name is Ramanujam and this is my wife, Aruna. I am a doctor at the Vizag district hospital. We've just escaped from Naxalites.'

The man's eyes widened momentarily and he quickly ushered them into the commander's tent.

'Aruna! Are you the lady who sent the message with the location?'

'Yes. But somehow the Naxalites found out about it and they moved us.'

The officer nodded grimly. 'We were in the Nallamalai forests at the time, so the police got there as soon as they could and they found your phone. Both we and the police have been combing the area since then, trying to locate you. But shouldn't there be more of you? Where are the others?'

'We're the only ones who've managed to escape. The others are still captive.'

'We had better go after them quickly. Do you know where they are being held?'

Aruna shook her head. 'I have no idea,' she said. 'We walked for hours going this way and that last night. They could be anywhere in this forest.'

Ramanujam smiled and said, 'I know almost exactly where the camp is.'

Aruna and the Greyhound officer looked at him in astonishment. 'Where?'

'If you go upstream about three miles, you will see that the river has a kink, going round a big rock. Just on the other side of the rock, there is a tree that seems to stand almost by itself. You can't miss it. It has great aerial roots that straddle the stream. On that banyan tree, I've carved an arrow towards the spot where we made a camp last night.'

Aruna blushed but neither man noticed. The officer was now writing down Ramanujam's words. Having caught up, he nodded to Ramanujam to continue.

'From there, go straight south for about six miles until you can see two hills on either side of you. The camp is by the base of the left-hand peak.'

Surprised, Aruna asked, 'How do you know that? It was dark and we were pretty blind.' Not to mention terrified, she thought.

'I was scared that we would make a big circle and end up in the guerrillas' hands again. So, I followed the Pole Star and I know we were walking for almost three hours by how much the Ursa Major, the Great Bear, moved in the sky.'

'Oh!' said Aruna, at a loss for what to say. 'How do you know these things?'

Ramanujam grinned. 'Only some of the times I left the hostel at night were to meet girls, remember,' he said.

The officer clapped Ramanujam on the shoulder. 'Shabhash!' he said. 'This is fantastic information.' He poked his head out of the tent. 'Break camp, boys. We are leaving in ten minutes.'

He turned back to the couple. 'We'll move faster without you. Also, it will be dangerous once we find them. The Naxalites are armed and we have to be careful because of the hostages, while they can fire indiscriminately. A couple of my men will remain here to protect you. And if we need to, we can get in touch with you on our radio.'

'One other thing,' said Ramanujam. 'Please don't make this news public yet. The Naxalites seem to have informants among the police. I think that's how they found out about Aruna's text message.'

The officer nodded. 'That's what my senior officers and I were thinking. You've given us very detailed information, so we'll rely on speed and surprise. But it means that you cannot call your families to let them know either.'

The couple nodded. While they were anxious to assure their parents that they were safe, it was the least they could do for their friends who had all helped them to escape and then remained behind to provide cover.

'Let's go, men.'

Aruna dropped to her knees and prayed for the success of the mission.

The phone rang in the old bungalow, making both the women jump in surprise. They went quickly into the living room. Mrs Bilqis picked up the receiver, listened for a moment and fainted on to the sofa, still clutching the phone.

'What—' said Nadira. She removed the phone from her friend's hand and put it to her ear.

'Hello, hello . . .' said a male voice.

'Dilawar?' shouted Nadira. 'Is that you?'

'Who? Nadira Aunty. What happened to ammi-jaan? Why isn't she answering?'

'What . . . Ya, Allah!'

'We've been freed by commandos. We are all fine. I can't talk for long. The others are waiting for their turn to speak. We'll be in town in a few hours.'

Nadira put the phone down. This was not the time to tell him about his father. She called the maid and together they splashed cool water on Mrs Bilqis's face, reviving her.

'I had a dream,' she said. 'I dreamed that my son was coming home.'

'It was not a dream, silly. You almost gave me a heart attack, collapsing like that. Dilawar and the others have been freed. Your son will be back home in hours.'

Mrs Bilqis jumped up. 'Come on, let's prepare a feast for Dilawar.'

Their eyes met and Mrs Bilqis slowly sat down again. This was now a house in mourning and no food could be cooked in it for several days. The household would have to rely on the community around to feed them.

Mrs Bilqis took off her black bead necklace, the traditional sign of marriage among Muslim women. Hers had finally ended. She then started to remove the gold bangle from her right hand, which was more difficult as it would not pass easily over her wrist. As a widow, she could no longer wear jewellery. The maid looked at her in astonishment and exclaimed, 'Madam, what are you doing?' Realisation must have struck her, because she said, 'Oh!' and rushed to the master's room.

Mrs Bilqis laid the bangle on the coffee table in front of her and turned to Nadira, surprised to see tears in her friend's eyes.

'Don't be sad, Nadira,' she said. 'My marriage finished years ago. Today was just another step on the way. Your Baba's prayers were effective, after all. I got my son back.'

Nadira shook her head. 'Yes, but at what cost?'

The ringing of the doorbell broke the silence in the Ali household. Mr Ali went to the verandah and opened the gate to a middle-aged man in a branded T-shirt that was too tight around his paunch, trousers and white sneakers.

'I want to join the marriage bureau for my son.'

'Sorry, sir,' said Mr Ali. 'The office is closed now.'

'When I called you last week, I was told that it was open from nine till twelve in the morning.'

'Yes, sir. That is normally the case. I apologise for any inconvenience, but we have some personal problems at the moment. We are closed until further notice.'

The man clicked his tongue. 'That is the problem with India,' he said. 'Everything is personal; there is no professionalism. I have just come back from America. My son works there, you know. It is not like this in those advanced countries. If a shop says that it opens at nine, it opens at nine. No excuses. If you invite somebody over for six o'clock, they come at six – not an hour and a half later. In fact, the only people in America who are not punctual are those who have moved there from here. It seems that they can leave India, but India cannot leave them.'

'This is not America, sir. And right now the marriage bureau is closed. I am sorry.'

'Rehmaaan . . . .' came a yell from inside. Mr Ali rudely closed the gate and rushed into the house.

Mrs Ali was sitting on the sofa, holding the phone and hyperventilating. Her brother Azhar and Pari were hovering around her, almost dancing with excitement.

'What happened?' asked Mr Ali.

Pari hugged Mr Ali, much to his discomfort. He was not used to physical displays of affection. She shouted, 'He is free! He is free!'

He disengaged himself gently. 'Rehman? How? What about Aruna? And Dilawar?'

A shadow passed over Pari's face. 'I don't know.'

Mr Ali looked at his wife. Without speaking and with tears streaming down her cheeks, she passed him the phone.

'Hello,' he said.

'Abba, it's Rehman. The Greyhounds stormed the Naxalite camp and rescued me and Dilawar. We will be back in town in a few hours.'

'And Aruna?'

'Oh! She and Ramanujam escaped earlier. In fact, they contacted the commandos and told them where to find us. We are all fine. One commando was shot in the leg, but they say that it is just a flesh wound.'

Mrs Ali grabbed the phone from her husband and started speaking to her son.

'You know something, ammi?' said Rehman. 'The leader of the commandos says it was crows that helped his men find us.'

'Crows?'

'Yes. He says that Ramanujam gave them very detailed directions, but because of the thick jungle they would have missed us even if they had gone just a hundred yards past us. But the guerrillas had got hold of a goat last night and roasted it over a fire. In the morning the bones and remaining meat attracted a large number of crows. It was their loud fighting over the scraps that gave the campsite away and also covered the noise of the soldiers while they got into position. I'll have to go now. I will see you all very soon.'

Mrs Ali put down the phone reluctantly.

'What was that about crows?' said her brother, Azhar.

Mrs Ali told him what Rehman had said.

'Subhan 'Allah,' said Azhar. Glory be to God. 'Last Friday, the imam at the mosque quoted a verse from the Quran in his sermon: *There is not an animal that lives on the earth, nor a being that flies on its wings, but forms part of communities like you. Nothing have we omitted from the Book, and they all shall be gathered to their Lord in the end.*'

'Truly,' said Mrs Ali. 'Everything is from the Lord and everything will go back to Him.' She was silent for a moment. 'But still, crows . . . Couldn't Allah have chosen a more . . . *suitable* bird?'

The car screeched to a halt beside the long row of scooters and motorbikes parked along the yellow temple wall.

'We two, our one,' declared a poster pasted there, but the man, in crisp white clothes, who leaped out of the passenger seat was too old for the family planning message. When he had been younger, the message had been, 'We two, our two.'

He ran as fast as he could through the wide wooden door and, pausing only to take off his shoes, climbed the steps where devotees were packed together on the hard, cool granite floor. Aruna's father looked up and saw the man looking around as if lost. Aruna's father got up, wincing at the pain in his knees and, for the first time in his life, broke the decorum of a temple.

'Viyyankulu-gaaru, daughter's father-in-law, why are you here? What happened?'

The old man, Ramanujam's father, saw him and smiled widely. 'Good news, sir. The children are free. They are coming home in a couple of hours.'

The devotees in the temple had stopped chanting, surprised at the sight of the two dignified men shouting across to one another. On hearing the news, they burst into a spontaneous cheer. A path was created for Aruna's father-in-law as the people sitting on the floor shuffled aside and he made his way forward. Aruna's father-in-law greeted him with a hug.

'These people have all been praying for our children,' he said.

Ramanujam's father turned to the crowd. 'My friends, our prayers have been answered. I have just spoken to my son and daughter-in-law. Their friends are safe too. They are on their way back now. Thank you. I am sure your prayers kept them safe while the police rescued our children.'

He looked sideways at the idol of Hanuman – with the body of a man, but the face and tail of a monkey. Ramanujam's father's eyes widened, as if seeing it for the first time. He made a deep and long obeisance before rising and turning back to the people with tears in his eyes.

'My son tells me that when they couldn't walk in the forest any longer, an old monkey reminded him that he was a doctor who knew how to make bandages.'

There was a stunned silence for a moment and then the devotees erupted. The girl, Anu, stood up and rang the temple bell loudly.

The priest, DK, raised a conch shell to his lips to produce a loud, primordial 'Om . . .'

'Hanuman ki . . .' somebody shouted over the noise.

'Jai,' came the victorious affirmation from the crowd.

DK put the conch shell away. 'Say it again for Lord Hanuman, devotee of Lord Rama.'

'Hanuman ki jai,' went up the shout. The bell tolled. The honking of the traffic outside added to the celebratory din.

# CHAPTER TWENTY-ONE

The tiny room was starting to irritate Pari intensely. It was like living in a hotel – but having to run a kitchen too, in the corner.

Before coming to Vizag, she had lived in a village with her parents. Later, she had lived in a small town with her husband. In both those places, her houses had been big with multiple rooms, a separate kitchen and a backyard with a garden. She had been so looking forward to moving into a two-bedroom flat and still could not believe that, because of the malice of one person, she had been thwarted at the last minute. And not only that, her reputation and that of Rehman had been called into question. It was really good of chaacha and chaachi to ignore the talk and still allow her into their house, even if it meant their son, Rehman, having to leave home and find another place to stay. In the last few days all this had been forgotten in the excitement of everybody returning safe and sound, but there was no doubt that the matter would raise its head again.

Now that Aruna was back, Pari's temporary job at the marriage bureau had come to an end too. She really had to find some work soon. Mr and Mrs Ali's comments that her

inherited money would not last for ever were beginning to
worry her and she was also getting bored with being idle.
Since Vasu had started going to school, time dragged heavily
in the confined space, especially because she did not want to
spend too much time with the Alis when Rehman was
around.

Her mobile phone rang and she fished it out of her handbag. The number was familiar but she couldn't immediately
place it.

'Hello.'

'Pari, it is Mrs Bilqis here. Have you got a moment?'

'Of course, madam. What can I do for you?'

'I have been thinking about your wedding. Now that
Dilawar has come back safely, I think we should go ahead
with it as soon as possible.'

Pari was surprised. Just a few days ago she had gone to Mrs
Bilqis's house with Mrs Ali, taking food, because of Dilawar's
father's death.

'Are you sure, madam?' she asked delicately. 'Under the
circumstances . . .'

'Oh, Pari,' said Mrs Bilqis. Pari could hear a sigh in the elegant woman's voice. 'Life has to go on. I am sure you know
that. But I think it should be a simple ceremony. We'll just call
a few family members and friends and have a small wedding – not more than fifty or sixty people.'

Pari thought back to her first wedding. It had been a grand
affair – with almost fifteen hundred guests and the ceremonies
had lasted three full days. A whole host of relatives and workers had descended on the house in the village, weeks before
the date, organising everything – constructing the marquees
from palm-tree trunks and fronds; finding chickens and lambs
for the meat; sourcing kilograms of ghee, quintals of rice,
mountains of onions and myriad spices for the biryani;

tracking down chairs, tables, saris and jewellery for the trousseau, and God knows what else. Pari certainly didn't know because she had been merely the bride, just a spectator, the calm eye in the whirlwind of activity round her, not allowed to help out in anything because she *was* the bride. She had been shocked by the amount of money that her father had spent, peeling off notes every few minutes from a big roll that never seemed exhausted. 'Abbu,' she had asked, 'why are you spending so much?'

'My princess deserves the best,' he had replied, before being distracted by the marquee-maker saying they were short of palm leaves. Several more notes had been stripped off the roll.

She certainly did not want a big wedding this time round. As far as she was concerned, the simpler the better. The last time, she had left her parental house with tears in her eyes but a song in her heart. She had been scared, both of leaving her father's home and of the mysterious wifely duty that she would have to perform for her husband – something that the married women round her would only giggle at and talk about in ways that made no sense. But married life was still an adventure that she looked forward to and her husband had been everything that a bride could dream of.

Marriages are made in heaven, her father had told her on the eve of the wedding. When Allah made a creature, He also made the creature's mate. Pari, the young Pari, had believed it. After all, her parents had been together, very happily, for a long time. The chances of any of her uncles and aunts ending up with their particular partners seemed pretty low too, but it seemed inconceivable to her that they could have spent their lives with anybody else.

This time round, married life did not hold any secrets, especially *that*, and there would be no tears in her eyes. Her heart would be a different matter. It belonged to Rehman and that in itself was wrong. He had no place in it. This marriage was the safest way to remain faithful to her dead husband. She would be the ideal wife for Dilawar, she decided. Because she could not give him her heart, she would make sure that he lacked nothing else. You were wrong, abbu, she thought. Not all marriages are made in heaven. Some, probably most, are constructed right here on earth, for any number of reasons.

'Pari, are you there?' came the voice on the telephone.

'Er . . . Sorry, madam. Of course, a simple ceremony is fine by me. In fact, even fifty guests are too many.'

'Arre beta,' said Mrs Bilqis, using an endearment to address Pari for the first time. 'I tried to reduce it but that is the minimum number I have to invite. Otherwise, there will be serious problems for me later on. As it is, many people will have their noses put out of joint that they weren't invited.'

'All right, madam. I am sure you know best,' said Pari.

'One more thing, Pari,' said Mrs Bilqis.

To Pari's surprise, the older lady sounded embarrassed. 'Yes, madam.'

'Dilawar wants to meet you again before the wedding. Will this evening be fine?'

'We've already met . . .'

'That's exactly what I said. I tried to talk him out of it, but he is adamant. Just humour him please, for my sake. It is at our place, so Nadira and I will also be there.'

'Of course, madam. That's not a problem. I'll have to leave Vasu with chaachi but I am sure that will be fine.'

'Thank you, dear.'

That evening, Pari was shown into the Bilqis house by the maid. The sun had not yet set and it felt good to get out of the heat. She was surprised to find Rehman there.

'What are you doing here?' she asked.

'Good afternoon to you too,' he replied.

Pari blushed. 'Sorry,' she said.

Rehman smiled. 'Dilawar asked me to come over.'

'Oh, his mother called me.'

The maid brought a glass of water for Rehman and asked Pari what she wanted. The two young people both sat stiffly on sofas opposite each other. Ever since that accusation about improper behaviour, Pari did not know how to act with Rehman. She had become self-conscious about the fact that she was in love with him and had to hide it.

Pari looked around the room curiously. It was elegantly decorated with items that spoke of old wealth. It would certainly be a big change from her cramped room, but that thought only depressed her. She felt none of the nervous butterflies and stomach tightening that she had when anticipating life with her first husband. She wondered whether it was because she had already been through that process once and it held no more mysteries for her. Yet she felt those same butterflies at the thought of spending time with Rehman – which didn't make sense.

A photograph of Dilawar's father hung on one wall, showing him when young and fit. He was sitting on a horse, with the sun on his face and smiling broadly. Pari imagined what it must have been like to be cut down in his prime and spend the next two decades in bed. If Mr Ali was right, and she had no reason to doubt it, Pari's own father had wanted to end his life within months of suffering the stroke that had laid him low. At the time he had already been much older than Dilawar's father and had lost interest in life after his wife had died. She shuddered. She would prefer to die than be helpless like that, she thought.

Rehman eyed her with concern. 'Are you cold?' he asked.

Pari shook her head and made a small sign, pointing to the photograph of Dilawar's father. He nodded in understanding.

Mrs Bilqis's friend, Nadira, came in and sat down next to Pari. Dabbing the sweat from her forehead with a tiny handkerchief that looked incongruous in her chubby hands, she said, 'I swear that the weather keeps getting hotter every year.'

Dilawar and his mother entered the living room and a volley of salaams followed.

'Sorry to keep you waiting,' said Mrs Bilqis.

The maid came in with tea and Mrs Bilqis fell silent. Once the maid left, Mrs Bilqis continued, 'I don't want to delay the wedding. I know that we are in a period of mourning but I am sure that Dilawar's father would have wanted us to carry on as normal.'

Nadira nodded. 'Did you know that Dilawar and his father are descended from the Mughal emperors?'

'No,' said Pari, slightly mystified by Nadira's going off at such a tangent. 'But I am not surprised.'

'When Babur finally conquered Delhi and established the Mughal dynasty after a lifetime of wandering stateless, he could have expected to rule for a long time. He was a healthy man with a zest for life, after all. But barely four years after Dilawar's ancestor had started ruling Delhi, his favourite son and heir, Humayun, fell ill. He got worse by the day and finally the physicians gave up. In desperation, the emperor circled Humayun's bed three times and prayed to Allah, offering his life in exchange for his son's. It must have worked, because almost from that day Humayun started improving, while Babur fell ill and took to his bed. Humayun recovered and his father died soon after.'

Rehman nodded. 'I remember reading that in our history lessons.'

Nadira continued, 'We did not tell Dilawar's father about

your kidnapping, but we couldn't keep it from him. He saw the news on television and he died, at almost the same time as you were being rescued. I have no doubt in my mind that, just like his ancestor, he offered an exchange that Allah, for reasons of His own, was willing to accept.'

Rehman and Pari nodded, not knowing what to say.

Nadira looked at each of them and said to Dilawar, 'We should not waste your father's sacrifice by delaying this wedding. Our elders have said that we should do today what we would do tomorrow and should do now what we would do today.'

Mrs Bilqis smiled at her friend and turned to Pari. 'Obviously we must have a simple ceremony. I was thinking that we should have just a nikah, the wedding itself, and not the valima, the reception. What do you say?'

'That's fine by me, madam.'

'Right, I have prepared a guest list. Have a look and tell me whether there is anybody else you would like to invite.'

Pari took the sheet of paper that Mrs Bilqis held out, glanced through the names and handed it to Rehman. Turning to Mrs Bilqis, she said, 'We really should discuss this with Rehman's parents. I will be guided by them in all these matters.'

Mrs Bilqis nodded. 'All right, I will do that. I also thought that because it is going to be such a small wedding, we could have the nikah in our house. I know that traditionally the wedding is held in the bride's house and the reception in the groom's, but since we are not having the reception, I thought we could bend the custom slightly. What do you say?'

Pari said, 'If chaacha and chaachi have no objection, then I don't have a problem with it either. On the face of it, it seems like a sound idea.'

Turning to Dilawar, she added, 'When we met the last time, I said that I would prefer to live in Vizag for a year or two after the wedding, so that Vasu had time to adjust to his new life before making the jump to a big metropolis like Mumbai. I've changed my mind. If you want me to come with you to Mumbai as soon as we are married, then that's what I will do. I am sure that a young boy like Vasu will fit in somehow.'

Rehman looked at Pari in surprise. She hadn't told him that. He wondered why he felt so unhappy about it. After all, ever since this proposal had been made, it was clear that Pari would leave Vizag and move far away.

Mrs Bilqis said, 'I've also picked out some dates for the wedding. The earliest one is next Friday, before the Jumma prayers and the final one is three weeks from now.'

'So soon?' said Rehman, before Pari could say anything.

'If we can do it while Dilawar is in town, that's all the better, isn't it?'

Rehman nodded. 'I suppose so.'

Mrs Bilqis opened the drawer next to her and took out an envelope. 'What do you think of this design for the invitation cards?'

Dilawar threw up his hands and said, 'Wow, this is really going very fast.'

He stood and paced up and down the room several times, furrowing his brow and rubbing his chin. Everyone in the room wondered what was going on in his mind. As he turned towards them at the far end of the room, his face was right next to his father's and grandfather's portraits and Pari realised how closely he resembled them. He had the same features: strong chin, the long, aquiline nose, the fair skin, broad neck and full lips. It seemed that their family bred handsome sons. Only Dilawar's eyes were different. He had inherited his mother's elongated eyes and thick lashes, giving his face a softer look than that of his ancestors.

Coming to a halt in front of them, he said, 'I don't think we should have this wedding.'

'If that's what you felt, Dilawar, you should have told me. I would have put it off for a bit. After all, the past couple of weeks have been very intense, what with your adventure and your father's death.'

'I didn't say that I wanted to delay the wedding, ammi-jaan. I said that we shouldn't have this wedding at all.' Dilawar turned to Pari. 'I am sorry, Pari. I've led you on and I apologise for that. You are entitled to be angry with me, but listen to me fully and, if you can, please forgive me.'

Dilawar looked away from them for a moment, seeming to stare at something out of the window. He turned back to them and faced his mother. 'Ammi-jaan,' he said, 'I don't like girls.'

'Nonsense,' said Mrs Bilqis. 'You get along very well with Nadira's daughter. You said you liked Pari. Over the years, so many of your female classmates and cousins have told me that you really seem to understand them and genuinely like them.'

'Not that way, ammi-jaan. I like girls as friends, certainly. I just don't want to marry a woman.'

'What do you mean, you don't want to marry a woman? Who else would you marry? A cat? Or a boy?' She laughed at her own witticism and then stopped when nobody else responded.

Dilawar kneeled down in front of her and took her hand. 'I think you have always known, ammi-jaan. I am gay. I don't find girls attractive in that way.'

His mother pushed his hand away. 'Don't be silly,' she said, laughing shrilly. 'It is just a phase you are going through. If you marry a nice girl like Pari, you will be cured. Though I don't know whether she will marry you, now that you've revealed your disgusting perversion.'

'Even if I grant you that being gay is a perversion of every animal's natural desire to procreate, it is no more disgusting than sex between a man and a woman, if you think about it. And it was not nice of us to keep a big secret like this from Pari and lure her into a marriage, was it? Some people might call it cheating.'

Mrs Bilqis drew herself up even straighter than usual and looked away from her son.

'Ammi-jaan, there is no *cure*, as you call it, for my condition. I am gay.' Turning to Rehman and Pari, he told them, 'I wanted you to hear it too. That's why I called you both over.' He faced his mother again. 'It defines me, in the same way that being a woman defines you or Pari. I can hide it; I can push it into a far corner of my mind and marry a woman. I might even be able to have children. But I will never be happy and I will never be able to truly love my wife, so she will not be happy either. Is that what you want for me?'

'At least you won't be committing a sin. Remember what the Quran says: *If two men among you are guilty of lewdness, punish them both. If they repent and amend, leave them alone; for Allah is Oft-Returning, Most Merciful.*'

Mrs Bilqis put a hand on his head and continued, 'Whatever you have done so far has been in the passion of youth. Change your habits now and, as the Quran promises, you will be forgiven.'

'Ammi-jaan, I don't really believe in God. I think we have one life here on earth and we have to live it in the best way that we can.'

Mrs Bilqis turned to her friend. 'Nadira, a spirit, a djinn, has taken possession of him. Does your Baba have an amulet to exorcise him?'

Dilawar replied before Nadira could answer. 'There are no spirits, Ammi-jaan. When I was a child, you used to say that

Allah is aware of the path of every single ant in this creation. Do you think He is unaware of what I am? If you believe in God, then who do you think created me as I am? Maybe in places like London being gay is accepted and taken as normal, but here, to be gay is to be afraid. Afraid of exposure and dismissal from your job; scared of losing family and friends; forced to skulk on dark street corners and face the danger of physical assault. When we were kidnapped by Naxalites, the police searched for us and fought to free us. If I was beaten up in a gay encounter, I would not even dare to go to the police. Until a few days ago, I would probably have been thrown into a cell and blackmailed by the police themselves. This is not a lifestyle choice that I am making. I want to be like everybody else: wake up in the morning, go to the office, come home in the evening to a loved one and be happy. Instead, what do I face? Stares, sniggers, petty police extortion . . . I don't do this for fun or to be lewd,' said Dilawar. Rising from his knees, he stood tall before them. 'No, I do this because I am made like this. I can no more stop myself from being attracted to a man than a young woman can stop cooing and becoming broody when she sees a bonny baby.'

Mrs Bilqis gave a sob and Nadira hugged her. Dilawar turned away and stood facing the window. Pari looked, embarrassed, at Rehman. He shook his head slightly and going up to Dilawar, patted him on the shoulder.

'That was very brave of you,' he said.

Dilawar turned towards Rehman, his eyes shining. 'Thank you,' he said. 'I thought you might not want to touch me now that you know I am gay.'

Rehman smiled. 'You haven't suddenly turned into a high-voltage electricity line that I cannot touch you,' he said. 'You are a good man today, the same as you were yesterday.'

Dilawar shook his head. 'Not many people think like you,

my friend. I myself kicked out Shaan, the man I loved most dearly, when people started making comments.'

Pari came up to them and said to Dilawar, 'Can I have a word with you in private?'

'Of course.'

Rehman excused himself, while Dilawar took Pari out into the garden.

He said, 'Are you angry with me?'

Pari shook her head. 'No. But if it is easier for you and will help you, we can still get married.'

Dilawar looked at her in surprise. 'But—'

'I won't interfere with your life. I already have a son and don't need any more children.'

'But why?'

'I have a secret too. I am in love with a man I cannot marry. It might be less trouble for both of us if we are together. We can each—'

Dilawar interrupted her. 'Sorry, Pari. Two people hiding their truths do not a marriage make. Why can't you marry the man you love anyway?'

'How can I love somebody else without betraying my beloved husband?'

Dilawar took Pari's right hand in both of his. 'Pari, Pari . . .' he said gently. 'You loved your husband. You will always love him. You will not be unfaithful to him by finding happiness elsewhere now that he is no more.'

Pari shook her head, unconvinced.

'Did your husband truly love you as much as you loved him?'

Pari gazed into his eyes. She had to tip her head back to do so. 'Of course,' she said simply.

'Then he will not have wanted you to live a desolate life by yourself. You are a young woman. Do you think his soul will be peaceful when he looks down on you from heaven and sees you lonely and sad?'

'No, but—'

'He will rejoice if you are happy.'

'I am not sure . . .'

'I am certain,' he said.

Pari turned to go inside once more. Dilawar took hold of the edge of her sari as it fluttered towards him on the breeze. She stopped when she felt the cloth tightening around her.

'There is no reason why you cannot marry Rehman,' he said softly.

She turned swiftly back to him. 'What?' she said, shocked.

'You are in love with Rehman, aren't you?'

She nodded. 'How did you know?'

'Apparently, all women in London want a gay man-friend, precisely because we know these things.'

'He is in love with Usha, the TV journalist. They were engaged to be married before she broke it off and he still pines for her.'

Dilawar smiled. 'He might *think* he is in love with some-body else. But I can put my hand on my heart and guarantee to you that he actually loves you.'

'What kind of love is it when he doesn't even know about it?'

'I loved Shaan too, but I still paid more attention to com-ments from people whom I don't even know. Rehman's love for you is just under the surface. One small pinprick from you and it will be exposed.'

'I am not sure that I can do it.'

'What is that quote in *Hamlet* about not doubting your love?' he asked.

'*Doubt thou the stars are fire; Doubt that the sun doth move; Doubt truth to be a liar; But never doubt I love,*' she quoted unfailingly.

'Exactly,' said Dilawar. 'Love can move mountains. You only have to get him to reveal to himself a truth that already exists. Of course you can do it.'

'And what about you?' said Pari. 'Why should I follow your advice if you yourself don't believe in it?'

Dilawar looked at her, shocked, for a moment. 'You are right,' he said softly. 'I have to be brave and show Shaan that I am worthy of his love.' He gazed into her eyes and smiled. 'Thank you, friend, for showing me what to do.'

Pari smiled back at him. 'You are a brave man. You showed that in the forest and now in your own house.'

She turned to go, but he stopped her again. 'I was really looking forward to being a good father to Vasu. I am sorry that can't happen now. But can I continue to be involved in his life?'

'Of course,' she said quickly. 'You will always be his special Bombay-uncle. The rich, slightly disreputable one who shows him the ways of the big, bad world.'

Another smile lit up his face and it was he who turned away. 'Thank you,' he said and he sounded as if he were choking up.

# CHAPTER TWENTY-TWO

In the past week, dark monsoon clouds had rolled in over the Bay of Bengal, and the weather had gone from searing to merely boiling. There had been a few showers, but more rains were needed to break summer's fevered grip.

It was five in the evening and Mrs Ali stood at the gate watching the world go past. She had just watered the plants from the well in the front yard. The rains had raised the water level and even though it was still very early in the rainy season, Mrs Ali felt confident that the well was safe from running dry for another year.

A thin, wiry man in his thirties walked up to her. He was wearing a shirt that appeared to be new, but he had an old panchi wrapped around his waist and a towel around his head like a villager. Mrs Ali noticed that he was wearing brand new flip-flops with blue rubber straps, even though his feet appeared rough, as if he had been walking barefoot all his life. 'Namaste, amma!' he said, raising his hand to his forehead in a respectful greeting. 'Do you need fresh milk? I can arrange for a buffalo to come here daily and milk it for you, madam.'

Mrs Ali was tempted. There was something satisfying about warm milk from a lowing buffalo that was lost when it was delivered in a chilled packet. And it brought back memories of the time when she had been younger and Rehman had been a growing boy, when they used to get their milk in just such a fashion. But then she reconsidered and shook her head. Full-fat milk was very rich and none of them needed it now – in fact, the doctor was always urging her to lose weight and she was sure it wasn't good for her husband or Rehman either. 'We don't need it,' she said.

'No problem, amma. My four buffalos are almost booked up anyway. I just need one or two more houses.'

'Four?' said Mrs Ali and raised her eyebrows. 'You are a rich man!'

The man laughed. 'May your mouth always speak the truth, amma. I am just leasing the buffalos from a farmer. My name is Sivudu. I've recently moved here from my village and, by God's grace, things are going well so far. My daughter is even going to school.'

A plump woman came towards them, walking with a waddle that spoke of years of easy living. 'Namaste,' she said to Mrs Ali, and turned to Sivudu. 'Did I hear you right? Can I get fresh milk in this city? My grandchildren think it comes from a *plastic* sachet and not from buffalos or cows.' She patted her forehead with a handkerchief. 'We live on the second floor next door. Go upstairs and tell the lady there that I sent you.'

Sivudu nodded and left, his flip-flops flapping.

'I moved in recently with my son and his family,' the woman said. 'I heard that your son was kidnapped by the Naxalites.'

Mrs Ali had never seen her before. 'Yes,' said Mrs Ali. 'It was very worrying at that time, but it has been almost a month now and we are just trying to forget the whole thing.'

Mrs Ali did not ask how the lady knew about Rehman's adventure. She would have been more surprised if there was somebody in the neighbourhood who had not heard of it.

'Where are you from?' she asked.

'We are originally from Guntur district,' said the lady. 'But we were transferred from city to city while my husband was in service. Now that my husband is no more, I left our ancestral house in the village and have come here to be with my son.'

'What else are children for, if not to look after their parents in their old age?' said Mrs Ali.

The old lady sighed. 'That's what I have always believed and I looked after my own mother-in-law but youngsters nowadays don't have the same sense of duty.'

This tickled Mrs Ali's ear for gossip. There was surely a story here.

'Oh,' she said. 'Is your daughter-in-law giving you trouble?'

'As soon as I came, she left the kitchen to me entirely. I have to cook all three meals every day. Then she complains that I use too much oil and make the food too spicy. I don't know what kind of bland food she was used to, but my son is so thin and my grandson is so fussy about food.'

Mrs Ali nodded in understanding.

The old lady continued, 'You have a lovely house here. I am not used to living in a flat, you see. Everything is so cramped. I like to have a basil plant growing out the front so that after my prayers I can water it. How can you do that if you are two floors above the ground? And my daughter-in-law gets angry if I ring the bell when I pray in the morning.'

'Yes, I can see that it is difficult. You still seem quite healthy. Why don't you go back to your house in the village? I am sure that you could hire a servant to help you. The children will respect you more when you are independent and they will treat you better.'

'You are right,' said the old lady. 'I've been thinking about it myself, to be honest.'

The maid Leela came down the road just then for the evening

shift. Seeing the two ladies together, she said, 'Did you know each other?'

Mrs Ali said, 'No, not really. I was just standing here and this lady was good enough to ask after my son.'

'She is the mother-in-law of the lady in the second-floor flat where I work,' Leela said, pointing next door.

'Oh!' said Mrs Ali, understanding. 'You are from *that* household. Is your daughter-in-law's name Swaroop?'

'Yes.'

It was the very flat where Leela had to work before going to Mrs Ali's house, causing such disruption to her morning routine. It was also Swaroop who had made those accusations against Rehman and Pari.

Mrs Ali turned to the old lady. 'Please come inside. Why are you standing by the doorstep like a stranger?'

The two women went through the verandah, where Aruna and Mr Ali were busy working, and into the living room.

'Would you like tea or coffee?'

Leela was surprised, but it wasn't her place to comment on what her mistresses did.

A few minutes later, the two ladies were sipping tea.

'I am not one to gossip,' said Mrs Ali. 'But have you noticed that your daughter-in-law keeps meeting her friends for, what do you call them . . . yes, kitty parties?'

'Yes,' said Mrs Raji, for that was her name. 'Yesterday so many women came over and they were eating and drinking all afternoon. It disturbed my siesta.'

'Some of these modern women do that. They get into these competitions about who has spent the most on a holiday or who has the best car and so on. And then they nag their husbands until they give in and spend the money.'

'It was not like that in our days,' said Mrs Raji. 'We met

only our neighbours or family members and we used to talk about how to save money, not how to spend it.'

'Exactly,' said Mrs Ali. 'But we cannot really blame them. They watch television and movies and get influenced by what they see. It is up to us, as elders, to guide them on to the right path.'

Mrs Raji sighed. 'That is easier said than done. My daughter-in-law refuses to listen to me. How can I guide her in anything?'

'It is not easy. But they say that anything worthwhile takes time to achieve. How long have you been here?'

'About a month.'

'See, that's not enough. You are talking about habits that have been established over years. How can you change them in days?'

'There is something in what you say.'

'Of course there is. It will mean difficulties for you. Instead of living a quiet life in your own house, you will have to put up with your daughter-in-law's tantrums as well as cook for the whole family. It is totally necessary for the sake of your son and your grandchildren.'

'Yes, but—'

'I totally understand if, at your age, you think that your son and his family will have to manage by themselves, make their own mistakes and do the best they can. After all, you have worked yourself to the bone over the years and now you deserve a calm, retired life.'

'There is no retirement for a woman when her family's future is at stake.'

'Spoken like a true Indian mother,' said Mrs Ali, taking a delicate sip from her cup. 'If you ever feel the need for some relaxation, drop in for tea and a chat.'

Pari and Vasu were the first people to arrive. Rehman came out, lifted Vasu up in the air and put him down again.

'Oof,' he said. 'You are becoming too heavy for this game. Your mummy has been feeding you well, I think.'

'Rehman Uncle, why was the ancient Egyptian boy confused?'

Rehman looked at Pari, who rolled her eyes. He turned back to Vasu and said, 'I don't know. Why?'

'Because his daddy was a mummy.'

Rehman laughed. Pari said, 'That's what he learned in school today.'

'It's good to see that your school fees are going towards something useful,' said Rehman.

Vasu went inside, leaving Pari and Rehman alone in the front yard.

'I've heard from Shaan. He and Dilawar are getting back together again, though Dilawar doesn't know it yet. Shaan is planning to tell him after the Mumbai Gay Pride march tomorrow,' he said quietly.

'What?' said Pari. 'You are truly a man who gives grave news coolly and without emotion. How do you even know Shaan?'

'I came across him when I was contacting various NGOs about the contract farming business.'

'Wow!' said Pari. 'What do you think Dilawar will say?'

'I am sure he'll start crying,' said Rehman and laughed.

'You and your stereotypes,' she said, shaking her head. 'By the way, Dilawar called me the other day.'

'Oh!' said Rehman. He couldn't help feeling surprised and just a bit put out. 'What did he want?'

'He invited me and Vasu to Mumbai. What do you think? Should we go?'

'Do you want to go?'

'I think it will be good for Vasu to see more of the world and get to know Dilawar better as well.'

'What's the point of Vasu and Dilawar getting close?

Dilawar lives far away and we are all here to look after Vasu, aren't we?'

Pari looked at Rehman oddly. 'Are you jealous of Dilawar wanting to be involved in Vasu's life?'

Rehman shrugged. 'Of course I'm not jealous. Why would I be?'

She shook her head. 'Don't you know that it is impossible for anybody to have too much love? Yes, Vasu has me and you and chaachi and chaacha. That does not mean he cannot also have the affection and support of Dilawar. Love is not like water to a plant that too much of it rots the roots.'

'Was that Shakespeare?' he asked.

'No, you idiot,' she said. 'That was me.'

They both grinned happily. Mrs Ali called from the house and they went inside, smiling.


Ramanujam and Aruna joined the gathering soon after.

'Both of you are looking very smart,' said Mrs Ali, when she saw them. Ramanujam was wearing a formal shirt and trousers, while Aruna had put on a dark-mauve silk sari with a pale-lavender border. Apart from the obligatory mangalasutram, her jewellery included a gold necklace studded with rubies and ear studs with a central diamond surrounded by nine rubies.

'Thank you, madam,' said Aruna. The light caught the diamond on one of her ears.

'I haven't seen this set before on you,' said Mrs Ali, leaning forward for a closer look. 'Are they new?'

'Yes,' said Aruna. She glanced at her husband. 'He bought them for me after we got back to town.'

Pari came closer as well and the two ladies examined Aruna's jewellery with many exclamations of delight.

Vasu said, 'This is boring. When are we eating?'

Pari turned to him with a frown. 'Shh . . .' she said. 'Don't be rude.'

Rehman said to Vasu, 'You'll never get a wife if you talk like that. Come on, let's go into the front yard and stop you from getting into any more trouble.'

'Yuck,' said Vasu. 'I will never want a wife.' But he followed Rehman out of the room.

Ramanujam joined them a few minutes later. 'Were you bored too?' asked Vasu.

'No,' said Ramanujam, laughing. 'I just have something to say to your uncle.' He turned to Rehman. 'The operation was successful. We removed the bandages today and he is fully recovered. The biggest problem has been keeping expectations realistic.'

'I don't understand,' said Rehman.

Ramanujam said, 'He and his mother were expecting that as soon as he came out of the operating theatre, he would be able to talk perfectly. But I still have to concentrate to understand him.'

'Ahh!' said Rehman.

'Exactly. I had to explain to them that talking is a skill just like herding goats and it does not come automatically. I told them that it would take months of practice before he could have a conversation with total strangers.'

'Who are you talking about?' asked Vasu.

'When we were rescued from the Naxalites, most of them were killed or captured by the Greyhounds. But their leader and a few other men escaped. A goatherd from a nearby village saw the men in the forest and led the police to them. We made sure that the good man got a reward and uncle here got his doctor colleagues to operate on him and fix him up.'

'What was wrong with him?'

'He had a cleft palate. The front of his upper lip and jaw were missing and—'

'I know what a cleft palate is,' said Vasu, interrupting. 'I have seen people like that. But why did he help the police? My grandfather told me that villagers should never get involved in these matters. He said that if we helped one side, the other side would get to know about it and take revenge.'

'The Naxalites stole one of his goats. So he was very angry with them and that's why he helped the police.'

Vasu nodded. He could understand that. He went over to the nearby guava tree. 'See how I can jump up and catch that branch,' he said.

'We all want to be noticed,' said Ramanujam, looking at the boy speculatively. 'I didn't realise until today just how big a boon it is to be anonymous.'

Rehman raised his eyebrows quizzically.

'After the bandages were removed, we had to cross the corridor from the nurses' station to the ENT surgeon's office. When we reached the doctor's office, the patient turned to me, smiling.'

'"Did you see what happened in the corridor?" he asked, his eyes shining.

'I was puzzled. "Nothing happened," I said.

'"Exactly. We went through that crowd and nobody even gave me a second look. I didn't have to avert my face or look at the disgust and pity in people's eyes."'

Vasu went back into the house. Ramanujam said to Rehman, 'It is really lucky that the insurgents stole the goat, you know.'

'Why?'

'I don't think Aruna or, for that matter, I, would have felt totally safe as long as Adi was alive. It became personal with him, not just political. After we operated on the shepherd he cried and begged my forgiveness. Apparently, after we were kidnapped, he had come across our trail but had misled the police because he was angry with them for beating him. He had hoped that we would be killed.'

Rehman appeared shocked.

'He told me that he loved each and every animal of his herd – they were his friends apparently, and he had names for all of them. That's why when the guerrillas stole Spinach Lover and killed it, he turned against them and led the police to Adi.'

'So much power, so many followers and so many guns – all undone by Spinach Lover . . .' said Rehman, musingly. 'Who can tell what trivial incidents lead to what terrible consequences?'

Ramanujam looked sharply at Rehman, thinking that he had sounded rather like Mr Ali, but he said nothing.

'All vegetarian food tonight,' said Mr Ali, appraising the cabbage and coconut fry with a jaundiced eye. 'Now that's a dish that would be improved immeasurably with the addition of a little mince.'

'Stop it,' said Mrs Ali. 'Aruna and Ramanujam don't want to hear about that.'

A generation or two earlier, no Brahmin would have eaten in a Muslim house or, indeed, any house in which meat was cooked, on pain of losing their caste. Even today it was not common for such invitations to be either issued or accepted.

The dining table was pulled forward from the wall and all six chairs set around it. Even so, Vasu had to sit on a stool in one corner. On the menu were steamed rice, brinjal and lentil sambhar, cabbage and coconut fry, ridged-gourd curry, sautéed spinach with red chillies, ridged gourd-skin chutney and aavakaai, the red-hot mango and mustard pickle, as well as home-made yoghurt and ghee. A steel plate held a salad of sliced onions, carrots and limes.

'Very nice, madam,' said Aruna.

'You people are the masters of vegetarian cooking,' said Mrs Ali. 'We can only try.'

Aruna said to the whole table, 'I got a letter today from Srinu and Gita.'

'Who?' asked Pari.

'The couple who were with us in the camp and helped us escape.'

'What do they say?' asked Rehman.

'They are doing well and are moving to Vizag soon.'

'Permanently moving?'

Aruna nodded. 'Yes, permanently.'

'Weren't they going to set up a biscuit factory in their village?'

'Yes, that was Srinu's plan, but now they don't want to stay in the village any more. They are just too scared.'

'That's the problem the Naxalites don't understand,' said Rehman. 'If entrepreneurs like Srinu and Gita don't create industries in villages, how can the villagers' lot ever improve? The Naxalites may have started off fighting for the poor, but now they themselves are one of the factors holding back progress.'

'I've written to Gita to tell her that whatever assistance they need to help them settle down in the town, we would provide,' said Aruna.

After some time, Mrs Ali said, 'Ramanujam, you seem to love the spinach. Aruna, please serve him some more.'

'It's very nice, aunty. Spinach Lover lives again!' said Ramanujam.

Rehman grinned but the others looked puzzled, so Ramanujam explained to them. 'Let's drink a toast,' he said and everybody raised their glasses of water. 'To Spinach Lover. May his legs forever take him to fields of green leafy vegetables!'

Mrs Ali took a sip of water and said, 'Did you read the paper today? They have given an award to the police inspector whose team killed the monster who kidnapped you. The police are hailing the killing as a major achievement and have even put up the inspector for promotion.'

'No, I didn't read the paper,' said Ramanujam. 'I was busy this morning.' None of the others had seen the article either.

Mrs Ali said, 'A human rights organisation is protesting against it. They think that the officer should not be promoted because the man was killed in an obviously faked encounter.'

Aruna said, 'You mean they captured Adi and then killed him in cold blood? How can the human rights people tell that? Even if they had done it, it is no more than what the rakshasas deserved.'

'According to the paper, there was a big blow to the back of the Naxalite leader's head at least twenty-four hours before he died. They said there were bruises on his hands and legs that showed that he had been tied up. They are asking for a full investigation.'

Ramanujam and Aruna glanced at each other, remembering the events of that hectic night in the forest camp.

Ramanujam said, 'I'll speak to the deputy superintendent of the police. He is a family friend. The human rights people are probably right most of the time, but in this case they don't know what they are talking about.'

Pari turned to Vasu. 'Stop drinking so much water. It will fill up your belly. That's the second glass you've gulped down.'

'The food is very spicy,' he said, refilling his glass from the big silver jug.

'Don't be silly, Vasu,' said Pari. 'It must be just the chutney. It's got ground green chillies in it. Leave that and eat the rest of your food.'

'We had a magic show in school yesterday,' said Vasu. 'The magician was dressed up like a genie. He took some money from his pocket, put it in his hat, waved a magic wand and it disappeared. He went to one of our teachers, checked her purse and the money was there. It was quite amazing.'

'That's a very common trick,' said Mr Ali. 'Any wife can do it with her husband's money. She doesn't even need a magic wand.'

'You should have married someone like that Swaroop woman in the next building. Then you would have known what spending is,' said Mrs Ali.

'Don't talk about that nasty woman,' said Pari. 'Why do you keep meeting her mother-in-law? She seems just as bad as Swaroop.'

Mrs Ali waved her hand without replying. As if to change the subject, she said to Aruna, 'You are looking very well nowadays. Your complexion has really improved. Is there any good news that you should be sharing with us?'

Aruna looked confused. 'No, no . . .' she said. 'There's no news.'

Mrs Ali, not wanting to embarrass Aruna, did not point out that she had single-handedly polished off all the lime pieces, leaving their desiccated skins in a pile on the side of her plate.

Ramanujam said, 'We want to go on a real holiday now, this time to Mumbai and Goa as we planned, but my parents don't want us to travel.'

Rehman said, 'I want to go back to the village and get the trunk of stuff that I left in Vasu's grandfather's house.'

His parents, Pari and Vasu all chorused, 'You are not going back there.'

Rehman looked at Aruna and Ramanujam and gave a theatrical shrug.

The next morning, Aruna came out of the bathroom holding a small plastic wand that looked like a toothbrush without the bristles and gazing at it intently.

Ramanujam sat up in bed, bare-chested, the sheet around his waist. 'What does it say?'

Aruna silently handed him the stick. He stared at the clear window in the plastic. Two blue parallel lines stared back at him. He read the instructions below the lines and examined the lines again. A wide smile appeared on his face and he opened his arms wide. Aruna blushed and walked over to him. His hug enveloped her and she clung to his neck.

'Can it be true?' she said. 'A baby. Our baby! I still can't believe it.' She pushed away from him and eyed him with concern. 'You are fine with this, right?'

'Of course,' said Ramanujam. 'You are the one who wanted to delay having children until your sister finished her college and was married off . . . And you had seen all the tourist spots of India.'

'I know I wanted to do that, but now, this just feels so right.' She closed her eyes and hugged her husband again. 'Ohhh . . . I love you! I love you,' she said and kissed his shoulder. 'I don't think we will be allowed to travel so soon after our own adventure anyway. And as for my sister and parents, I'll just have to work something out.'

'That's the spirit,' he said.

Aruna lay against her husband's chest for a moment. 'The only time I missed the pill was when we were in the forest.'

'I told you that you were a tigress that night,' said Ramanujam.

Aruna blushed again and hugged him even more tightly.

'When shall we tell people? Our parents will be ecstatic.'

Aruna shook her head. 'I don't know. I want to wait just a bit,' she said.

On the way back from dinner the previous night, the thought that she might be pregnant had struck both of them almost simultaneously and they had picked up the testing kit.

'How did madam guess that I was pregnant? My period

was a little late, but until she asked me the question, I did not even imagine . . . I just thought all the stress of the kidnapping had somehow delayed it.'

Ramanujam said, 'Nothing escapes her eye. She is one sharp lady who can count your guts if you just yawn in front of her.'

Aruna laughed. 'It's lucky that she likes us.'

The thief had a sneaky look in his eye as he crept closer to his target. Mrs Ali was sure of it.

She watched as the crow dropped on to the ground from the lower branches of the guava tree. Mrs Ali was in her cane chair, on the verandah, keeping her eye on the front yard where she had laid diced pieces of tomato on a plastic sheet to dry in the brilliant post-rain sun. Once the tomatoes had been dried for several days, she would add them to heated oil, red chilli powder, fenugreek seeds, curry leaves and other spices to make a pickle that would last all year.

'Shoo! Shoo!' said a voice at the gate. Leela, the tall, lean servant maid, was not sporting her habitual smile. 'Oh! You are right here, amma. Why are you letting the crows eat the food?' she asked.

'It's OK,' said Mrs Ali. 'I deliberately put that tomato piece a little away from the others, so the crows could get to it. They are God's creatures too and need to eat, you know.'

Leela looked at her mistress as if she was going mad, but, perhaps out of politeness, made no comment.

'You are right,' said Mrs Ali and laughed. 'Put out the stick so the crows know what their limit is.'

Leela took the stick out of the side alley, wiped it with a clean cloth that lay next to the tomatoes and laid it across the sheet. When she turned, Mrs Ali saw that her expression was unusually grim.

'What's wrong Leela?'

Leela sighed. 'I've decided to drop the second-floor flat, madam. I cannot stand the daily fights. If I wash the dishes before sweeping the house, the mother-in-law complains. If I sweep the house first, the younger woman says that she is getting delayed in packing the lunches for her husband and children. The two women are constantly at each other's throats. I lived with my mother-in-law in a small, one-room shack, but that big flat with multiple rooms is not enough for those two. I tell you, amma, I have finally realised that property and material things do not bring happiness if people cannot get on with each other.'

'Then why the long face? Go and tell them that you are not working there any more and that's the end of it.'

'It is not so easy for poor people like us, is it? I really need the money. My grandson's medicines still take a big chunk of my son-in-law's income and I help them out when I can. I also need to save for my second daughter's wedding.'

Mrs Ali nodded. The money that Leela had saved over the years for her younger child's wedding had been used up to pay for treatment when Leela's grandson had needed surgery.

'Can't you get some other housework?'

'I have asked, amma, but all the flats are already serviced. Unless I go far away, there is no other work available, but then I'll be spending all my time walking from one place to another, too tired to actually sweep and clean.'

'We don't want that, do we?' said Mrs Ali. 'Well, I have some good news for you. I know a family in the next building who want a servant maid.' She smiled.

Leela was astounded. 'Who, amma?' she asked. 'I am sure that there isn't a free flat next door. The watchman's wife and daughter do most of them and they won't give up any of their families.'

'Swaroop's mother-in-law came by earlier today. She said that she and her daughter-in-law had a big showdown in front of her son. Swaroop wanted to kick her out, but the old lady stood firm. She told them that if they wanted to inherit a single cowrie shell from the ancestral property, they would have to put up with her and not just for six months, either. And it wasn't as if she was a burden. For the first time, everybody in the house was eating proper food instead of instant noodles and other junk.'

'I've heard you and . . . Did you . . .'

Mrs Ali inclined her head. 'Anybody could tell this confrontation would happen sooner or later. I might have prepped the old lady beforehand.'

Leela smiled, for the first time that morning. 'Then what happened, amma?'

'The son, in desperation, agreed to move out of the flat into a bigger house, further away from town, so his wife and mother could each have more room.'

'A town is not big enough for those two,' said Leela. 'You said another family—'

'I've just got off the phone to the flat's landlord. You know the Raos who used to live there before?'

'Yes, I remember them. I used to work for that family too. They had a daughter and that tall son who did not want to study.'

'Those people, exactly. I had kept in touch with the lady of the house when they moved out. Anyway, as soon as the mother-in-law left, I called them up and took over the flat for Pari and her son. In about two weeks, they will be moving in.'

'That's very good news. Pari-amma has been wanting to move out of her room for such a long time now.'

Mrs Ali said, 'Right. Pari also has a job now and she says she needs a maid to help in the flat. Anyway, that's all for later. Right now, I've rinsed out the men's shirts and trousers in the orange bucket. Hang them out first because I want them to dry before the sun comes round the house. Then you can start on the dishes.'

'Yes, amma,' said Leela. There was a spring in her step as she went through the house.

Mrs Ali sat back in the cane chair on the verandah and surveyed the front yard. The stick had kept the crows away. A pair of sparrows landed on the wall of the well, chattered to each other, as sparrows do, and then flew away. A motorcycle honked on the road. A boy in flapping clothes ran past the house on some errand. The tomatoes were drying nicely in the sun.

The only tiny note of dissatisfaction was the fact that Pari's engagement with Dilawar was definitely off. She didn't know why it had been broken, nobody was saying anything, but the important thing was that Pari seemed happy. Maybe it was for the best. Mrs Ali couldn't imagine how anybody could live in a crowded city like Mumbai where everything was always such a hurry-burry. And Mrs Bilqis was such a good woman – despite the broken engagement between her son and Pari, she had gone out of her way to use her influence and get Pari's job back at the call centre. Mrs Ali and Pari had gone to Mrs Bilqis's house to express their gratitude, but Mrs Bilqis and her friend Nadira, who was also there, had both appeared embarrassed and had waved their thanks away. Real ladies – the two of them.

A car stopped by the gate and Aruna got out. 'Morning, madam,' she said. Her complexion *was* glowing. The girl's cheeks had filled out a bit more than normal.

Mrs Ali smiled contentedly. The previous few weeks had seen problems, but she could feel life returning to its usual path once more.

# EPILOGUE

The sun was a red ball hanging low in the west when the group of men and one woman pulled up on the outskirts of the small town. The men wore dark-green fatigues and were all carrying guns – self-loading rifles for the seniors and country-made pistols for the juniors. The woman, in a lemon-yellow salwar kameez, looked like a fresh hibiscus flower amid foliage. The leader of the men, Leninkumar, spoke quietly into her ear.

'I am having doubts about the latest mission.'

'Didn't you tell me that you have doubts before every mission?'

Leninkumar nodded.

'Then this is no different.'

'I love you, Roja,' said Leninkumar softly, so the other men would not hear him.

Her cheeks reddened slightly, but Leninkumar wasn't sure whether it was because of the sun's rays. She turned to him and said, 'I know.'

'Should we have taken the ten million rupees as ransom for your father's release?'

Roja's father was Mr Reddy, the landlord, who had been

kidnapped after his 'trial' on the same night that the guerrillas had captured the four young people from Vizag. Leninkumar had seen Roja for the first time that night, but had got to know her better when negotiating the ransom. It had been love almost at first sight.

So much had changed since then. He had come back to their camp that evening to find that Adi had been trying to molest that girl, Aruna, in the hut. He had let the couple go, but knew that Adi would never forgive him for it, so that very night he had gathered together this group of loyal men, taken the landlord with him and left the camp. He still felt guilty about it, wondering whether he and his men could have made the difference against the Greyhounds the next morning.

He and Roja had met several times over the next couple of weeks, neogtiating about her father, and had finally agreed on the ransom amount. When she had come to deliver the money, Roja had surprised him, and her father, by opting to remain with the men in the forest.

'I want to marry you,' she had told him later.

He loved her confidence.

'You were a student with a bright future. Why did you leave all that behind and join the Naxalite movement?' she asked him.

'To fight for the poor and the weak,' he answered.

'The money will help you in that struggle,' she said. 'If it remained with my father, it would just have languished in a steel safe or been used to trap more poor people into a cycle of debt.'

He turned and addressed his men.

'This mission is strictly for volunteers. Do any of you want to drop out?'

None did. His chest swelled with pride. 'Comrades, let's go!'

Roja started moving with them, but he stopped her. 'This is a dangerous assignment and we don't know how it will end. I don't want you there.'

Roja looked into his eyes for a moment, then nodded and peeled off from the group.

The squad swiftly covered the distance to a modest single-storey structure with a red-tiled roof. A low wall surrounded the house, enclosing a small well-tended garden with orange kanakaambaram, white jasmine and several creepers with showy yellow flowers that bore marrows and gourds. A blue-berry tree shaded the far corner.

A line of crows, sitting on the telephone wires leading to the house, took off with loud caws as soon as the armed men came in sight. Other crows in nearby trees took up the warn-ing calls.

Leninkumar, the son of a revolutionary Marxist, in name if not in fact, knocked on the wooden door. The elderly man who opened it was tall and slim, bespectacled and stooped with age. He wore a long white cotton hand-loom shirt with a white dhoti around his waist that hung down to his knees. His eyes widened in shock when he saw Leninkumar and his men. He fell back and was pushed to one side as they barged their way into the house and bolted the door behind them.

Leninkumar scrutinised the room. It was as he had expected. A medium-sized television stood on an aluminium stand in one corner with an old cloth covering it. A coffee table in the middle of the room held the day's papers – in English and Telugu – neatly folded under a glass paperweight, chipped from some long-ago fall to the cement floor. A ceil-ing fan moved the air slowly. A picture of Mahatma Gandhi hung on one wall and that of a young man in a soldier's uni-form on another, with a garland around both photographs.

The soldier was the old man's son who had died in some long-forgotten border skirmish. Leninkumar knew that the old man also had a daughter, married to a schoolteacher in a distant village. Everything in his house showed the orderly life of an old couple with modest means. What was unusual was that the man was an MLA – a member of the state's legislative assembly. Most MLAs lived in big houses with dozens of flunkeys to serve them. The old man was universally respected and not a little feared because he eschewed the scores of money-making opportunities that abounded within a politician's reach.

The old man made his way to the front of the Naxalites and said, 'What can I do for you gentlemen?' He spoke calmly.

An inner door opened and a grey-haired woman came in, holding a platter with an oil lamp and some flowers on it. 'Did you hear the crows—'

The platter dropped from her hands as she took in the scene. The flowers scattered. The lamp sputtered and almost went out, struggling to stay lit as most of the oil in the small clay pot splashed on the floor.

Leninkumar saw a flicker of fear for the first time on the man's face.

'Leave my wife out of this,' he said. 'She has nothing to do with politics.'

Leninkumar licked his lips in uncharacteristic nervousness and stepped forward. Dropping to one knee, he laid his rifle at the man's feet.

'We have heard about the government's offer of asylum. We wish to surrender.'

The men behind him dropped their guns too. The man looked at his wife in stunned surprise. Turning back to the men in front of him, he said, 'Why did you come here? You should have gone to the police.'

Leninkumar shook his head. 'We don't trust the police. They are just as likely to shoot us after they've taken our arms as to accept our surrender.'

'But why me?'

'My father respected you,' said Leninkumar. 'He used to say that you were an honest man.'

The old man bent down and raised Leninkumar to his feet.

'What is your name?' he asked.

'Bharatkumar,' said the young man, claiming his rightful, parent-given name for the first time in years. Son of India.

The flame in the lamp took hold, shining bright and steady once more.

# THE MARRIAGE BUREAU FOR RICH PEOPLE

## Farahad Zama

What does somebody with a wealth of common sense do if
retirement palls?

Why, open a marriage bureau, of course. And soon Mr Ali, from
beautiful Vizag in South India, sees his new business flourish as the
indomitable Mrs Ali and able assistant Aruna look on with careful
eyes.

But although many clients go away happy, problems lurk behind the
scenes as Aruna nurses a heart-rending secret; while Mr Ali cannot
see that he rarely follows the sage advice he so freely dishes out to
others. And when love comes calling for Aruna, an impossible
dilemma looms …

A colourful coastal town and contemporary marriage bureau prove a
perfect backdrop for a splendid array of characters making sense of
all sorts of pride and prejudice – and the ways in which true love
won't quite let go – in this witty and big-hearted debut.

ABACUS

978-0-349-12137-6

# THE MANY CONDITIONS OF LOVE

## Farahad Zama

Mr Ali's marriage bureau is flourishing. But trouble lurks in the beautiful surrounds of Vizag in South India, as son Rehman is set to embark on a secret (and very ill-advised) romance with TV journalist Usha.

Meanwhile Mr Ali's lovely assistant Aruna has a problem too. She's indispensable, has a wonderful husband, and lives in a mansion that's a far cry from her parents' one-room home. but how long can Aruna remain happy once spiteful sister-in-law Mani comes to stay?

A bustling marriage bureau proves a perfect backdrop for a splendid array of characters, making sense of the collision between modernity and Indian tradition in this magnificent return to the world of *The Marriage Bureau for Rich People*.

ABACUS

978-0-349-12139-0

## Now you can order superb titles directly from Abacus

☐ The Marriage Bureau for
    Rich People                Farahad Zama        £7.99

☐ The Many Conditions of Love    Farahad Zama        £7.99

*The prices shown above are correct at time of going to press. However, the publishers reserve the right to increase prices on covers from those previously advertised, without further notice.*

⎯⎯⎯⎯⎯⎯ ⟨ABACUS⟩ ⎯⎯⎯⎯⎯⎯

Please allow for postage and packing: **Free UK delivery.**
Europe: add 25% of retail price; Rest of World: 45% of retail price.

To order any of the above or any other Abacus titles, please call our credit card orderline or fill in this coupon and send/fax it to:

**Abacus, PO Box 121, Kettering, Northants NN14 4ZQ**
Fax: 01832 733076   Tel: 01832 737526
Email: aspenhouse@FSBDial.co.uk

☐ I enclose a UK bank cheque made payable to Abacus for £
☐ Please charge £              to my Visa/Delta/Maestro

☐☐☐☐☐☐☐☐☐☐☐☐☐☐☐☐☐☐

Expiry Date ☐☐☐☐     Maestro Issue No. ☐☐

NAME (BLOCK LETTERS please) . . . . . . . . . . . . . . . . . . . . . . . . . . . . . . . . . . .

ADDRESS . . . . . . . . . . . . . . . . . . . . . . . . . . . . . . . . . . . . . . . . . . . . . . . . . .

. . . . . . . . . . . . . . . . . . . . . . . . . . . . . . . . . . . . . . . . . . . . . . . . . . . . . . . . .

. . . . . . . . . . . . . . . . . . . . . . . . . . . . . . . . . . . . . . . . . . . . . . . . . . . . . . . . .

Postcode . . . . . . . . . . . . . . . . Telephone . . . . . . . . . . . . . . . . . . . . . . . . . .

Signature . . . . . . . . . . . . . . . . . . . . . . . . . . . . . . . . . . . . . . . . . . . . . . . . . .

Please allow 28 days for delivery within the UK. Offer subject to price and availability.

**I would like to thank . . .**

. . . Suketu Mehta, author of *Maximum City: Bombay Lost and Found*, for his help on Bombay and its gay scene. Any inaccuracies are, of course, the result of my own artistic licence and my responsibility.

. . . Will Francis, my agent, for always being at the end of a phone to discuss the book, and for his good editorial eye.

. . . Jenny Parrott, my editor, for buzzing with ideas to improve the book and the series, and then leaving me alone to do the writing. It's a difficult balance but Jenny gets it right.

. . . my wife Sameera, for the recipe, and much else.

*Farahad Zama moved to London in 1990 from Vizag in India, where his novels are set. He is a father of two, and he works for an investment bank.*